WINGS OF GRACE

VANESSA DAVIS GRIGGS

BET Publications, LLC
http://www.bet.com

NEW SPIRIT BOOKS are published by

BET Publications, LLC
c/o BET BOOKS
One BET Plaza
1900 W Place NE
Washington, DC 20018-1211

ISBN: 1-58314-468-4

First Printing: February 2005
10 9 8 7 6 5 4 3 2 1

Printed in the United States of America

To the women of the world who have lived life, demonstrating both strength and grace. Women who have continued to believe even when it appeared there was nothing visibly available to grab onto. Women who have sacrificed for those they loved, fought when necessary, risen up boldly, took a stand gallantly—"No matter what or come what may!" Women who judged the word "quit" and transformed it into "**Q**ueen, **U**'re **IT**." From women who have wielded broom and mop to those whose names seem to forever float from the lips of those—male and female—who wish to impress others by simply speaking their name. To you— women of glory, honor, majesty, authority, spirit, and grace—I dedicate this book.

ACKNOWLEDGMENTS

Always first, honor and praise to God: Jehovah Jireh—my provider, Jehovah Shalom—my peace; Jesus—my Lord, Savior, and Big Brother; and the Holy Spirit—my comforter and my guide. "For every good and perfect gift comes from above."

Loving thanks to my mother, Josephine Davis, who has always believed in me and what God's intended me to do. My father, James Davis, Jr., for his encouraging words to "Stick with it; things take time." To my husband, Jefferey Griggs, for being supportive of me and my dreams. My children—Jefferey, Jeremy, and Johnathan—who define me as "mama." My daughter-in-law, Philicia; "Nana's baby," Asia; my sisters, Danette Dial and Arlinda Davis; my sister-in-law, Cameron; my brothers, Rev. Terence Davis and Rev. Emmanuel Davis—I thank each of you for being such a blessing in my life.

I've had some really faithful people who have remained in my corner: Rosetta Moore, Zelda Oliver-Miles, my cousin Mark Davis, Sylviaette Simmons, Vina Lavendar (spreading the word at Mi-Lady Beauty Salon in Tuscaloosa), Alice Gordon Carrillo, Vanessa L. Rice, Linda H. Jones, Shirley C. Walker, Pamela Hardy, Mary R. Woolridge, LaShanna R. Price, Mary Chavers, Pam Kingsbury, Marissa Monteilh, Ruth Washington, Delois Davis, the Children of Love, Pam Douglas, all of my aunts, uncles, nieces, nephews, and cousins. How richly blessed my life is for your life having crossed my path. Thank you for being there through it all.

Psalm 75:6–7 states that promotion comes from God. There are so many who have and continue to spread the word about my work. Thanks to the librarians, booksellers, churches, and book clubs (both on and offline), as well as those who host Web sites keeping others informed about all the many books available. A special thank you to Sistas Book Club in Birmingham, AL; Regina Biddings and Sisters Reading; Suzetta Perkins and Sistahs Book Club in Fayetteville, NC; Avis Williams and Soulful Expressions Book Club in Huntsville, AL; Evelyn G. Pelt and Sister's Book Club in Tuscaloosa, AL; Tee C. Royal and RawSistaz.com; Phyllis Fuqua and Sensational Readers Club in Rogersville, AL; Cover-to-Cover in Champaign, IL; Lisa R. Cross and The Sistah Circle Book Club; Reflections of Soul, Nubian Circle Book Club, and Sisters in Shape—all in Maryland; LaShaunda C. Hoffman and *Shades of Reading Magazine* (sormag.com); Cydney Rax and Book-Remarks.com; Yasmin Coleman and Apooo.org; Joyce Dixon and Southernscribe.com; Wayne Jordan and RomanceinColor.com; Ken Reed and BlackBoston Online.com; and the Black Expressions Book Club.

I tip my hat to *The Birmingham Times*; Dave Baird and ABC 33/40s "Matters of Faith"; Greg Garrison with *The Birmingham News*; Greater Mt. Nebo Bookstore in Upper Marlboro, MD; Glenda Howard of BET Books/New Spirit—I thank you for all you've done! To those who encouraged me, yet have now "crossed over Jordan" to be with the Lord: Maurice Plemmons, Johnnie Peoples, Oliver Brewer, Peggy Wiseman . . . I can feel you cheering me on in spirit.

A huge thanks to you for reading my work, the e-mails, letters, prayers, and words of encouragement that have blessed my heart more than words could ever convey. It's impossible to name every name here, but if you have been a blessing to me in any way, thank you. Thank you! Thank you! Thank you!

Now go, people of God, and possess the land. Feel free to visit me at my Web site: www.VanessaDavisGriggs.com. I do love hearing from you.

PROLOGUE

Get wisdom, get understanding.

(Proverbs 4:5)

Willie B (His story)

I had a hard time believing that one baby was my child. Yet they were twins, born December 4, 1935, while I was away on business. A boy and a girl: the boy looking as though I had spit him out. Didn't need no wife to carry him for nine months. Just puckered up my mouth, stuck out my tongue, blew hard, and literally spit a miniature me out. But the girl was a mystery to me. Couldn't find a hint of Mamie or me in her nowhere. Possibly the nose, but who can be sure just yet?

Mamie kept emphasizing that they were "fraternal twins." Her explanation of why they weren't a matching set. More like an overdone pound cake. That's what they reminded me of when I saw them the first time at ten days old lying side by side: a dark brown crust next to a golden light yellow. Like a hand: dark on the back, light in the palm.

"Mamie, I got something to ask you," I said, realizing there was no other way to say it but to say it. "Are you sure you've been totally faithful to me?" That seemed to arrest her attention right away. I never was no count at sugarcoating things.

"Willie B, how can you even question such a thing? Frankly, I'm offended you have allowed a thought like that to even form inside that big old head of yours." She picked up the baby girl and began to nervously, but gently, bounce her to quiet her slight fussing.

"Then, why that one baby there got so much white in her?" I looked down at my dark chocolate hands. Rugged hands responsible for building countless, artistic, beautiful, and expensive furnishings in and around wealthy homes from Asheville, North Carolina, to parts of New York. I studied my hands; my eyes not wanting to bear witness to what her eyes might end up confessing, and in the process, betray what her mouth might otherwise refuse to admit. In that moment, my hands demanded my attention. Back. Forth. Light. Dark. Light . . . dark . . . light . . . dark.

"Willie B," Mamie said in a tone more of surrender than anger. "I do have something I suppose I need to tell you. I vowed not to reveal this to another soul, but it's not fair or right to keep a thing like this from you. You're my husband. But more importantly, I believe you have a right to know the truth." She laid the baby down and slowly eased into a chair conveniently away from me. Both babies remained quiet.

Here it comes. What I've known in my heart for a while. I've seen how Mister V at the house where she works looks at her. Anybody with a grain of grits sense can see it. Mister V loves her, loves him some Mamie. I caught the way he looked at her the first day she started working for him. It didn't matter that she was dark—colored as they come and him white as light. He treats her as though he would give her the world were it in his power. Not own her. Not possess her. Not abuse or misuse her. But love her as Christ loves the church. One who'd give his life for her if it came down to it. Loves her the way I love her. Only Mamie's mine.

Or is she?

So I steeled myself, hard, to hear those possible, dreaded words: "You are not their father." The only part I can't seem to wrestle my brain around no matter how I grab at it is: *How can that boy there be the spitting image of me and not be my blood?*

Mamie (Her story)

There are times when it's not the answer that is the problem, but the question that was asked. I noted how Willie B looked at the twins. I knew then he would eventually have questions, with Junior looking so much like him already and Memory (that's what I named the baby girl) looking so white.

My answer could have shown my disbelief and hurt that he would dare question my faithfulness to him or our marriage. But he had commented too many times on how Mister V seemed undeniably in love with me. Had seen how we were around each other. It was just I knew how to handle Mister V, whereas most folks didn't dare even try.

I knew Memory's light skin and too silky hair would spark questions, what with Willie B and me both being so dark skinned. Just never expected it to be so soon. Still everybody knows the blood that flows through our Negro veins can, at any time, produce many shades of color no matter how dark or light we might be.

But the question Willie B asked was about my being faithful to him. And that question renders an entirely different answer than the one—I'm sure—he truly seeks.

Now the question I must ask myself is: *Do I answer his question? Or do I answer the question he should have—but did not—ask?*

Sarah (My story)

Ransom was his name, although as far as I knew, no one ever personally told him why. I, for my part, concluded it was because he had a way of holding a heart hostage. Any heart. Many hearts. My heart. His mama probably took one look at him, whispered, "Ransom" and the midwife mistook that for his name. Or maybe she'd said "Handsome," as I, myself, have declared about him under my own breath. In any event, that's what he did with my Southern belle heart. Held it ransom. "Sarah, I'm taking your heart. It'll cost much if you are ever to get it back" is what he should have said to me, but didn't. And instead of my heart being released or rescued, it has remained forever in his possession.

No, this is not a love story.

The year was 1935. I was twenty, young, and impressionable. As for all that was to happen to me over the next 66 years, one might peg me gullible, unsuspecting, trusting, an idiot for believing that things would get better or that family would never do anything deliberately to hurt those they claim to love. But insane?

Never insane.

That much I am sure about. In love, naïve, too trusting of those charged to love me, but never, I don't care who alleges differently, was I insane. Never should have been sent away. I just believed the wrong would right itself someday. Only someday never came. Today, May 16, 2001, I celebrate my birthday—well aware that, for me, time is winding down.

Mamie. It seems the older I get, the more I think about Mamie. We were like sisters, even though folks maintained it wasn't right for coloreds and whites to be that close. I never did get to see Mamie's babies. "Twins," Mother said when I pressed her. Mamie sent word to me she had something important to tell me. Then, suddenly, I was sent away.

"Memories," I say when people ask what kept me pressing on in life in spite of all I was forced to endure. My memories. Not heaven, not yet anyway. You see you have to die to get to heaven. And honestly . . . I'm not ready to die just yet. Somehow I believe truth will eventually prevail. Memory—yes, memory: my wings . . . my saving grace.

CHAPTER 1

The Lord will perfect that which concerneth me.

(Psalm 138:8)

The chime of the doorbell interrupted Theresa Jordan. With two months left before her baby was due to be born, even Theresa wondered how much more her body—only seven months ago a misses size 8—could possibly expand. Since moving into her newly built, two-story home in Atlanta, it usually took more than one press of the doorbell from an impatient visitor before she eventually reached the door. Looking out of the side window, she saw it was an elderly woman. No one she knew, though. "Who is it?" Theresa asked.

"I'm sorry to bother you, but I'm looking for a Lena Patterson," the woman said.

Theresa cautiously cracked open the door, mainly to get a better look at the inquirer. "Lena's not here. Would you care to leave a message for her?"

The woman looked down briefly at her feet as though the answer were scribbled somewhere on her runover, worn-out shoes. "Can you tell me when she might be back?"

Theresa thought for a second. "I'd be glad to take your business card or let her know you stopped by," Theresa said, opening the door completely now. She wasn't about to divulge information about her mother to some total stranger. But since Lena was planning to stay with her until well after the baby came sometime in September, Theresa didn't want to be rude to a possible friend or guest of Lena's. *Lena must have given her this address*, Theresa thought. *How else would she know to come here?*

"I don't mind waiting," the woman said. She looked at Theresa and for some reason began to squint, like she was memorizing some complicated mathematical equation etched on Theresa's face.

"I'd really hate for you to do that since I can't say how long Lena will be. Sitting in your car, in Georgia's July weather at that, can be dangerously hot." Theresa was seven months pregnant, home alone, and not about to take a chance on some stranger scamming her way into her house: old, woman, or not. *If you wait, it will definitely be outside.*

"Thank you. But as long as it's okay, I'll just hang around." The woman grinned crookedly at Theresa, then glanced at her stomach. "So, when's your baby due?"

"September eleventh," Theresa said, feeling even more uneasy about the visitor. There was something sneaky about her. "Are you sure you wouldn't rather tell me your name? It truly might be a while before Lena's back. I'd be happy to give her a message."

The woman smiled again. "No. But thanks just the same." She turned and walked away. When Theresa reached a window near the driveway and looked out, it was empty.

The front door opened and closed. "Theresa!" Lena said as she struggled with two large bags into the den. "Theresa, are you in the kitchen?"

Theresa made her way into the den. "Did you just see a woman out there?"

"A woman?"

"Yes. Outside. When you came in. There was a white woman, I'd guess in her sixties, here to see you not five minutes ago. She said she was going to wait for you."

Lena shook her head. "There was no one out there when I came up. You say she asked for me?"

"She asked for you. No one I know or have ever seen before, though."

"A white woman? And she asked for me? Specifically? By name?"

"Yes. She asked for 'Lena Patterson.' I tried to get her to tell me her name, but she insisted on waiting for you. I let her know it could be hours, but she still wanted to wait."

"Hmmm. Interesting. Strange, but interesting."

"Maybe not. Who have you told you're staying here? Since we've only been here a month, it would have to be someone you told, wouldn't you think?"

Lena cocked her head to the side. "See, that's what's bothering me a little. No one I know even knows I'm here except Richard, Beatrice, and of course, Maurice." She smiled, then shrugged. "Well, let's not dwell on it. Oh you *must* see what all I bought for the baby's nursery. We don't have as much time as we think to finish it up, you know." Lena spoke as though her mind were far from the mysterious visitor. But she couldn't help but wonder: *Who's looking for me here when no one, not even my employees in North Carolina, knows my whereabouts? And why wouldn't the woman leave her name?*

"I've always been partial to chocolate," Sarah Fleming said with a thick Southern drawl as she sipped a cup of steaming, hot cocoa.

Johnnie Mae Taylor had first met the white-haired, medium-sized woman in May of 1999 in Selma, Alabama, when she was working on a nonfiction project. Interviewing some thirty elderly people residing in an assisted-living apartment building, Johnnie Mae had been recording the oral history from this unique mixture of black and white people, along with a noted photographer named DeRamus, capturing their glory in black-and-white pictures. Sarah had kept to herself since arriving at The E House, causing some occupants to whisper of her obvious resentment about having to live under the same roof with blacks.

The E-House director contacted Johnnie Mae in mid-May of 2001 when the eighty-six-year-old, sophisticated Sarah (who had originally refused to tell Johnnie Mae anything much about her life) insisted she had to speak with "that colored author" as soon as possible.

"I'm sort of like oatmeal," Sarah said when Johnnie Mae finally arrived two weeks later. "Add hot water and it becomes soft and mushy. But leave it out long enough, it'll turn hard and can be quite difficult to budge." She then proceeded to tell Johnnie Mae a captivating tale in such unbelievable detail; Johnnie Mae could only attribute it to an old woman's delusional, or apparently overactive, imagination.

Sarah looked into her eyes. "You don't believe a word I'm saying, do you?" She then leaned back in her chair. "All right. If it's proof you need, then I'll provide some. The next time you come, I'll have something for you. Then will you agree to help me?" Johnnie Mae nodded, smiled, patted Sarah's hand twice, and later said goodbye.

A month later, Johnnie Mae stood at the counter of Dulles Airport in D.C. to check in for her Houston trip before finally being able to head home to Birmingham, Alabama, just in time for the Fourth of July. Her thoughts kept wandering back to Sarah and whether or not she should even bother visiting her again. But there was something about the elderly woman's words that continued to replay in her head like a stuck record.

"There are times when all you have left are your memories," Sarah had said. "You reach out. You want to touch something. But when you grasp for something to show somebody else it really happened, you only come up with wisps of air. You can see it. You can feel it. You know it's there. But you can't prove it exists to anybody else. Yet without it, you know . . . you realize, a part of you might cease to exist."

Can't prove it. Can't prove it. Can't. Can't. Can't prove it.

"Excuse me, Miss. I believe you may have dropped this," a man said, bringing Johnnie Mae's thoughts back to the present.

Johnnie Mae glanced down at the white slip of paper with the handwritten number on it the 5'11" man held out to her. "No," she said. "No, I don't believe I did."

Extending his right hand so she could get a better look, he gripped the bag he held tighter, then smiled, flashing pearls of white. "Don't you want to check it out and see?"

Johnnie Mae half-glanced at the paper before looking without flinching into his hazelnut-colored eyes. "No," she said. "I'm really not interested in seeing it in the least bit." She picked up her folder from the counter, turned, and strolled defiantly away.

"Okay," he said loud enough for her to still hear him. "Your loss."

Johnnie Mae's schedule had been hectic the past few months. Nothing could have prepared her for the twister headed her way after being on some of the most popular shows in the nation. Radio shows; newspaper and magazine interviews; television; book signings, speaking at luncheons, dinners, and banquets to business folks, at colleges and expos. Success seemed to birth more success: things producing more of their own kind. People recognized her now. She was being pulled in so many directions—flying from the East Coast to the West Coast many times in the same day. She'd catch a flight at one o'clock P.M. out of New York into California, tape a late-night show that afternoon, then back to New York in time to get maybe three hours of sleep before appearing all perky on a live morning show. Her internal clock, weeks ago, had become all out of whack.

Then someone you don't know stops you in the airport just so he can "inform" you that you dropped a piece of paper you know you didn't drop? Please! she thought.

Johnnie Mae conceded she had enough going on in her life already with her fiancé, Pastor George Landris, being eager to exchange wedding vows, while she was seemingly the chief holdup.

"Johnnie Mae," Landris had said two weeks after she agreed in April to become his wife, "let's pray." They were on bended knees as they kneeled together in prayer. He'd taken her hand—the left one to be exact—and begun.

When he finished, he looked at Johnnie Mae. She opened her eyes to see him smiling at her with so much love. He then changed to a one-knee stance.

"Johnnie Mae," he said, facing her and gently stroking her finger—the one connected to the heart: the ring finger. "I love you. My desire is to be one with you. To be your confidante, your lover, your husband, your friend. My eyes, may they forever focus lovingly on you. My ears, be radars for your voice. My nose to know it's you even before you enter a room. Oh to taste and see how truly good the Lord is as my heart beats as one with you. J. M. Taylor: Will you become bone of my bone and flesh of my flesh and honor me by becoming my wife?" He then slipped a three-stone, three-carat Elara™ diamond ring exactly squared with cut corners, onto her finger. (Experts' translation: "Fire, brilliance, and beauty set in platinum: Rare, elegant, sophisticated. The brilliance of an ideal-round diamond [with 61 facets!] unsurpassed uniquely in a square.")

Tears began rolling down her face: *The official proposal.* She looked deeply into his eyes. Searching? For what, she did not know. *Is this too soon? Am I moving too fast? Do I really want to spend the rest of my life—the rest of my life—with Pastor George Landris?*

Johnnie Mae searched frantically through her purse, then in the pockets of everything.

It was nowhere.

"I'm sorry, Ma'am, but I don't show a reservation under any of the names you've given. If you could provide me with the confirmation number, then maybe I could—"

"But I can't *find* my confirmation number," Johnnie Mae said with a snap. "I told you, the woman at the car rental counter in D.C. made the reservations when I rented my car there. Can't you call them and see how she reserved it?"

"Ma'am, if she reserved it, she should have given you a confirmation number. That's our best way of tracking it, for just these kinds of cases."

Johnnie Mae let out a sigh. *Where did I put that number? It was on a small piece of paper. I was in a hurry . . . what did I do with it?*

The woman in D.C. had been efficient enough to let Johnnie Mae know that Houston's rentals were quickly becoming slim pickings—a huge convention was taking place that week. She had informed Johnnie Mae that she could reserve a car for her Houston trip at the same time she rented her car in D.C. She had then handed Johnnie Mae a piece of paper.

"Make sure you keep this confirmation number. Should you have any problems, this number will guarantee you a vehicle," she had said. "You shouldn't have any complications, but you never know."

Now Johnnie Mae knew.

She remembered sticking it inside her itinerary envelope along with her Houston airline ticket. Or so she thought. But now it wasn't there.

"Looking for this, perhaps?" A heavy voice loomed as a whisper in her left ear. Johnnie Mae turned around to look into familiar eyes. Eyes she now realized she had seen before, though not on him. *But who?*

He again held out the paper with a number on it. Something inside of her insisted that she look at it this time. It was indeed her rental confirmation number. Turning to the woman behind the counter, she handed the paper to her.

"Oh," the woman said after keying the number into the system. "That's why I couldn't find it." She smiled at Johnnie Mae, who had yet to thank the man slightly grinning beside her. "Looks like they hooked you up. It'll be just a minute now. Then you'll be all set. I do apologize for the delay."

Johnnie Mae turned to the man: dark chocolate; neatly trimmed hair, moustache, and beard. "Thank you," she said in an even-toned voice. "So, are you following me?"

He laughed, throwing his head back as though that was the funniest thing he'd ever heard. "Your curves appear to be in all the right places, your face seems pretty tight. Based on your demeanor, I'd guess you're *much* older than your look of, say, late twenties, early thirties. But . . ." he said as he placed a card down on the rental counter, smiled at the woman working behind it, then turned and looked again at Johnnie Mae, "you're not *that* compelling. Just be thankful I didn't throw that paper away."

The woman handed Johnnie Mae her paperwork, thanked her, and smiled first at Johnnie Mae, then at the gentleman next to her.

Johnnie Mae had two book signings tomorrow, then home to see daughter Princess Rose and get some much needed rest. Next week, it would be Philadelphia, Maryland, then Dallas. But that man's laugh, for the rest of the day, played over and over in her ear.

CHAPTER 2

The steps of a good man are ordered by the Lord.

(Psalm 37:23)

"Johnnie Mae, are you planning to stop in Atlanta on your way home from Dallas?" Landris asked.

Johnnie Mae knew Landris wanted to talk about the wedding plans. Neither of them had really cared about having an elaborate ceremony. Landris, in fact, had let her know he truthfully desired nothing more than to begin their life together as quickly as possible: "Right now," he'd said. "If you would agree to it." He'd suggested they could have a small, simple ceremony at one of their homes. Both sides of the family had quickly squashed that idea. Johnnie Mae conceded she was too busy to plan a wedding "of any size right now." So the earliest she saw them marrying would be sometime maybe in early spring of 2002. They had a serious discussion about it when she was at his house around the end of May.

"You do want to marry me, right?" Landris had said.

"Yes."

"And you're not just stalling or looking for some way to get out of it completely?"

"No. I'm just really busy, and planning a wedding, even a simple one, will take more time than I can spare right now. You know this book tour has me out-of-pocket a lot. A wedding would be too much." She looked at him and wrinkled her nose as she smiled. "But I do want to marry you. So don't take my suggestion to wait wrong. Okay?"

"What if . . ." Landris smiled, "I plan the wedding and all you have to do is show up?"

"You? George 'the Macho' Landris? Plan a wedding? Our wedding?"

"Yes." He adjusted his body on the couch more comfortably.

She laughed. "In that case, I'd have to agree just so I can see you do it."

He tapped her on the nose. "So, what you're saying is you don't think I can do it?"

"I didn't say you *couldn't* do it. I'm just *saying*," she sang the word "saying" back to him as she muffled a laugh. "I'm saying, this is something I've got to see."

"All right. You're on." He rubbed his hands together as though he were trying to start a fire with two sticks. "Then I'll see you on . . ." He got up and looked at his planner. "Saturday, September 8, 2001, at four o'clock in the afternoon walking down the aisle. Oh, and be sure to wear something dazzling for the occasion. Okay?"

Johnnie Mae laughed. "You mean I have to dress up, too? You sure ask a lot of a woman," she joked.

Landris leaned over and kissed her softly on the tip of her nose. "Yeah, and you'd better believe I give as good as I get."

"So, where should I show up? You know I need to log all of this on my schedule. It would be a shame if I were to somehow miss it because of that small technicality."

"I'll let you know 'the where' later. In the meantime, can you at least provide me with a list of the people you'd like to invite?"

"See, what did I tell you? Work, work, work. I suppose next you'll be wanting addresses to go with those names?"

"I hope I don't have to ask. Johnnie Mae, can you just work with me?" He held his thumb and index finger up in the air about a half-inch apart. "Just a little bit?"

Now that it was confirmed, Landris couldn't wait to tell Johnnie Mae where their wedding would be taking place. *She is going to flip! Or else think I have*, he thought.

* * *

Murmuring was brewing at Wings of Grace Faith Ministry Church about Minister Fulton preaching in Pastor Landris' upcoming absence. His thoughts reflected back to the first time when this had reared its ugly head. He thought he had laid this question to rest; it seemed he hadn't, since remnants appeared not only present, but also seeking to thrive again.

"We are *not* having no woman in the pulpit!" Sister Ida Jean Pickett had said just six months after Landris became the pastor. "You're trying to go too far! It's not biblical. It's against our tradition. And I for one am not gonna stand for it."

Pastor Landris looked at her and smiled. "Now Sister Ida Jean, I must beg to differ. Although I do thank you for pointing out to me just how much teaching I obviously have ahead of me. Hosea 4:6 states, 'My people are destroyed for lack of knowledge.' This proves what we don't know *can* and does hurt us."

"Well, know this: You're not ramming nothing down my throat! I know the Word."

"Sister Ida Jean, my job is to teach the Word of God and we are all required to rightly divide the Word of Truth. Thankfully, 'ramming' is not my style." Pastor Landris tipped his head toward her in a nod of respect.

"Well, when you bring it, you'd just best not come half-stepping, I can tell you that much before you even come bucking out of the starting gate."

"Sister Ida Jean, with a Bible scholar such as yourself to keep me on my toes, I wouldn't dare come any other way except with my . . . steps together." He smiled.

She nodded. "Better not. So, when can we expect this here teaching you think is gonna make me and a host of others see things differently? 'Cause you probably realize, I'm not the only one around here who feels this way."

"Soon, and apparently the sooner the better."

"All right," she said. "I'll be waiting. And it had *better* be good." She frowned, then smirked when she turned and walked away.

As Pastor Landris thought back to that day with Sister Ida

Jean, he recalled it to be the first of many hurdles he would have to overcome as a pastor.

It all started when Juanita Fulton came to him with a church question. What folks didn't know, or more correctly didn't wish to acknowledge, was that she had graduated divinity school with honors. More importantly, she was saved, with a heart for God's people. A rare find: one who genuinely loved the people and didn't just talk it.

"Pastor Landris?" she said, stopping by without prior warning.

"Yes, Sister Fulton. Come in, come in." Pastor Landris ushered her into his small, closetlike office.

She didn't sit down or begin with small talk. She just came right out with it. "I've been called to preach." Watching his reaction, she then continued. "I've been a member of this church a long time. Long enough to be aware of the sentiments toward women in general, but particularly, toward women who announce they've been called to preach. A teacher, an evangelist, a missionary, all of these—in some churches, anyway—is a different matter and more readily accepted by the masses. But God called me to preach."

Pastor Landris looked at her intensely. "And?" he said, gesturing with one hand.

"And, I want to know your view on this matter." She continued to gauge him.

"Sister Fulton, I have my own *personal* thoughts and views about this. But if you would allow me the opportunity to check first with my superior, my boss actually—"

"Your boss? Pastor, I already know pretty much what the general consensus is going to be concerning this question. I know these people—"

"Well, I am bound to take it to a higher authority. You know my superior? My boss? God." He smiled. She laughed. That caused her to relax a little. "Sister Fulton, I'm going to seek God's face and His Word for myself as I allow the Holy Spirit to lead, teach, and guide me. It shouldn't take too long. I'll get back with you on this soon."

Two days later he phoned, requesting to see her. "Sister Fulton. I don't quite know how to say this other than just say it. I did seek God. I searched His Word. The Holy Spirit was my guide to understanding and truth. Please allow me to be the first to welcome you to Wings of Grace Faith Ministry Church as Minister Fulton and to our church's pulpit."

Juanita was so excited, she screamed. "Praise God! Oh, thank you, Pastor. I thought I was going to have to leave the church in order to fulfill my calling. Thank you so much!" She then got quiet.

"Is something wrong?" Pastor Landris asked.

"Pastor Landris. I know you're new to all this, but you do realize what you're about to do? This may not go over well with the congregation, but especially those in leadership. I'm telling you, I know these people. And trust me, it's not just in our church either."

"I'll tell you what: if you'll concentrate on your initial sermon I'm scheduling in say about four weeks, I'll handle the people. Deal?" She nodded and flashed him a huge grin.

Little did Pastor Landris know the trouble he was unleashing. Turns out, Sister Ida Jean's exchange with him was one of the more pleasant ones he would encounter.

CHAPTER 3

For every creature of God is good, and nothing to be refused.

(1 Timothy 4:4)

Pastor Landris found himself addressing the matter from the pulpit prior to Juanita Fulton's first sermon. Now in 2001, he was reflecting on what he might have to do again.

"I believe it was Dr. Richard D. Dobbins who said, 'Until the pain of remaining the same hurts more than the pain of change, most people prefer to remain the same.' My dear brothers and sisters . . ." Pastor Landris had said as he looked out over his flock of the once small, but now growing congregation of around 300 people, "I have been made deftly aware of a topic we as Christians must address this day."

Pastor Landris bounced on the balls of his feet as he used the podium to lift up his body slightly in a light rhythm. "We need to ask ourselves: Why is the devil so afraid of women? More specifically: Why does it *seem* to be so important to keep women from ministering, prophesying—which means to preach . . . to tell the good news? Why? Why? Turn with me to Acts the eighth chapter, the first through the fourth verse." He waited until the sound of turning pages ceased.

"It reads: 'And Saul was consenting unto his death. And at that time there was a great persecution against the church which was at Jerusalem; and they were all scattered abroad throughout the regions of Judea and Samaria, except the apostles. And devout men carried Stephen to his burial, and made great lamentation over him. As for Saul, he made havoc of the church, entering into every house; and haling'—that means dragging off—'haling men *and* women committed them to prison. Therefore they that were scattered abroad went every where *preaching* the word.'

"Acts 2:16 tells us, 'But this is that which was spoken by the prophet Joel.' So, let's turn to Joel 2 beginning at verse 26. It reads: 'And ye shall eat in plenty, and be satisfied, and praise the name of the Lord your God, that hath dealt wondrously with you: and my people shall never be ashamed. And ye shall know that I am in the midst of Israel, and that I am the Lord your God, and none else: and my people shall never be ashamed.'

"The 28th verse says: 'And it shall come to pass afterward, that I will pour out my spirit upon all flesh; and your *sons* and your *daughters* shall prophesy.' Prophesy or prophecy here does not mean the telling of or prediction of the future or what is to come. It is *God* speaking *through* humans *to* humans in a known language in order to build up, exhort, comfort, and encourage. It is declaring, pro-*claiming* the gospel. Gospel is the 'Good News.' Truthfully, every Christian is responsible for the sharing of the gospel."

Pastor Landris continued. "It says in Joel, 'I will pour out *my spirit*,' and we know that 'will' and 'shall' are future tense, 'I will pour out my spirit upon all flesh; and your sons *and* your daughters shall prophesy, your old men shall dream dreams, your young men shall see visions. And also upon the servants and upon the *handmaids* in those days will I pour out my spirit.' In Acts 2:15–16, Peter declares, 'For these are not drunken, as ye suppose, seeing it is but the third hour of the day. But *this is that* which was spoken by the prophet Joel.' In other words, the 'will' and the 'shall' in Joel became the 'is' in the book of Acts," Pastor Landris said with enthusiasm. "But this *is* that."

He stepped out from the podium, came down out of the pulpit, and began to walk among the congregation with a solemn look. "So, again I ask the question: Why is Satan so afraid of women working in certain capacities in the church? Could it be he heard God say in Genesis 3:15, 'And I will put enmity between thee and the woman, and between thy seed and her seed;

it shall bruise thy head, and thou shalt bruise his heel'? Satan knew *what* but not how, since he's not omniscient. He didn't know when or where, since he's not omnipresent. And he didn't know how to stop it because he's not omnipotent.

"So, when you minimize the potential, you minimize the possibility. Yet Jesus was born. And being born of a woman gave Him a legal right to get back what the first man Adam gave away. Then Satan put a 'hit' out on the Word. How? After Jesus was born, Herod ordered that all children two years and under be killed. John 1:1 plainly tells us, 'In the beginning was the Word, and the Word was with God, and the Word was God.' John 1:14 further explains, 'And the Word was made flesh, and dwelt among us (and we beheld his glory, the glory as of the only begotten of the Father) full of grace and truth.'

"Satan failed to kill the Word after the Word was born in flesh. Then his plans totally backfired when Jesus laid down his life on the cross, went to hell, took back the keys, and arose with *all* power. Power He gave to we who believe. So I surmise that Satan is now waging his battle using different tactics. Tactics that could prove effective in minimizing or slowing down the spread of the good news about salvation if we play into his hands.

"The fewer folks to spread the gospel, the fewer souls receiving an opportunity to hear the Word and be saved. The more folks accepting Satan's lies that God wants us sick or dying early because 'God needs flowers in His garden or angels'—the more eliminated. Lies pitting us against each other using Godly differences among ourselves as a human race: gender and color—superiority among dust of the earth. Lies Satan needs us to buy into so he can carry out his plan to limit us and take as many unsaved souls to hell as possible.

"Or to lessen the number of people who might bless those saved already by teaching them of their God-given authority through Jesus' name and benefits Jesus purchased on behalf of those who accept Him. If Satan can get us to carry out his plans, he wins. His strategy is to minimize the soldiers by getting us to dilute our power and strength, to fight ourselves—plain and simple. Jesus said, 'A house divided against itself cannot stand.' "

Pastor Landris stopped to see if the people were getting this message. He could clearly see that many were allowing the words to soak in, but still a good many seemed to be purposely tuning him out.

"I'm aware there are many scriptures that we have believed supported a campaign against women preachers, women in authority, women teaching men, and even women speaking in church. Many of you here are convinced and believe you can arguably prove that women should never be in any type of leadership role. For me to speak to all of these scriptures would take much more time than I'm allotted in one sitting. But I do want to address some of these scriptures before concluding this teaching today.

"When scripture is taken out of context or not interpreted properly, and it distorts God's character, robs believers of their *God-given inheritance*, and/or causes the believer to come to a position of nonresistance, it is likely being used as a doctrine of devils. First Timothy 4:1 warns of this. 'Now the Spirit speaketh expressly, that in the latter times some shall depart from the faith, giving heed to seducing spirits, and *doctrines of devils.*'

"That's why it's important we study scriptures ourselves, employing the Holy Spirit to assist with its interpretation and illumination, praying Psalm 119:18, 'Open thou mine eyes,' and that we be under a good teacher or preacher. It also helps to learn the history behind a situation happening, especially during the time certain passages were penned.

"Many people quote several scriptures written by Paul out of First Corinthians as their basis to keep women in their 'places.' Let us be mindful of the time and place these writings were set— a time when women were second-class, many times treated as subhumans. A close example of the attitudes toward women still flourishing today would be a place like Afghanistan. Research it for yourself. See how these women are treated. Not being allowed to learn. Having to always be covered from head to toe. A mindset about women and their being evil and useless actually began with the ancient Greeks like Aristotle, Plato, and Socrates, and has continued throughout history and countries. Study this for yourself.

"For years women were not allowed to learn scriptures. So

when the opportunity presented itself for them to teach and prophesy, it's natural they'd have questions the men had already been taught. Let me say here that contrary to popular belief, Paul did not have a negative stance about women. Women were ministering during his time. But there are times when we find we have to work within a system in order to change the system.

"Sometimes things may be offensive and a stumbling block that might hinder people from hearing the ultimate message. My dreadlocks, for instance—I know some of you had a hard time listening to me at first because you wanted me to get rid of them."

People laughed and a few responded with, "Amen!" Pastor Landris laughed also.

"Some of you had scriptures about it." He shook his dreadlocks. "Say, First Corinthians 11:14, where it says, 'Doth not even nature itself teach you, that if a man have long hair, it is a shame unto him?' If this were an absolute Word from God, then it would have to apply to all men. So, explain God's Word to Samson sanctioning his hair being long?"

He smiled. "But most of you have gotten past my hair and now focus on the Word of God. Of course, had my hair been a huge deterrent, I might have, *might*, have cut them. Not because I believed they were wrong or inappropriate, but because the greater good would have outweighed my need to express myself as I please: culture and style. Having said that, in the days of the early Christian church, Paul was mindful of these things as well. Many of Paul's statements were relative to a period, culture, and laws and not an absolute, across-the-board mandate from God. This is why it's so important to allow the Holy Spirit to guide you through scriptures, distinguishing between relative and absolute.

"Paul knew they had to first gain people's ear for them to hear. And, ultimately, the Word of God would do the changing from the inside out. A side note here: Paul was also not an advocate of slavery either, but then, that's another sermon for yet another time."

He wiped sweat from his head and continued. "People quote First Corinthians 14:34–35, where it states, 'Let your women keep silence in the churches: for it is not permitted unto them to speak; but they are commanded to be under obedience, as also saith the *law*. And if they will learn any thing, let them ask their husbands at home: for it is a shame for women to speak in the church.' Here's what you need to note about those passages.

"Number one: They should be looked at in context with the preceding scriptures that address order and how to maintain order without causing confusion. Number two: Women at the time, *by law* as I said earlier, were considered second-class citizens. There were laws about how women should act at all times. Number three: Not all women had husbands, so the order seemed to address wives, not women, who may have disrupted the services by asking clarifying questions of their husbands. Relating to an era and situation.

"In verse 36, Paul seems to be making a point of what some people believed and he appears to be mocking them by saying, 'What? came the word of God out from you? or came it unto you only?' If Paul really meant for women to be quiet in church, why then in First Corinthians 11:5 give them speaking instructions? 'But every *woman* that *prayeth* or *prophesieth* with her head uncovered dishonoreth her head.' Paul was instructing prayer and prophesying in the church—the mouth. He was addressing situations advising both women and men how to behave and how to dress without unnecessary distractions.

"Had Paul meant for women to be quiet as an absolute, it would have to apply to all sounds. No singing, praying aloud, testifying, teaching, and no saying, 'Amen!' If that was Paul's intention, then why instruct women how to speak and what to wear when they were speaking?" Pastor Landris paused a minute as he walked around.

"Now let's look at superiority and submission, in First Corinthians 11:3 and 11:12. 'But I would have you know, that the head of every man is Christ; and the head of the woman is the man; and the head of Christ is God.' First off, this is speaking about responsibility and accountability, not superiority. The Father and Christ are coequal, fulfilling different functions. Christ is also *not* the head of every man, only those who receive Him. So, if you can see equality and personal worth, but distinction, in the responsibility and function between God and Christ, then it would be wrong to interpret the woman and man differently in this same scripture. The 12th verse says, 'For as the woman is *of* the man, even so is the man also *by* the woman; but all things of God.' This is referring to creation and procreation. Mutual dependency. Submission: like a lock and a key. Both needing the other to function as *designed*. Purpose. Paul explains 'in Christ there is neither male nor female.' You see? One Body of Christ, but all things of God."

Pastor Landris let out an audible sigh. "I believe when you have an enemy, you should look at the strategy your enemy may be using to bring you down. So I ask: What purpose would God have in keeping women silent? How does it serve God to keep any worker on the sidelines when the harvest is plentiful and the laborers few? On the other hand, were I trying to limit the Word of God from being spread, what better way to muzzle the ox that treads the corn? The enemy, who is outnumbered and already declared defeated, appears to have devised a way to employ the believers' services and limit our effectiveness. Look around you. How many bodies would be unemployed in the work of the Lord if women were nonexistent? totally silenced?

"Ask yourself: Why would God allow people to miss hearing about Jesus, miss having the opportunity to be saved just because the Word is coming out of the mouth of a woman? Oh, I know some of you still want to blame Eve for sin entering into the earth. But I'd like to remind you, God commanded the man. Read Genesis 2:16–17. Eve wasn't even created then. He commanded Adam, 'Of every tree of the garden thou mayest freely eat: But of the tree of the knowledge of good and evil, thou shalt not eat of it: for in the day that thou eatest thereof thou shalt surely die.'

"Now flip over to Genesis 3:3. I have often wondered exactly what Adam told Eve that God told him, since Eve's response to the serpent's question was, 'But of the fruit of the tree which is in the *midst* of the garden, God hath said, Ye shall not eat of it.' That scripture didn't say the tree in the midst. Look back at it. That's why it's imperative we're taught correctly and know God's Word ourselves. That's why Paul encouraged wives with husbands—who had been taught already—to ask questions at home. Believers need to know so we don't miss God. Lives are at stake; this is too important."

Pastor Landris smiled as he came to a close. "Beloved, do you truly believe that God would prefer folks be lost because the creation He created and that is speaking His Word is a woman? that He would silence potential laborers but declare that if these should hold their peace He would make the rocks cry out? Does this sound like the intent of God? preferring souls be lost, never the possibility to hear about the death, burial, and resurrection of Jesus Christ, and end up going to hell because God would never use a woman? Correct me, but sounds more like devil doctrines than God's nature or intent."

Pastor Landris waved his hand. "The Bible is full of women whom God used in the ministry. Women were spotlighted in Jesus' life: His birth; when He ministered; His death, burial, and resurrection. It was Mary Magdalene whom Jesus showed himself to first after His resurrection. A woman. John, Chapter 20. Check it. Don't be deceived by Satan and his deceptive devices. Deception is Satan's only weapon against us. He causes *us* to believe the wrong thing. Speak the wrong thing. Then we just lie down and allow him to walk all over us because we *believe* we are in God's will. Let's not partner with Satan and allow him to use us against ourselves. Now if you still don't get this, then pray and ask God to speak to your heart about it." He wiped his face with his handkerchief.

"Well, that was my best shot. But understand: I must move how the Lord moves me. And if that puts me against some of you desiring to hold on to the '*traditions of men*,' then that's the position I find myself in. I'll not say that God has not called a woman to preach because she's a woman. God's ways are not our ways; his thoughts, not our thoughts. I pray Minister Fulton preach the Word in and out of season. That she plants licks upside Satan and the demons' heads, and truly bless God's people. You see, I'm pulling for *our* team." He smiled. "Like Peter said in Acts 11:17, 'Forasmuch then as God gave them the *like gift* as he did unto us, who believed on the Lord Jesus Christ; what was

I, that I could withstand God?' " He looked up. "In other words: Who am I . . . to question God?"

He opened his arms. "The doors of the church are open," he said. And at that moment, one-third of the congregation—about 100 people—stood up and marched out. Landris knew that that same fraction now, in 2001, would be closer to 1,300 people.

CHAPTER 4

In the house of the righteous is much treasure.

(Proverbs 15:6)

A guy from GDS express courier delivery service handed Lena a package addressed to her after she signed for it. Opening it again left her questioning: *Who knows to send me something at Theresa's new address?* She looked at the contents, disbelieving her eyes.

"What is it?" Theresa said, gauging the expression on Lena's face. "Bad news?"

Lena shook her head, then handed a photo to Theresa as she continued reading the one-page paper enclosed along with it. "Goodness," Lena said. "My goodness."

Theresa stared at the photo. "This looks like the necklace you gave me last year." Theresa had worn it once, when she and Maurice attended a gala two months ago.

"Not looks like. It is."

"How can you be so sure?"

Lena handed Theresa the paper and waited for her to finish reading it. "But this paper says the stone they're looking for is an 'alexandrite set in platinum.' The necklace you gave me is an amethyst set in antique sterling silver," Theresa said. "I don't get it. What makes you think it's the same necklace?" Theresa gave the paper back to Lena.

"It says, 'An alexandrite viewed under sunlight or fluorescent light appears medium to bluish green, but under artificial light or twilight it appears violet or a purplish red.' When I gave you that necklace, we were inside a room: artificial light. It appeared it was an amethyst. But I've seen it in sunlight. The color was totally different. Back then I couldn't explain it; just figured my eyes were playing tricks on me. This says, 'The alexandrite stone came from Russia long before their resources were depleted.' "

Theresa looked at the paper again. "It claims, 'A stone over five carats is almost unknown.' "

"Yeah. And the stone in the necklace you have is enormous," Lena said.

"According to this: Ten carats. Apparently around 1830, rare stones were discovered in Russia and named for Czar Alexander II: alexandrite. If the stone we have is the same one they're looking for, it carries some kind of history with it." Theresa studied the photo closer. "Probably why they're offering a reward for its return. Do you think George Kunz of Tiffany really ended up resetting the czar's personal stone in platinum like this says? Can you imagine who might have owned this before you got ahold of it?"

"I can't imagine."

"I still don't think this is the same piece of jewelry you gave to me, though." Theresa looked again at the photo. "Maybe somebody had a knockoff made of it. You know, folks are known for doing that sort of thing. Especially rich folks trying to impress each other."

"It's the same one, Theresa." Lena took the photo from her daughter. "You do still have the necklace?"

"Yeah."

"Can you get it?"

"Right now?"

Lena was studying the photo. "If possible. I realize everything's not unpacked yet."

Theresa got up and came back with the necklace a few minutes later. "Wow. To think somebody could be offering $1 million for this. That's if it's the same one."

"Turn it over," Lena said. Theresa did as instructed, sitting down gently next to Lena. "Look here." Lena's nail touched one particular spot.

Theresa looked where Lena pointed on the back of the necklace. "You mean this mark? It looks like a symbol or some foreign inscription." She would have thought it just a defect if Lena hadn't pointed it out. Theresa could see now the mark was intentional.

"Now look at this." Lena pointed to the photo.

Theresa brought the picture closer to her face. "It's the exact same mark."

"Yes," Lena said with a sigh.

Theresa turned toward Lena. "But how did you know that was there? I never would have noticed something so small like that."

Lena shook her head. "This necklace was all I had left of Big Mama's. I studied it to where I knew every scratch, every etch, every detail about it. Nobody knew I had it. Nobody. When Big Mama gave it to me right before she died, she told me not to let anyone know it existed. 'No matter what, no matter who: No one can know you have this! Not 'til you're grown. It's your inheritance,' she had said. 'And I've kept it safe.' "

"So where did she get it?"

"All she ever told me was it came from a family she'd worked for. Some woman gave it to her, and she was passing it on to me. She made me promise I wouldn't let anyone take it no matter what they might later try and tell me. 'Nobody!' she said."

Theresa ran her hand across the stone. "You think she got this legally? I mean it is a pretty elaborate piece of jewelry. And if these people are offering a $1 million reward for its return, 'No questions asked,' I can't even begin to conceive what it's really worth."

Lena drew back. "What are you trying to say? That Big Mama stole it?"

"No, not stole it. Maybe it was just some sort of misunderstanding?"

Lena shook her head. "Not Big Mama. She always said it wasn't but two things she couldn't stand: a liar and a thief. The worst tongue-lashing I ever got was when I took this quarter that was on the piano. Then I lied about not taking it. Funny thing was, she had left the quarter there for me. So, in essence, I actually stole from myself. And that's what she told me: 'When you steal, you mainly take something valuable from yourself.' " Lena took the necklace and smiled. "No. Big Mama said this belonged to me. Something I should pass on someday. 'Keep it in the family.' When Big Mama died, my mother returned two days after the funeral. She didn't even care enough to make it to her mother's funeral. Just came looking for what she could take. 'Where's the good stuff?' she said. 'What have you done with it? I know she had more than this knickknack junk!' She tore the house up looking, then took what she pleased. Told me I didn't have a right to nothing. Sold the house. Since I was only sixteen and Big Mama had no real will, just written wishes on a signed paper leaving me everything, there was not much I could do." Lena dabbed at her eyes. "Well, no need of torturing myself about the past. It's just . . . the first time I get to see my mother and know it, and she comes in taking all she can. Then she leaves me without a second thought, again, all alone to fend for myself."

"That was when you moved into that duplex house?"

Lena smiled. "Yes. I had to live somewhere. I went to school and worked to provide food and a roof over my head. Nobody questioned me about adult supervision. There was no reason to. Then I learned I was pregnant with you, and my life changed again."

"Why didn't you just sell the necklace? And where was it during the fire?"

"Questions . . . questions. I didn't sell the necklace because Big Mama gave it to me. It was all I had left of her. Our inheritance—mine, then yours. I had it hidden, but good."

"But nobody knew you had it."

"If I had sold it, I wouldn't have known the true value anyway. I probably wouldn't have gotten much for it: at least not what it was worth. They could have told me it was just costume jewelry, and I wouldn't have known any better. According to this paper, 'No more than one person out of 100,000 has ever even seen a real alexandrite.' The way that thing changes color, they probably wouldn't have known it was a genuine alexandrite either.

Besides—" she handed the necklace lovingly back to Theresa—
"I saved it for you. It belongs to you now."

"Yeah, but that was before we knew what it was worth." She
handed it back to Lena. "You take it. And if you want to contact
these people about it, I can't think of anything better to happen
for you. You deserve it. That much money can change your life."

Lena refused to take it. "Put it back up. I don't know what's
going on, but I do think you need to find a safer place to store it.
Not here. The sooner, the better. Whoever sent me this package
must believe I have the necklace. Or at least that I know where it
is."

"Do you know who might have sent it?"

"No. And there's no return address or name on the package."

Theresa got the courier envelope. "I'm going to call the
courier service to see what they can tell me about where this may
have come from." Theresa looked at the contact number on the
paper. "Let's call the number on here and see who's on the other
end."

Lena called; it was some kind of automated answering service.
The paper provided an ID code to be used when calling. Lena
opted not to use it. Not yet. There were entirely too many questions Lena wasn't comfortable about with answers, she was reluctantly being forced to conclude. Foremost among them: *Who
on earth even knew I had the necklace?*

CHAPTER 5

For the lips of a strange woman drop as a honeycomb.

(Proverbs 4:3)

Johnnie Mae couldn't stop thinking about Sarah, but she had decided not to go back to see her. She was too busy to waste time on delusions or fairy tales. Sarah, allegedly from a family of wealth, couldn't prove it. She told Johnnie Mae all about Asheville, North Carolina, and seemed an expert on Biltmore Castle. Sarah spoke of visits to "Otto the Magnificent—Otto H. Kahn's" mansion in Cold Spring Harbor, New York.

"Oheka Castle?" Johnnie Mae said. "It's in Cold Spring Hills," she corrected her.

Sarah looked confused. "Oheka Castle? And they changed it from Harbor to Hills?"

Johnnie Mae smiled. *How can she possibly claim to know so much about Otto Kahn's place, the second largest residence ever built in America, and not know what it's called?* "Oheka Castle, that's what it's called these days."

"Where'd they come up with that name?"

"Oheka. It's a monogram for Otto H. Kahn's name. 'O' from Otto, 'h-e' from—"

"Hermann. That was his middle name," Sarah said. "Herman with a double en."

"Yes. Hermann," Johnnie Mae said, somewhat impressed. "And 'k-a' from Kahn."

"He died in 1934, you know. Heart attack. Tragic. I was nineteen years old at the time."

"Oh."

"I met many of the people who worked on his house. Did you know much of the intricate work at both Biltmore and Oheka, as you call it, was done by colored folks?" She sat back. "Biltmore's owner, George Vanderbilt, even commissioned a beautiful, multilevel, Tudor-style building specifically for the hundreds of colored craftsmen who worked on Biltmore Castle. It was called the Young Men's Institute. That was in 1892. It later became a cultural center. The Vanderbilts celebrated the house's completion with a Christmas party in December of 1895. Twenty years before my time, but my mother would reference back to it every year when she compared other gatherings that didn't measure up. Colored folks around Asheville held quite powerful and prominent positions."

Johnnie Mae frowned. "Sarah, why do you call African Americans 'colored'?"

"I'm sorry. Is that offensive? I don't mean to offend anyone. I just always hated saying 'Negro.' Mamie said most Southern whites didn't always utter that word correctly. Colored was what most of the folks I knew called themselves." She sipped her cocoa.

"People say 'African American' now. Although many still say 'black.' Me, for one."

Sarah smiled. "See, that's my problem. It keeps changing. It's hard to keep up or know what's not offensive. Colored seemed to have worked for me, so I kept to what I knew. What would you advise me to say and do these days?" She took another sip of cocoa and shook her head. "Oh I do so miss Mamie! I've mentioned her to you."

"Briefly."

"Mamie was my best friend in the world. We were like sisters. She worked at our house, but if you ask me, I'd say she was the one who ran it. Of course, my mother was pretty strong-willed herself. Unlike some of the high society women during that time, she would speak her mind if you pushed her. She never cared much for Mamie, though."

"Do you want to talk about Mamie?" Johnnie Mae asked.

"No. I was just thinking if Mamie were around, she'd help me navigate what was appropriate to say or not. I declare she was one of the smartest folks I knew. Mamie spoke quite properly, though she refrained around many folks—both colored and white. People expected things of you, but I knew the truth. It's a shame the way people regarded colored—I mean African Americans. Acting like they weren't smart. A lot of them were some of the most brilliant folks I ever met, even if they never got proper credit. My uncle took credit for all the inventions this one African-American man came up with. Oh, he gave him a little money from them, but wasn't nothing compared to what he made from certain inventions that history still credits with the wrong name." Sarah leaned forward. "If you haven't been, you should visit Biltmore Castle," she said. "It was the most beautiful place back in my day, especially around Christmas. Oh, you should have seen the decorations! I hear they have kept things up and still make a big to-do for Christmas. I heard it's open for tourists again. First time was 1930. But go, if you ever get the chance."

"I may do that," Johnnie Mae said, eyeing closely Sarah's every move.

"Biltmore had about 250 rooms, 31 of them guest bedrooms, 43 bathrooms, a two-lane bowling alley, indoor heated swimming pool, 65 stenciled fireplaces, a baronial banquet hall I believe they say was 45 feet wide by 72 feet long and about 70 feet high with a triple fireplace that was so large you could walk into it. That hall seated 64 people! Can you believe, built in 1895, Biltmore was already wired for electricity—had central heating and refrigeration, and an Otis elevator? The first passenger elevator in Asheville, yes it was.

"But the library was my favorite room! The ceiling had this seventeenth-century Pellegrini canvas from Italy: a rare Venetian ceiling painting that 'opened the doors to heaven' if you took the time to look up. Angels everywhere. There was this black marbled fireplace surrounded by two stories of shelves filled with 23,000 books. A spiral staircase took you to the main level of the library. And the library terrace, oh—provided the most beautiful, endless scenery imaginable of the site and those majestic mountains! There was a passage behind the fireplace mantel that led to the house's second floor." Sarah stopped. "Oh, I'm just going on and on. I get a bit carried away when I speak of the house that George Dub-ya built. I mean, but it took 1,000 stone-cutters and 1,000 craftsmen. Skilled artisans were brought in from all over the world. Working around the clock, it took six years to build that French Renaissance chateau that overlooks the French Broad River. Pristine, dear!"

In awe, Johnnie Mae found it hard to believe Sarah could be accurate with such tall facts. But she did possess a gift with words. "Sarah, how did you end up here?"

"Here? I believe someone drove me."

"Drove you as in a vehicle. Or drove you as in . . ."

"Crazy? Is that the word you're looking for, dear?"

"No, not really."

"That's what they said originally when they put me in that other place: that I was crazy. Delusional. 'Unable to separate reality from fantasy.' I was no more crazy then than I am now. Although many may argue the point." She laughed. "Coming through all I have, it's amazing I haven't *gone* crazy, though. But to answer your question: I was driven in a vehicle commissioned by my family. Traitors." She leaned back. "Now I'm here. But I'd like to get home once before I die. It's been 65 years since I was last home."

"And where is home, Sarah?"

"Why Asheville, North Carolina. Haven't you been paying attention, dear? I am a woman of means, and I desire to reclaim what is rightfully mine. Now, there's one woman who might be able to help me if she's still alive. She has a box I gave her. It will prove I speak the truth. I just have to find the key. You'll need it to get inside the box."

"The key?" Johnnie Mae asked, unable to mask her true skepticism.

"Yes. There is a key to the box she holds. Of course the box is locked, and I am the only one with the key. With all of this moving from one place to the other, and having to keep it hidden, I seem to have misplaced it. But a woman in Dixon Town has my box. I need you to find my Pearl. Then you'll see. See that I'm not some delusional old woman making up stories." She looked at Johnnie Mae. "That's what *you* do, don't you, dear?"

"What?"

"Make up stories."

Johnnie Mae laughed. "I write fiction. So, yes, I suppose you could say that."

"Well, if what I'm saying proves not to be true, feel free to use this tale to pay for any time of yours you believe I may have wasted."

Johnnie Mae smiled. *Yeah, and who'll publish it? They'll probably say it's unrealistic. A rich white woman's family institutionalizes her to bury a secret surrounding a stillborn baby. When she insists there's more to the story than they admit, she's hidden away in Alabama with no family willing to bring her home or allow her to reclaim her rightful place.*

"Sarah, about Mamie? Would you happen to recall her last name?"

"Mamie married that fellow who did that fancy, intricate-type work. 'He creates art out of iron,' Mamie would brag. 'In constant demand by the big shots.' She'd said he worked on Otto's house in 1920. Was in Virginia in 1935 when their twins were born. Willie B. Now what was his last name? Was 15 years Mamie's senior. What was—?"

"Look. Don't worry about it. If you should think of it later, just let me know."

" 'Pitter-patter of little feet.' That's it! Peterson. She became Mamie Peterson."

Johnnie Mae had written all this down with Sarah promising proof upon her return. *What am I doing? I don't have time for this nonsense. Forget this*, Johnnie Mae decided.

CHAPTER 6

For it is a good thing that the heart be established with grace.

(Hebrews 13:9(b))

"Mama Lena. Would you please tell your daughter to stop fighting me about everything?" Maurice said to Lena.

Lena was finishing her last forkful of macaroni & cheese. She and Theresa had played around using seven different cheeses at once to come up with the best macaroni & cheese either of them had ever tasted. "Now Maurice, you know the child barely listens to me."

" 'Barely' is better than never," Maurice said as he grabbed the bowl of mac & cheese. "Does anybody else want any more of this?" He looked from Lena to Theresa. Theresa burst into a laugh. He had eaten half the bowl already.

"Go on, child. Knock yourself out." Lena laughed and fanned her hand at him.

"We just appreciate your allowing us to at least taste it. Otherwise, we wouldn't have had a clue whether it was any good or not," Theresa said.

Maurice raked the rest of the macaroni & cheese into his plate. "Oh, you would have had a clue all right." He set the bowl back on the glasstop table. "That empty bowl right there would have been clue enough. You know I don't play about my macaroni & cheese."

"So, Maurice, what is it you think I can convince my daughter of doing?"

"Marrying me, for starters."

Theresa sat back in her chair. "Maurice, not again. I've already told you . . ."

Maurice stopped chewing. "And I told you. I want our child to have his—"

"Or *her*," Theresa said with a smirk.

"Or her parents living together," Maurice said.

Lena leaned in and looked at him. Maurice caught her stare.

"*Married* and living together," he said, clarifying his statement for Lena's benefit. "Theresa knows what I mean," he said to Theresa.

Theresa speared a broccoli floret and twirled it around in the air. She didn't say a word, but the broccoli seemed to say, *Whatever*.

"Theresa. Why won't you marry him? He seems honorable."

"Because . . ."

Lena waited a second. "Because what?"

"Because I don't believe having a baby with someone means you have to marry him. Do you know how many people get married because the girl's pregnant, then end up divorcing later because the two can't stand each other?" Theresa said. "Too many."

"Do you know how many people date for years, some even living together—"

Lena gave Maurice that look again.

"Not that we're ever planning on living together without marriage," he said more to Lena than Theresa, then back to Theresa. "But people date for years and still end up divorcing. And I'm not going to marry you because of this baby."

Theresa got up from the table and went to the great room. Maurice followed.

"Theresa, let's face it. I've always loved you. I've wanted to marry you since we were young . . . er. Younger. Since we were younger. You were the one about to marry the good old reverend last year. Otherwise, I would have asked you then. You know I tried to get back with you years before, but you didn't want to hear a word I had to say."

"Look, Maurice. I know it seems ridiculous, but I don't want to rush into anything. I'm having your baby. Now, you gave me money to put down on this house, although I told you I had my own money and I didn't need your help, and I appreciate that."

"The baby is both our responsibility. I'm not going to let you bear the burden of raising our child by yourself. This house is good for you and for our baby. I'd just like to be able to enjoy the both of you as a family: mother, father, and child. I'd like the baby to have my last name. I would like for *you* to take my last name if you would."

"Oh, Maurice. That is so male thinking. What if I don't want to change my name? What if we get married and I keep my maiden name? Or hyphenate it with yours?"

"Hyphenate it? So you can drop it more easily if things don't work out between us?"

"I know: Why don't you take my last name? Why does the woman have to give up her name? How about you become Mr. Maurice Greene Jordan? Or Greene-Jordan?"

Maurice took her hand. "Marry me?"

Theresa laughed. "Give it a rest."

"Think about it then—for me . . . and for our baby? I want us to be a family, Tee. I'd like to spend as much time with the two of you without having to get up and go home or sleep on the couch."

Theresa chewed on her bottom lip. "Maurice, let me be honest with you. I'm not sure whether the two of us have enough going between us to be discussing marriage."

"I love you," he said. "I'd make you happy."

She smiled.

"Do you love me?" he asked.

"Yeah. I suppose I do." She sat down. "But is love enough?"

"I suppose not enough for you to marry me?"

"Maurice, I just don't know right now."

"Then you have a little over a month. Can you know before the baby comes?"

She laughed. The doorbell rang. Maurice looked at her stomach. "Sit tight, I'll get it."

Theresa got up and walked with him. "Like you'd know who it is if they told you."

Maurice looked out the side window and shrugged. It was a

woman, but it was too dark out for him to see well. "Who's there?" Maurice said as he flipped on the outside light.

"I'm looking for Lena Patterson, please."

"And who may I tell her is asking?" Maurice said as he watched Theresa peek out.

The visitor hesitated. "Elaine. Tell her, Elaine."

Theresa got a look at the woman and hurriedly started for the kitchen. "Mama!" she whispered. "Mama! It's that woman! At the front door. Asking for you. You remember, the one who came here about two weeks ago but wouldn't leave her name?"

"Did she say who she is this time?" Lena dried her hands on a dishtowel.

Maurice walked into the kitchen. "Lena, somebody named Elaine is here to see you."

"Elaine?" Lena looked at the ceiling as she thought out loud. "Elaine? Elaine?"

"You want me to see what she wants?" Maurice asked.

"No. I'll see."

Theresa started walking in step with Lena. "I'll go with you."

"I haven't a clue who Elaine is. Maybe she's a salesperson or something."

Lena went to the door and opened it. "Yes? May I help you?"

"Lena?" Elaine looked at her and smiled. "Lena, it's so wonderful to see you."

Lena looked at her closer. She felt as though she might have seen this person somewhere before years ago. But for the life of her, she couldn't place when or where.

"May I come in?"

Lena was hesitant at first. But Maurice was there, and the woman seemed harmless. "I suppose. For a minute. Actually, we were just finishing up supper."

Elaine came inside and looked around, then back at Lena, who was practically being shadowed by Theresa. Neither Lena nor Theresa offered her a seat.

"I suppose you're wondering why I'm here."

"You say that as though I should know you," Lena said, still studying her face.

Elaine let out a tiny chuckle. "And you're acting as though

you don't." Elaine walked closer to Lena. "My name is Elaine Robertson."

Lena smiled. "Elaine Robertson? Still not tickling a familiar ivory tune for me."

"What about Memory?"

"Oh, my memory is fine, thank you very much."

Elaine reached out and touched Lena's hand. "Dearie, *my* name is Memory; Memory Elaine Patterson Kane Stone Robertson. Married three times, and the man I'm with now is not my husband." She smiled. "Memory was my given name, although I go by my middle name of Elaine."

Theresa looked at a solemn Lena for an explanation. "Mama, who is she?"

Elaine smiled at Theresa. "Why, dearie. I'm Lena's mother. So I guess that would officially make me your grandmother." She extended her hand to a frozen Theresa.

Maurice looked at Theresa. Theresa looked at Lena. And Lena stared hard at Elaine.

Definitely no love lost or found at the present time between them.

CHAPTER 7

Let brotherly love continue.

(Hebrews 13:1)

Pastor Landris opened an official letter from the Internal Revenue Service. He started laughing. "Boy, when you guys make a mistake, you sure make one worthy of arresting one's attention," he said to the letter.

Landris originally had some stock left in his account. It was really only one stock: Microsoft, but he still owned shares of it. His brother was the one who handled all that for him. George had instructed his brother, Thomas Landris, to sell some shares back in 1998. When he relocated from Birmingham to Atlanta, that was how he had purchased his house and that 1999 Mercedes-Benz with cash, debt free. It was silver, with a fully independent suspension, a 5.0-liter V-8 engine that produced a peak output of 302 with a horsepower at 5600 rpm, a five-speed automatic transmission, napa leather upholstery the color of Starbucks latte, and a convertible top made of Panorama glass hardtop instead of the standard aluminum roof—a dream come true.

Thomas was two years older than George. He'd always had a good head for business and speculative-type ventures. If only he were better about holding on to money once he acquired it. George, on the other hand, hadn't been interested in investing in the least. But Thomas had talked George into letting him invest a few thousand dollars from George's company management incentive program back in January 1987. That was how George ended up with 2,000 shares of Microsoft stock in the first place.

Thomas had had a "feeling" about a new company that was going public called Microsoft. Only Thomas, as usual, was long on "feelings" and short on cash.

"Man, what does this have to do with me?" George had asked.

"I'm just asking for a loan. And I promise when this stock hits it big—and it will—I will pay you back every nickel, every dime I owe you and then some," Thomas said.

"Thomas, that stock would have to make it really big for you to pay me back every cent you owe me. Man, how many times are you gonna do this? Why don't you just get yourself a real job and work for a living like everybody else?"

"I had a job. You know how these folks are. The Man is always trying to keep the black man down."

"You can't blame your last job loss on 'the Man,' Thomas, so don't even go there."

"Oh. You talking about 'cause I was late, right? Look. Things happen. They were wrong to fire me for being late that last time, and you know it. It wasn't my fault. I got robbed. At gunpoint—"

"You didn't have any business being in a place like that in the first place, Thomas."

"Oh? The best party in town and you think I wasn't going just because it was in the boonies? Man, please! Everybody who was anybody was up at that party."

"Yeah," George said, laughing. "And you see what you got for your good times? Robbed, then knocked upside your head because it wasn't even worth their time and effort to rob you. Then you got to work the next morning and *what*? They fired you."

"I got there late! But that time wasn't my fault. I went straight from the emergency room to work. Most folks would have just called in sick. Doing right just doesn't pay."

"Thomas, they fired you because you'd already been late five times in ten days that particular month, twelve times the month before, fourteen times—"

"George, you don't have to go there." Thomas placed his foot on George's coffee table. George gave him a baleful eye and he took his foot down. "The first and only time I was late for a truly legitimate reason, and they fired me. Canned. Now how fair is that?"

"But they warned you: 'One more absence or tardiness this month, and you're gone. No exception.' They told you, Thomas."

"It was still wrong, and you know it." He stood up straight. "But listen. Just let me have about two thousand of your bonus money, and I'll make us both rich. You watch."

"I'll tell you what. You can invest half of that for me and the other half for yourself."

"Ah, man. Really? That's great!"

"But—" George walked over to him. "When I tell you I want to sell my shares, I had better have some to sell. And whatever my money makes, I want it. No rationalization and no exception. Whatever you make from the part I'm fronting you is yours to keep. But Thomas, I'm not playing about my part you're investing on my behalf."

"So you believe me? You believe I'm right about this one?"

"I don't know. But I'm going to try you with it. I mean it, though. If I tell you to sell my shares, I want them sold. I don't want to have a discussion or debate about it. And then I want all of the money my investment earns, too. That's if there is any. *All*."

"Oh, there's going to be plenty. I feel it. You and I are going to be rolling in dough."

"Yeah. I've heard that one before, too. How much did you lose of Mom's money on that last 'feeling' you had?" George got his checkbook, wrote Thomas a $2,500 check, and handed it to him.

"Well, this check—minus your investment, of course, just my part, mind you—is going to make me enough to pay yours and Mom's money back. Just watch and see."

George allowed Thomas to deal with his investments. And Thomas turned out to be right. When George told Thomas how much money he needed in 1998, Thomas sold the corresponding number of shares and wired George the funds. Almost a million dollars, and it would have been had George not opted for taxes to be taken out of it first. Thomas had told George he still had shares left to demonstrate to him he was keeping his end of their agreement.

"When you need more cash, just let me know and I'll take care of everything," Thomas said. "Would you like to know how many shares you have left?"

"No," George said, figuring it couldn't be that much, since he'd cashed in such a large amount already. "You just remember what I told you. That's all we need to know."

"I know I wished I hadn't sold my shares so early," Thomas said. "You really were wise to hold on to yours, George. Really wise."

George didn't know how wise, but he decided in March of 2000 he wanted to sell all the shares he had left. The past few times he had called Thomas, it had taken him months to return his call. George didn't want to be dependent on a brother who pretty well might have already sold his shares and pocketed the money. Or worse, George might really need his money and Thomas would be nowhere to be found until long after the fact.

Thomas had called him later that year to let him know he'd gotten his message. "I'll catch up with you soon," he had said. "I really need to talk to you. It's important." George didn't know what that meant, but it didn't sound good at all. More than half of 2001 was gone, and he hadn't received any money nor heard a word from his brother.

Now the IRS was sending George a bill for taxes due on an amount that couldn't possibly be right. Impossible. So George called the number listed to straighten it out.

"Yes, my name is George Landris. I need to speak with someone about a notice I received today dated July 9, 2001." George gave the woman—Ms. Tatum—his caller ID and social security number, then waited.

"Mr. Landris, our records indicate you sold some stock in the year 2000, and that income was not reported on your 2000 federal income tax return," Ms. Tatum said.

So Thomas did sell my stock. Not that George had seen one red cent from it yet.

"Look, Ms. Tatum. I don't deny having owned some stock that may have been sold. Someone else was managing it for me.

But I can assure you: There is no way I owe taxes on the amount
listed on this notice. No way. I owned shares of Microsoft stock,
but it couldn't be much, since I sold a pretty good chunk back in
1998. This clearly has to be a computer error. So what do I need
to do to get it straightened out?"

"Well, Mr. Landris, all I can do is place a note on your record
to indicate you dispute the amount reported. You'll need to contact the brokerage firm and have them check into it." She gave
him the name of the firm that reported the investment income
to his social security number. "They will either prove their
records correct or see it was actually reported incorrectly, and
correct it. I agree with you, though; this does appear grossly
overstated. If what was reported is incorrect, they are required
by law to send a correction."

"So you're not going to remove this until you've heard back
from them?"

"Can't. Unless and until we receive information from the re-
porting firm to change it, we have to assume this information is
correct. Just please keep our office informed."

George wasn't worried. As soon as he contacted the firm handling the original sell transaction, he'd get this error straightened out. Then there would be only two lingering questions to
be answered: *Where is my brother? And where is the money, however
much it truly turned out to be, from the sale of my stock?*

George tried calling his brother again. The answering service
he generally used when he was "out-of-pocket" (which usually
meant he was somewhere in the United States or abroad) took
the message. But when George pressed her on the urgency of his
reaching his brother, the woman admitted she didn't know when
he might call in for messages. And, additionally, she had no way
of getting in touch with him otherwise.

George called his mother, Virginia. "Mom, have you talked to
Thomas lately?"

"Why yes, as a matter of fact. He called me the other week.
So, what's he done now?"

George didn't want to trouble his mother with their sibling
quandary. "Oh, I left a few messages for him, and I've not spoken
with him yet. It's kind of important that I talk to him, but he

doesn't seem to be retrieving messages from his answering service."

"How much?"

"How much what?"

"How much money are we talking about this time?"

George laughed. "What makes you think it's about money?"

"I know my child. And if you're searching this hard, it must be a pretty big amount this time around." She let out a sigh. "Five thousand? Ten thousand? Fifteen? How much? Come on. Spill it!"

George laughed to keep his mother from wondering or worrying. "Mom, I just want to talk to him. So would you happen to have a number where I can reach him?"

Virginia thought a second. "I was trying to remember where he was when he called. He *is* in the states, though. I think he called from D.C.? Or was it Houston? No, I believe he said he was going to Houston later. In pursuit of a hot lead or something. Said he had places to visit in a short span of time. And he sounded *so* excited, too."

"So I take it he still doesn't have a cell phone?"

"That's your brother. He hates for people to have easy access to him. He likes being the one in control. 'You want me? You call and leave a message with the answering service.' He decides when he checks for messages and whether or not he'll return your call. When he wants you, he calls you direct and will repeat-dial you until you finally answer the phone."

George heaved a long sigh. "All right, Mom. Thanks anyway."

"If I hear from him, I'll make him call you."

"Yeah, telling you always works. Now he'll be calling me a tattletale again."

"Well now, son. You really were when you were younger, you know. 'Mom, make Thomas stop!' 'Mom, tell Thomas to give it back.' 'Mom—' "

"Okay, Mom," George said in his most charming voice. "I get your point, okay?"

"Speaking of which: How's that wedding coming along?"

How she can switch from tattling to a wedding is beyond me. But that's my mom: versatile, vibrant Virginia.

With that, George told his mother what he hadn't yet told Johnnie Mae about the wedding plans. He was really looking forward to seeing Johnnie Mae when she arrived in Atlanta from her tour in Dallas.

CHAPTER 8

But that which beareth thorns and briers is rejected.

(Hebrews 6:8)

Elaine turned to Maurice. "May I sit down?" Maurice looked at Lena.

"Why? You're not staying long," Lena said matter of factly.

Elaine turned to Lena. "Old age, dearie. These old bones ain't what they used to be."

"Oh, you mean when I was young and you didn't have time to sit, let alone stay? Just breezed in and out—*when* you came at all. So don't let me hold you now," Lena said.

Elaine sat gingerly in a winged-back chair. "Nice," she said. "Just like the chair in Madear's living room. Minus the plastic covers, of course." Elaine chuckled a little. "You remember those, don't you, Lena? The sofa, chairs, and the plastic that covered them. And what about her car? You remember? The hard bubble plastic?"

Lena refused to sit, choosing instead to tower over Elaine as she spoke. "You mean the sofa, chairs, and car you took along with all the other things in her house?"

Elaine tilted her head back to look up at Lena. "Please don't tell me you're still upset about that?" She waved her hand. "Pshaw. Believe me, there are more important things to be concerned about these days. Trust me, none of that stuff was worth much anyway. Even preserved in plastic." She looked Lena up and down. "Your face, your hands. Want to talk about what happened to you?"

"Life happened." Lena sat down on the couch across from Elaine. "But then, since when have you ever cared?"

"I cared. Care now. That's why I'm here."

"Meaning?"

"Meaning, I want to be with my family."

Theresa and Maurice sat next to Lena.

"Mama, you want me and Maurice to give you some privacy?" Theresa practically whispered.

Elaine smiled. "You know, Theresa. That would be really nice. Give your mama and me here some time to get to know each other again."

"Again?" Lena said to Elaine as she grabbed Theresa's wrist to keep her seated next to her. "Lord, give me grace. Thirty-five years ago I didn't even know you. I was sixteen, your child, and I didn't know you from a stranger off the street."

Elaine seemed to tense up, then just as suddenly, she relaxed. "Fifty-one years?" She shook her head. "Has it been *that* long ago since you were born?"

"Yes. Big Mama died 35 years ago. I was sixteen. And I've not seen or heard from you since." Lena released Theresa's wrist, then began to brush her own thighs downward through her long, blue-jean skirt. "Thirty-five years," she said with conviction.

"Oh, Lena, don't be so theatrical. It wasn't like I was *ever* there for you." Her voice softened. "But I'm here now. I want to get to know my family. You of all people shouldn't have an objection to that." She smiled.

"But what if *I* do?" Theresa said, staring directly at Elaine, willing her to look at her.

Elaine smiled, first at Lena, then Theresa. "She's definitely from our side of the family. A beautiful little thing, too. Just like you were. My precious, beautiful little Lena."

"And would you quit talking about me as though I'm not here?" Theresa said, getting more and more agitated with this stranger who only minutes ago was no one in particular ringing her doorbell.

"Sorry, dearie. You're right. I do have a few nasty habits; I suppose you'll get used to them, though."

"*Used* to them?" Maurice asked before he could stop himself. He had intended to stay out of this.

Elaine looked at him. "You two married or just living in sin together?"

"Neither, not that it's really any of your business," Theresa said. "And I'd like to know as well what you mean by us getting used to them?"

"I need a place to stay," Elaine said.

"So, get you somewhere then." Theresa checked to see Lena's reaction to all of this. Lena was rocking slightly.

"We're family. I'm old. I have nowhere else to go. Surely Lena . . . Theresa, you wouldn't leave me to the streets? From what I understand, you're both good Christian women. Now what does the good book say? 'When I was hungry—' "

Lena stopped rocking. "That reminds me: How did you know where to find me?" she asked.

Elaine's mouth broke into a huge grin. "Pretty simple, really. I went back home to Winston-Salem, talked to a few people from our old neighborhood. I heard about you and something about a fire. I went to the library to search archives, but modern technology—oh, it's such a marvelous thing! I discovered I was possibly a grandmother." She said the word "grandmother" with a smugness. "One of the young folks volunteered to help me 'surf the net' as they say, while I was in the library. And voilà! It's amazing how helpful folks can be to a defenseless old woman. Especially an old woman who looks like me."

Theresa gave a start, disgusted by her insinuation. "What do you mean looks like you?"

Elaine smiled at Theresa. "Wouldn't you really like to give me and your mother some time alone? I assure you, we'll have plenty of time to get to know each other as a family; and that little one you got there in the oven as well. September the eleventh, you said?"

Theresa stood up. "Listen, I don't know who you think you are or what you think you're doing here, but you're not coming in my house messing over us," Theresa said.

"Big Mama." Elaine said it to Lena, then leaned back satisfied, contentedly in the chair.

"What about her?" Lena asked with a face of stone.

"Aren't you at *all* curious about what happened? Me. Her. Why I never came back to get you? Why I look so white?" She grinned, then stood up to leave. "Well, dearies, I can see my visit is not being well received. Suppose I'll see if I can't find a nice bench to sleep on or a bed available for me this time at the shelter." She started toward the door.

Lena stared at her, willing her mouth to cooperate with her true desire. "Wait," she said. *Betrayed by my heart yet again.* "Theresa, I'd like to speak to . . . Memory. Alone."

Elaine turned around and grinned first, then realized that Lena had deliberately called her Memory. A name she despised being called. *Lena must surely know this.*

"You sure?" Theresa asked Lena.

Lena looked at Elaine—"Memory" being the name she had grown up hearing her mother called. That is, on the rare occasions Big Mama would speak of her or say her name at all. "I'm sure," Lena said to Theresa.

Theresa and Maurice started out of the room. Theresa turned and glanced back. "If you need us, we'll just be in the kitchen."

"Are you always so dramatic, too?" Memory asked Theresa. "Like mother, like daughter. I suppose it must be hereditary, apparently skipping my generation."

Theresa rolled her eyes at Memory. *Who would ever guess we're from the same blood?* Theresa thought. *And who would believe someone so evil could have produced someone with such a wonderful and caring heart as Lena's?*

Maurice looked at Theresa, and she knew that he was probably questioning the exact same thing.

CHAPTER 9

Even so the tongue is a little member, and boasteth great things.

(James 3:5)

"**D**id you know I was a twin?" Memory asked Lena as she sat down to continue their conversation. "A brother they called Junior. Willie B and Memory. Good rhyme, huh?"

Lena thought a second. She did recall Big Mama mentioning something about someone named Junior once or twice, but she had never met him or known whom Big Mama was referring to. "No, I didn't know that."

"So, after all those years, she still wouldn't talk about him, huh?" Memory grunted, then took out a cigarette. "Mind if I smoke?"

"Yes, in fact I do. If you want to smoke, you'll have to go outside."

Memory smiled, then smirked. "Okkkaaay. So you're one of *those* kind, huh?" She slid the cigarette across her nose before sticking it back inside the pack.

"You were saying about being a twin?"

"Was. I *was* a twin."

"What happened?"

Memory sat back and adjusted her body to fit more comfortably in the chair. "He died." Her eyes glazed over for a second. "Pepper died."

"Pepper?"

"Yeah, that's what the kids in the neighborhood called him. I was Sugar; he was Pepper. I was white; he was dark. I was sweet; he was spicy: the one who made people struggle to find their next breath." Memory looked at Lena and smiled. "He was so funny, he could make you laugh until you forgot *how* to breathe. Pepper—spicy at home, school, church, the ball diamond. And *ath-le-tic*?" she sang. "Oooh, he had some major skills!"

Lena found Memory's tale an attention-grabber. Here she was this horrible woman Lena had thought of all of her life, and now she sat there—after attacking everyone in the house—all sentimental. *You are definitely some piece of work*, Lena thought.

Lena's gaze didn't go unnoticed by Memory. "Pepper had been the best part of my young life. That's the truth. Then he went and fell into a well. He *died*, Lena. And you know what? Even then, she wouldn't take responsibility for her part in his death."

"She?" Lena asked.

Memory looked hard at Lena. "Dear, sweet Big Mama: the woman who kept me from taking you—my own child—with me. The woman who probably would have eventually beat down the spirit of her own flesh and blood had he not taken flight. Ten years old . . . Junior and I were only ten when he ended up dead, and I was left to cope and try to understand the purpose of living in an unforgiving, meet-my-need-first world."

Lena looked puzzled. "But Big Mama never whipped me. Never."

Memory laughed. "And why, pray tell, do you suppose that was?"

Lena shrugged. "I never really thought about it. She was . . . who I knew her to be."

"She never whipped me either. I couldn't figure it out at first. Lord knows I did my devilment: in and out of church. But Pepper had spunk. He had a certain strut about him even at a young age. He got in trouble all the time for talking back to grown folks. She said he was a little too confident, not understanding when to show it and when to keep it hidden. Actually, she only intended for him to suppress it around white folks. Told him if he didn't learn how to 'contain' his self-confidence, meaning to not look white folks head on when he talked to them or, worse, to say exactly what he thought, they were going to find him dangling from a tree someday. A black mother's worst fear."

Memory laughed, shook her head, then cocked it to the side. "So she beat him with limbs from a tree. Ain't that ironic? And whenever I challenged her about it, do you think she actually gave me a 'taste of a licking, too,' as she threatened she would?" Memory smiled. "Not her sweet little Memory. Not her fair-skinned, precious baby girl. If only Pepper and I had known the truth back then, things might have turned out differently."

"The truth?"

Memory closed her eyes. "The truth it took me until I was fifteen years old to learn. The truth explaining more about the true Madear: our great and virtuous mother. A truth that, in some ways, is partly responsible for my being back in your life right now."

"And that would be?"

"And that would be . . ." Memory looked at the clock and stood up, "another subject for another day. I suppose I should get going to find somewhere to lay my head tonight."

"Memory, how did you get here? Who brought you here to Theresa's house?"

"I got here the same way I got here the last time I came. I took the bus as far as it would bring me, then walked the rest of the way." She glanced around the room.

"So, where will you go when you leave here?"

Memory smiled. "Worried about me all of a sudden, huh?" She walked to the door. "Well, don't be. I'll be in touch." She opened the door. "And we'll chat some more." She reached in her pocketbook, took out a cigarette, stepped outside, lit it, and blew her first puff away from the house. "Ta-ta, my dear." She strolled away, with Lena's stare on her back.

Theresa walked in just as Lena closed the door. "Is she gone?"

Lena nodded as she walked toward Theresa.

"You want to talk about it?"

Lena shook her head. "I don't know about her. She has a way of telling you something without telling you anything, yet you know there's still more she plans to tell."

"Will she be back?" Theresa said as she bit down on her thumb.

Lena looked at Theresa. "I don't know, but I have a feeling she will. She wants something, but I haven't figured out what that something might be."

"Mama, if you want her to stay a few days, I don't mind. I mean, I won't object."

Lena laughed. "Yeah. Right. I don't know who you think you're fooling, but I am not the one. You don't trust her any more than I do."

"But you have good reasons. I just met her. But still—she *is* your mother."

"And she has answers to questions I never even thought I'd get to know or that needed to be answered . . . and then some."

"And . . . she is your mother." Theresa smiled. "I know you; you've got a good heart. It must have pained you to let her leave knowing she claims to have nowhere to stay."

"It was hard, but I need time to pray about a few things. I have a strange feeling in my spirit, and I'm not so sure which way I should go. I do know I'm not planning to put you in harm's way of her if I can help it. Mother or not."

"I can take care of myself."

Lena smiled. "Yeah, but that woman who calls herself Sugar, who just left here—she ain't. Theresa, we've both got to be careful until we figure out exactly what she's after."

CHAPTER 10

For God hath not given me the spirit of fear.

(II Timothy 1:7)

Johnnie Mae took a cab to the Dallas airport. Running late, she missed checking in her luggage at the curb and had to carry it inside to the airline counter. Just as she was lifting her one bag, she happened to glance to her left. The guy she had seen a few weeks ago, first in D.C., then in Houston, was headed for the metal detector line. At the exact same time she spotted him, he grinned, then looked away.

She didn't see him anymore after that and breathed a sigh of relief. "I'm being paranoid," she said under her breath as she boarded the plane, took her window seat, and stared out. On her way home, she was stopping in Atlanta to see Landris. Excited about the wedding plans he'd made, he couldn't wait to share with her all he had accomplished. Admittedly, his excitement had gotten her equally keyed up without any specifics as yet.

She and her mother talked every day. Her mother always spoke highly of Landris.

"Pastor Landris is such a dear sweet person," Mrs. Gates had said when she was home during the Fourth of July. "Did you know, he calls and checks on me and Princess Rose every few days?"

Johnnie Mae smiled. "Is that right?"

"Yes. And he absolutely adores you!"

So, when Johnnie Mae spoke with her mother again last night, she became a little concerned.

"Pastor Landris is such a dear person. Did you know he calls and checks on me and Princess Rose every few days? That man absolutely adores you!" her mother said.

Had Mrs. Gates not said the same words twice during the week she was home, three days ago when she called, then again last night, Johnnie Mae might not have been so troubled. She had noticed her mother was forgetting things that Johnnie Mae knew she knew. Marie and Donald hadn't said much to her about it lately. Not since they'd mentioned how she was forgetting things a few months back and Johnnie Mae reminded them how none of them were as sharp in the memory department as they once-upon-a-time had been, either.

So when she got home, she had planned on talking to her mother about seeing a doctor: definitely another mêlée waiting to be fought between mother and daughter.

Landris and Johnnie Mae had made dinner plans for her arrival in Atlanta. She could tell from the lift in his voice when they spoke earlier that he was pretty pleased with himself regarding his wedding-planning skills. But there were some other things going on that seemed to be overcasting his excitement with a cloud of distraction.

"Is something bothering you?" Johnnie Mae said.

"Why do you ask?"

"A question with a question. Then I'll take that as a yes."

"Nothing for you to be concerned about. Just working to contain a situation at the church, and I received a letter from the IRS a few days ago. They, or at least somebody, have made such a huge mistake it's almost funny. But I'll get everything straightened out soon. Since our wedding plans are progressing fine, I'll let that take me higher when I don't care to reflect on problems. Imagine: you'll be Mrs. Johnnie Mae Landris soon."

Okay, Johnnie Mae thought. *Now is not the time to bring up the fact that I may become Mrs. Johnnie Mae Landris legally, but from a work standpoint, I'll still be writing as Johnnie Mae Taylor. We don't need to get into this discussion just yet. Just in case he has a problem with it.*

"Landris, have you heard from your brother yet?"

"Not yet. But my mother's on the lookout, so I'm sure I'll hear from him soon."

Johnnie Mae told Landris she would meet him at the restaurant, since it was near the hotel.

"No, I'll pick you up."

"Landris, what sense does it make for you to have to find a parking place when I can just meet you at the restaurant? Besides, that'll give me time to finish up a few things before I meet you."

"In other words, you're planning to make me wait at the restaurant?" He laughed. "Okay, Miss Johnnie Mae. Then I'll meet you at the restaurant. Around seven o'clock?"

"Seven is good."

After Landris hung up with her, his telephone rang.

"What's up, my brother?" said the voice on the other end.

"Thomas? Man, where have you been?" George said, glad to finally hear from his elder brother.

"Yeah, I missed you, too," Thomas joked, calling from a pay phone. "And listen, you didn't have to go run and tell Mom on me. I was going to call you as soon as I got a chance."

"Now you know I wasn't telling. I just hadn't heard from you in months, and I didn't know if something had happened to you. I asked Mom if she'd heard from you lately."

"Man, you know Mom does not play that. You, I can ditch for a few months. Mom will hunt me down. Or at least she has threatened she would do it."

"Yeah, like you're really scared of Mom."

"I hear you're about to get married," Thomas said, changing the subject.

"Yeah, I am."

"Who would have thought? My little brother first becomes a preacher, then a pastor, and now you're about to settle down?" He laughed. "What's next? Fatherhood?"

Landris laughed too. "Well, she does have a beautiful little girl already. So . . . yeah."

"A ready-made family?" Thomas looked away. "Hey, hold on a second." He put his hand over the mouthpiece and watched a woman walk by. "Sorry, I just saw the cutest little number stroll by. I didn't want to be distracted talking to you."

"Thomas, you need to quit. And where are you anyway?"

"In a hotel lobby. I just checked out. Usually, I make my phone calls from a pay phone because they charge from fifty cents to a dollar per call from your hotel room just to dial out," Thomas said.

"I thought you were doing well these days financially," Landris said. He was thinking about that tax notice he had received and the cash from the sale of the stock he had yet to receive from Thomas.

"Come on, you know how it goes. And with me it goes more than it seems to come." Thomas glanced at his watch. "Listen, I have to get off here so I can get to the airport."

"Thomas, I need to talk to you. About my stock."

"You told me to sell the rest of your shares."

"Okay," Landris said with a nudge in his voice for Thomas to continue. "So . . ."

"So, I did. Now I guess you're wondering where's your money?"

"Yeah, that question has presented itself lately, along with some other questions." Landris took his time to choose his words carefully. He knew Thomas. If he got off the phone before they finished, it could be a while before George got another chance.

"Let me make this easy for you, George. I'll be in Atlanta this evening. We can talk then and iron out things."

" 'Iron out things'?" This wasn't sounding too encouraging. George started twisting his mouth to keep himself from blurting out the wrong thing, especially over the phone.

"Yeah. I'll be in Atlanta for about a day."

"What time should I pick you up from the airport?" George asked.

Thomas looked at his watch again. Five minutes until the shuttle was due to arrive. "I'm not planning on staying with you. I reserved a room already. I'll just take the shuttle or catch a cab to the hotel and contact you from there."

"Thomas, why would you stay at a hotel when you know there's plenty of room for you at my house?"

"Hey, brother. I didn't know what you might have had planned already. There's nothing tackier than somebody imposing on somebody else on short notice, I know."

"Well, you're not imposing. So cancel your room reservation, and I'll pick you up."

"Look. I sort of have some other plans already. You know how it is? A hotel room is cool. Why don't we meet for a bite to eat at one of those soulful Atlanta restaurants you're always bragging about? How about Sylvia's?"

"Thomas, I already have plans for dinner. My fiancée is stopping in today. We're trying to get our wedding plans set."

"Women, they are something about weddings, aren't they? I know you're dreading having to go through all the hoops she's probably laying out for you to do for a ceremony that will probably last all of what? Twenty minutes?" He laughed.

"Actually, I'm doing the planning."

"Ah, man. Don't tell me she's already got you whipped."

"Not whipped. Just can't wait to become one with the one who completes me."

"Whoa! My man is becoming poetic about a woman? I can't wait to meet this one. She's got to be something else!"

George knew Thomas was in a hurry to get off the phone. "Why don't you come eat dinner with us tonight?"

"A threesome? While the two of you discuss a wedding? Thanks, brother, but no thanks. Methinks me will pass on this one. We can just get together sometime tomorrow before I leave out."

"Thomas, I really do need to see you." George then gave him his cell phone number. "I hope you'll change your mind about dinner. I would like for the two of you to meet, since you'll both be here. Besides that, I wanted to ask about your being my best man at my wedding, if you will."

Thomas looked outside. "My shuttle's here. I've got to run. We'll talk."

"Call me when you get here," George said.

"Will do." Thomas hung up the phone, then wondered how much George actually knew about the stock sale, and how on earth was he going to tell him the rest of the story?

CHAPTER 11

Deceit is in the heart of them that imagine evil.

(Proverbs 12:20)

"I should have gotten your phone number," Memory said when Theresa answered the door. "Then I could have called instead of just showing up."

"Yes, and I could have saved you a trip."

"Does that mean Lena's not here or that she's here but she doesn't care to see me?"

Theresa rubbed her stomach. *Five to seven more weeks give or take two weeks and this baby can kick all he or she wants without kicking me.* Theresa really didn't know what she should tell Memory. Lena had gone to the grocery store with Maurice. They'd just left. In fact, Theresa was surprised that Lena and Maurice hadn't passed Memory on their way out. But if they had, they would have certainly doubled back in a hurry.

"She's not here," Theresa said.

Memory pointed at Theresa's stomach. "You're carrying low. It's a girl."

"I really don't care to know my baby's sex yet. Otherwise, they could have told me when I had my sonogram, which is a lot more accurate than some old wives' tale for sure."

"Regardless. It's a girl." Memory looked around Theresa. "Can I come inside this time or would you prefer we stick to our routine of me waiting outside in now the late July Georgia sun and you safely inside?" Memory flashed a slightly crooked smile.

"Look, Memory—"

"Elaine." She corrected her. "Although I love being called Sugar by my friends."

Theresa looked at her. "Look, Memory. You're welcome to come inside and wait."

Memory grinned. "Then I suppose Memory it will be." She nodded, then stuck her chin up with an even larger grin on her face as she strolled inside past Theresa.

"I'm in the den watching TV. You can come in there with me."

"Don't trust me too far out of your sight, huh, dearie?"

Theresa stopped walking and looked at her. "Let's you and I get something straight."

"By all means."

"I don't particularly care for you. I don't know what you're up to—"

"Moi? I just came to find my family. What could possibly be wrong with a sixty-six-year-old woman wanting to make amends with long-lost family?" They reached the den and both sat down eyeing the other.

"Perhaps because your past motives have been 'suspect' to say the least?" Theresa said as she clicked through the channels of the cable stations.

"Yeah, and I suppose you've been perfect all your life, too? Probably the model daughter, friend, employee, girlfriend, soon-to-be-mother, etcetera, etcetera."

Theresa looked, checking for signs that Memory might know something and was using that information to get under her skin. "No. I'd just like to identify your real motivation for showing up here and cut through all the fat."

"What else would there be, other than family?" She smiled. "You should never listen to one side of a story and judge a person based on it. If you're going to dislike me, at least see where I'm coming from first, then conclude with your own evaluation."

"I'm not basing my feelings about you on anything other than how you came in here acting like you were God's gift to daughters." Theresa settled back gingerly on the couch.

"Well, dearie, I'll be the first to admit my department of parenting skills is lacking somewhat. But then, children don't come with warranties or instruction manuals themselves. And no matter how old they get, you still feel like you need to look up an answer to a question." Memory glanced around the room. "What's your air-conditioner thermostat set on? It's kind of warm in here." She fanned her face with her right hand.

"I'm fine; quite comfortable, in fact. Maybe you're experiencing hot flashes?"

"That was late forties, early fifties. My personal summers are over." Memory began to smack her lips. "Would it be too much trouble to ask for something to drink? I'll be happy to get it if you'll politely offer me something, then point me in the right direction."

Theresa sighed loudly. "The kitchen's that way." She pointed to the right. "There's some orange juice and tea in the refrigerator. Knock yourself out."

Memory stood up. "Would you care for anything? A sandwich maybe with something to drink?"

"If you'd like a sandwich, there's some luncheon meat in the refrigerator as well."

Memory stood waiting.

"What now?" Theresa snapped as she looked up at her.

"I asked if you wanted something. I don't believe you answered my question."

Theresa shook her head. "No, but thank you for asking." She blew out air with a short laugh and continued to shake her head.

"You and your mother both have issues," Memory said as she started for the kitchen.

Theresa wasn't going to let that slide. "*What*?" she said, following her. "You come up in *my* house, wanting to eat and drink up *my* food, complaining about *my* thermostat setting when you could have very well stayed outside, and you think *we* have issues?"

"No one can say your eyes and ears don't work. You see and hear just fine."

"Okay. All right. I'm really trying here, but you are truly working my last nerve."

"Could you be any more cliché? How about, 'You're not going to stand for this!' or 'You're going to make me go off on somebody in a minute.' Those are all good, too," Memory said as she washed her hands in the sink, then dried them with a paper towel. She took out the sandwich meat and found the bread on the counter in the breadbox. "Are you sure you don't want me to make you one? A sandwich, I mean?"

Theresa walked out of the room counting to ten. Memory came in the den about five minutes later with a sandwich, some potato chips, two bread-and-butter pickle slices, and a tall glass of tea.

"Who said you could open the chips or get a pickle?" Theresa asked.

Memory handed the plate to Theresa. "Just thought maybe you would like some chips and a pickle with your ham sandwich." Theresa wouldn't take it, so Memory set it on the end table.

"It will be there when you're ready." She went back in the kitchen and returned with a plate identical to the one she had fixed for Theresa.

"Okay," Memory said while chewing. "You're the Christian here. I'm just a backslider: a fallen one with dedicated years of past service. What do you and I need . . . to be civil to each other and move forward? Show me how you Christians do it these days."

Theresa hated this. *Now she's using Christianity to make me feel wrong about how I'm acting. Oh, she's good*, Theresa thought. *She is good!*

"If I have a problem with you, I'm supposed to confront you," Theresa said.

"I hope that means to confront me in love." Memory smiled. "I was a pretty diligent student of the Bible myself back in the day. Couldn't help but be with Mamie for a mother. Sundays at Sunday school, eleven o'clock services, three o'clock programs, 5:30 P.M. BYTU. Mondays, Young Missionary Society. Tuesdays, required teacher's training. Wednesdays, prayer meeting. Thursdays, choir rehearsal. Fridays, fish fry, hot dog, or spaghetti dinners for the building fund that coincidently never seemed to build or add on to the building." She giggled. "Whew! I for one understood why God rested on that seventh day."

Theresa was determined not to laugh, since it made being confrontational a bit less effective. "How could you leave your own child and never come back to even see about her or your own mother?"

"Is that what you heard?"

"Am I wrong?"

"No, that's pretty much accurate. But I don't think you're the one who should be questioning me about it."

Theresa laughed. "What?"

"I mean, have you always loved your mother? Always did right by her yourself?"

Theresa sat there unable to say anything.

"Thought not. There were times when I didn't like mine either. Then when I learned information that almost turned my world upside down, do you know what she did?"

"No, I do not."

"She stood there and first tried to deny it without actually denying it. Then she tried to explain her actions away and wanted me to agree that she had been right. I saw her six months before she died. We exchanged words. She told me that as long as she was on this earth, she never wanted me to step foot in her house again. Sooo, I didn't. Then two days after I knew for sure she was six feet *under* the earth, I came home." Memory looked past Theresa into the hallway.

"But what about Lena? What did Lena ever do that would cause you to treat her the way you did?"

"She was born."

Theresa pulled herself back. "What an awful thing to say about your own child."

"Well, it happens." Memory looked at Theresa's sandwich as she licked the crumbs off her finger. "Are you planning on eating that?"

Theresa looked at her with disgust. "No."

Memory got up and took the plate off the table. "Bon appetit!"

"Theresa, we're back!" Lena said. "Where are you? In the den?" She walked in and stopped in her tracks when she saw Memory. "You?" she said staring at Memory.

Memory smiled as she shoved a potato chip into her mouth. "Yes. Me. And I've been sitting here having a lovely time with my wonderful granddaughter." She looked at Theresa. "Haven't we, dearie?"

Theresa rolled her eyes, got up, and walked out.

"What did you do to her?" Lena asked.

"Talked. We were just sitting here chewing the fat. It must be her hormones. Up. Down. You know, with her baby being due shortly. Oh, and she's carrying the baby low. I told her it's a girl."

Lena left Memory to go find Theresa.

CHAPTER 12

Be not overcome of evil.

(Romans 12:21 (a))

Landris received the information by express mail from the brokerage firm an hour after he hung up from talking with Thomas. He had gone through a lot to get the printout of all past activities on his account. Because Thomas had set things up, everything had gone to an address Thomas had on file. Since it was George's social security number and he proved that much, they didn't have a problem sending him the information. When he had spoken with them, they maintained that their records were indeed correct. Landris was anxious to see how they erroneously came to such a conclusion.

Thomas said he'd be in Atlanta for only a day. So, maybe Thomas could help him straighten this out once and for all while he was in the city.

"Thomas is going to have a fit when he sees how they've messed up my account. Brother," Landris said to the bulk of stapled pages he held with his name and account number on top, "you are going to hit the ceiling when you see how much they're claiming I received." He laughed even though this wasn't the least bit amusing.

* * *

Johnnie Mae was about to get into a cab when a man stepped up just ahead of her.

"Excuse me, Miss. But—"

"You again?" Johnnie Mae said, recognizing him as the guy in Houston who had found her lost confirmation number. "Why do you keep showing up everywhere I go?"

"Me? Well, maybe because it's a free country. At least the last I checked it was."

"Look, this is my cab. Why don't you just get another one?" Johnnie Mae said.

"Maybe because it was actually the cab I summoned first and when I turned to get my bags, you slipped in and tried to take it."

"Do all of your sentences begin with 'Maybe because'?"

He laughed again. The laugh she hated. The one that made her feel like he thought he was better than she was.

"Okay. I tell you what," he said. "You can have this cab. You know why?"

She looked away from him. *Who cares why?*

He laughed again. "Maybe because," he said the word "because" with an explosive *b*, "I'm a better person than you are. And maybe because it's not worth wasting my valuable time about it. Or maybe because, you'll get some wild notion in your head that I might *actually* be 'following you.'" He laughed and stepped back.

"I tell *you* what," she said, backing away. "You take this cab, and I'll just take that limo there instead." She then spoke to the now totally-confused-about-what-to-do-next cab driver. "Could you please give me my bags back?"

She walked over and talked to the limo driver as she watched the cab drive away a grinning, sneaky, dark-chocolate passenger. After he was gone, Johnnie Mae thanked the limo driver for his time and got inside the next available cab.

When she arrived at the hotel, she called Landris. Then she planned on resting a little before their scheduled dinner date.

"I spoke with my brother today," Landris said with a triumphant bounce in his voice.

"Oh, Landris, that's great! So, he's okay?"

"Yeah. He said he was coming to Atlanta today, but he hasn't called yet, so I don't know. You can't ever be sure about Thomas. He didn't tell me what time his flight was arriving, and he's planning to stay in a hotel instead of here with me. Probably just up to his old tricks again. You know: make me think he's coming, then he'll call a month from now to tell me some bizarre tale of what 'actually' ended up happening instead."

"As Tavis says, 'Keep the faith.' I believe he'll show up and surprise you this time."

Landris chuckled. "Anywhere Thomas shows up, there's usually a surprise lurking. I gave him my cell phone number, and I invited him to dinner with us. But of course, he declined. Just as well. I'd hate for you to get your hopes up expecting him to show, and he ends up disappointing two people instead of just one."

Johnnie Mae yawned. "Landris, I'm going to take a nap before I see you. I am really bushed. In fact, I was so tired, this guy at the airport almost made me forget I have been commanded to 'love ye one another.' Over a cab."

"A cab?"

"Yes. I'm kind of ashamed. But he jumped me for a cab I had hailed already. Well . . . And it's that same guy I told you who keeps showing up everywhere I seem to be. If I didn't think it was ridiculous, I would truthfully believe the man is following me."

"That's not entirely a far-fetched idea. The legal terminology is 'stalking.' "

She yawned again and covered her mouth. "I'm an author. I don't believe authors attract that kind of following. Most people don't even recognize us when they see us."

"Don't fool yourself. It's not impossible. Even regular folks have stalkers. Johnnie Mae, you need to be careful. And if you think somebody is really trying to hurt you, you need to pay attention to that feeling and act accordingly to protect yourself."

"Well Landris, I'm going to lie down for a few minutes so I'll be refreshed for these wedding updates you've been teasing me with." She looked at the clock on the nightstand. "I'll see you at the restaurant in about two hours."

"Can't wait," Landris said.

Johnnie Mae didn't bother taking off anything else, having already slipped off her five-inch heels. In two minutes flat, she was out like she'd been sucker punched by somebody with a lifelong grudge to resolve, and they had just settled it.

CHAPTER 13

To me belongeth vengeance, and recompense.

(Deuteronomy 32:35)

"Theresa, what did she say to you?" Lena asked. She found Theresa in her bedroom lying across her bed. Maurice was up there with her.

"Nothing, Mama."

"Then, why are you upset?"

Theresa sat up and looked at Lena. "I'm not really upset. I just don't . . ." She thought about how to say it. "I just don't know about her. What is she after? She just shows up and says whatever she wants. What comes up, comes out."

"Okay, that's it! I'm telling her to leave and not to bother you ever again."

Theresa rubbed her stomach and smiled. "Mama, don't. She's your mother. I know you want to know more about her and things that possibly only she can tell you."

Lena looked at Maurice. "Maurice, go downstairs and don't let that woman out of your sight, please."

Maurice looked at Theresa, then at Lena as he left.

"You really don't trust her, do you?"

"She hasn't given me a reason to trust her yet," Lena said, sitting down next to her daughter. "But I admit there was something else Big Mama wanted me to know. And I believe Memory might know something, if not all, about what it was."

"But Big Mama didn't tell you what exactly or leave you a clue?"

"No, although she struggled to tell me something a little before she died. She couldn't talk, so she tried writing it. 'Find Grace' was all she scribbled. I thought she was consoling me. But when I happened to say something about grace the other day when Memory was here, she reacted strangely. Like the word 'grace' had meaning to her, too."

"I remember her reaction. I thought it was because you were telling her how long it had been since you'd last seen her."

Lena was in deep thought, talking things out as she went along. "So did I. But I happened to have said an old quote I'd heard Big Mama say: 'Lord, give me grace.' Now that I think back to the words Big Mama kept trying to relay, maybe I was wrong about grace. Maybe Big Mama was really talking about a person or a place called Grace."

"Or maybe not. Maybe she really was telling you to find God's unmerited favor. You know . . . grace." Theresa looked into her mother's eyes. "So what do you want to do about Memory? She's downstairs waiting with poor old Maurice on watch duty."

Lena smiled. "What would you like me to do?"

Theresa shook her head. "I'd like to find out what she's really after. And if she's genuine about hooking back with family, then we've gained a family member."

"And if she's not, then I'm going to find out the truth. But Theresa, if at any time you don't feel comfortable with her around, say the word, and she's as good as gone."

"Oh now, that's a given!" Theresa smiled.

Lena smiled back. "I'm going downstairs to talk with her. Do you need anything?"

"No, I'm fine." She hunched her shoulders. "Well, maybe I am a *little* hungry."

"I'll get you something and bring it back up. Then why don't you lie down and take a nap. You're looking a bit drained to me today."

Lena went downstairs and fixed Theresa soup and a sandwich. She peeped in on Maurice and Memory. Lena quickly concluded: *The boy looks in dire need of rescuing.*

"Memory, I'll be with you in a minute," Lena said.

Memory saw the tray of food Lena was carrying and smiled. "Oh, take your time. I'm rather enjoying myself with this fine young man here."

Lena saw the pleading on Maurice's face. *Please hurry*, he seemed to be saying.

"Maurice," Lena said when she returned to the den. "I'm sure you have something you need to do. Don't let us keep you."

Maurice was out of that chair in one heartbeat. "Yeah, Mama Lena. I'm going to let Theresa know I'm leaving. I'll be checking with you guys later."

"Bye, Maurice. We'll have to do this again soon!" Memory said, waving her fingers at him in a toodle-loo fashion. "I helped him put away the groceries," she said to Lena. "That was a hoot." She giggled.

"Memory, why are you here?"

"How many times do I have to answer this question? I'm here because of you. Okay? I came because I'd like to get to know you. Is that too much for a mother to ask of her only child? It's just you and me left; and, of course, Theresa and the baby soon. I've come to realize the importance of family these days. I'm trying to make things right. Okay?"

"Who is Grace?"

"What?"

"Grace. I was wondering if you knew anybody named Grace." Lena eyed Memory's reaction closely.

"Grace?" Memory squirmed, then readjusted her body. "Grace?" She shrugged.

Lena thought before she answered. She didn't want to tip her empty hand and cause Memory to hold back any information she might otherwise disclose.

"Big Mama mentioned Grace a few times," Lena said.

"Did she ever say any more?"

Lena hesitated. She wasn't about to tell her what Big Mama scribbled on the paper, just in case it was important. "Not a whole lot. I was just wondering what you knew."

"There was a white woman who visited Madear occasionally. No big deal. She said something once, I believe, about a little town called Grace. I wouldn't worry myself about it if I were you. Madear knew lots of people all over the place."

Lena searched Memory's face. *She's holding back on me. I can see it.* Lena couldn't shrug it off. "Okay. Then, do you think she possibly meant Grace, North Carolina?"

"Not sure. But listen, dearie. Madear had a sort of like jewelry box, handmade, with a lock on it. By any chance, would you happen to know what became of its contents?"

Yes I know, Lena thought. "You mean the contents weren't in those things you took when you ransacked the house?"

" 'Ransacked' is a bit harsh, don't you think, dearie?"

"Then, how would you describe it?"

"Okay. So apparently you and I need to settle this misunderstanding about the things that were inside Madear's house. First of all, I was her legal, rightful heir. Still-living heir. Were I not alive, you would have had the right to her things."

"She wrote a letter with her desires to leave me everything. And you knew it."

Memory let out a sigh. "So you're mad about things? Is that what this is all about? Things? Things, Lena?"

"I'm upset because you knew what Big Mama wanted, and you disregarded her wishes even in her death."

"They were things, Lena. T-h-i-n-g-s. Things! You-bring-no-thing-into-this-world-and-it-is-certain-you-will-take-no-thing out kinds of things. Most of it was junk anyway."

"Big Mama's 'junk,' as you call it, I didn't see as being junk. They were things from her life. She wanted me to have them. She wanted me to have her house. Instead, I was left with nothing. And then left to find somewhere else to live after you were gone."

Memory put up her hand. "Please, spare me. Madear just wanted to still control things after she was gone. She always had to be in control. Well, guess what, I was the one who ended up making the final decision of her 'things.' *I* decided, not her. If she wanted you to have her stuff, she should have made better legal arrangements."

"I should have gone to a lawyer and showed him the letter expressing her wishes."

"A lawyer? You were sixteen. Do you really think you would have won against me back then?" Memory laughed. "Come on. Let's say you had found a lawyer, took Madear's handwritten note leaving everything to you. Don't you think I would have pointed out that you were still my daughter, therefore putting me in charge of a minor—meaning you? I still would have ended up with everything, Lena. This way, we cut out the middleman. Actually, you should thank me for being such a good steward."

"Why didn't you ever come home? Why didn't you come visit Big Mama or me?"

"I did come home. A few times when you were a baby, again when you were about five years old, and once or twice when you were a teenager."

"Then, when was the last time you actually saw Big Mama?"

"About six months before she died."

Lena looked stunned. "That's a lie."

"Nope. It's the truth."

"Then, where was I?"

"Six months before Madear died, I came home. You weren't there. You'd gone on an all-day church trip is what she told me. That's probably why she let me in her house that day." Memory thought back to the last time she saw Madear alive.

"What do you want this time?" Madear said as she stood on the other side of the screen door, just one more thing separating mother and child.

"You're not going to let me in?" Memory asked, sweet and sincere.

"I didn't let you in the last time, but you managed anyhow. I think the technical term for that is 'breaking and entering.' "

"I don't know what you're talking about, Madear," Memory said as she fidgeted.

"I'm talking about you and one of your hoodlum friends coming in my house when I wasn't here. Do you think I'm crazy? I know it was you here snooping around about seven years ago when my house was broken into. How you could put us in danger—"

"What makes you so sure it was me?"

"Because you didn't find it."

"What are you talking about? I keep telling you, it wasn't me."

Madear nodded and smiled. "And you're not going to find it either."

"But it belongs to me!" Memory pressed closer to the screen door. "This is ridiculous. Please let me come in. We can sit down and talk like two civil adults. Look, I brought a present for Lena." She held up a medium-sized, shabbily wrapped box.

"Lena's not here."

Memory looked scared. "Where is she?"

"Don't go acting like you care. She's gone on an outing with the church."

"Please, Madear, let me come in."

"You're not getting it, I don't care what you try to convince me of."

Memory pulled open the screen door and stepped inside. "But that necklace belongs to me! You know it's mine. You have no right to keep it from me."

"I have every right. And it's not yours."

"But I heard that white woman when she gave it to you. She said for you to be sure I got it. 'Keep this for Memory,' she said. I heard her. I walked in when you were holding that necklace. You had taken it out of that beautiful wooden and gold locked box. It belongs to me, and you have no right . . . no right to keep it from me!"

"Memory, that necklace doesn't truly belong to just you."

"Yes, it does. Why are you trying to take what's rightfully mine?"

"It belongs to Lena now. She's—" Madear caught herself before revealing too much.

"That woman said, 'Let her know this came from Grace.' Who or what is Grace?"

Madear sighed heavily. "Who or what grace is, is of no concern of yours. That woman who came here from time to time, I worked for her for many, many years. She appreciated my loyalty, okay? She was fond of you. What you think you heard was not at all what was going on between she and I. You only heard a piece of the conversation."

"That necklace belongs to me, and I want it. Please don't force me to have to take it."

"What did you say?"

"You heard me."

"Are you threatening me?"

Memory smiled. "Me? Threaten you? Please. You took my brother from me, then the one person who truly loved me for me. Me and Percy could have had a life together."

"You talking about that boy who got you pregnant? Both of you were children. He was sixteen and you were only fourteen. What could you have possibly known about love?" Madear stared Memory down.

"I know that Papa really loved me. In spite of everything, he did. I know that much."

Madear's face softened at the mention of her late husband's name. She sat down on the sofa. "Yes, your papa did love you." She looked up. "But so did I. And I still love you, Memory. More than you'll ever know."

"Then, why are you keeping something that's mine?"

"There are things that you don't understand yet. Things . . . things I need to tell you about someday."

Memory came over and knelt beside Madear. "Then, tell me. I'm thirty-one years old now."

Madear thought about Memory—how irresponsible she had been and still was. "Are you still floating around like a drifter with those hoodlums? No job to speak of?"

Memory stood up. "Blue is not a hoodlum! He has vision, Madear. All he needs is enough money to finance this one idea he has, and he and I will be on easy street for life." She started searching with her eyes subtlely around the room. "Just one break."

"What are you looking for?" Madear stood in front of her to block her vision.

"I'm just looking, Madear." She put her hand on her hip. "Just looking. Gosh!"

"You're not getting it. It's not yours, Memory; I don't care what you think you may have overheard that day. So just let things be."

"Madear, I'm going to have what's mine. I love you and appreciate all you've done for my child and me. But you can't keep taking what belongs to me and doing as you please. You just can't. I let you keep Lena. Give me the necklace, and you can have her."

"I would like for you to leave now."

"Then give me the necklace!"

"Leave, Memory. Now!"

"Give me what's mine, and I'll go and promise never to darken your steps again."

"One day, I have something to tell you. Until that time, I have to do what's best."

"Best for who?" Memory stepped up close to Madear. Madear stepped back, but Memory kept advancing toward her with every step back Madear took. "Best for Junior? Best for Papa? Best for me? Best for Lena?" She laughed and shook her head. "Oh, I know. Best for you. In that case, you'd best give me what belongs to me or else."

"Or else what?"

Memory's laugh sounded roped with pain. "I'm getting what's mine. And if you get in my way, Mamie Patterson, then I'll not be responsible for what you'll force me to do."

"Don't ever think you can threaten me and get away with it! Not after all I've done for you! I love you, Memory. But I want you to leave! And as long as I'm on this earth, don't you *ever* step foot in my house again without my invitation. You understand me?"

Memory started for the door. "Oh, I understand perfectly, *Ma . . . dear*. Per-fect-ly!"

Memory looked around. Now thirty-five years later, here she sat talking with the last person on earth who might know where the necklace was. "Big Mama told me she loved me," Memory told Lena. "Six months before she died, she told me . . . she loved me."

CHAPTER 14

A good man out of the good treasure of the heart bringeth forth good things.

(Matthew 12:35)

"Landris, I am so sorry," Johnnie Mae said as she quickly slid into the booth.

Landris looked at his watch and laughed. "Late, late, late." He leaned over and kissed her softly on the left cheek. "Oh, have I mentioned that you're late?"

She laughed, too. "I don't know what happened. I was going to take a short nap and the next thing I knew, it was seven-fifteen. Please forgive me."

"Don't sweat it, Johnnie Mae. While I waited for you, thinking maybe you had stood me up, my brother called. He is in the city. We talked for a few minutes, although I still was unable to convince him to come here so the two of you could meet."

"Well, I would have loved meeting him. So, is he coming to our wedding?" Johnnie Mae began to glance over the menu.

"I don't know, but I did mention to him my desire that he be my best man." Landris looked at his menu. "See anything you like?"

"I see *lots* of things I like. I am starving!" The waiter came over and took their order. Johnnie Mae smiled at Landris. "You're looking mighty fine these days." She leaned in.

"Thank you." He smiled as he handed her a golden envelope. "For you, my love."

"What is it?"

"Open it and see."

Johnnie Mae opened the envelope. "Our wedding invitation?" She ran a finger over their names scripted with raised, gold-foil letters on fine, black linen. "It's so elegant."

"So, you like it?"

"Like it? I love it."

"You don't think it being on black sends the wrong message do you?" Landris said as he rubbed down his moustache.

"It reeks of royalty. That's the message I get when I see it." Johnnie Mae opened it and read the inside. "Oh my goodness! You're kidding? Is this for real?"

Landris smiled, shook his head, then nodded yes. "You approve?"

"Our wedding is going to be at Oheka Castle? *The* Oheka Castle?"

"The one and only."

She covered her mouth with one hand. "Oh my goodness!"

"I've secured it for approximately 200 guests. And it's not going to cost them a thing because I plan to take care of the cost for their travel and overnight expenses."

"Landris, that's too much. You can't do that. Do you have any idea how much that's going to cost?" She took a big sip of water. "Of course, you know. What a silly question! I don't know, but I do know it has to be expensive. Landris, I can't let you do this by yourself. Listen—"

"Oh, you can't *let* me?" He laughed and handed her a brochure from Oheka Castle. "It's already done." He sat back. "I just need you to help pick out the menu, since we'll be having a sit-down dinner following the wedding." He just happened to glance down at her left hand. "Johnnie Mae, where is your engagement ring?"

She followed his eyes to her hand. "It's in the safe in my room. I take it off sometimes so as not to draw too much attention. You know, with all my traveling from city to city. I'm around all kinds of people." She started scooting to get out of the booth.

"Where are you going?"

"To get it."

"You don't have to do that. I was just asking."

"I want to. I want you to see it sitting just where it should be. It'll only take about ten minutes. Tops! Besides, I have something I must show you."

"Then, I'll go with you." He started to get up.

"No, you sit tight," she said. She had all this information back in her room about Oheka Castle she wanted to show him. Talking with Sarah had led her to do research on both Oheka and Biltmore Castles. And now their wedding would be at Oheka.

Johnnie Mae made it back to the restaurant in record time with ring on hand and a folder full of Oheka information. As she strolled back to their table, she noticed Landris talking with a guy. His back was to her, but they sat there seemly enjoying an animated conversation. The man was laughing hard. Johnnie Mae put on her best smile.

"I'm back," she said to Landris just as she was about to slide in and sit next to him.

"Wow, that was fast," Landris said. "Look who showed up while you were gone—"

The guy smiled as he looked up at Johnnie Mae. His smile quickly faded.

"You!" she yelled when she saw his face. "What are you doing here?"

"What am _I_ doing here?" he said cocking his head to the side indignantly. "You just came up."

"Look, I am tired of you following me!" She slammed the folder down on the table. "If you don't leave me alone, I will report you to the police. Do you understand me?"

"Woman, please! I understand you're a nutcase!"

"Johnnie Mae, what's wrong with you?" Landris stood and pulled her close to him.

"This," she said as she pointed at him, "is the man who's been following me!"

"Following you? Oh, you wish!"

"Then, what are you doing here now? How did you know I would be here?"

"Johnnie Mae," Landris said, holding her hand. "This is Thomas. My brother Thomas." He turned to Thomas, who seemed equally as disturbed. "Thomas, this is Johnnie Mae Taylor; the love of my life. My soon-to-be wife."

"*This* . . . is the love of your life?" Thomas said, almost spitting out the words.

Johnnie Mae shook her head. "Thomas? This is Thomas? This is your brother?"

"Yes, I'm Thomas. And just in case you still haven't gotten it yet, I am *not* following you."

Landris sat down quickly, bringing Johnnie Mae down along with him.

The waiter came over with a tray in the air. "Turkey Tetrazzini," he announced.

Johnnie Mae raised her hand. "That's me."

Thomas looked at his brother, then Johnnie Mae. Landris glanced over at Johnnie Mae. Johnnie Mae practically glared at Thomas.

"Pleased to meet you," Thomas finally said, extending a hand to Johnnie Mae.

"Likewise," she said with half-a-smile as she rubbed her forehead with her left hand.

"Woman, put that thing down!" Thomas said. "You're about to blind me with those high beams! Look at that thing." He beckoned for her hand to get a closer look. "An Elara™ diamond ring, three carats, estimated cost around one hundred grand," he said.

Johnnie Mae's eyes widened as she quickly looked over at Landris. "What?" Johnnie Mae said as she turned her body completely toward Landris. "What?"

Landris avoided her obvious attempt to stare an explanation out of him.

"Katie Couric and Diane Sawyer favor the three-diamond Elara™ pendant, while Sela Ward and Jennifer Love Hewitt have been known to sport the diamond solitaire necklace. And now, it looks like you got my man here hooking you up in style with a three-stone Elara™ diamond ring. Go 'head, George! A man with style *and* class. My brother."

"Sir, what can I get for you?" the waiter came back and asked Thomas.

"How are their ribs?" Thomas asked George, who nodded a quick approval. "Then, hook me up with some southern barbecue ribs and the works," Thomas said to the waiter.

The waiter nodded. "And to drink?"

"Tea. Sweet tea with a twist of lemon."

The waiter left.

Thomas grinned at George; invisible bird feathers seemed to dangle from the corner of his mouth. "Well, well. So we're all here together. Yes, siree. Well, Miss Johnnie Mae, George tells me you're an author? What exactly do you write?"

"Fiction."

"I hope not that religious stuff. You'll never make any money if it's that kind."

"You talking about Christian fiction?" Landris said. "Why do you say that?"

"I'm no expert, but I've noticed the world seems to support other type books a lot better than the Christian folks seem to support Christian fiction . . . unless you're some big name with a huge following. I'm saying I wouldn't look to get rich doing it. That's all."

"Thomas, I'd have to disagree with you on that," Landris said.

"Disagree all you want. I have two words for you: *Harry Potter*. Christian folks preach against it, sell books telling you why you shouldn't read or buy it, but do you find them making any real statements where it counts by supporting Christian fiction with the dollars? making those type of books hit many, if any, mainstream, best-selling charts? Talk is good: it don't cost a thing. But money rules what the industry will put out and what you might end up seeing eventually get to the big screen."

Landris glanced at Johnnie Mae, who wasn't saying much. She had said grace and was picking her way through her tossed salad. Johnnie Mae didn't write Christian fiction. Landris had mentioned a few times she should consider it, since she wasn't that far from it already. Now Thomas was sitting there proving the very reason why she shouldn't do it.

"Well, I have two words for *you*," Landris said to Thomas. "*Left Behind*."

"Left behind what? What's left behind?"

"A series of Christian fiction that has and is doing quite well in the publishing world."

"Yeah, and I bet even with that, some Christians have attacked it."

"Well, I learned a long time ago, you can't please everybody," Johnnie Mae said, finally looking Thomas' way. "Fifty percent of the people will like what you do, and fifty percent of them will dislike what you do. Either way, fifty percent of the people will probably end up unhappy with what you do or how you do it. So, I've learned not to sweat it, to follow my own heart, and to be true to what I believe."

"Your meal, sir." The waiter placed Thomas' plate with a half-slab of ribs slow-cooked over a hickory fire, baked beans, coleslaw, and fresh hot yeast rolls in front of him.

Thomas inhaled, smiled, and instantly became no talk and all eat. Johnnie Mae and Landris exchanged looks several times while trying to keep from laughing as they watched Thomas go at it like he hadn't eaten a meal in days.

CHAPTER 15

But he giveth grace unto the lowly.

(Proverbs 3:34)

"Where are your things?" Lena asked Memory with a gentleness in her voice.

"Why?"

"Theresa and I have been talking, and she's agreed to let you stay here for a few days."

"How many is a few? Until you come up with a reason for me to leave?" Memory asked as she scratched one side of her itching head.

Lena readjusted her body in the chair. "Tell me something. When you came here, how long were you originally looking to stay?"

"A few days. A week maybe. I don't know. Maybe more. However long it took me to accomplish what I came here to accomplish. I mean I do have my own place to live."

"And where is that?" Lena leaned forward so she would be sure not to miss a thing.

"Detroit."

"And what were your plans again?"

Memory stood up and walked around the room. She picked up a jade elephant and ran her hand over its trunk. "To find you. I stopped off in parts of North Carolina, my old neighborhood, then Winston-Salem, which eventually led me here. Lena, I came in search of you." She set the elephant down carefully and looked up at Lena. "To see how you were after all these years. When I discovered you had a daughter, I followed the trail, and it led me here. So here I am."

"But, see, that's where you lose me. How did you know we were *here*? In this house?"

Memory frowned. "Public records. Theresa had a closing when she bought the house. The address is listed with the owner's name. How else would I have known?"

Lena didn't blink. "Then, how did you know I was here?"

Memory shrugged. "I didn't. I just took a chance that you might be, and if not, Theresa or someone would eventually tell me where to find you."

"You can stay a week," Lena said. "After that, you'll need to be on your way."

"Fair enough."

"But the first time I suspect you're not on the up-and-up with us or you do anything to hurt my child, you're gone."

Memory smiled. "Thank you. Now we'll have a chance to really talk. Catch up on what we've missed all these years." She walked over to Lena and held out her arms.

Lena allowed the hug, but that by no means meant she was being easily fooled.

Lena and Memory talked quite a bit. Memory insisted on helping them get situated from the move. Lena and Theresa were beginning to relax around Memory. They looked at photos of a young Theresa. Then Memory pulled out a scrapbook with pictures Lena hadn't seen or remembered seeing before. "This is a young me," Memory said, pointing.

"Memory," Theresa said as she examined closer. "You looked like Mariah Carey."

"Look at Mama Lena," Maurice said, laughing at a black-and-white photo of a mischievous-looking Lena around four years old sporting two long pigtails.

"I was so skinny," Lena said, laughing. "My legs looked like pipe cleaners."

"Who are these people here?" Theresa asked, pointing to a dark-skinned couple in a sepia photo, sitting with a dark little boy and a white little girl in front of a fake flowery background, apparently taken several decades ago inside of a studio.

"That," Memory began with a smile on her face, "is Madear, Papa, Junior, and me."

Both Theresa and Maurice exchanged looks.

"Junior and I were twins."

"Mama, you never told me you have an uncle," Theresa said. "Where is he now?"

"Junior died when we were ten," Memory said. "He fell down an old well shaft. And as you probably can tell, I don't much favor either of my parents. There was a rumor that Madear and this white man she worked for had a thing going on. Madear denied it when I asked, but I heard her and Papa arguing one night when they thought I was asleep." She ate a spoonful of her buttermilk stuffed with cornbread mixture. Maurice frowned as he watched her repeat the action of spoon to glass to mouth.

"Papa told her he didn't care who that child—me—really belonged to. As far as he was concerned, I would always be his little girl. Madear kept telling him it wasn't right, though. That everyone had a right to know about their own offspring if they so chose. She wanted to get the truth out into the open. It was obvious to me, even at that age; it was a burden on her conscience. She kept crying about how grace had kept us safe thus far. 'But how much more can grace keep intervening?' She kept saying she didn't know what to do and Papa kept telling her he would fix everything somehow," Memory said. "Then Papa had to leave for about six months to work on a big job in Richmond, Virginia. It was just me and Madear then. No Papa to step in-between us when we clashed."

"I don't get it. What makes you think they were talking about you or that Big Mama had . . . you know?" Lena asked.

Memory smiled and took another bite. "Because, dearie. After I had you, Madear and I exchanged words. I was so upset, I told her I was going to go live with Papa until he came home. We really went at one another's throats. I told her I wasn't staying with her any longer. 'I'm going to stay with my father, and you can't stop me! You're just jealous of me and Papa's relationship,' I said. That's when she blurted out, 'He's *not* your father, Memory!' I was devastated." Memory recalled it just as it had happened 51 years ago.

"Liar! You're lying. He is my father. How can you say something like that?" Memory said. "How? How can you go to such great lengths to be so cruel?"

Madear looked more disappointed with herself than she was at any disrespect Memory had just shown her. "Baby, I'm sorry. I didn't mean it. Not like I said it."

But it was out there then and nothing she could say could ever take it back. "Then who is my father?" Memory asked. "Who? Tell me!"

"Madear wouldn't tell me," Memory said, returning to the present with all eyes glued on her as she told the story. "So I left her in search of Papa. Only Papa couldn't answer my questions either. All he ever told me was my answer was likely in Asheville, North Carolina, where we lived right before we moved to Winston-Salem."

Memory's smile was genuine with warmth for a change. "That's where I originally met your father, Lena. You see, Madear and Papa lived in this grand house in Asheville. One day, Madear was in a panic. Out of the blue, she said we were moving. I didn't want to leave, so I ran away with a guy named Percy James. We were trying to get married so I wouldn't have to leave Asheville. I was gone for days, ended up getting pregnant before Papa tracked me down and brought me home. We left our home in the middle of the night and moved to Winston-Salem. As far as I know, neither of them ever went back again."

CHAPTER 16

That ye be not slothful.

(Hebrews 6:12)

George took Johnnie Mae to the airport to catch her 10 A.M. flight home to Birmingham. It wouldn't be long now before they would be husband and wife.

George called Thomas at the hotel. He and Thomas had agreed to hook up around 11 o'clock. Thomas had yet to ever visit George's house since he'd moved to Atlanta. An automated voice-mail message requested the caller to leave a message. "Hey brother," George said as he wondered why Thomas hadn't answered the phone. "I'll be outside waiting for you as planned in about fifteen minutes. See you then."

George waited in his car for thirty minutes. No Thomas.

"Valet parking?" he was asked a third time when he got out of the car.

"No thanks. I just need to check on one of your patrons real quick. May I leave my car here a minute while I run in and see?"

"Only for a minute." The young man flashed him a signature, full-tooth grin.

George's long strides carried him quickly to the front desk, where a friendly-looking woman stood waiting behind a green marble counter. "Excuse me, Miss. Would you please see if a Thomas Landris has checked out yet?" he said.

She typed in some information. "I'm sorry, but we don't show a Thomas Landris as ever having checked in," she said.

"Are you sure? That's L-a-n-d-r-i-s. He told me he was staying here."

She nodded; no typing necessary. "I'm sure. Might it be under a different name?"

"Not that I'm aware of. But thanks for checking." George left and walked quickly back to his car. "Thanks," he said, tipping the guy who was practically guarding his car.

"George!"

George turned around. "Thomas?"

Thomas was carrying his luggage and a briefcase as he walked briskly over to George's car. "Sorry I'm late. I hope you haven't been waiting too long. Pop your trunk so I can put my things in."

George did as instructed, then unlocked the car doors. "So, where were you?"

"Trying to straighten out my hotel bill. Would you believe they were trying to charge me for a bunch of extra stuff? It took a little longer than I expected to get it cleared up."

"You're talking about here? This hotel here?"

"Of course, here." Thomas slipped into the seat on the passenger's side and leaned forward as George slid in.

George stared at Thomas. "That's funny. I just came from inside asking whether you'd checked out, and the woman in there told me that you had never checked in."

Thomas shrugged. "See what I mean? They apparently need a better system or some employees who know what they're doing." Thomas looked out of the window as George pulled out onto the one-way street. "Well, did you get your little woman off okay?"

George hesitated but decided to let this one go. This time. "You mean, Johnnie Mae? Yeah, she got off all right."

"She's a feisty little thing. You're definitely going to have your hands full with her." He glanced over at George. "And that ring you got her—wow! Bling! Bling! I didn't know my little brother had it in him. You got taste, that's for doggone sure."

"I really didn't appreciate your bringing up how much it cost in front of her either."

"Well, it's not like it's a secret or anything. If she really wanted to know, all she had to do was take it to a reputable jeweler. Where did you find it anyway? It's not like Elara™ diamond rings are available in every jewelry store."

"Tapper's. West Bloomfield, Michigan."

"In Orchard Mall?"

"Yeah, you're familiar with them?"

Thomas smiled. "Let's just say I know my way around jewelry and jewelry places."

"Is that what you've been up to lately?" George asked as he looked briefly at Thomas, then set his gaze back on the road to complete his right turn.

"That, among other things. Just trying to make my way in the world. Everybody ain't got it like you, my brother."

"And how is that?"

"You're a man of God these days. What was that you told me a couple of years back? 'The blessing of the Lord, it maketh rich, and He adds no sorrow with it'?" ———

"Yeah, Proverbs 10:22."

"That's what I'm talking about. You even remember where the scriptures are found."

"It's about more than just quoting scripture or impressing people because you know where a scripture is in the Bible, Thomas. It's getting it in your heart. So when the storms come—and Jesus said storms will come—when they come, whatever is inside of you is what will come out. Faith in, faith out. Peace in, peace out. Fear in, fear out. 'Out of the heart the mouth speaketh.' Words—right or wrong—have power to become manifested."

"Please, no preaching. Okay. No disrespect, but you know how I feel about religion."

"You're still mad with God about Makaila, aren't you?"

"Why do you have to bring this up, George?"

George looked at Thomas as he drove into his subdivision. "She was our sister. We both loved her. You can't be mad at God about her death."

"I'm not mad at God. I'm mad at so-called Christian folks who think they are the only ones with the right answers. I'm mad about so-called Christians who claim they represent, or are ambassadors, or are 'Children of the King,' yet God is love and they're displaying a totally different image to the world. Being judgmental, impatient, and arrogant. Believing they're so right or so perfect and that God only speaks through them, or to them, or just to certain people."

George pulled into his garage. "Thomas, not all Christians are like that. What happened with Makaila was wrong. So wrong. But you can't blame all Christians for what happened to her." George turned off the car as he kept his eyes on Thomas.

"I just don't want to hear about religion, George. Not today. I can imagine God must be so pleased with his 'children' down here. How they're portraying him as a Father. Some poor. Some barely making it. Begging the world for a handout or hand up. Sick. Tired. Defeated. Unloving. Unforgiving. Unkind. Can't give. Won't give, even when they have it to give."

"So what's your beef, then? God's people are being defeated because of a lack of knowledge. Many of them don't know who they are in Christ. They don't know about their God-given authority in Jesus' name. Some don't realize their strength in the Lord because many have not and are still not being taught. Yes, God's children do miss it, many times and many opportunities where we should have been the light in darkness."

"My beef, George, is that I don't want to hear some dull sermon about ignorance and knowledge, light and darkness. About the blind who think they are walking in light when, in fact, they are still in a sort of darkness. Folks who—were I inclined to believe them—would force me to conclude that God is a racist, a sexist . . . that He has problems with people of certain color and gender. But you know what: I do know better. So you'll have to excuse me, but I truly don't want to hear anything about religion, *if* you don't mind."

"Then, don't hear about religion. Hear about a relationship. Because Thomas, that's what I'm talking about: a relationship with God, not religion. Not dogma. Not fanatics who believe they are the only ones who can possibly be right and anything contrary to their belief about God is wrong. I'm talking about a personal, spiritual relationship with the one and only, Almighty, All knowing, All-seeing God! A relationship. One-on-one."

Thomas looked hard at George and shook his head. "A relationship?"

"Yes! Two people getting to know each other on an intimate basis."

Thomas stared again, then laughed. "Point served. Point taken. Point received."

"Oh, and Thomas?" George said as he popped open the trunk and got out.

"Yeah," Thomas said, stepping out of the car and meeting George at the trunk.

"I'll have you know that my sermons are not—I repeat, *not*—dull!"

Thomas retrieved his luggage and briefcase, stood back, then looked George over from head to toe. "Makaila would be proud of you, man. Because you know she did love herself some good preaching."

"Yeah," George laughed, opening the door to his house. "Only thing: She probably would have been the one doing the good preaching. And who knows, maybe our lives would have turned out completely different a lot sooner."

"You mean, maybe I wouldn't have become so bitter?" They stepped into the house.

"Our whole family pretty much quit attending church, so you weren't the only one who was affected by her death. Our foundation was weak. We shouldn't have quit."

"George, I've never told you this. But back when that happened, I told God if He would save my sister's life, I would give Him mine and serve Him for the rest of my days. When she died, I decided that day: What good is it to pray to a God who may or may not come when you need Him most? So I walked away and never looked back."

"But God is real, Thomas. What happened or didn't happen doesn't define who God is. He is God just because He is. Not based on whether or not He answered your prayer. You have to have faith in God. Not always understanding what's going on or why."

Thomas set his things down on the kitchen floor. "George, I know you mean well. I just don't want to go there with you. Not today. When you can explain to me how God can let things happen to innocent people . . . children who can't take care of themselves, why God allows evil to happen to good people, allowing monsters to molest, abuse, and mistreat the weaker ones of society—when you can explain that, then maybe we can talk."

George smiled and patted his brother on the back, knowing it was going to take some fervent prayer and the right words to get through to him.

Thomas looked around. "Man, this is a beautiful home."

"Yeah. Paid for with the money from the investment you convinced me years ago to buy into." George walked over to the kitchen table and picked up the papers from the brokerage firm he had received. Now was as good a time as any. He handed them to Thomas.

"What's this?"

"I requested that from the brokerage firm that handled my investments."

"You did what?" Thomas looked at the first page. "Why did you call them?" His voice began to escalate. "Why didn't you call me if you had a question?"

"I did call you," George said. "Remember? You wouldn't ever call me back."

"But I don't understand. What would make you go around me and get a . . ." He flipped through the pages. "You had them send you your record from day one?" He looked from the paper to George's face. "What's up? You didn't trust me?"

"Thomas," George looked at him. "Apparently, there was an error reported to my account. I received a notice from the IRS accusing me of failing to report and pay taxes on some investment income. Turns out, it was the recent sale of my Microsoft stock."

"But you told me to sell it."

"And I don't deny that. But Thomas, I've not seen any money from that sale, nor did I get a 1099-B letting me know what I should have included in my 2000 tax filing. Why are you so upset that I requested copies of my own statements anyway? It's obvious there has to be some kind of error. Just look at the amount they report as being paid out." George cocked his head to the side. "Look at it."

Thomas looked down.

"I just need for us to straighten this out," George said. "I see what they show. I see how they say they came to that amount. You tell me. What do you think happened? Did they add too many zeroes? Miscalculate? Mix up my account with someone else's? What?"

Thomas had already seen and was well aware of the amount. He had seen it when he'd cashed in the shares and taken receipt of the funds. Still, Thomas sat down at the table and studied the summary page of George's portfolio as though he were really trying to figure it out. "Let me look at this a minute," Thomas said, stalling. *Now what do I tell him? Think.*

George Landris

Stock: Microsoft

Account Opened: January 29, 1987   *Account Closed: March 31, 2000*

Date	Action	Shares	Amount
01/29/1987	Purchased	2,000 shares @ $ 000.53	$ 1,060
09/21/1987	Split 2:1	4,000 shares @ $ 000.82	$ 3,280
04/16/1990	Split 2:1	8,000 shares @ $ 1.61	$ 12,880
06/27/1991	Split 3:2	12,000 shares @ $ 3.19	$ 38,280
06/15/1992	Split 3:2	18,000 shares @ $ 4.37	$ 78,660
05/23/1994	Split 2:1	36,000 shares @ $ 6.71	$ 241,560
12/09/1996	Split 2:1	72,000 shares @ $ 21.53	$ 1,550,160
02/23/1998	Split 2:1	144,000 shares @ $ 45.46	$ 6,546,240
07/28/1998	Sell	20,000 shares @ $ 59.81	($ 1,196,200)
07/28/1998	Held	124,000 shares @ $ 59.81	$ 7,416,440
03/29/1999	Split 2:1	248,000 shares @ $ 95.00	$ 23,560,000
03/31/2000	Sell	248,000 shares @ $115.00	$ 28,520,000
03/31/2000	Held	0 shares	$ 0

Thomas knew the $28,520,000 was correct. But he kept his head down. Thinking. He wasn't expecting to have to deal with this yet. *Why didn't I send him some of the money when I got it? Why didn't I have them withhold taxes? Why didn't I call him back when he left me a message? Then I could have, at least, handled this without his having requested this printout. And I wouldn't be in a mess right this minute. Think, Thomas. Think!*

George noted that Thomas was intense in reviewing the figures. He had his pen out and seemed to be scribbling all kinds of figures on the back of a piece of paper.

"Although $2,852,000 is a lot," George said, breaking the thickened air of silence, "I could have believed that figure considering what I got on the last sale back in '98. Truthfully, I was expecting the sale to be closer to maybe $50,000. But $28,520,000? Improbable. So what do you think happened?"

Thomas looked up and shook his head. "Wow." He passed his hand over his mouth several times. "And you say the IRS is looking for taxes to be paid on this amount, huh?" Thomas tried to laugh it off while he continued to process various prospective scenarios.

"Oh, and that's not counting the penalties they're assessing: all total, a mere $5,704,000 and some change. What's that . . . about 20 percent? I guess I shouldn't complain. It still leaves me with around what . . . $22 million?" George sat down. "That's, of course, *if* I had ever *received* the money, which—as you and I both know—I did not. So, how do you suggest we make this right?"

"George, why don't you let me take these papers with me, including the tax bill, and while I'm off doing my thing, I'll get this straightened out for you." He managed a smile.

"Thomas," George said, matching his brother's smile, "why don't you just bring everything into my study, and you and I get this straightened out right now . . . together? While you're still here." George stood up, took a few steps, then looked back at his brother, who wasn't following him. "Or is there something else you need to tell me?"

CHAPTER 17

I have been young, and now am old.

(Psalm 37:25 (a))

Johnnie Mae drove to her mother's house after she arrived at Birmingham's airport, having formed a habit of leaving her car in long-term parking to get home quickly and easily.

"Well, hi," Johnnie Mae said when she walked inside and found her siblings, Donald and Marie, in her mother's kitchen in the middle of a workday. "What a surprise."

"Hi," Marie said.

Johnnie Mae noted Marie's smile was like watered-down coffee: weak.

Marie and Donald then exchanged quick looks. Johnnie Mae caught it. "Okay, what's wrong? Where's Mama? Where's Princess Rose?"

"Johnnie Mae—" Donald began.

"What's wrong? Donald, tell me what's going on. Marie, has something happened to Mama? To Princess Rose? What?"

"Please sit down," Marie said, touching Johnnie Mae's hand.

"No, I will not sit down! Just tell me what has happened!"

"Mama had a slight accident," Marie said. Johnnie Mae covered her mouth and began shaking her head as she sat in a chair. "Johnnie Mae, now don't go getting upset."

"They're both all right, Johnnie," Donald said as he massaged her shoulders.

"Then, where are they?"

"Princess Rose is in Mama's room taking a nap," Marie said. She stood and began to pace as she started to wring both her hands.

"And Mama?"

"They wanted to keep her in the hospital overnight. Just for observation, that's all."

"Why? Was she badly hurt? I want to go see her." Johnnie Mae got up and started out of the kitchen.

"Johnnie Mae, we need to tell you something. I know you don't want to hear this," Marie said.

Donald stepped forward. "We've tried to tell you this before, but you never want to talk about it."

Johnnie Mae didn't want to hear a prelude. "What is it? Just spit it out, will you?"

"Apparently, Mama forgot how to get home," Donald said, looking down at the black-and-white linoleum floor. "She was riding around lost. She got frustrated, and that must have been when she ran through the stop sign and ended up hitting another car."

Marie walked up to Johnnie Mae. "She was over on Highway 280, Johnnie Mae."

"Highway 280? Why was she all the way over there?"

"Confused, apparently," Donald said. "She's still upset because she doesn't understand how she got all the way over there to begin with. She was going to the grocery store: two miles from here. And she ended up all the way over there."

"What did the doctor say?"

Marie hugged Johnnie Mae. "Possibly the onset of Alzheimer's."

"Johnnie, I know you don't want to think about that, but we need to address this."

"How bad is she? Did the doctor say?"

"Not as bad as she might get later." Marie sat down at the kitchen table and folded her hands into each other. "But she's been trying to cover it up for a while now. Johnnie Mae, some things have happened while you were away traveling and she made me promise not to mention it to you."

Donald turned Johnnie Mae to face him as he wiped the tears

that were now flowing from her eyes. "She didn't want you worried on top of everything else in your life."

Johnnie Mae sighed hard. "I knew something was going on. The last time she and I spoke, she couldn't remember things she had just said the day before."

"We told you about this once," Donald said, "but you said—"

"Donald, I know what I said!"

"Johnnie Mae, you don't have to snap my head off. This is not any of our doing. But we do have to think about what course we might need to eventually take from here."

"Course?" Johnnie Mae said, cutting off her tears. "What do you mean 'course'?"

Donald sat down at the table across from Marie. "Like checking into a place to put her where we know she'll be looked after, taken care of, and kept safe."

Johnnie Mae looked hard first at Donald, then at Marie. "You want to put her in a nursing home? You want to put our mother in a nursing home?!"

"Not a nursing home, per se. One of those assisted-living facilities," Marie said as she looked away from Johnnie Mae's now demanding stare.

"No, we are not! We will not be putting our mother away! She has been there for us when we needed her, and I will not," Johnnie Mae said, "*will not*, allow it! No way!"

"Oh yeah, right? Right. You, Miss Fly-All-Over-the-Country-World-Renowned-Famous-Author, won't allow it? So I suppose that means you're going to stay and take care of her?" Marie looked directly into Johnnie Mae's face. "Oh, I know, maybe you'll hire somebody to sit with her in your stead. What's the plan, Johnnie Mae? You have all the answers; we're just her children in need of direction. Tell us, what do you suggest?"

Johnnie Mae's voice remained controlled. "I am going in to check on my daughter. And then, I'm going to the hospital to check on Mama." She started out of the room.

"Johnnie Mae, why are you always in denial?" Donald said.

"Donald, what you call denial, I call faith. I just choose to believe God and His Word. Now, if you'll excuse me . . ." Johnnie Mae left them to go get Princess Rose.

* * *

Johnnie Mae arrived at the hospital to see her mother an hour later.

"I don't know what happened to me today," Mrs. Gates said, "but I'm fine now. Ask me anything. My address. My birthday. My children and all of my grandchildren's birthdays. Ask me. I know all of this. I just got a little confused today. I don't know."

"Mama, don't worry yourself about it. I'm home, and we'll figure this out together."

"But I promised to help you with Princess Rose. And your wedding! Oh, I can't wait for your wedding to Pastor Landris. September the eighth. See, I remember. Has he told you where the wedding's going to be yet?"

Johnnie Mae smiled. "Oheka Castle. In Cold Spring Hills, New York."

"Oh my. A castle. That sounds grand. I have money saved up, so I'll make all my reservations just as soon as they release me tomorrow—"

"You don't have to do anything but show up, Mama. Landris is taking care of all the arrangements and the cost."

"You are kidding! Is the man that well-off or just plum crazy?" Johnnie Mae laughed.

"I know he's plum crazy about you," Mrs. Gates said. "Pastor Landris is such a dear person. Did you know he calls and checks on us every few days? I mean that man absolutely adores you, Johnnie Mae."

Johnnie Mae smiled and caressed her mother's hand. "Is that right, Mama?"

"Oh yes. I keep forgetting to tell you." Mrs. Gates adjusted her head on the pillow. "I guess you know the doctor thinks I might be in the early stages of Alzheimer's? I'm trying to tell him it is just signs of old age. What do they expect? So, what do you think?"

"I think we should see what the doctor suggests medication-wise and work at getting you some rest. I'm going to be home for the rest of the week. I'm going to take you home with me and take care of *you* for a change. That's what I think."

"Johnnie Mae." Mrs. Gates looked at her and squeezed her

hand. "You're not going to take Princess Rose from me, are you? I told you I'd keep her while you're doing your thing with the book. I don't want you to think I'm not well enough to take care of her."

Johnnie Mae stood up, leaned down, and kissed her on the forehead. "Mama, let's not talk about this. Okay? You're what matters right now. And I'm home."

Johnnie Mae and Princess Rose left for home. She stopped by the post office on her way to pick up what had to be by now a pile of mail.

"This says I have a certified letter," she said to the postal worker handing her a card.

The postal worker came back with a letter requiring Johnnie Mae to sign for it. It was from the director of The E House. Johnnie Mae turned the envelope around in her hand. *I wonder what this is about.* She decided to wait and open it after she got home, when she and things were a little more settled.

CHAPTER 18

Yet have I not seen the righteous forsaken.

(Psalm 37:25 (b))

Johnnie Mae placed her hand slightly over her heart when she finally got a chance to read the note from Ms. Latham of The E House the following day.

July 11, 2001
Sarah Fleming asked me to get this to you. She said you would know what to do.
Sincerely,

Edith Latham

Edith Latham

It was one o'clock in the afternoon by the time Johnnie Mae's mother was released from the hospital. Johnnie Mae brought her home with her to Coffee, Alabama. After her mother and Princess Rose laid down to take a nap, Johnnie Mae called The E House.

"Ms. Latham?"

"Yes."

"This is Johnnie Mae Taylor."

"Oh, Ms. Taylor. Thank you so much for calling me."

"I got your note and that key Sarah Fleming asked you to send me. How is she?"

"Oh dear, I'm sorry. Sarah's no longer with us."

"No longer with you? What do you mean? Is she—"

"Two people came and took her away about a week ago. She was waiting on you to come back, that much I do know. Anxious, actually. It was the strangest thing. When they showed up all of a sudden with no prior warning, she came to me as she was leaving and said, 'Ms. Edith, I appreciate all you've done for me. I want to return your key to that back room.' Well, I didn't have a clue what she was talking about, as we don't have a back room. So I said, 'The key?' And she had this look on her face that pleaded for me to go along with her. 'Oh yes. The key,' I said. So I took the envelope she held out to me and thanked her for having kept it safe. 'You just don't know how many people forget all about that key,' I said, just because that man kept looking at her and me all funny. Evil. Like he suspected we just might be up to something. He made me nervous."

"So, did her family come to take her home?"

"I'm not sure where they took her. When they have a right, they don't have to say."

"Well, did they leave a forwarding address for her?" Johnnie Mae stood ready with pen and paper to write down the information.

"No, but she never got any mail here anyway. In that envelope, she left specific instructions for me to get that key to you. She said you would know what to do with it."

"Except I'm not so sure that I do," Johnnie Mae said. "Ms. Latham?"

"Yes?"

"Would you happen to know and can tell me whether or not Sarah was wealthy?"

"Wealthy?" She laughed. "Oh, Sarah did like to pretend that she was. Claimed she was from a well-to-do family out of Asheville, North Carolina. I always loved hearing her pronounce the word 'Carolina.' But our place is mainly for those who need help subsidizing their cost. Now if she were rich, do you think she would have been here?"

"Did she happen to say anything else? Mention a name or anything that might help me to make sense of this key?"

Ms. Latham was quiet a second. "On the bottom of the note, she wrote the words 'pearl black.' I don't know if that helps you or means anything at all to you."

"Pearl black? Do you think she meant it like a name, maybe?"

"She didn't write it in capital letters, but I suppose it could be a name. Then again, it could be referring to a piece of jewelry. You know: a black pearl?"

"But she wrote 'pearl black.' Right?"

"Yes."

Johnnie Mae jotted that down. "Ms. Latham, if you happen to hear from Sarah or her family, would you please let me know? Or at least, ask them to contact me?"

"Sure. But I have to tell you, I don't expect I'll be hearing from any of them again."

"But if you do . . ." Johnnie Mae said.

"I'll let you know."

"Thanks. Goodbye." Johnnie Mae set the phone quietly back onto its cradle.

She picked up the key and turned it around. It was definitely old; the kind with the decorative end and teeth that resembled a capital letter F. "Pearl black," Johnnie Mae said, recalling some things Sarah had said to her. And "Dixon Town." But Johnnie Mae thought back to her brief attempt to verify Sarah's story, when she discovered there was no such place as Dixon Town. Yet, she couldn't shake the feeling that she was being pulled to visit Asheville, North Carolina, for herself. One thing could not be disputed: Sarah had been accurate in her descriptions of Biltmore Castle. Johnnie Mae had tons of information that confirmed everything Sarah had told her. Even down to the width, height, and depth of the infamous banquet hall inside the castle.

But how can I go to Asheville with what's going on with my mother? There were things she really should have been doing for her wedding, some six weeks away. She hadn't even found her wedding gown yet.

"Johnnie Mae, what are you doing?" Mrs. Gates asked, hugging her daughter. She sat next to her at the kitchen table and polished an apple from out of the fruit bowl.

Johnnie Mae smiled at her mother. "Just thinking."

Mrs. Gates bit down hard into the apple. "Anything I can help you with?"

Johnnie Mae cocked her head to the side. "Mama, what would you say to us taking a trip to Asheville, North Carolina?"

"Asheville, North Carolina? What on God's green earth is in Asheville, North Carolina?"

"Biltmore Castle. And if I'm correct, possibly remnants of a person's life."

Mrs. Gates patted Johnnie Mae's hand. "Sounds like fun. I'm up for it if you are."

"Then, how about tomorrow?" Johnnie Mae stood up, looked around the kitchen, then grabbed an apple and took a bite. "We could drive up and not have to be in such a hurry. We could stay over a few days. I could get us a room at Biltmore Inn. You'll love it."

"You're up to something, aren't you? I can see that little twinkle in your eye."

Johnnie Mae smiled. "I just got a feeling, Mama. This is something I believe I have to do. I might be too late already, but I've got to see this thing through."

"Then, I'd better get packing," Mrs. Gates said with a refreshing giggle. "Three generations of Gates women on an adventure. Princess Rose is going to love this!"

CHAPTER 19

God having provided some better thing for us . . .

(Hebrews 11:40)

FedEx delivered a letter addressed to Lena at ten o'clock in the morning.

"What is it this time?" Lena said as Theresa looked on. Memory was busy in the kitchen with one day left before she was to leave her newly found family.

"Open it and let's find out," Theresa said as she rubbed her stomach a few times.

Lena noted the return information. "It's from New York." She ripped the zipperlike opener off and retrieved the contents. "It's a letter from Lawrence Hatcher, an attorney in New York. My presence is requested in a matter of importance. They want me to call them. All of my travel expenses and arrangements will be handled out of their office."

"Do they say what they want with you in New York?"

"No. But I suppose I'll just call this number and find out." Lena went to the den and called. She talked for about ten minutes before hanging up.

"That was his secretary. Seems someone left something for me in a will and a Mr. Hatcher is in charge of the execution of it," Lena said, still gazing at the paper.

"A will? Did she tell you who left you something?" Theresa was getting excited.

"No. She couldn't tell me anything over the phone." Lena stared as she spoke, her eyes focused on nothing in particular. "I have to fly to New York to find out any more."

"So?" Theresa said, finding it hard to contain herself now. "When are you going?"

Lena looked at Theresa. "Who said I was?"

"Why wouldn't you go? I'd want to know who left me something as well as what they left me."

"It seems Mr. Hatcher is only available the week of September 10–14. After that, he'll be working on some high-profile something or other. When he finishes that, he'll be vacationing for three weeks. So I don't see me finding out anytime soon, since she said it would be the first of December before he would be able to see me after September fourteenth. And, unfortunately, he can't possibly meet with me before September tenth."

"Then go on one of the days between September 10–14 when he's available," Theresa said.

"Your baby is due September eleventh. I'm not going anywhere that week."

Theresa laughed. "Why not?"

"Theresa, I'm not planning to be out-of-pocket when you're due to have the baby. I came here to help you during that time, and there is no way I'm going to let anything keep me from being here when this little one makes his entrance into the world. Nope."

"Who's going somewhere?" Memory said as she strolled into the den munching on a bagel splattered with cream cheese.

Theresa and Lena instantly exchanged looks. Memory had been better the past few days. In truth, the three women had shared a lot with each other. But Lena still wasn't ready to trust Memory totally. Not just yet. Lena had walked in on her yesterday in Theresa's room rummaging through her closet. She'd claimed she was seeing if anything there needed to be organized. Lena hadn't bought that story worth a wooden nickel.

"Mama's going to New York," Theresa said, missing Lena's apparent hesitation.

"For what?" Memory wiped her mouth with the back of her hand.

"Business," Lena said before Theresa could volunteer any more information.

"Business, huh?" Memory smiled. "So, when are you leaving?"

Lena showed reluctance again. "I haven't decided I'm even going."

"She's going," Theresa said. "She's going if I have to drag her to the airport myself."

Memory looked at the two of them. She sensed Lena was trying to hide something from her. She smiled. "Then, when is this trip that you might not take scheduled?"

"Any day between September 10 and 14. But I am not planning on going anywhere and run the risk of possibly missing out on the birth of my grandbaby. I'm just not."

"So you'd only have to be gone for one day?" Memory asked.

"Yes," Lena said. She wondered where Memory was trying to take this conversation.

"And you would be flying, right?"

"Yes, if I were to go."

"Then why don't you fly up the night of September tenth, schedule your business meeting for the morning of September eleventh, and leave as soon as your meeting is over?" Memory said as she sat down and took another bite of her bagel.

"Memory, I don't know if you're listening or not. But Theresa's due date is September eleventh. Why in heaven would I schedule myself to be gone on her due date?"

"How about," Memory began, "for the simple reason that most people hardly ever deliver their baby on the exact due date? What better day to *not* expect a baby to arrive than the actual date?" Memory smiled at the sheer genius of what she'd just said.

"That's right." Theresa was getting excited again. "Mama, that would be a perfect plan. You fly up late on the tenth and meet him early the next morning. Because let's say the worst-case scenario is I actually go into labor on September eleventh. By the time I deliver, you could be on a plane back here, and you wouldn't miss a thing!" Theresa looked at Memory, who was nodding in agreement with her.

"Theresa, why are you so determined to make this hard?"

Lena said. She bore into her with eyes of steel. "I'm not doing it. There's nothing that man in New York could have for me that can compare to the rewards of being with *my* baby when she has *her* baby. So it's settled. End of discussion."

The doorbell rang, interrupting any more debate on the subject.

"Now what?" Lena said with a bit of frustration. "Another FedEx? And I still would like to know why it appears I'm getting more mail here than I ever did in North Carolina. Did somebody take out an ad in the paper telling everybody where to find me?"

"Present company excluded?" Memory laughed as she quickly headed to answer the door. She looked out. "It's Maurice," she yelled as she opened it. He hurried in.

"I've got some great news!" he said, giving Theresa a quick hello peck on her cheek. "Good morning, Mama Lena." He hugged her.

Lena smiled and hugged him back. "Morning, Maurice."

He rubbed his hands together. "I've got great news! I've been granted an opportunity to pitch a reality television show idea I've been working on to a producer in New York who is interested in discussing my proposal further. So what do you think of that?"

Lena looked at Theresa, who was grinning like she'd just won some grand prize.

Confused, Maurice looked from Theresa to Lena. "What? Did I miss something?"

"No, Maurice. It's just, Mama got something today, and *she's* going to New York."

"I am not going." Lena said, stopping Theresa before she got wound tight again.

"Why aren't you?" Maurice asked Lena, but looked at Theresa for the answer.

"Because she doesn't want to possibly miss being here when the baby is born, dearie," Memory said. She wiped her hands on her shirttail.

"But Memory was just making an excellent point. See, Mama needs to go sometime between September tenth and fourteenth or she'd have to wait until December. She's afraid I'll have the baby if she goes now. So Memory was pointing out how hardly anyone ever—"

"Hardly ever . . ." Memory chimed in like this was call-and-response time.

"Hardly ever goes into labor on their *exact* due date. So, if Mama were to fly up, say, September tenth, the night before, meet with them early that next morning—"

"The earliest time available that morning," Memory said.

"Then she could be finished and on her way back without much time lost."

"I don't care for flying, Theresa, and you know that," Lena said.

Theresa turned to Maurice. "I have a great idea. You and Mama could fly up to New York together—"

"Oh, and neither one of us be here?" Lena drew back to get a better look at the person who was spewing such nonsense. "Child, have you lost your everloving mind?!"

"She needs to go, Maurice. It's sounds important." Theresa wouldn't look at Lena.

"Oh, you just want to know what it is, that's why you're pushing so for me to go," Lena said, turning up her nose.

"I hope y'all don't mind this suggestion and think I'm out of place," Memory said. "But I was just thinking. It wouldn't be any problem for me to hang around a little while longer. At least until after Lena goes to New York and comes back. And if Maurice wants to go with her, y'all would at least know that someone is here in the house with Theresa. Just in case she needs anything. It's just an offer here. But I sure wouldn't mind."

Lena looked suspiciously at Memory. "That's not necessary, Memory. If Theresa needed someone around, her father and Beatrice are nearby. But I'm not going, so I really don't know why we're even still having this conversation."

"Well, my offer's out there. And I would love nothing more than to do something to repay y'all for these past few days you've shown me kindness. I could keep the house clean, cook, and do whatever else needs to be done. It's not like I have to be anywhere in the next few weeks. And besides, I hadn't planned on leaving Georgia just yet anyway." *Not until I get what I came for,* Memory thought, then smiled. "So y'all think about it, and if you decide you want me to stay, just say the word, and I'm here. But realize I am due to leave here tomorrow sometime."

"Thanks, Memory," Theresa said. She was convinced her mama needed to find out what that letter was all about. And if she had to get Maurice to go with Lena, then so be it. But she wasn't going to let her mama pass up this opportunity. Plus, she had to admit, she was curious to learn what was beckoning Lena to New York in such grand fashion.

Theresa took the letter Lena received and called the number. The secretary Lena had spoken with earlier answered the phone.

"Yes, I'm calling for Lena Patterson. I believe you spoke with her earlier today."

"Yes, I did."

"And what did you say your name was again?" Theresa asked.

"Frances Stillman. So, has Ms. Patterson decided on what she wants to do?"

"Yes, she's decided to fly up on the latest flight possible out of Atlanta on Monday, September 10," Theresa said. "And meet with Mr. Hatcher at 7:30 A.M. Is that possible?"

The secretary was quiet a second. "He usually doesn't see clients until 8 A.M. But I'm sure he'll make an exception in this case. Mr. Hatcher will require about one and a half hours with Ms. Patterson, so I'll put her down for Tuesday, September 11, 2001, from 7:30 A.M. to 9 A.M."

"Perfect," Theresa said. "That sounds perfect."

"Our office is located in the World Trade Center, Tower One, on the eightieth floor. Now, will Ms. Patterson be traveling alone or will someone be accompanying her on her trip? Provisions are available for a travel companion, if she desires one," Ms. Stillman said.

Theresa thought about it. *Oh this really is perfect!* "Why yes," Theresa said, trying to hold back her bursting excitement. "She does, Ms. Stillman. His name is Maurice Greene." She spelled his last name for her.

"Okay, then. We're all set," Ms. Stillman said. "And what was your name again?"

"Theresa Jordan. I'm Ms. Patterson's daughter."

"Then, I will make arrangements for two, from Atlanta to New York, arriving on a late-evening or night flight, on September 10, 2001—"

"The latest one they have, please. I'm pregnant, and we're trying to limit my mother's absence to a bare minimum."

"I understand. I'll be making hotel accommodations for two, with both of their checkout times and flight departures from New York to Atlanta for September 11, 2001, sometime after noon. That should give everyone time to conclude the business at hand and arrive in plenty of time at the airport. I'll call back when I have confirmed reservations along with confirmation numbers, which I will follow up with in a package to include all of these details in writing," Ms. Stillman said.

"Could you possibly call me back instead of my mother? It's just much less burdensome for her with me handling this. You understand?"

"Oh, sure. I'll call you, Ms. Jordan, once I have secured the information. Could you give me your phone number again, please?"

Theresa gave her the phone number, hung up, grabbed a sofa pillow, and smiled.

Lena walked in and saw Theresa hugging a pillow. "What are you up to, smiley?"

"Oh, nothing. You know, Mama, I was just thinking. Let's let Memory stay a while longer. Maybe another week or two? *Or three or four or five.* I'm sure the two of you still have lots more to talk about . . . more to learn about each other. Your past. Her past—"

"Theresa, what are you up to?"

"Nothing, Mama. I was just thinking how great it's been hearing about days gone by. Learning about our family. Honestly, she's really gotten better. She's been a big help."

"So, you're telling me you want Memory to stay? Here? A few more weeks?"

"Yes. I really do."

"Yeah. Right. Just like I really want to be out-of-pocket when my grandchild is born. You're not fooling me, little Miss Theresa. You're up to something, sure as I was born to die. I just hope whatever it is, it's not something you're going to regret later."

Theresa smiled. "You mean me?"

"Don't try that innocent act with me." She wrinkled her nose. "Memory is fixing something Italian with parmesan. She said it should be ready in about ten minutes."

Theresa hugged Lena. "Great, I'm starved!" She started skipping to the kitchen.

"You'd better slow your roll before you set off something really too soon. And I know that skip, too. You're up to something." Lena shook her head. "I just know it."

CHAPTER 20

For the thing which I greatly feared is come upon me.

(Job 3:25)

George stood with the phone held out for Thomas. He had picked up the portable phone for him to call the brokerage firm.

"George, listen," Thomas said. "I've sort of run into a little problem. I was working to resolve it, which is why I've been doing so much traveling lately."

"So, where is the money? Twenty-eight million dollars, and I haven't seen a cent of it! Now I'm standing here with a letter addressed to me from the Internal Revenue Service requesting taxes on $28,520,000, Thomas, and I don't have a clue where the money is?" George put the phone down.

Thomas stood up and backed away. "I can explain."

"I'm waiting."

Thomas walked to the other side of the great room and stood near the marbled fireplace. "My original plan was to shelter your money. I knew when I heard your message to sell your entire remaining shares it was going to generate a huge tax bill. Personally, had I been you, I would have only taken out what I needed, because as long as you don't sell, there's no tax consequence due. Microsoft wasn't even paying dividends on their stock, so you hadn't had a tax liability for anything except your 1998 sale."

"When I sold it."

"Right."

"So, I suppose what you're trying to say is: This is partly my fault?"

"Now, George, I'm not saying that. But I wouldn't have sold all my shares had it been me. But you told me years ago, when you got ready to sell your stock: You didn't want to hear any arguments from me. So, I followed your wishes to a T and sold it."

"So far, I've got that much. Had you been me, you wouldn't have sold it all. Correct me if I'm wrong, but didn't you sell all your shares earlier on?"

Thomas rubbed his forehead, then cleared his throat. "Well, yeah. I did sell mine early on. So I didn't acquire as many shares as you ultimately did. In fact, I sold mine in the mid-1990s and got a measly $13,000 for the 8,000 shares I had accumulated."

"So, had you been me and saved yours, then you would have had enough to not resort to keeping my money? Does that about get us to the top of this mountain without us having to take the scenic route?"

"You always were direct and to the point."

"Then how about you getting direct and to the point. Where . . . is . . . my . . . money, Thomas?" George waited.

"You know, if I recall correctly, the Bible says when you pray you should stand and forgive. And I know you, if anybody, wouldn't ever preach one thing and live another."

"Thomas, don't play with me. We're talking about the IRS. I'm a pastor of a church with almost 4,000 members. The IRS is looking for somewhere in the neighborhood of six million dollars from me. I don't have *six . . . million . . . dollars* to give them, Thomas! So please don't keep me in suspense any longer. Tell me: Where is my money?"

"All right! All right. I had an opportunity to possibly double your money. What I was thinking was that I could take it, make it work for you—"

"Oh . . . make it work for me?" George said it before he could stop himself.

" 'Be angry and sin not,' " Thomas said, quoting yet another scripture he recalled.

"Please don't stand there quoting scriptures to me." George bit down on his lip. "I'm preparing to get married in about six weeks. I've planned this wonderful day for Johnnie Mae and me to exchange our vows before God and those who care about us—"

"George, you know I care."

"And now, you stand here and tell me that you *took* money that didn't belong to you, and you took it upon yourself to use it without my knowledge or consent. And if I'm following you even remotely here, it sounds like you might not have any of my money left." George sat down on the chaise lounge and shook his head. "Stop me at any point you believe I have gone astray in summarizing any of this."

Thomas came over and sat next to George. "I was really looking out for your best interest, George. Had this worked out the way it should have, your money would have been sheltered from taxes, at least for a while. And yes, I'll admit, I would have had an opportunity to double your money, meaning I would have had millions as well."

"I have one question for you?"

"Anything, George. Anything."

"Is there any possibility that I might see any of that money? I just need to know." George's vein was pumping harder than usual in his left temple, and it showed.

"A slight possibility."

"Slight?"

"Yes. I messed up and I have been working for the past year to get your money back. I know it's my fault you owe a penalty with the IRS, but I have a tax expert who is right now working on how we might get that reversed off you." Thomas stood up again and began pacing the floor.

"When do you think I'll know something for sure?" It was difficult, but George was working hard to keep his cool.

"That, I can't say. I thought I would have had this straightened out before you even discovered it, actually."

George hung his head and began to pray silently. *God, you said the battle is not mine, but it's yours. You told me to forgive, although I confess I'm doing it by faith right now. Please, Holy Spirit, order my steps, in Jesus' name. Lord, you said the prayers of a righteous man availeth much. I thank you it's done now. I thank you, Father, for hearing me always. In Jesus' name . . . Amen.*

George looked back up at Thomas, who was now looking toward heaven.

"George," Thomas said, looking at him. "I don't suppose you still want me to be your best man at your wedding? Not with all that you now know about all of this."

George began to laugh uncontrollably. *Forgive. Forgive. Forgive. Do good to them that spitefully misuse you.* "Yes, Thomas. I still want you to be my best man."

"I'm going to get this mess straight. I promise you, George. Don't doubt me now."

"Me, doubt you, Thomas?" George said. Then he laughed some more. *Thank you, Lord, that it's done now. I thank you because I believe I have already received now. You said in Mark 11:24, 'What things soever ye desire when ye pray, believe that ye receive them, and ye shall have them.' I believe I have received now. I thank you right now. I believe it is already worked out now. Now. Now. I thank you now . . .*

CHAPTER 21

Let every soul be subject unto the higher powers. For there is no power but of God.

(Romans 13:1)

"You're going where?" Landris asked Johnnie Mae when she called.

"Biltmore Castle in Asheville, North Carolina."

"Why are you going there?"

"It's just a feeling I have that I need to go there. There's this woman named Sarah Fleming. I met her in Selma. Landris, they came and took her away. I told her I would come back, but I didn't get a chance to. She left a key for me and the name of a woman I believe will either prove what she told me as truth, or release me from a wild turkey chase." Johnnie Mae walked around her room gathering things she needed for this trip.

"I would have loved to have gone with you, but I have a few crises here to work on. Thomas has decided to stay a little longer. And I'm meeting with the board of directors on Friday morning. It seems a few people are making a ruckus about me having Minister Fulton fill in for me the two weeks I'll be gone during our wedding and honeymoon."

"Minister Fulton is the woman preacher, right?"

"Yes. And apparently there's more opposition than I originally realized about our church having a woman preacher at all. She's been doing things around there since after I became pastor. But putting her in total charge has stirred up a hornet's nest. On a different note, I'm having the wedding invitations addressed and they'll go out before July 24. I need the RSVPs back fairly soon to lock in the transportation and room accommodations. So, that's on track. Now, are you riding up to Asheville alone?"

"Mama's going with me," Johnnie Mae said as she placed her favorite pair of white sandals in the bottom of her suitcase.

"She's feeling up to it?"

"Yeah, I believe so. And it will be good for her to get out and away."

"Your sisters and brothers still talking about her going to live in a home?"

"Landris, I really don't want to think about any of that right now. She seems fine. Like her old self. Or young self." Johnnie Mae began to stammer, "I-I-I . . . I just don't know."

Landris let out a sigh. "I understand. But if she's feeling up to traveling, I know she's going to enjoy spending time with you and Princess Rose."

"Well, if Biltmore is anything close to the way Sarah described it and the brochure I have on it, Mama's going to feel like a queen."

"And well she should. She certainly deserves to."

"Yeah." Johnnie Mae stopped and looked at herself in the mirror. Her eyes looked tired.

"When are you coming back?" Landris asked.

"We'll probably be gone for about five days. I don't want to say, just in case something comes up and we stay longer. I figure one day to drive up, a day to drive back, a day or two to explore Biltmore the way it should be done, and possibly a day for me to look for some woman in a place that doesn't even exist on any map, called Dixon Town. If I get a good lead on either the woman or the place, I may stay another day or two. But I'll let you know whatever I end up doing."

"I guess I won't hold you up. The invitations will likely be arriving before you get back. Just a forewarning, in case you start getting inquiries from people about it."

Johnnie Mae stopped. "Thanks, Landris. You're really being a great sport about all of this. First I say I don't have time to plan a wedding, and now you're left still having to do everything.

Meanwhile, I seem to have time to traipse off on a possible dead-end trail that has nothing to even do with me personally."

"Yeah, but look on the bright side. Because of this possible dead-end trail, you're going to spend some quality time with two fabulous people: your mother and daughter. Time is precious and shouldn't be wasted. Besides, in a little while, you and I will have loads of time to spend together. And I promise you, I'm not planning to waste not even one minute of my time with you."

She smiled. "Oh yeah?"

"Yeah," he said. "Drive carefully."

"I will."

"Johnnie Mae?"

"Yes?"

"I love you."

She smiled again. "I love you, too."

CHAPTER 22

And be ye kind one to another, tenderhearted, forgiving one another.

(Ephesians 4:32)

"My name is Thomas Landris, I'm calling on behalf of George Landris."

"I'm sorry, sir, but I cannot give you information about this account without his authorization," the woman at the IRS said.

"But he has authorized me. I can give you his social security number if that helps."

"Sir, you don't understand. He would have to call us and authorize us to speak with you himself." She spoke on as though she were reading from a script. "Anybody could have obtained information illegally and call us saying that person authorized them to speak on their behalf."

"What if I get him on the phone and let him tell you it's all right for me to speak to you?" Thomas knew George wasn't at home to authorize it, but he also knew George was expecting him to fix the mess he had made and in a hurry.

She didn't miss a beat. "Sir, he would have to call us himself. Anybody could get on the telephone now and claim to be him by your direction. Not that I'm accusing you of doing that, but that's why we have certain policies in place. So, if he desires for you to speak on his behalf, he will need to contact us himself and let us know."

Thomas thought a second. "What if I just have a general question? Not for a specific account, but just a question in general. Could you answer that?" he said.

"What's your question?"

"If a person happens to own stock maintained by a brokerage firm and he or she authorizes the stock be sold—say they never receive the cash from the sale, although the investment income is reported to you guys: What recourse would that person have?"

"The stock is sold but the money is never received, although it is reported as being disbursed and the check was cashed?" she asked, ensuring she understood the question.

"Correct."

"Then, legal proceedings against the person who illegally cashed the check should commence. Proper authorities should be notified and charges brought against them."

Thomas laughed a little and shook his head. "No, I don't think I explained that right. The brokerage firm sent the money, but the person whose social security the money is assigned to never got it. Yet, he's now responsible for taxes on money he never got."

"Sir, if someone cashed another person's check and that person never received their money, that is referred to as theft. And the proper authorities should be contacted immediately with a full police investigation conducted. The person responsible for the theft of those funds should be prosecuted to the full extent of the law. And if this were the case, of course we would handle the tax liability differently for the innocent victim of the crime." She took a second before proceeding. "Sir, does that answer your question?"

"Yes. Thank you." Thomas then hung up the phone. "Police. Prosecution. Oh man, I have got to get that money back. Brother or no brother, I could end up in prison!"

Thomas couldn't believe the mess he had gotten himself into. He had had a simple enough plan: Sell George's stock as he had asked and wire him his money. But then he had started thinking about the taxes George would have to pay on that much money and he'd thought it ridiculous to give up that kind of cash to taxes. So, he'd investigated his options.

"The rich folks do it all the time," Sammie, his advisor had said. "It's called tax shelter."

Thomas had checked out the various suggestions from the tax advisor. But whatever he did, when he sold the shares, the cash amount would hit the account and alert the tax authorities. He had looked into transferring the account to an offshore firm where income wasn't reported to the United States IRS. Then there were Swiss bank accounts, although taxes would have to be paid if the shares were cashed out first, but at least the money wouldn't be sitting in an account possibly creating interest that would generate more taxes on it.

"You could invest it in a business or property. That would be a way to minimize the impact of so much money," Sammie had suggested.

"I know my brother. He's already told me that when he asks that his stock be sold, he wants it sold, and he wants his money. I've been stalling for a while, refusing to return his calls. But I have got to do something soon. When I sell it, he'll want his money to do with as he chooses. I'm barely making it here, and he'll be rolling in dough. Yet, he doesn't even have a clue how much he has," Thomas said, pacing the floor in Sammie's office.

"He doesn't know how much he has now?" Sammie asked.

"No."

Sammie laughed. "Then why don't you pay the taxes out of the sale, send him most of the money, and keep a little for yourself."

"Keep some for myself?"

"Yeah." Sammie began twirling his pen between his fingers like a majorette twirling a baton. "For his own sake. You know, he'll have money he doesn't even know about. What a lucky thing for him later in life when you present it to him," he said with a smile.

Strangely intrigued, Thomas sat forward. "I couldn't do that. That'd be dishonest."

"Not really. Your brother obviously wouldn't have any of this had it not been for you and your savvy efforts. You tell me it was your idea to purchase the stock. You've been the one to manage his account. Didn't you say when you tried to tell him a few years back how much he had, he didn't even care to hear about it? It's like found money."

"But I couldn't do something like that to him. He's my brother."

"Thomas, look. You've told me you're in a bind for cash," Sammie said, halting the pen's spin in midair.

"I could just cash out his money like he asked, and let him worry about the taxes and the consequences of what to do about it. I'm sure he'll be so grateful to me for it having grown so much, and for the work I've done that he hasn't had to do, he'll probably want to give me ten percent of it as a gratuity."

"And maybe he'll look at the money he gave you to invest, as you've previously told me he never asked for or got back from you, as payment enough. You both started out with the same amount invested, didn't you?"

"Don't remind me." Thomas stood up and walked to the window. "I wish I could have gazed into the future back then and seen what being patient would have netted me. I'd be rich now just like him. Instead, I'm so broke, I can barely afford the air I breathe."

"I do have another idea you *might* want to consider."

Thomas turned and looked at him. Sammie gestured for him to sit back down. Thomas did. "I'm listening."

"It would essentially be a short-term investment with possible maximum return, minimal effort, and only a slight, very slight, risk involved. So . . . are you game?"

"You have my undivided attention."

"It's possible to double your money in a matter of weeks. Possible—now you know I can't guarantee anything. But all the numbers add up to me. And the best thing about this type of investment: You use the cash from the sale of the stock, double it taking possibly months, and keep the extra for yourself. Problem solved. And . . ." he leaned back in his seat, "the extra made would be tax free for you. Hard to track and virtually untraceable."

"But is it legal?"

"Of course it's legal. And the best part is: you don't put all of your eggs in one basket. So, if something goes wrong with one of them, your risk has been minimized."

"And how do you fit in? Where do you get your pay?"

Sammie smiled, held the pen up, and used it as if he were a drum major directing a band. "Finder's fee. If you're interested, I get ten percent of what you put up." Sammie stood up and walked over to Thomas. "Tell you what: you sleep on it, pray about it if you're the praying kind, and get back with me when you've decided."

Sammie went into his filing cabinet and retrieved a packet. "Here's a little information on what I'm talking about. Look it over. See if you don't see not only the possibilities financially, but the implications this could have on history. Why, you'll not only get rich, you'll be a hero to scholars and historians around the world who will unknowingly be singing your praises." He slapped Thomas on the back as Thomas took the package.

Of course Thomas had said yes. How could he not? It had been an opportunity to make some much-needed money in a short time, while helping society retrieve historical artifacts, masterpieces, and gems that could tell or refuse to tell their tales.

Only a year later, and Thomas was in a mess! Sammie wasn't returning his calls. He had been to see him and learned he had relocated his operations to D.C., then Houston. He found him in Houston. Sammie told him things weren't moving like they wanted them to, but assured him that everything was on the up-and-up. "Something is about to happen soon," Sammie said. "Just hold on a little longer."

"My brother is going to find out that I cashed in his shares, and he's going to be looking for me and his money," Thomas told Sammie in June. "Not counting the tax situation, which I'm sure the IRS will be looking for him on. That's if they aren't already."

"Look, we have a few leads that seem poised to pay off any minute. You're going to make enough money to pay your brother's tax bill and any penalties with money to spare, plus his original entire amount intact. Listen, I probably shouldn't be telling you this, but do you remember that necklace—?"

"You mean the ten-carat alexandrite necklace?"

"That's the one." Sammie smiled. "Well, I think we have a lead on it. At least we've narrowed it to where it probably is. There are people interested in getting their hands on it at a great cost. Because of you, we have a million-dollar reward out there for its return. Ten packages were delivered, and we've received three callbacks so far on the automated line we set up. Somebody's going to turn that gem over soon to claim the reward. If they only knew how much that thing is really worth, they would laugh at our reward offered."

"Yeah, okay. Just as long as something is happening. But how much longer do you think this is going to take? I'm sweating bullets here. And my brother keeps calling me. I'm going to have to call him back at some point."

"You know what the good book says: 'Patience is a virtue.' "

"Yeah, and the good book also says: 'God is not mocked. Whatsoever you sow, that shall you also reap.' I just wish I'd never done this in the first place."

"You'll be singing another tune shortly. You have to get in the water to swim. But didn't you keep some of that money? You didn't hand all of it over to me."

"I kept some. I'm not completely stupid," he said, shaking his head. "I bought him a CD [certificate of deposit] and a Treasury bill. You know I can't cash those yet. And the cash I did keep, I've gone completely through already. In fact, I'm planning to go see my brother, and I don't even have money for a hotel. I sure don't plan to stay with him to get grilled while I'm there. I can't tell him any of this yet. He thinks everything is fine.

"What about that lead your guys had on those missing pages, 1–6 and 11–14 of *The Gospel of Mary*, Mary Magdalene's lost manuscript?" Thomas asked, recalling off the top of his head some of the things listed for recovery in that packet Sammie had enticed him into investing in more than a year ago. "And that 1913 nickel: the nickel with the Liberty Head on it that's been missing since sometime in the early 60s? Anything?"

Sammie seemed to be thinking. "The missing manuscript pages are still not panning out the way we were promised. And the 1913 coin . . . 1913 coin . . ." he looked up at the ceiling as though the answer were written there, before he got up and looked in the files.

He checked the folder. "There's a $1 million dollar reward for it. Yeah, that's the nickel that a U.S. Mint employee illegally minted in 1920 with the Liberty Head when it had been changed to an Indian/Buffalo piece. It says, 'Five of these coins were produced by that employee specifically to trigger a collector's market. Two of them are held privately, one is in the Smithsonian, and one is in the possession of the American Numismatic Association. In the early 60s the fifth nickel vanished. Collectors believe it was lost when a North Carolina dealer transporting it died in a car crash around 1962. The police never recovered it. So far, it has never been found.' There appears to be a lot of copies of this coin turning up, but nobody has recovered the real thing yet."

"Kind of funny, huh?" Thomas said.

"What's that?"

"What was supposed to be such a sure, quick deal hasn't turned into anything for me but a sure, quick bust. You, on the other hand, at least got a finder's fee."

Sammie raised one eyebrow. "What, you don't trust me on this?"

Thomas got up to leave. "Hey, my brother trusted me, his own flesh and blood, and look what that's gotten him. You and I aren't kin at all. So what do you think?"

"Just give it a little more time. I'm telling you, it's going to pay off. You'll see."

"If not, we'll need to salvage what we can. I don't want to end up dead because of some stupid stuff."

"Dead? Do you really think your brother would kill you over this?"

Thomas laughed. "My brother the preacher? Oh no. But my 'I brought you in, I'll take you out!' mother—now she's a different story."

"Thomas, what are you thinking about over there?" George asked when he walked into the room and saw Thomas staring into space.

"Just working on how to best fix the mess I created."

"Glad to hear that. I think I'll call the IRS and see what recourse is available to me at this point. I mean I didn't ever actually receive the money. They can't possibly hold me on something I never received. So, what do you think?"

"I think you should let me see what I can do first. Give me a chance to make it right."

"Two weeks, Thomas. Then I'm going to take steps to make it right myself. Understand?"

"George, you do know I could possibly go to jail for my part in this, don't you?"

George looked at him. "Thomas, every action holds a consequence. You're my brother, and I have to forgive you because God's Word tells me it's the right thing to do. But forgiveness is a different act than allowing people who do wrong to get away with it. I could have reacted differently when I first learned of this. I chose—the operative word being 'chose'—to allow you the opportunity to reconcile your actions. But I am not going down for this one. And if you have to reap what you've sown, then that's called the Word not returning unto God void." George put his hand on Thomas' shoulder. "Two weeks. Then I'll have to take care of my business however necessary."

"George," Thomas looked into his brother's eyes. "Thank you for letting me stay here."

"No problem. Just don't lie to me again. You should have told me when you came to Atlanta you didn't have any money or a place to stay. Instead of pretending like you had a hotel room when you clearly knew you didn't. Hobo-ing around."

Thomas gave him a manly hug. "No more lies. And I'm going to make this right, George. Then, when you get your money back, I promise I'll do a better job next time."

"I forgive you, Thomas. But I'll not be dealing with you in this area again. I have to be a good steward of God's money. And the honest truth is, I wasn't. I love you, but forgiveness is not the same as reinstatement. You'll not be over my finances ever again."

CHAPTER 23

And having a high priest over the house of God.

(Hebrews 10:21)

Pastor Landris had a meeting with the elders and board of directors on Friday morning at 10 A.M. Presiding over the meeting, Elder Fuller got right to the point. The majority of them were not pleased with Pastor Landris' decision to put Minister Fulton in charge of Sunday services and the church matters in his absence.

"We rejoice with you in your upcoming nuptials," Elder Fuller said, "but we would feel better if someone other than Minister Fulton was left to preach and conduct business in your stead, Pastor Landris."

"I'm sorry. I'm not quite understanding the problem," Pastor Landris said. "You don't feel she's capable of handling matters in my absence?"

"No sir, that's not it at all. Without a doubt, she has the credentials and potential."

"Then, what's the problem?"

Deacon Pritchard stood up. "Pastor, I realize I'm new to the board. But I'm not sure whether you realize Minister Fulton is a woman."

Pastor Landris looked at him, then leaned forward. "Oh, I may be a man of God, but I'm not blind or oblivious to the fact that she's a woman. And your point being?"

"My point being, the church's original bylaws plainly state that women are not to be preachers. They have their place. Although I for one love Minister Fulton's teachings and would be the first to agree she is more than capable of instructing anyone on any level—"

"But," Deacon Perkins stood and said, "we don't believe women should preach."

"Speak for yourself," Deacon Thomas said, then angled his body toward the door.

Deacon Perkins nodded at Deacon Thomas. "I stand corrected. *Many* of us here don't believe a woman should be placed in the positions you appear to insist on doing."

"In other words, a woman can teach you, bless you, sing for you, put her money in church, fix dinner for church functions, and visit the sick and shut-in, but you don't want her preaching God's word? Is that about right?" Pastor Landris asked.

Deacon Perkins sat down. Elder Fuller began speaking. "No, that's not at all what we're saying. We're saying that when this church was founded, there were certain rules and regulations set in place. Now, we have turned our heads regarding many things you have come in and implemented; even allowed you to ordain and license Minister Fulton, although some of us didn't actually support that decision either. Granted, she does an excellent job for the Lord; no one can deny or take that away from her—"

"It's just we don't care to have a woman preacher at our church," Sister Sweeny said. "I happen to be a woman, and I know I don't want one. I just don't think it's right or scriptural, and nothing you say can alter my belief."

"Pastor Landris, we have several ministers here at the church. Why don't you ask one of them to occupy your position while you're gone?" Deacon Fuller said. "Then we can drop this whole ridiculous thing altogether and move on to more important matters."

"Why don't I? Because I asked one: Minister Fulton, who has graciously consented."

"See there. Now you're just trying to force others to accept what you want because you think your way is right," Deacon Perkins said. "You can't come into our church, change things to reflect what you believe, and totally disregard the majority's voice."

"The only majority voice I'm concerned about is God, Jesus, and the Holy Spirit's. Just because a majority believes a thing, doesn't make it right. If you have concerns I can address specifically that so far I haven't, I'd be more than happy to do that now. I don't know if you're aware of it or not, but there were women leaders recorded in the Bible: women preachers, women prophets—not prophetesses: *prophets*, and teachers throughout the Bible.

"Deborah was a leader and a prophet. Miriam was a worship leader and a prophet. In Romans 16:1, Paul said, 'I commend to you our sister Phoebe, a servant.' The Greek word used and translated to 'servant' was *diakonos*. Almost everywhere in the New Testament, that word *diakonos* is translated as 'minister' to describe a minister of the gospel. Paul goes on to tell the church to receive Phoebe 'in a manner worthy of the saints . . . for she herself has also been a helper of many, and of myself as well.' The Greek word that was translated to 'helper' here is *prostatis*. Although the *chosen* translated word used was 'helper,' Paul was actually describing Phoebe's exceptional leadership.

"God used a woman named Anna to announce the arrival of the Messiah. Huldah, a prophet who verified the scroll of the Law found in the temple, was a woman. Isaiah described his wife as a prophet. Philip's four daughters were all prophets. That's Acts 21:8–9. A definition of prophecy is found in Revelation 19:10: 'For the testimony of Jesus is the spirit of prophecy.' In Romans 16:7, Paul called Junia—another woman leader, as has been affirmed by Dr. Gordon Fee, a professor at Regent College in British Columbia, Canada, and other scholars—an apostle 'who also was in Christ before me.' "

"Okay, hold up," Elder Fuller said. "Now you've gone too far. Jesus only had twelve disciples and they were men. That means we ought to follow Jesus' example to a T."

"Then, that would mean, since all the men following Jesus were Jews from Galilee speaking Aramaic, that a lot more folks right now right here would be knocked out of being Disciples of Christ. Including you, Elder Fuller." Pastor Landris shook his head. "Just because something is a tradition," he said, "doesn't make it what Jesus would have us as a body to do. When you go home, why don't you read up on Mark 7:1–23, paying close attention to verse 13, where it warns against, 'Making the word of God of none effect through your tradition, which ye have delivered,' which means handed down 'and many such like things do ye.' Jesus' argument was not with God's Word, but with human beings' misuse of it. Jesus came not to bind us, but to set us free. We have to look at traditions of men and ask what is God's desire for us in order for us to move forward. If what we're doing is contrary to God's nature and desire for us, we need to change. There's no harm in change. There's no disgrace in having done a thing a way in the past, to learn better, and then go forward in the future."

"Pastor Landris, we hear you. But I have to tell you: If you pursue this, there will be repercussions that you may not like," Elder Fuller said. "We are charged with being the governing body of our church, having to discern what is of God and what is of Satan."

"Yeah. Because this is your church." Pastor Landris looked at faces peering at him. "Not God's church. We don't have time to seek God about what He prefers. We're too busy creating and enforcing our own laws and rules. Well, here's a mathematical solution to know if it's of God or of Satan. If it adds or multiplies, it's of God. If it subtracts or divides, it's of Satan. Seems to me, *this* is subtraction and division. You do the math."

"You have a problem with authority, don't you?" Deacon Perkins said.

"I am a man under authority," Pastor Landris replied. "The question is, whose? 'What is man that thou art mindful of him or the son of man that thou visiteth him?' I don't have a problem with authority. But, last I heard, I was the shepherd here. And Jesus told me if I loved Him, to feed His sheep. I do love Him, and I *will* feed His sheep with His Word. Our lives should be better—going from glory to glory. Instead, we keep letting Satan deceive us. And instead of us meeting to strategize how to add another blow to Satan by adding another soul to the kingdom of God, we're discussing how to keep a preacher—"

"A woman preacher," Sister Sweeny said. "We're talking about a woman preacher."

"A preacher nonetheless." Landris shook his head and laughed. "And here we are trying to implement ways we as saints of God can keep the Word from going forth."

"It's not keeping the Word from going forth. There are plenty of men capable of doing the job. There's an order in things. We need to adhere according to that order," Deacon Pritchard said. "God does things decent and in order, but this is out of order."

"And if you can't abide by what is set up already for this ministry, then maybe you should consider stepping aside," Deacon Woods said.

"Now, let's not get carried away," Elder Fuller said. "Pastor Landris, all we're asking is for you to get another preacher in your absence. That's all. No reason for this to get all out of hand. There's Minister Huntley, Minister Tucker," Elder Fuller pointed to the ministers sitting at the conference table. "Also Minister Elton, he's . . . he's okay, coming along, and could certainly use the practice."

A few heads nodded. "Minister Elton? I know that's the truth!" Sister Sweeny said.

"The point is: We represent the congregation. There's lots of talk since word got out that you'd be gone for two weeks and Minister Fulton would be left in charge," Elder Fuller said. "Some folks aren't taking kindly that they can't attend your wedding either."

"And I'd like to point out, even though we haven't directly brought this up as yet," Sister Sweeny said, "many of the more prominent members believe you might be headed toward that co-pastor movement that seems like it's becoming prevalent here of late."

"Co-pastor movement?" Pastor Landris said, clearly puzzled by the phrase.

"Yes. A lot of preachers lately are bringing their wives on as co-pastor. Well, you just need to know before you even get that notion in your head," Sister Sweeny said as she looked from one person to the other before directing her attention back to Pastor Landris, "we hired *a* pastor. We didn't hire a pastor and a co-pastor.

After you're married, she can be the pastor's wife. But don't be trying to force that two-for-one stuff on us. Now, if you'll agree to reconsider and rescind your appointing of Minister Fulton to serve in your absence, we could dismiss and all go home."

"Pastor Landris," Deacon Perkins said, "even though I don't believe in women preachers, I will admit Minister Fulton has certainly been a blessing to every member here. She's a dynamic speaker, an anointed warrior for the Lord. If you could just play down the preacher status bit a little. Allow her to continue doing what she's doing, but just don't call attention to her, everybody will be fine with things as they already are."

Pastor Landris nodded his head and bit down on his lower lip. "Okay, so the bottom line is: Minister Fulton can preach, but let's not call her a preacher. And if we can put her in a place where we don't call attention to what she's doing, but let her do it, that's good, too." He watched their faces as a few of them nodded and smiled. "Oh yes, and I need to get another person to preach while I'm gone for the two weeks in September as long as *he's* a man. It doesn't matter whether he's anointed or not or has a Word from heaven; just as long as *he's* a man." He stopped and smacked his lips. "How's that so far?"

"That's about right," Deacon Woods said, smiling.

"And don't forget the co-pastor thing," Sister Sweeny said, smiling as she raised her index finger to mimic the number 1.

"Right. And when I get married, don't even think about making my wife co-pastor. Not here, anyway."

Elder Fuller stood. "So, I suppose we're all in agreement then?" He looked around the room. The five minority votes that hadn't agreed on this in the first place still refused to support any of it now. They just sat there like marble statues with their arms folded.

Pastor Landris held up his hand as though to ask permission to speak.

"Yes, Pastor Landris," Elder Fuller said with a strong, reassured voice.

"I'm not in agreement with it. And I don't plan to reconsider or rescind my request to Minister Fulton. I prayed about this before I even asked her. I have faith she will be a blessing to the people in my absence. She has my full support and confidence. And I am now, as in the past, pulling for her to continue to grow in God's Word and His grace," Pastor Landris said.

"Then this matter is *not* closed," Deacon Woods said with a trembling in his voice.

Mumbling and unrest began among all of those in attendance.

"Order! Quiet! Everybody, let's get quiet!" Elder Fuller shouted over the fever-pitched voices of his fellow members. "I suggest this discussion be tabled until a later date, when cooler heads can prevail. This meeting is adjourned for today!"

Pastor Landris still couldn't believe what had happened. He had just invited Thomas to come hear him preach on Sunday and had gotten him to agree. Now George wasn't sure he would still be the pastor come Sunday based on the way that church meeting had ended. Especially behind some of the stabbing looks he'd gotten from a few of the attendees as they'd filed past him out of the conference room.

CHAPTER 24

Out of the same mouth proceedeth blessing and cursing.

(James 3:10)

Lena and Theresa were whispering in the nursery as they began putting away stacks of gifts Theresa had received from the baby shower her friends had surprised her with.

"Have you decided what you want to do about the necklace?" Theresa asked Lena.

"No, and I'm not calling that number yet. So don't bother asking," Lena said. She stopped to admire a mint green crocheted top, bottom, hat, and booty set. "The necklace is safe, so at least that's one less thing to worry about."

"I still would like to know if that reward is on the up-and-up. And whether we actually have the necklace they're looking for."

"You just watch yourself with Memory around, you hear me?"

Theresa picked up a multicolored blanket and pressed it against her face. "This is so soft." She looked at Lena, gauging her demeanor before she spoke. "Mama, I think Memory is okay. She's been really helpful around here. Even you have to admit that."

"I admit she's snooping around this house. I'll admit that much." Lena took the blanket from Theresa, folded it back, and placed it inside the open drawer. "You just heed my words and don't let your guard down with her. Not for a second."

"Where is everybody?" Memory asked as she climbed the

stairs. "You got company pulling up in the driveway." Memory waltzed in and flashed them her best smile.

"It's probably my mother and father." Theresa put several packages of sheets in the drawer, then surveyed the truckload of things she still had left to put away.

"I can't wait to meet them." Memory looked around the room. "If you like, I'd be happy to finish up in here for you. That way you can visit with your folks."

"Oh, don't worry about it, Memory," Theresa said. "We can all visit with them. I know they're eager to meet you."

"Oh, I bet they are." Memory jabbed one hand on her hip. "Then, I suppose I can start a fresh pot of coffee brewing." She turned around and left, humming an unfamiliar tune.

Theresa started out of the room. Lena stopped her. "Just don't let your guard down. It's possible she's sincere, but in my spirit, I feel a tad of grit has not quite sifted out yet."

"Mama, I believe Memory is just a lonely old woman without anybody, and she's trying to hang on to the only family she has left, the best way she knows how."

The doorbell rang.

"I got it," Memory yelled loud enough for them to hear her.

When Lena and Theresa came downstairs, Memory handed Theresa a FedEx package. "It's for you. Overnight delivery. I signed for it."

Theresa looked at the return address. It was from the lawyer's office in New York.

The doorbell rang again, saving Theresa from having to open the package in front of them: especially Lena. Theresa had already convinced Maurice to take the trip. He didn't want to be gone during that time either, but the way Theresa had "explained" things to him, he wasn't left with much choice. So he'd reluctantly agreed.

Lena looked at the package, then back at Theresa. "Aren't you going to open it?"

"After 'while." She smiled and hurried to open the door.

"Theresa!" Beatrice said, stepping in first and hugging tightly the really pregnant mother-to-be. "Look at you; you practically light up the room with your radiant glow!"

Bishop Jordan came in behind Beatrice. He used a cane now to help him walk, but he was getting around remarkably. "Well, I'll be," he said. "It won't be long now."

"Yeah. About another month." Theresa kissed her father, who appeared shorter since having the stroke. He didn't have to bend down for her to kiss him as in years gone by.

After everybody was inside, Theresa made the introductions the easiest way she knew to do it. "This is my mother, Beatrice; my Daddy—who everybody calls Bishop Jordan except Mama, who calls him Richard. Everybody, this is Memory."

Beatrice offered her hand to Memory, who stepped up and smiled as though she were elated to make her acquaintance. Bishop Jordan stared at first, leaving Memory to wonder whether it was the effects of his stroke that made him slow to shake her hand, or his knowledge of how she had treated Lena in the past.

"Nice to meet you, Bishop Jordan," Memory said, offering her hand.

He didn't say a word; just shook her hand and nodded once.

"I have some fresh coffee made if anyone cares for any," Memory said.

"It appears you've just made yourself right at home," Bishop Jordan said.

Again, Memory couldn't tell what he was really thinking. He seemed to be maintaining a polite but respectful distance.

"That's me, dearie," Memory said as she headed for the kitchen. "Little Miss Make-Myself-at-Home."

Everybody else went to the den and sat down.

"I'll be with you guys in just a second," Theresa said, clutching the package close to her. "I need to check on something, but I'll be right with y'all."

"Baby, do you need me to help you with anything?" Beatrice asked. "I'm sure you got a lot of nice gifts at that shower."

"Thanks, Mother. But I'm good. This will only take a minute." Theresa went into the hallway and ripped the cardboard zipper off the package. Inside were two tickets to New York, hotel confirmation numbers, instructions for taxi fare, and directions to the lawyer's office. The lawyer was taking care of everything and bringing Lena to New York in style. Theresa smiled at her own cleverness so far. *All that's left now is to convince Mama to go.*

Theresa slightly waddled back into the den still smiling. "Mama, here's your airline ticket." She held out a small folder to Lena.

Everybody turned and looked at Theresa first, then Lena.

"Lena, where are you going? And I thought you didn't like to fly?" Beatrice said.

"I'm not going anywhere—"

"Oh, she's going to New York," Theresa said, purposely sitting next to her father.

"No, you see, Theresa thinks I'm going to go to New York, but—"

"Mama is going to see a lawyer in New York about some important business. Everything's been arranged. Airline, hotel, meeting . . . everything."

Lena looked at Beatrice, then Richard. "I've told that child I am *not* going."

"Yes . . . you . . . are. I've made the arrangements and you're going. You will be on that plane come September tenth." She waved the package in the air. "And Maurice will be accompanying you."

"Theresa, this is ridiculous!" Lena sighed heavily. "I am not leaving so close to your due date, and that's final!"

"What's final?" Memory said as she walked in with the coffee pot and some cups.

"Mama's going to New York. Leaving September tenth," Theresa said with a smirk.

"That is wonderful, dearie." Memory set the tray on the coffee table. "I'll be around, so there's nothing to be concerned about, Lena." She smiled.

"And we're here," Beatrice said, getting up to pour her and Bishop a cup of coffee.

Lena stood and began to pace. She sensed they were all ganging up on her now. "But what if she goes into labor while Maurice and I are gone? Theresa, this is wrong. Maurice is the father of your baby. Why would you go and do something like this when I specifically told you I didn't care about going up there just yet?" She stopped pacing. "Well, I'm canceling those reservations."

Theresa smiled. "What if I promise not to go into labor before September eleventh or at the very least, to wait until you're officially back on the plane coming home?"

"You can't promise something like that. You don't have control over when your baby will decide he—"

"She," Memory said, interrupting. She then looked up. "It's a girl. See? She's carrying the baby low. It's a she. A girl."

"Listen," Theresa said, ignoring Memory. "I don't feel like arguing. It's my baby, and I have made my decision. I want you to go and find out what those people want with you in New York. Memory is here. She's already agreed to stay until after you return."

"And we're not that far," Beatrice said. "We'll do whatever she needs to help out."

"I'm not helpless people," Theresa said. "Women have babies every day and folks aren't sitting around watching their every movement up until the minute labor begins."

"But—"

"End . . . of . . . discussion." Theresa went over and poured herself a cup of coffee. "Mama, please don't force me to have to ban you from my labor and delivery. Because if you keep acting like this, I might not let you in with me when I *do* go into labor."

"You wouldn't dare!"

"Try me," Theresa said. "Mama, I'm telling you. I'll be fine. Just go. Pleeeease. For me. You know I want to know what this is all about. I don't want to wait until December, or who knows how long, to find out."

"All right. All right! I give up. You win," Lena said. "I'll go. But if you so much as look like you're about to go into labor on the day we're getting ready to leave, reservations or not, I am canceling everything. I don't care what it might cost me. Deal?"

"Deal." Theresa arched her back and began to massage a faint ache with both hands.

When Beatrice and Richard were getting ready to leave, Lena

went over to them. "Keep an eye on things while Maurice and I are gone, will you please?" she whispered. "Especially on Memory."

Beatrice patted Lena's hand. "Bishop and I are already way ahead of you. Don't worry; we're on it. We just finished saying that exact same thing ourselves." She winked at Lena, then gave her a hug.

CHAPTER 25

A man shall be satisfied with good by the fruit of his mouth.

(Proverbs 12:14)

Countess Gates, Johnnie Mae, and Princess Rose were having a grand time in Asheville. Sarah Fleming had been so right about everything—Biltmore Castle, the view of the mountains, and the people. Johnnie Mae couldn't resist viewing the castle through the eyes of a writer. She just wasn't sure she'd ever be able to translate into words what her eyes and heart beheld. This place cried out with history, both told and untold.

Frederick Law Olmsted, the landscape architect who designed Central Park in Manhattan, directed the landscaping of Biltmore Castle. The architect for this home that was four acres in size—the house, not the original 125,000 acres of land—was Richard Morris Hunt, who also designed the Young Men's Institute, just as Sarah had told Johnnie Mae. Originally commissioned by George W. Vanderbilt, the YMI was created explicitly for the black laborers, then in later years purchased by the black folks of the community.

In Johnnie Mae's research, she learned about the special railway spur that was built specifically to bring in all of the transported tons of Indiana limestone and the massive amount of other material for the castle. Mrs. Gates's breath was practically taken away when she came upon the Winter Garden inside the castle, with its spectacular glass-roofed, light-filled, sunken garden room and a serene fountain occupying its center.

Johnnie Mae discovered that Dickson Town (or "Dixon Town," as some folks recalled it being called "back in the day") did, but didn't really, exist. She had asked around, only to discover that she would have to go deeper in her search to locate anyone who knew enough to assist her in finding what she was looking for.

"Ma'am," a forty-something-year-old man said, "you need to talk to Angela Gabriel. She lives with her great-grandmother, who probably knows 'bout everything there is to know more'n anyone else 'round these parts. Especially if it weren't never documented."

"Could you tell me where I might be able to find this Ms. Gabriel?" Johnnie Mae asked as she fanned away a swarm of gnats.

"She not hard to find. Not hard to look at neither," he said, grinning with missing teeth. "Just go down about three blocks and turn right at the church. It's a big old church, so you cain't help but see it. She lives about two blocks up from the church. It's a big old white house with them nice kinda columns. Just tell her Pleasant told you about 'em."

"Pleasant?"

"Yes, ma'am. That's my first name, although everybody excepting Angel calls me Moose." He grinned again.

"Thank you, Mr. Pleasant. Would you happen to know the house's address?" She stood ready to write.

"Ad-dress? Ma'am, I s'pose it do have one. But don't nobody go by no ad-dresses 'round these parts too much. When we say turn right at the church, the big one, everybody knows what we talkin' about. When I tells you the big old white house with the columns, there ain't but one like it left. So, if you miss it . . . Well, you ought not be able to miss it unless you're blind or stupid. And you look like you can see pretty well."

Johnnie Mae smiled. There was no further explanation necessary for that statement. She hurried. She had left her mother and a two-and-a-half-year-old hyperactive Princess Rose back at Biltmore Inn eating the ice cream they'd gotten from the Stable

Courtyard. She had assured her mother she wouldn't be gone long.

"Fourteen flavors of ice cream to choose from?" Mrs. Gates had said. "Johnnie Mae, you run on and take care of your business. Princess Rose and I will be fine getting our ice cream and then getting back to our room for a little R & R. Go on. We'll be all right."

"Oh, I'll go back to the room with you, Mama. I'll have enough time."

Mrs. Gates looked at her daughter and shook her head. "You're afraid I'm going to get lost or something? I believe little Princess Rose and I can find our way back to our room by ourselves. Can't we, baby?" Mrs. Gates looked at Princess Rose, who nodded and caused her twin, ropelike pigtails to swing back and forth.

"I know you can find your way back, Mama. But I just want to see you back safely to the room myself. Besides, I need to get another pad and paper out of my suitcase, since I'm sure I'll need to jot down a few more details while I'm out."

Mrs. Gates looked at Johnnie Mae. She could see she was worried, so she decided not to fight Johnnie Mae about it. If it would get Johnnie Mae gone, she could play along.

Johnnie Mae found the house, just as Pleasant had described it. She stepped up onto the porch in search of a doorbell. Unable to locate a button, she knocked. After a minute and hearing no movement inside, she knocked harder, stinging her knuckles somewhat. Seconds later, she heard soft footsteps slowly approaching the door.

An elderly woman cracked open the door. "Yes?"

"Hi, my name is Johnnie Mae Taylor, and I'm from Birmingham, Alabama."

"Yes?"

"I'm looking for Angela Gabriel. Is she here?"

"Angel stepped out for a minute."

"Would you happen to be her great-grandmother?"

The woman looked closer at Johnnie Mae. "And who'd you say wants to know?"

Johnnie Mae smiled. "Ma'am, my name is Johnnie Mae Taylor. I'm an author. Actually, I'm doing some research, and when I was looking for information on a place called Dixon Town, a gentleman by the name of Pleasant suggested I come talk to you."

"Dickson Town? That was Isaac Dickson's property. People called it Dickson Town like it was an officially assigned town name. Should have been, but it never did make it to a map. There is an elementary school named after Dickson now, though."

Johnnie Mae took out her business card. "Ma'am—"

"Call me Pearl, baby."

Johnnie Mae's eyes widened. "You wouldn't happen to be Pearl Black, would you?"

The woman began to laugh. "It's been some setting suns since anyone's called me by that name. Oooh, child. Those were the days! 'Git back, it's Pearl Black. And she don't, play, Jack.' Who told you my name? Got to be somebody from way back." She took the card from Johnnie Mae. "Now, I hope you know I can't see a thing without my bifocals."

"Ms. Black—"

"I told you to call me Pearl, baby. Why don't you come on in and shut the door." She turned and started walking away. Johnnie Mae followed her, closing the door behind her.

When Pearl reached the "sitting room," she offered Johnnie Mae a seat. On the wall were framed pictures of Dr. Martin Luther King, Jr.; President John F. Kennedy; a white, blue-eyed Jesus; and a black Jesus with lamb's wool hair. "So, who told you about me?"

"A woman named Sarah Fleming. Would you happen to know or remember her?"

"Did at one time. Decades ago. I heard she'd died some years back." Pearl sat in a burgundy, velvet-covered rocking chair.

"No, ma'am, she didn't. I just saw her this past May, and she was very much alive."

Pearl rocked slowly. "Her family claimed she lost her mind. Her brothers said that."

"Did you know her family?" Johnnie Mae leaned forward.

"Know them? I worked for them off and on for almost half-a-century of my life. I'm ninety-eight years old now. Not the spring chicken I once was. But my mind is as tight as a fishing line with a twenty-pound bass on the end of it fighting with all its might to stay free."

Johnnie Mae smiled. "Then, would you remember when Sarah was pregnant?"

"Remember?" She stopped rocking and snickered. "Shoot. I delivered her baby."

Johnnie Mae almost inhaled too fast to talk. "So, she really was pregnant?"

Pearl began rocking again. "I delivered two babies that day."

"Two babies? For Sarah?"

Pearl scratched her head full of silver curls. She looked like she'd just come from getting her hair pressed and curled; her curls were still that tight. "No, not for Sarah."

"Great-granny!" a woman's voice yelled as steps could be heard coming closer.

"Hi, baby. Look a' here. We have company. An author from Birmingham, Alabama." Pearl smiled, then looked at Johnnie Mae. "Sarah Fleming sent her. She came to talk."

Johnnie Mae looked at Pearl, then the young woman standing before her.

"I'm Angela Gabriel. But everybody calls me Angel. And you are?"

"Johnnie Mae Taylor," she said standing up. "Pleasant told me about you."

Pearl started laughing. "Old pleasant Pleasant sent you looking for our angel Angel Gabriel, and you stumbled onto the black pearl Pearl Black. Ain't God something!"

CHAPTER 26

And I will give unto thee the keys of the kingdom of heaven.

(Matthew 16:19 (a))

In the tradition of the African *jelis*, who traditionally passed down memorized history, Pearl began recalling details surrounding places and people around Asheville.

"The Patton family owned what was called The Henrietta before the Civil War," Pearl said. "It had the words *The Henrietta* etched on its front. It was over yonder on Biltmore Avenue. Later the name was changed to White House Inn—of course, that was before they made it into the YWCA's first headquarters," Pearl said. She turned and addressed Angel. "Why don't you bring us some of that cake I made?" She looked back at Johnnie Mae. "You like German chocolate cake? I made it from scratch."

"From scratch? Oh, I love German chocolate cake," Johnnie Mae said.

"And bring us something to drink with it," she said to Angel. "Milk or tea, baby?" Pearl asked Johnnie Mae.

"Tea, please. With honey if you have it."

Pearl nodded. "Milk for me." Angel smiled and hurriedly left the room.

"She's so protective of me," Pearl whispered. "She got an offer from this big company in Vance, Alabama. Some place dealing with expensive automobiles."

"You mean, Mercedes-Benz?"

"Yeah, that's the one. Turned them down because she didn't want to leave me. I told her I'd be fine, but she won't leave her 'Great-granny' for all the money in the world."

Angel returned with the richest-looking German chocolate cake Johnnie Mae had ever seen. Not the box-mix kind with store-bought icing. Not even the box-mix kind with homemade icing. It was the real deal absolutely made from scratch. Johnnie Mae took one bite and moaned, "Oh this is good! Could this be any moister? Wow, this is good!"

Pearl smiled. "Glad you approve."

"That's one thing people will tell you about Great-granny," Angel said, smiling. "Whenever she cooks, she *always* puts her foot in it."

Pearl waved her off. "Oh, baby. Is that why I can't get rid of you?"

"Of course, Great-granny. Where will I ever find anyone who can replace your good cooking?" Angel turned her attention to Johnnie Mae. "This woman has a mind like a seasoned rapper: spitting out information word for word and she rarely misses a beat."

"Don't be comparing me to those noisemakers. Now, you were asking about Dickson Town." She took a bite of cake and closed her eyes as she let the cake melt in her mouth. "Slave quarters were originally behind The Henrietta along Valley Street. As the story goes: sometime around the early 1880s, a man named Thomas Walton Patton sold those quarters to a colored man named Isaac Dickson. Folks often made the mistake back then, spelling his name D-i-x-o-n when the correct way was D-i-c-k-s-o-n. Anyhow, he ended up renting out homes he fixed up there, and it became its own little community. Folks called it Dicksontown like one word and Dixon Town, two words, misspelling the first."

"Then, where is Dickson Town currently?"

"Oh, it's the City Garage now." She took another bite of cake, followed by a swallow of milk. "Back when it was a town, there was a coal shop on what was Valley Street. It's called South Charlotte Street now. But Isaac Dickson was well respected by coloreds and whites alike. They say Dickson's father was the Dutch immigrant slave owner of Dickson's mother." She smiled. "Dickson came here in the late 1860s with a letter of recommendation. That was highly unheard of back then for a colored person."

Johnnie Mae wrote in between listening to Pearl's tale and snatching bites of that irresistible, mouth-watering cake. She ate slowly, just to keep it from ending too soon.

"Isaac Dickson was the first colored appointed to the school board. He demanded public education for coloreds back in 1887. George Vanderbilt was the one who made the Young Men's Institute a reality, but it was Edward Stephens who thought of it and got Vanderbilt to have it built. Colored folk then had a nice place to go. Vanderbilt gave land in 1895 for St. Matthias Episcopal Church because All Souls Cathedral wouldn't let colored folk attend. Funny, huh, souls are colorless, yet All Souls Cathedral didn't have a place for all souls. Sounds like false advertisement to me." She shook her head. "In 1906, colored folks purchased the Young Men's Institute—they called it the YMI— and took things to another level. We even had a public library in there. Oh, it was something."

"Pearl, Sarah told me about her having a baby," Johnnie Mae said, leading her back to the questions she had come all this way to find out.

"Did she happen to mention the baby's father?" Pearl set her empty plate on the table beside her and wiped the corners of her mouth daintily with her napkin.

"Yes. Ransom. But that's all she said about him: just that his name was Ransom."

Pearl nodded. "And the key?"

"Pardon me?"

"Did Sarah give you a key?" Pearl looked intensely at Johnnie Mae. "If you spoke with Sarah, I need the key." Pearl sat back and waited on Johnnie Mae's next move.

"She did give me a key," Johnnie Mae said as she began to search her purse. She looked inside pockets and zippers. "I had it with me. My mother, daughter, and I have been visiting Biltmore Castle. I put that key in a safe place to ensure I wouldn't lose it."

Pearl didn't utter a word. She just continued to rock in her chair like she didn't have a care in the world.

Johnnie Mae held the key in the air. "Here it is," she said, then sighed with relief.

Pearl perked up when Johnnie Mae handed her the key of decades past. She held it up close to her eyes and examined it thoroughly before turning and nodding at Angel. Angel got up and left the room.

"Johnnie Mae, what I am about to tell you, I have never told another living soul. Over sixty-odd years, three people lived to bear witness to the truth, and as it stands today, I am the only one left living to tell it. It's as if God has kept me on this earth this long to wait for you to show up on my porch." Pearl laid the key on the table next to her. "As a midwife, I have brought many a babies into this world. A few died for various reasons. Only once was I ever instructed to deliberately kill a baby . . . to just let a baby die. What I tell you today, I want you to pray and ask God what you should do with it, as I will leave that decision entirely up to you."

Angel came back carrying a handsome, gold-and-wooden, antique-looking box and placed it carefully in her great-grandmother's lap.

"Do either of you need anything else? Ms. Taylor? Great-granny?" Angel asked.

"No, baby, just leave us be for now."

Angel smiled and kissed her great-grandmother on the cheek. "Holler if you need me. I'll be somewhere close."

CHAPTER 27

And whatsoever thou shalt bind on earth shall be bound in heaven.

(Matthew 16:19 (b))

Landris called Johnnie Mae after she got home on Wednesday. She'd stayed an extra day in Asheville, having located a woman who had given her more information than she'd imagined possible. Johnnie Mae had taken that additional day to check out some things.

"How are things going with you and Thomas?" Johnnie Mae asked, knowing Thomas was staying—for some reason, although she didn't know quite what—a while longer.

"Fine," Landris said. He hadn't told Johnnie Mae about the problems his brother had created for him. That wasn't a conversation for the telephone. And if things went the way he desired, he'd be reflecting on what might have been a major problem instead of what was a major problem at present. "Thomas went to church with me this past Sunday."

"Is that right? So, how did he enjoy himself?"

Landris laughed. "He didn't have much to say about the service, but it seems he did meet someone he's interested in talking to. It's just like my brother: supposed to be going to church to spend time with the Lord, and he ends up trying to spend time with someone else he meets in the House of the Lord instead."

"Anybody I know?"

"Sapphire."

"Wow. Sapphire. Okay then."

"He wants me to invite her as his guest to our wedding," Landris said.

"She's Theresa's friend, isn't she?" Johnnie Mae remembered the day she first met Sapphire, then later when Bishop Jordan had his stroke. "Do you think she'll accept?"

"I don't know. But unless Thomas changes his mind before the week is out, she'll be invited. We're getting RSVPs back in already. There's such a short window now. The event director I hired, Tiffany Graham, is really working hard to coordinate everything for the wedding. Tickets have got to be secured."

"I came home to so many messages. People are in shock that they're being invited to a wedding at Oheka Castle and that it's all-expenses paid," Johnnie Mae said. "I'm sure there are going to be lots of folks upset who didn't get invited."

"A lot of my members are, a few voicing opinions. Mostly, they can't understand why we aren't getting married at the church so everybody can attend," Landris said.

"Oh, don't say that. I feel guilty enough that I've let you end up doing everything."

He laughed. "Oh, but you don't believe I can do it. So, I'm really enjoying myself, proving you wrong—thank you very much." He was quiet for a few seconds. "Tell me, have you changed your mind about the number of attendants you're having?"

"There's a flower girl and one attendant. I think I'll leave it at that."

"Okay. Just checking to be sure. If you do change your mind—"

"You'll be the first to know."

Johnnie Mae got off the phone with Landris. She had a lot to sort out. Now that she knew all about Sarah Fleming, she had no clue where Sarah was. Her mother was on her to go home, but Johnnie Mae didn't feel comfortable letting her leave just yet.

"You can't keep me here forever," Mrs. Gates said. "You're getting married in a little over a month. And I don't plan on moving to Atlanta with you. And that's final."

"Mama, I'm not trying to hold you here. I just want to be sure you're feeling okay."

"I'm feeling fine. Ask me anything. My mind is working well. A little worn, but what do you expect with years of constant use?"

Johnnie Mae hugged her. "Mama, I know. I just don't know what to do just yet."

"I have an idea. What if I promise not to go anywhere without checking in with someone first? Upon my return, I'll let them know I'm back." She looked at her daughter as Johnnie Mae frowned. "Johnnie Mae, listen. I'm a grown woman, and you can't hold me captive against my will."

"Then, tell me what I should do. What would you do if you thought someone you loved was in trouble? needed you to protect them? your children or grandchildren?"

Mrs. Gates looked away from her daughter. "Take me home, Johnnie Mae."

"But—"

"Just take me home. Now."

So, Johnnie Mae took her mother home to Edgewater, then called her siblings later to see what they thought. But she was adamant about not letting her mother go into a nursing home— assisted-living facility—whatever. She wasn't hearing that as an option.

A few days later, Mrs. Gates showed up at Johnnie Mae's house. "I want you to visit a place with me. I've gone myself, and I like it. There are lots of people my age there, but I would like to know what you think about it."

Johnnie Mae agreed to go with her. "Mama, what is this place?"

"It's where I can rent a nice small apartment and you nor the others will have to be concerned. I'd have my own bedroom, kitchen, living area, and bath. There are people on staff full-time, so there would be someone available all the time," Mrs. Gates explained as they sat outside in the car. "Just come in and see it. We don't have to make a decision today, but it's something to consider. There are people living here my age, Johnnie Mae. I get lonely sometimes at the house all by myself. And with you moving to Atlanta and taking Princess Rose from me, I'll be even more bored. This way I can be around others my age with something to do. They sponsor all kinds of activities here."

"Mama, I can't believe you're looking into something like this. Has somebody said something to you? Donald? Marie? Rachel? Has someone put you up to doing this?" Johnnie Mae was bouncing one of her crossed legs off the other in a tick-tock rhythm.

Mrs. Gates touched her hand. "This is all my idea. I still plan to keep my house. I'll just be like the senior citizens who have condos. But instead of me going all the way to Florida, I'll be right here in good old Alabama." She got out of the car. "All I'm asking is for you to take a look around and tell me what you think. That's all."

"Just look around? And if I don't like it, will you listen to me?"

"I'll listen. But Johnnie Mae, I still have a mind that works fine, and I can still make decisions for myself; what I believe is best for me."

Johnnie Mae got out. "We'll talk to the doctor again. They have medications that can help these days. Besides, he's still running tests on you. They haven't come up with a conclusive diagnosis on what is happening with you for sure."

Mrs. Gates smiled. "That's not going to change my age. Come on. Let's go in," she said in a cheery voice.

Johnnie Mae shook her head and walked alongside her mother, who was apparently just as determined as she was. Truthfully, that's where she had gotten some of her stubbornness, determination, and stick-to-it-iveness from: her mother, Countess Gates.

CHAPTER 28

And whatsoever thou shalt loose on earth shall be loosed in heaven.

(Matthew 16:19 (c))

Thomas noticed Sapphire when he saw her marching in leading the choir on Sunday. George had insisted that Thomas sit in the front row. He wanted to let the congregation know that his brother was visiting with them. Thomas wasn't thrilled about sitting so close, but when this beautiful, dark-chocolate, satin beauty glided into the sanctuary, he couldn't have felt more divine. He had apparently gotten her attention, too. He caught her sneaking looks at him a few times before she could turn away.

After services, she came over with a few others in tow to greet and welcome him. That's when he took the opportunity to let her know he would like to know more about her if she was available. "I'm not all that familiar with the area," he told her. "My brother is extremely busy with church things and his upcoming wedding. I'd love the company."

Sapphire didn't see any harm in being nice to Pastor Landris' big brother. They went to dinner after church, and he made her laugh. A lot. She liked a man who could put a laugh in her heart. So, when she asked him the question she asked any gentleman who made references to spending more time with her, she was somewhat taken aback by his answer.

"So. Are you saved?" Sapphire asked as she finished off the last of her pilaf rice.

"I believe in God." Thomas smiled. *Her eyes are so inviting.*

"But are you saved?" she asked again.

"I just told you I believe in God."

"The devil and the demons believe in God. Mark 3:11 says, 'And unclean spirits, when they saw him, fell down before him, and cried, saying, Thou art the Son of God.' There is a difference in being saved and believing in God." She waited on his response.

"I believe there is a God who sits high and looks low. I believe He is the only God, and that He's powerful, and ever-present, and all knowing. I believe He created the world, and that there are things we don't know about Him and may not ever know."

"But are you saved?" She leaned in closer, so as not to cause a scene. "I have no intentions of pursuing any type of relationship with anyone who is not spiritually equal."

"So, you're saying you and I would have to be in the same place spiritually to talk?" Thomas leaned in, mostly to get closer to her as he moistened his lips. "Just talk?"

"I'm saying, the number one thing I must have before I even spend time on any relationship, especially one that could escalate into more than just friendship, is someone who is first of all saved. From there, we can work on and work out anything. So, for the final time, Mr. Thomas Landris 'Extraordinaire,' are you saved?"

He smiled, knowing the answer she was seeking. "So, what you're asking me specifically is: Have I believed in my heart and confessed with my mouth the Lord Jesus Christ and believed that God has raised Him from the dead? Is that what you want to know? Am I saved in that respect?"

"Precisely." She leaned back; he had gotten a little too close for her comfort. She needed to keep her wits about her. *It's obvious . . . he has skills.*

"I did that back when I was twelve, at a revival. Sat on the 'mourners bench' for three solid days. Six of us had to sit on that bench and couldn't leave until we had 'tarried' and felt the 'move of the spirit' to accept Jesus," Thomas said, smiling. "I was baptized and everything. Now, why is that so important to you, again?"

"Pastor Landris has been teaching us about wise decisions and taking responsibility for some of the things that happen in our lives because we allow the flesh to dictate our actions. One message to the single folks was: 'Don't go out and get an unsaved man thinking you can change him after you get him.' Life is challenging enough sometimes when there are two touching and agreeing. It's a formula for chaos to start out with someone who has different beliefs. Right now, I have the power to put a thousand angels to flight on my behalf. If I'm to be with someone, I desire the power of two in agreement where God then deals in multiplication and ten thousand angels are put to flight on our agreement's behalf." Sapphire took a sip of her cola.

"So, one can put a thousand angels to flight and two can put ten thousand angels to flight?" He smiled. "I see you are also a woman with ambition and great vision."

"Guilty as charged. I've been accused and convicted of that a few times in my life."

"Nothing wrong with that," Thomas said as he tumbled deeper into her eyes. "I believe it's Proverbs 29:18 that says, 'Where there is no vision, the people perish.' Now George, my little brother, that man has vision."

"A family trait?" Sapphire watched his lips for his answer to emerge.

"I suppose." He bit down on his lower lip. "Like right now, I have this vision of you accompanying me to a wedding in September."

"And why on earth would you be seeing something like that at the end of July? You might end up finding someone else you'd rather have accompany you instead by September."

"Maybe because I am really interested in getting to know you better. And I have a feeling, come September, we'll be even closer than we are now. So, since the wedding is RSVP, I need to provide them with your name now."

"If I were to agree?"

"If you were to agree . . ." he said, grinning and pronouncing each word with emphasis.

"Can I give you an answer later?"

"As long as it's by tomorrow. George probably won't give me any longer than a day, since he and the wedding coordinator are wrapping up travel plans and all."

"Travel plans? Is this Pastor Landris' wedding?" She sat up with a different energy.

"Yes. And it is exclusive and by invitation only."

"So, what I heard is true? The wedding is not going to be held at our church?"

"Nope. It will be at Oheka Castle in Cold Spring Hills, New York. That's on Long Island. He's picking up the travel tab for all who are attending. If you say yes, you will be added as my guest."

She shook her head. "That sounds rather pricey: booking travel so close to the date. You generally get a better deal the earlier your reservations are made."

Thomas leaned in, putting his elbows on the table as he rested his chin on his fist. "The wedding coordinator has made special arrangements with a travel agency that has locked in certain prices, because from what I understand, he's planning to purchase quite a few flights with them. It's ingenious really and smart business for all parties involved. He gets a set discount price, giving him time to find out who will be coming, and they get all of his business for the affair." He leaned back. "I'm going to be his best man. And I would really love having you come as my special guest."

"*If* I were to agree, you know there will be nothing sexual happening between us?"

"Of course. That's why I need to know your answer by tomorrow. I'll need to let George know so he can get your room and airline-ticket reservations made."

Sapphire agreed to give him an answer shortly. She couldn't wait to tell Theresa and Maurice's sister, B, about Thomas.

"He seems quite different from Pastor Landris," Sapphire said on the three-way call. "Sometimes you can't help but wonder what he's really up to."

"Sounds like he's not boring," B said.

Sapphire could hardly contain herself. "Guess what, though?"

"Spill it, girl," Theresa said. "You sound like it's bursting to get out."

"He asked me to be his guest at Pastor Landris' wedding in September."

B clicked her tongue. "Girl, I thought you were about to tell us something good. So, he invited you to the wedding. We'll probably all go, except Theresa, who might be having her baby around then, if she hasn't already."

"The wedding is not going to be here."

"What?" B said. "Then, where? In Birmingham?"

Sapphire laughed. "No. Oheka Castle."

"Oheka what?" B asked.

"Oheka Castle in New York?" Theresa said. "The Oheka Castle in New York?"

"That one." Sapphire tried not to sound too excited. "Theresa, would you be okay if I were to go?"

"Okay with you going?" Theresa asked. "Of course I'd be okay. It's safe to assume I won't likely be getting an invitation." She laughed.

"If I get one, I won't be paying to go," B said. "They should have it here, where it's convenient for everybody. I'm not paying my money to go see somebody get married."

"It's not open for everybody," Sapphire said. "It's invitation only."

"So, I'm still not going to pay to go even if it is a privilege to get invited. Sapphire, you're actually going to spend your hard-earned money just to attend their wedding?"

"Well, you see, according to Thomas, Pastor Landris is picking up the tab for it: all of it. The travel cost, hotel, and of course once you get to the wedding there will probably be an overflow of food."

"He's paying for everybody?" Theresa asked, sitting up and switching the phone to her other ear.

"That's what his brother said."

"I wouldn't doubt it, then. George is generous like that," Theresa said.

"I think that's stupid and a waste of money," B chimed in. "Do you know how many poor people he could feed with the money he throws away?"

"B, I don't think it's really any of your business." Theresa sat back against her stacked-up pillows to get more comfortable. "It really is his money. Sapphire?"

"Yeah."

"Are you going to accept Thomas' invitation?" Theresa asked with a lift in her voice.

"What do you think I should do?" Sapphire asked.

"Go!" B and Theresa said in perfect E-flat harmony.

"For real?" Sapphire began to smile. "You won't be upset with me or think I'm being a traitor?" Sapphire was really more concerned about what Theresa thought—since she had almost married George—than what B thought about it.

"No," Theresa said. "It sounds like fun to me. I'd go if I wasn't pregnant, and of course, if I was invited."

"I say you should go. We need an inside spy in the place," B said. "We want details when you get back. And, if possible, take pictures—just in case you think something isn't important that turns out to be."

"B!" Theresa said. "That's a terrible thing to tell somebody."

"I told her to go. I just figure since *we* aren't getting to go, it's good to have someone on the inside keeping us informed. If anyone from church goes, they'll probably be the ones who wouldn't report back dirt even if they were standing right in front of it when it happened," B said.

"And you think I will?" Sapphire said in her most serious voice.

B started laughing hard. "Oh, you had better! Tell the brotha you'll be glad to go. Then let me hook your hair up before you leave. You might have dreadlocks, but I can work with them and make you like the gold in a four-inch-wide herringbone chain."

Theresa was quiet.

"Theresa?" Sapphire said. "Are you sure you're all right with this? Because I can tell him no now. You're my girl and—"

"Sapphire. Go," Theresa said. "And please, have fun. For all of us."

So Sapphire called Thomas on Monday night and agreed to be his "guest" for the wedding in New York.

CHAPTER 29

And grieve not the Holy Spirit of God.

(Ephesians 4:30)

By August, Johnnie Mae was back on the road doing another round of book signings. While in Michigan, she ended up finding the most perfect wedding dress. She also bought the "best woman's" (as Landris dubbed her one adult attendant) and the flower girls' dresses. Landris had a confirmed 176-guest list and everything was booked and ready. Tiffany was pleased with how things were really flowing together. "I prayed the prayer of petition, and now I thank God daily it is already done," Pastor Landris told her.

"Thanksgiving is the voice of faith," he said when she inquired further. "I learned that from my mentor years ago. And it's true. In the natural, when we believe something is already done, we thank the person for having done it. I asked, I believe I have already received—which in truth I have received in the spirit world—so I thank God every day that it is done. 'Thank you, Lord, this wedding is anointed. Thank you, Lord, it is blessed and it is a blessing right now.' See?"

Tiffany laughed. "Yes. I see. And right now I need to bless some people with some money they can see. So, do you want me to stop by your house and pick up the check?"

George's thoughts switched to Thomas, who had managed to recover at least some of his money. Whatever other risky things he had done, fortunately he had put some of the money in more secure things with maturity dates of six months to a year. Some CDs and Treasury bills had just matured and were promptly handed over to George—or more accurately, most of it was promptly handed over to the IRS for the payment of his tax bill.

"Almost six million dollars for taxes," Thomas had said. "Look, if you let me invest this money, there's a stock I know can make a quick return in a few weeks. Enron is a hot stock. I'm telling you, you can't lose with it. People are making money hand over fist."

"No, Thomas. If this tax bill goes unpaid, *you* are most likely going to jail, not me. So, you should be the first person happy that there's money to pay it," George said.

"But I'm telling you, George. I've got a real good feeling about Enron. Real good."

"Is it a Holy Ghost–anointed feeling?"

"Well, no."

"Then, I don't want to hear it. Because the Holy Spirit is advising me to save you from going to jail by rendering unto Caesar that which is Caesar's." George smiled.

"Okay, but any other money we get after this, you should invest it and give me a chance to recoup some more of what I've messed up."

"Any other money after this that comes in, my tithes will be paid first, and I'll seek God's face about what to do with the other 90 percent," George said as he walked away.

Johnnie Mae called Landris to see what else she needed to do for the wedding. He was pleased to inform her that everything was pretty much set now.

Johnnie Mae's old friends, Honey and Sister, were excited about getting their tickets and could hardly wait for September to arrive. All of the immediate family members on both sides were also packed and counting down the days until September 8.

Mrs. Gates was still visiting facilities geared toward the elderly, against Johnnie Mae's wishes. Johnnie Mae asked her mother to travel with her the last few weeks of the book tour, but she flat-out refused.

"You take Princess Rose away because you don't think I'm re-

sponsible enough to keep her. Now you want to baby-sit me,"
Mrs. Gates said, crying. "You don't trust me."

"Mama, that's not it. I just want to spend time with her. I wish
you'd reconsider and go with me. You could keep her while I'm
doing my thing, then the three of us could hang out like we did
in Asheville." Johnnie Mae paused. "So, why won't you come
with us?"

"Because I need to find me a small place, and I don't have time
to waste jetting across the country with you. Johnnie Mae, you
have a life and pretty soon you'll be living all the way in Georgia,
and I'll be here all by myself."

"Mama, you're not all by yourself."

She started crying again. "I don't want to be a burden on anyone."

"After Landris and I are married, you could come live with us."

Mrs. Gates stopped crying. "I'll do no such thing. I don't want
to leave Alabama. I'm still looking around and checking out
places. Oh, did I tell you I met this woman at one of the places I
visited, and of course, she's an elderly woman. She claims she's
financially well off and hiding out from her family. She was reading your latest book!"

Johnnie Mae's stomach began to flutter. "Mama, do you recall
her name?"

"I don't remember it offhand, but she was telling me she had
met an author once who was now doing her story. When I told
her I have a daughter who's an author, she perked right up. I didn't
tell her that was your book she was reading, though. You know,
sometimes that makes people uncomfortable. Especially if they
end up not liking the book, and they think you're going to ask
them about it. Then they have to lie to not hurt your feelings. I
told her I'd be back to see her because she really seems alone.
No one ever talks to her." She tapped her temple with her index
finger. "What is her name?"

"Mama, could you possibly take me there? I'd like to meet her.
She sounds like someone I might know and desperately need to
find. Could her name be Sarah?"

"Sarah? Sarah?" Mrs. Gates repeated. "Sounds familiar, but I
can't say for sure."

"But you can take me there?" Johnnie Mae asked. "Could we go right now?"

"I suppose. But what's the hurry?"

"It's important. I told you, I'm trying to find this woman named Sarah Fleming."

"Have you checked the telephone book?" Mrs. Gates picked a piece of lint off her favorite polka-dot dress.

"The phone book won't help. Sarah could be anywhere in the world by now. But if she's the woman you met, then I have some important information she really needs to hear."

They left, dragging a sleepy Princess Rose with them. Mrs. Gates directed Johnnie Mae to the place. Johnnie Mae located the person in charge.

"Excuse me, I'm looking for someone named Sarah Fleming. Is it possible she's a resident here?"

The woman looked at Johnnie Mae and was about to answer her when she noticed Mrs. Gates with her. "Countess! Darling! Don't you look well." They embraced. "So, you did come back, just like you said."

"Yes, and I brought my daughter with me, just like I told you I would." Mrs. Gates looked at the director, then Johnnie Mae. "I'm sorry, your name has slipped my mind."

"Frances. It's Frances. You said you were going to bring your daughter. Would you like to look around now? I'm free at the moment and can show you all that we have to offer here at our facility," she said, looking more at Johnnie Mae as she spoke.

"I'd love to look around," Johnnie Mae said politely. "But I'm actually looking for a woman named Sarah Fleming. I'm not sure if that's the name she would be listed here by, but my mother was telling me about a woman—"

"Here she is," Mrs. Gates said as she started away. "How are you?" Mrs. Gates said as she hugged the woman. Johnnie Mae turned quickly. "I want you to meet my daughter. Now, I'm not so great with names lately, but you two can introduce yourselves."

Johnnie Mae smiled at a woman she had never seen before. The woman extended her hand. "I'm Mary Jane. Plain Mary Jane," the woman said, true to her name.

Johnnie Mae continued to smile. "My name is Johnnie Mae—"

"Taylor!" Mary Jane said loudly while covering her mouth. "I just finished reading your book. Oh my goodness. It's really you. But I thought you were taller."

Johnnie Mae laughed a little. "I get that a lot."

They chatted. Johnnie Mae then excused herself so the two of them could get home.

"Don't you want to see the empty apartment?" Frances asked, still waiting.

Johnnie Mae looked at her watch. "Maybe another time," she said.

"Johnnie Mae. While we're here, the least you could do is look at it. I'm running out of time, and this is important to me," Mrs. Gates said. "We are already here."

So, Johnnie Mae consented and they looked around. Johnnie Mae couldn't hide her disappointment that Mary Jane had turned out not to be Sarah. Even more disheartening, she really liked this place. But if she told her mother she did, it would appear as if she were endorsing her decision to commit herself to a nursing-home type of facility.

So, Johnnie Mae turned up her nose, frowned, and shook her head quickly when her mother asked her what she thought.

CHAPTER 30

Let them shout for joy, and be glad, that favor my righteous cause.

(Psalm 35:27 (a))

One week before Johnnie Mae's wedding, her mother stopped by her house in Coffee.

"I think I've found the perfect place," Mrs. Gates said. "One I'm certain you will approve of. They have a community garden. It's secure. And a space is available now. I know you're getting ready for your wedding, but I'd really like you to take a look at it."

"Today?" Johnnie Mae asked. She had just gotten in from LA, and the trip had been exhausting.

Mrs. Gates looked away. "Well, not if it's a bad time. I just thought maybe we could run up there real quick, and you could tell me what *you* think. But if you'd rather wait until another time, it's fine. I understand you're busy with other, more important things."

Johnnie Mae could see the disappointment in her mother's face. "No, Mama. If you'll let me finish up a few things, we can go today."

"Anything I can help you with?"

"No. In fact, why don't I go up and get Princess Rose, and we can be on our way."

"Oh, let me," Mrs. Gates said. "Princess Rose!" She yelled. "Grandma's here."

Princess Rose ran out of her room, down the stairs, and into her grandmother's arms. "Grandma! Your hair is pretty." She stroked her grandmother's freshly styled silver hair.

The place Mrs. Gates had found was only twenty minutes from Johnnie Mae's house. When they arrived, Johnnie Mae was surprisingly impressed. It was attractively gated, with a superbly manicured lawn. Flowers were still blooming out front. The backyard had a place for them to grow vegetables. Ms. Phillips, the director, was a sweet, soft-spoken woman who genuinely seemed to care about all of the residents.

"Well, Mama, I must admit: I like it."

"Good!" Mrs. Gates said. "Because I really like it too. It has a real homelike feel to it. A feeling of community, like back when I was coming up."

Just then, a woman came in. She was a large, heavyset woman who seemed to command attention just by entering a room.

"I'm so hungry," the woman said. "I feel like a gutted fish!"

Johnnie Mae turned.

"Hey baby, you came back?" the woman said to Mrs. Gates.

"Yes, and I was wondering where you were," Mrs. Gates said. "I was wanting you to meet my daughter. She's an author, you know."

"Is that right?" She stepped up closer to Johnnie Mae. "My name is Azile," she pronounced it Az-a-lee. "You know, like the flour? My mama named me after a sack of flour, baby. It ain't hard to spell. Ain't nothing but A-z-i-l-e. That's all, sugar. I s'-pose if I had'a come a little later in life, she would have named me Betty after the cake mix. Or Sunflower after a sack of corn-meal."

Mrs. Gates laughed and looked at Johnnie Mae. "She's a char-acter, isn't she?"

"Oh baby, Ms. Azile wouldn't hurt a flea. The most loving woman in all the world," Ms. Azile said. "I was out with my new neighbor. She stays locked up in her room all the time with no-body to come visit her. I finally dragged her out, and we went to the store. Hey baby," Ms. Azile said, beckoning for her friend. "Come over and meet Countess. She thinkin' 'bout moving here with us."

"She's just looking," Johnnie Mae said. "We haven't decided that she'll be actually moving—"

"Sarah, I'd like you to meet Countess," Ms. Azile said. "And this is her daughter—"

"Johnnie Mae Taylor!" Sarah said, covering her heart with both her hands, hardly believing her eyes.

"Sarah Fleming!" Johnnie Mae said ecstatically as she drew closer to her. "Sarah! Thank God!"

Sarah quickly found a seat and sat down. Johnnie Mae went over to her.

"I've been trying to find you," Johnnie Mae said, sitting down beside her.

"They took me away." She looked into Johnnie Mae's eyes. "Did you get the key?"

"Yes, I got it. And Sarah, I found Pearl Black."

"You did? Did she still have the box?" Sarah looked intensely at Johnnie Mae.

"Pearl not only had the box, but she told me some things you need to know. Sarah, I have to talk to you," Johnnie Mae said. Mrs. Gates cleared her throat. Johnnie Mae looked up. "Oh, Mama, this is Sarah Fleming. I met her in Selma. Sarah, this is my mother, Countess Gates."

"Pleased to meet you, Sarah," Mrs. Gates said.

"Your daughter has been a godsend. I don't know how she was able to find me, but I had been praying so hard she would." She turned to Johnnie Mae. "And God answered my prayer. Somehow, you found me. But we don't have much time."

"What's wrong?" Johnnie Mae asked.

"Ms. Phillips, the director, she thinks I'm not stable. That's what my family told her when they brought me here. I have no phone in my room, and I'm not allowed to talk with anyone. The only reason I was able to go out with Ms. Azile is because Ms. Phillips is partly afraid to cross her and partly believes Ms. Azile isn't a real threat to anyone here. If Ms. Phillips suspects anything, I believe she'll call my family, and they'll be here to take me away."

"What if I were to take you home with me?" Johnnie Mae asked.

"They'd probably accuse you of kidnapping."

"Even if you tell them you went with me voluntarily?"

Sarah frowned. "You don't know my family. They're powerful and quite convincing about my mental state, or lack thereof."

"Not if what I know comes out. I've got to tell you what Pearl told me," Johnnie Mae said as she kept a watch out for Ms. Phillips.

"Let's go to Ms. Azile's place. It will appear we're still together, and Ms. Phillips won't suspect a thing." Sarah stood to her feet. They found Ms. Azile chatting with Ms. Phillips, who wore a pasted smile on her face while her head bounced like a bobblehead toy.

"Ms. Azile, I was just telling these fine folks about your grandbaby," Sarah said.

"I would love to see a picture of her," Mrs. Gates said, instinctively stepping in to aid the situation.

"Oh baby, I have a whole album of her. Would you like to come up to my room and see her pictures?" Ms. Azile started walking away. "I'll be back, Ms. Phillips. I need to go show them my little heart."

Ms. Phillips laughed. "Now, Ms. Azile's not going to turn down a chance to show off that beautiful grandbaby of hers. You ladies should plan on being up there a few hours." She smiled, exhibiting her gratification for such a well-timed reprieve.

Countess, Johnnie Mae, Princess Rose, and Sarah followed Ms. Azile into the elevator that traveled between the four floors. When they got to Ms. Azile's apartment, Countess kept Princess Rose as she sat with Ms. Azile, oohing and aahing over her grandbaby's pictures. Sarah and Johnnie Mae went into the bedroom and closed the door to talk.

"Pearl is ninety-eight years old," Johnnie Mae began. "But she is alive, with a mind like a teenager. At first, she wouldn't tell me anything worth telling—just talked about the history of the area, things like that. Wouldn't tell me anything—that is, until I showed her that key."

"I told you that you'd have to have the key."

"She gave me this beautiful golden-and-wooden box. The key fit perfectly; but I didn't open it or look to see what was inside."

"Then, why are you glad to see me? You don't know any more about what I have told you concerning my life than the last time we talked."

"Pearl told me about you and your baby. She was the midwife who delivered her."

Sarah nodded, reflecting back on that day. "Pearl is from a generation of midwives." She took Johnnie Mae's hand. "So, what did Pearl tell you?"

Johnnie Mae took a deep breath and wondered. *How much do I tell her?* Pearl had left that decision totally up to her.

"Pearl told me your oldest half-brother instructed her to let your baby die."

"What?" Sarah touched her heart again. "They told me the baby was born dead already. Stillborn. But Pearl told you my brother Heath said for her to let my baby die?"

Johnnie Mae swallowed hard and nodded.

"How *could* Pearl? I don't understand. How could Pearl do something like that? All this time. And I trusted *her* with the information and things in my box? When she had let my baby die? She and my mother, they lied to me!" Sarah began to cry. "They lied."

"Sarah, please wait." Johnnie Mae tried to calm her. "There's something else."

"What? What else matters? They let a sweet, innocent little baby die. My baby. And then they lied to me about it. They told me she was stillborn when in fact, they had watched my baby die without doing anything to help her."

"Sarah!" Johnnie Mae grabbed her by the shoulders to hold her steady. "Pearl didn't let your baby die. Your baby lived, Sarah! She didn't die."

"What?"

"Your baby didn't die." Johnnie Mae nodded her head firmly as she smiled and kept speaking. "She lived. And your daughter might very well still be alive somewhere out there today. It's been years, but who knows?"

"But how?" Sarah asked. "How is this possible? They had a funeral for the baby. So, how is it possible?"

Johnnie Mae thought back to the conversation she'd had with Pearl in order to give Sarah the answers she was so desperately seeking.

CHAPTER 31

Redeeming the time.

(Ephesians 5:16)

Johnnie Mae and Pearl sat alone with the box on Pearl's lap. She beckoned for Johnnie Mae to take it, after she herself had tried the key and saw that it fit perfectly.

"Never knew what was in here," she said, lifting the lid a crack, but not even then looking inside. She closed it, locked it back, and released it into Johnnie Mae's custody.

"Ransom was my friend. He and I grew up together. All of us loved going to Candy Land, hanging out at the Young Men's Institute, especially the library. Ransom had what we called 'gifted' hands ... artistic. He could take a piece of wood and other hard material and make the most exquisite things out of them. You see that design on top of that box? That's his handi-work. He started by creating requested projects for folks around the area. My old Ransom." She smiled. "Would you care to hear how he came about that name?"

Johnnie Mae nodded, not fully knowing where or how this ac-tually fit into the tale.

"My mother was the midwife when he was born. She told me his mama was in hard labor. Said she had put scissors under her mattress, but even that didn't ease her pain. When that big, strong boy pushed his way into the world, his mama motioned for the Bible. They gave it to her. She turned the pages and pointed. 'His name,' my mother said she said. 'What? Ransom? You want to name your son Ransom?' my mother asked her.

"She died with her finger on Matthew 20:28: 'Even as the Son of man came not to be ministered unto, but to minister, and to give his life a ransom for many.' So that's what my mother wrote in her midwife record book: Ransom. My mother told me she was never sure if that's what his mama really meant to name him or if she was telling her something important. Something spiritual that took place during her moment of crossing over. His name might have been her finally seeing Jesus." Pearl wiped her mouth with her napkin. "Ransom grew to be a handsome thing. So, when Mr. V had him doing work around his place, it was no surprise Sarah fell for him. I mean she fell hard. When Mr. V got wind of it, he put a stop to it before anything got started good. Or so he thought. People in our community used to say, 'If that ain't the pot calling the kettle black.' "

"What do you mean?" Johnnie Mae asked.

Pearl smiled. "It was common knowledge, Mr. V was in love with a colored woman named Mamie. You talk about a tiny little thing. And that girl had some book knowledge in her. She learnt plenty from school, 'cause we had dedicated teachers around these parts back then. But that girl read with the same fervor as a man dying of thirst devours water."

"Mr. V was white," Johnnie Mae said, thinking aloud more than asking Pearl a question.

"Yes, as was his daughter Sarah. Both of them seemed predisposed to dark chocolate if you ask me. And I ain't talking candy bars either. Of course, Mr. V would never let on to that. He was trying too hard to make folks believe he was a racist." She shook her head. "He wasn't. Just didn't want his daughter caught up in that. It was hard for coloreds and whites to be together, even as friends, back in those days. I think his wife knew he had strong feelings for Mamie. That's why she didn't care for her too much. But she couldn't get rid of Mamie either." Pearl held up her glass. "Could you take this in the kitchen for me and bring me back a glass of ice water out of that jug in the Frigidaire?"

"Sure," Johnnie Mae said, rising and taking her glass. She came back with a cold glass of water and handed it to Pearl.

Pearl took a drink, then set the glass down. "Mamie and Sarah were best friends. Then Mamie ended up meeting this man who did pretty sharp work himself. Mamie married that fellow. Sarah wanted to marry Ransom, but that was not going to happen. So she pretended to be interested in a neighbor up the road from their place. When Sarah ended up pregnant, her father went to the young man's house to force him to make things right by his daughter." Pearl nodded her head as she remembered. "You guessed it. Denials and truths came from everywhere. Then Mr. V found out the father was Ransom. Ransom asked Sarah to go away with him. But then Sarah's father started acting like he was okay with the baby being Ransom's. Leastwise, Sarah believed him. Ransom got offered a job out of state making more money than he'd ever dreamed. Mr. V talked Sarah into staying until after the baby came, then she could meet up with him. Two months and not hearing anything from Ransom, Sarah believed he had left her for good. But her father was in her corner. He told her they would take care of her child, as a family. He loved his daughter. She had no reason not to trust or believe him.

"That's when her brother, Heath, came to me. Told me when the baby came, he didn't want that baby to live. His stepmother, Sarah's mother, overheard him when he told me. She tried to talk him out of it. But he wasn't the type to listen to women. Mr. V didn't believe her. If Mamie hadn't been about to have her baby, she probably could have gotten Mr. V to see his son was up to no good. But Mamie was about to have her own baby. It took a lot out of her just to get her work done. Mamie happened to go into labor at their house. I was her midwife, too. Mr. V had early on insisted she stay at their house when her baby came. At least until she felt well enough to be home alone, what with her husband out of town at the time. The day Mamie went into labor, Mr. V was away on business himself. But that vulture of a son of his was there circling like a hawk."

"What about his wife? Sarah's mother?" Johnnie Mae asked.

"She was there. None too pleased that Mamie would be staying in a guest room with her newborn child at her husband's insistence. But she didn't cross Mr. V when it came to Mamie. I always wondered if Mrs. V had thoughts that the baby Mamie was carrying might possibly be her husband's. Mamie had already told her on more than one occasion that her heart belonged to only one man: Willie B. So when Mamie went into labor, I was sent for. Then Sarah went almost two hours behind her. They were so much like sisters."

Pearl took another sip and got more comfortable. "Mamie delivered first. She was resting four doors down. Sarah's baby came hours later. I'd been given orders to make sure Sarah's baby didn't live. So right before she was to push for that final time, I gave her something to drink. The baby was barely out before she was out like a light."

"But Sarah told me she was sure she heard the baby cry," Johnnie Mae said. "That's why she didn't believe the baby was stillborn."

"Yeah. When she woke up, and we told her the baby had been born dead, she kept insisting, 'But I heard the baby cry! I heard her with my own ears. I wasn't dreaming.' Oh, she was tore up. Her mother cradled her and assured her she had been there the whole time. 'You never heard her cry, Sarah,' her mother said. 'You couldn't have.' "

"Was her mother really there the whole time?" Johnnie Mae asked.

Pearl nodded. "She didn't leave her side the entire time. Sarah's mother took one look at that baby, picked her up, and held her in her arms: a gorgeous baby girl with the faintest touch of yellow-brown around her ears. That's how you can tell the shade level of a colored baby: the edge of their ears. She rocked that baby. I knew what the brother had told me, and I wasn't sure how I would defy him. But there was no way I was going to let that baby die. I worked too hard to make sure they all came here all right. I looked at her rocking and singing to that baby with tears streaming down her face. Sarah, lying there, unaware of what she would face when she finally opened her eyes.

" 'Give me the baby,' I said to her. 'I have a job to do. Heath gave me strict orders. You know if I don't do it, he will someday.' I only said that for her benefit. So she could let him know I had done what he told me to. She looked at me. 'No,' she said. Then she took off with the baby. I just knew she had gone to kill that helpless little thing herself, and that I had failed both Sarah and her baby. Mrs. V came back with empty arms."

"Sarah's mother didn't have the baby anymore?"

Pearl shook her head. "I was about to ask what she had done when she said, 'The baby's dead.' I heard my own heart thumping. 'You killed it?' I asked her before I could stop myself. 'No, she was stillborn,' she said. That's when I tried to figure it all out. I had planned to take the baby and give her to a family that would love and keep her safe. Nobody needed to know the truth. But the baby would have lived. Now this woman was telling me she had killed the baby. Then she grabbed me and made me look in her eyes." Pearl wrapped her arms around herself. "She then told me what she had done and what I would have to do. And she told me I couldn't tell it. Ever. Not to Sarah. Not to Mr. V. And she didn't have to tell me not to tell it to that devil Heath." Pearl became quiet.

"What did she do?" Johnnie Mae couldn't take this much longer. She could imagine a mother who'd utterly flipped out; and a poor, twenty-year-old Sarah lying there not realizing her world was about to be turned upside down, inside out, and back again.

"She had taken the baby down the hall to where Mamie was, placed the baby in Mamie's arm, and told her, 'You had twins today. A boy and a girl.' Well, Mamie didn't know what to think. She thought Sarah's mother had lost it. 'No, I had a little boy. That baby there is not mine.' Sarah's mother told her if she didn't claim that baby, the baby would end up dead before the night was over. If Mamie wanted to help Sarah—if she truly loved Sarah like she claimed—she would say she had birthed twins on this day.

"Then I was sent into Mamie's room to record in my book a twin birth. Mamie asked me to tell her what was going on. I told her if she wanted to save that baby's life, she had to claim her for her own. I told her how serious Heath was about this baby not living. That if he ever found out the baby hadn't died, he might take it upon himself to make it so. Three of us knew the truth. We had intended to make it right when we could. Mr. V came home that night. When he learned Sarah had delivered, he went in to see her. That's when his wife told him how horrible it had all been. How Sarah's baby had died."

"How could you pull something like that off?" Johnnie Mae asked with a puzzled look on her face.

"We had a funeral: a quick one. Mr. V didn't care for anyone to know anything, so not only didn't he attend—it was okay that the ceremony was only with a few of us, privately, and the very next day. Sarah was too distraught to attend. So we cried over an antique doll in a box and buried it under a cloak of secrecy, in the family plot." Pearl laughed. "It's funny now. It wasn't so funny then. So the three of us were bound by a secret: Me, Mamie, and Sarah's mother—Grace."

"And no one ever told Sarah?" Johnnie Mae asked, as more of a statement of fact. "Ever?"

"Mamie was going to. Right after her husband got back. The baby was so white, he didn't know what to think or believe. Mamie had no choice but to tell him. He told her it wasn't right for Sarah not to know the truth. Mamie wasn't working there at the time. She was home keeping the babies. But Mamie knew their cook. Asked her to sneak Sarah a note telling her they needed to talk. From what I hear, Heath found out about it even though the note got delivered. He figured out how to get Mr. V to send Sarah away. Made it look like she had stepped off the deep end. Nobody ever heard from Sarah again. Her father's health quickly went downhill after that. And when he died, the two brothers took over most all of the family dealings. They had no interest in sharing the wealth. It was perfect having Sarah away. They decided to make sure it remained a permanent thing."

"What about her mother? Grace? Why didn't she ever do anything?"

"She did. She made sure her daughter and her granddaughter were taken care of. That was tricky, since her husband didn't will her much power upon his death. I know, having spoken to Mamie before they moved away, that Grace kept in touch with them. Grace was trying to figure out how to make things right for her daughter without permanently ending up on the outside herself. Grace possessed the house and all of its contents. Mr. V's boys controlled the money and all the legal say-so. Grace didn't know where her daughter was, but she knew about her granddaughter that neither of them knew existed."

"Pearl, you're saying there's a chance that Sarah's baby might be alive?"

"She was doing well last I saw her when she was around fourteen. Sarah thinks her baby died at birth. I assure you, that was not the case." Pearl pointed to the box. "That box may have something to help Sarah. I hope so. She gave it to me right after the baby incident. Frantic and scared, it was like she knew something was off. She asked me to take the box, and to keep it until she came to get it. She didn't want anyone to know I had it. Sarah showed me the key and said if she were to ever send anyone else on her behalf for the box, they would have that key. Sixty-six years later, you show up."

Johnnie Mae stood up and hugged Pearl. "I thank God for you," she said. "Sarah told me she believed her baby didn't die. I thought she was mistaken or just in denial still."

"Well, it's been a long time. I just pray it's not too late to make things right."

Johnnie Mae felt Sarah squeezing her hands hard. "My baby is alive. I feel it, Johnnie Mae. Please help me find her. Please. I beg you. Please. Help me find my family."

Johnnie Mae smiled. "I don't know what I can do. I've searched for information on Mamie, but I haven't found anything that matches. Sarah, I'm getting married next week, so I can't spend time on this right now. But after I return from my honeymoon and things settle down, I'll see if I can't locate this Mamie Peterson."

"Mamie *Peterson*? Did I tell you Peterson?"

"Yes. I wrote it down. You said, 'Mamie Peterson.' That's exactly what you said."

"Then, I should have said Patterson. It's Mamie Patterson." She looked concerned, having made such a costly error. "Johnnie Mae, when you get home, feel free to open the box. And if you find anything that you believe will help you in this matter, use it."

"Why don't I just bring the box here to you—?"

"No. I don't want my family getting wind that I'm getting any outside assistance. And if they get their hands on what's inside that box, I'll never be able to reclaim what's rightfully mine." She smiled at Johnnie Mae. "I trust you. Whatever you need to do, whatever the cost; I'll gladly repay you when things are finally set right."

CHAPTER 32

But without faith it is impossible to please him.

(Hebrews 11:6 (a))

"**B**elieving in God is not enough." Pastor Landris began the last Sunday morning service before he would be leaving on Thursday for his wedding ceremony, being held on Saturday, the eighth of September.

"Satan believes in God. There are many who believe there is a God. James 2:19–20 tells us, 'Thou believest that there is one God; thou doest well: the devils also believe, and tremble. But wilt thou know, O vain man, that faith without works is dead?' So you see, belief can become a state of being. Let me take you to school for just a minute if you'll allow me. A verb can be a state of being as in *is*, *am*, or *were*. Or a verb can show action as in *run*, *fight*, and *stand*. Hope is a good jumping-off spot. To believe something or in something is admirable. But it is possible to believe, yet never take any action on what you believe. 'Faith,' on the other hand, is an action word requiring you to not just believe, but to act on what you believe.

"Romans 10:9 supplies the formula for faith. It is how we who are saved became saved. 'That if thou shalt confess with thy mouth the Lord Jesus, and shalt believe in thine heart that God hath raised him from the dead, thou shalt be saved.' Confess. Believe. Receive. Belief can be a state of being. It's wonderful to believe something, but you shouldn't stop at belief. There must be action behind your believing. Confess. Say. Do. All action words. Doing something with that state of being. Now *that* is faith. Have you ever wondered why a perfectly good battery sitting inside of a perfectly good piece of equipment, making electrical contact but not required to work, eventually goes dead? The battery started out being good and strong, but it wasn't required to do any work just sitting there waiting. So it *became* dead. And so it is with your faith: Without works, it's dead.

"The scripture in Romans tells us that by believing in our heart the Lord Jesus Christ, and confessing with our mouth that God has raised Him from the dead, we shall be saved. Saved? Saved from what? Not persecution, I can tell you that much from experience. Saved from going to hell? Okay, that's one good benefit. But by applying this faith formula in your life across the board, you can also be saved from sickness. Saved from poverty. Saved from lack. You need to take your believing beyond just a state of being. I believe if I walk out of this building and go get in my car, I can drive home. Believing that is great. And what I just said is a true statement. But if I don't act on what I believe, it doesn't matter how much I believe it or how true it really is, nothing—*no thing*—will happen. If I say I believe God's Word but don't act on my belief, it profits me nothing."

Pastor Landris began to walk around. "Some folks think we are saved so we can obtain eternal life." He shook his head. "I submit to you today: Everybody will have eternal life." He looked at the many faces, some with looks of confusion, and smiled. "Yes, you heard me correctly. I said *everybody* will have eternal life." Pastor Landris glanced briefly at Thomas as he walked back up to the front.

"The question to be answered is not, '*Will* I have eternal life?' The question to be answered by each of us is, '*Where* will I spend eternal life?' the eternal life where you will be raised with a *spiritual body*. So, yes, you will experience eternal things with an eternal body that will live forever: a body that no longer gets sick or dies. So, will you be spending your eternal life in your eternal body in heaven?" He took a few steps to the other side. "Or will your eternal body end up burning eternally in the lake of fire?"

He paused. "People, don't let Satan deceive you. He already

knows *his* outcome. There's nothing he can do about it. He can't make a choice that can change his fate. He and his demons are doomed to the lake of fire. But Satan likes company. When Lucifer was kicked out of heaven, a third of the angels went with him. Of course he wants you to party with him. Oh yes, make the wrong decision—and no action one way or the other is still making a decision—make the wrong decision, and you'll be singing, 'It's getting hot in here' for real. And taking off all your clothes will take on a whole new meaning."

Some of the older people nodded. The younger folks bucked their eyes, sat up, and paid closer attention to what he was saying. Pastor Landris didn't miss any of this. *Yes, I've heard the song,* he thought, then smiled.

"Don't let the Pied Piper dance you right into the lake of fire 'partying like it's 1999.' As you can see, 1999 has come and gone, and we're still here. That's just how eternity will be. Time won't matter because nobody will be keeping time. Forever will be forever. How do you measure forever?" He walked down another aisle as he spoke.

"And for all of you who believe you can work your way to heaven 'anyhow': Let me help you out. Your works are not enough to get you into heaven. You will fall short of the perfect score heaven requires. 'Ninety-nine and a half won't do.' But when you decide to accept Jesus as your Savior, when you make Jesus the Lord of your life, your getting into heaven is then based on Jesus. God sees Jesus in place of you. Over 2,000 years ago, your sins became His sins. Your sickness became His sickness. Every curse, including poverty, all became His. The sentence for sin happens to be death. You were supposed to be on that cross, pierced in your side, wearing that thorny crown, buried, then sent to hell. But Jesus! Somebody say. 'But Jesus!' "

"But Jesus!" the congregation said.

"*But Jesus* paid the price. He died on the cross. People seem to want to keep Him on the cross. Some folks wear crosses so big— bling! bling!—for all to see. But there was no power in the cross. You see, had Jesus only died on that cross—like many others before and after Him—and that was all there was to it, we'd still be in a mess today. But Jesus . . ."

"But Jesus!" the people sang out again.

"*But Jesus* went down and paid a visit to old man death and old man hell. Jesus, the Son of man and the Son of God. And for all you women haters out there—you know, those of you who don't believe God uses a woman in the ministry—I hope you know when the Bible says Son of man that no earthly 'man' had anything to do with this. Jesus was born of a woman. Wo . . . man. Because God knew some of you men might think more highly of yourself than you ought—be strutting around with your chest out—had man had anything to do with the conception and birth of Jesus. Hence, He fixed it so divinely, using the one whom some of you still consider unworthy of your respect. Jesus was born of a woman, people. Excuse me. I just had to take that little side journey right there.

"I want you to know that Jesus did all that He did on this earth as a man. Not as God. As a man. You see, it would have been unfair of God to require things of us that could only be done by God. So Jesus stripped himself, became poor in the sense that He left the riches of heaven to come down to dirt, rich earth. Jesus was the last Adam. Not the second, not the third, but the last Adam. 'Last' implying finished. The end. You know, 'The End,' roll credits, the end.

"Jesus, the last man Adam, went to hell, walked boldly up to Satan, and took BACK. Oh, y'all don't hear me! I said Jesus took *back* . . ."

"Go on and preach it, preacher!" someone in the congregation shouted out.

"He took *back*, which implies man had possession first. Jesus took *back* the keys. And had Jesus taken the keys and remained dead or in hell, it would have done us no good. But Jesus! I'm talking about the last man Adam, y'all."

"Go 'head, Pastor! Preach the Word!"

"Jesus took the keys and on the Jewish-counted third day, He arose from the dead. God raised Him from the dead. Jesus restored to man that which the first man Adam gave away. Our power. Our authority. Our keys. Restored to the believers. Keys," he said as he reached into his pocket, took out his ring of keys, and jingled them, "that can keep out. Keys that can allow in." Pastor Landris wiped his brow. " 'Whatsoever you bind on earth—' "

" 'Shall be bound in heaven!' " the collective voice of the congregation rang out.

" 'And whatsoever you loose on earth—' "

" 'Shall be loosed in heaven!' " the congregation yelled even louder.

Pastor Landris took a moment to look up to heaven, then at the sea of people praising God. He smiled.

"Church, Jesus our High Priest—oh, I wish I had time to fully explain how the Old Testament high priest system operated. But Jesus, our High Priest: You see, the high priest was the only one allowed into the Holy of Holies to offer the sacrifice, the blood sacrifice—to atone for the sins of the people. They would have to tie a rope around the high priest's waist just in case something happened and he didn't come out, to be able to pull him out, since nobody could just go in and get him. *But Jesus—*"

"But Jesus," the congregation said quieter and with more reverence.

"Jesus, our High Priest, rose on that third-day morning. It was His blood: the ultimate sacrifice. His blood, poured out on the Mercy Seat in the Heavenly Holy of Holies. Jesus told Mary Magdalene when she was about to touch him after He rose, not to because He had not yet ascended to His Father. Jesus then went to heaven and poured out His blood on the Mercy Seat for you. And you. Oh, and you, too," Pastor Landris said as he pointed to various sections in the audience.

"The ultimate sacrificial lamb. No more yearly atonements: now eternal redemption. Already done. Jesus has already done it. He doesn't have to pay to redeem you when you decide to come into the body of Christ. Jesus already paid your price. And all you have to do is accept Him as your Savior, ask Him into your heart and to become Lord of your life. Then receive Him. Now if you believe what I've just said, that's great. But as I said earlier, believing is not enough. If you believe but don't act on a thing, it does you no good. If you believe God can heal, but don't act on that fact, that's not faith. If you believe Jesus died on the cross, was buried, and that God raised Him from the dead, then take the next step and act on that. Confess it with your mouth, and you shall be saved."

Pastor Landris backed up. "Or, you *can* go it alone and be judged solely on your works. Because if you don't accept Jesus—literally have Jesus to stand in your stead—then you're left to be judged by your perfect works. If you believe you can go through this life without ever doing anything wrong, then, hey—all I can say is this: Abraham, 'the Friend of God,' couldn't do it. David, 'a man after God's own heart,' couldn't do it. Solomon, 'a man of wisdom,' couldn't do it. Moses—oh, y'all remember parted-the-Red-Sea Moses. He was only allowed to *look over into* the Promised Land. Now if you think you're saved, when in fact you came forward maybe as a youngster who felt pressured to go shake the preacher's hand, but you didn't give your heart to the Lord, didn't believe out of your heart, please don't leave today without setting things right. I'm talking about a relationship. Realizing how much God loves. He sent His only begotten son, Jesus, just for you. Jesus came that we might have life, and have it more abundantly. Jesus lived to show us how to live a fruitful and victorious life on *this* side of heaven. Jesus rose with all power so you could have all power. And when you accept Him as Lord and Savior, it's just the beginning of the best that is yet to come for you. When you believe, act on it. The just shall *live* by faith. 'Live'—an action word. Don't just be satisfied with believing. Act on what you believe. Be in faith. Faith is action. Faith causes things to happen."

Pastor Landris concluded, then opened the doors of the church. People came for salvation, to be restored, to receive the baptism of the Holy Spirit, and for church membership.

Pastor Landris looked at all those lined in front of him and saw his brother, who had just said to him that morning as they'd entered the church, "What must I do to be saved? I mean, really saved. What can I do to have a better life than what I'm experiencing now? You've changed so much, George. I believe in God. But what do I do to have peace and joy? What do I have to do . . . to have what you have?" Thomas had no idea that God had already prepared George with this sermon for today, before George even had a clue why.

Thomas had tears streaming down his face as he looked toward heaven. And George gave thanks to God for all those who were making one of the best decisions of their lives.

Little did any of them know, including Pastor Landris, that that sermon on that Sunday would be the last one that Pastor George E. Landris would preach at that church.

CHAPTER 33

For he that cometh to God must believe that he is.

(Hebrews 11:6 (b))

Landris had arranged for he and Tiffany to arrive at Oheka Castle that Thursday night, with the other key wedding members arriving on Friday morning. The ceremony was scheduled for Saturday, September 8, 2001, at four o'clock in the afternoon. Two limousines had been reserved all day Friday for the various arrivals throughout the day. Johnnie Mae, Princess Rose, and Mrs. Gates flew into LaGuardia Airport on the morning flight together and boarded one of the limousines headed east to Long Island.

"We're almost there," Johnnie Mae said, recognizing where they were from the signs as they prepared to exit the freeway.

"Jericho Turnpike," Mrs. Gates said, reading the sign. "How ironic you would be getting married, and there's your father's name, Jericho, just as we're approaching the castle, no less." She shook her head. "God is something else, ain't He?" She smiled.

Oheka was a French chateau–style castle, different in design from Biltmore Castle. Johnnie Mae couldn't help but reflect on the history behind all of this, as well as the many black folks who had made contributions to things and places that had never been recorded—only whispers linger from past ancestors, who plead, *Find a way and tell our stories.*

"This is enormous," Mrs. Gates said, scooting out of the limousine before the driver had a chance to assist her. Tiffany greeted them at the entrance and got them all situated.

Johnnie Mae marveled as she looked around inside. She reverently touched the handcrafted wrought-iron railing of the grand staircase. Her mother and daughter walked up one side as she herself walked up the other, only to meet them at the top of the stairs in the middle.

"It took two years for them to refinish this staircase," Tiffany said, noticing Johnnie Mae's attention to the elaborate features.

"Imagine back during the time this was first done how long it probably took them just to create it. Or the person who did such intricate, detailed work," Johnnie Mae said.

Tiffany smiled and shook her head. "This whole place is mind boggling: the formal gardens, reflecting pools, spraying fountains. Oh, and the rooms . . . I can't wait until you see yours! We have escorts posted all around to guide you in locating various places, although I took the liberty of creating a map of the places affecting us during our stay."

"This is so nice," Mrs. Gates said. "How many rooms does this place have?"

"I believe 126 originally," Tiffany said, walking ahead of them but turning around to answer. "Of course, I'm not the expert." She smiled. "And the weather appears to be cooperating this weekend, so the wedding will be held outdoors in the Castle's Garden."

When they reached their "room," which really was like an apartment unto itself, Johnnie Mae was more than pleased. Princess Rose ran inside, pulling her grandmother, who stumbled a few times keeping pace. "This takes my breath away," Johnnie Mae said.

"Pastor Landris said you wished to share a room with your mother, so I'm glad this is to your liking. If you need anything, here is the number to my room, and of course my cell phone number, as I will be in and out finalizing things before tomorrow's ceremony."

Johnnie Mae and Mrs. Gates unpacked and made plans to venture around the grounds. Landris stopped by to be sure everything was all right and to their satisfaction.

"Landris, this is wonderful!" Johnnie Mae said.

He smiled. "Well, it's only going to get better. Tiffany said she only needs you and your attendants later on for rehearsal. Since the wedding is so small, it won't take long."

"Small?" Johnnie Mae said. "You call flying in 176 guests and 14 wedding-party participants small?" She laughed.

"The actual wedding party is small," he said. "So it will be mainly you and I getting our parts right. My group has already rehearsed, so we're all ready. Now it's your group's turn."

She smiled. "I'm sure we'll do just fine."

He made funny moves with his mouth. Like someone wanting to smile but fighting not to let it happen.

"What?" Johnnie Mae asked.

"What? What?" Landris grinned.

"You're up to something, aren't you?" Johnnie Mae stepped up closer to him.

"Who, me?" He laughed, then stepped back. "Well, I need to take care of a few more things. I suppose I'll see you after your rehearsal in about two hours. We're all meeting for a rehearsal dinner. And the next time I see you following that, you'll be taking steps toward finally becoming my . . . wife." He couldn't help but smile after those words left his mouth.

She smiled, too. "Yeah. Your . . . wife."

CHAPTER 34

And that he is a rewarder of them that diligently seek him.

(Hebrews 11:6 (c))

The guests were seated in chairs in the Castle's Garden: a perfect afternoon for a wedding, inside or out. Johnnie Mae arrived in a horse-drawn carriage along with Princess Rose and her mother. In the front, centered on the lawn, a golden arch overflowed with a snowfall of white roses. The presiding minister stood underneath it. Thomas and the ring bearer, equally decked out in a three-piece, vested silver tux, matching shoes, and matching bow tie, stood before the audience. But there was no sign of Landris anywhere.

The processional began. Johnnie Mae's mother came in from the left side instead of down the middle aisle, as everyone was expecting. Still no sign of Landris. Princess Rose walked in, dropping red and white rose petals from a white wicker basket. No Landris. The wedding march began to play, the audience stood, and after a minute Johnnie Mae made her way to the left outer edge, where all could see her. She then stood motionless. People glanced over to see if Pastor Landris had shown up yet. Still no groom in sight.

Everyone looked at Johnnie Mae. How could they not? She was adorned in what appeared to be a dress made of diamonds, although it was of only embroidered jewels. The thin straps made of crystals sparkled while suspending the gown from her shoulders to a shimmering, V-shaped, nineteenth century–style bodice adorned with thousands of hand-sewn crystals. Silver lace shimmered up, over, and down, swirling to a bottom that flared out—standing as if by its own accord. She looked like royalty. Her gown, from the Paola D'Onofrio collection, was purchased at Roma Sposa in Birmingham, Michigan. An iridescent tulle veil flowed from the back of her hair like a translucent blanket and trailed behind her. No other jewelry adorned her anywhere. There was no need. She wore long gloves, a perfect match to the material of her dress, which although white, hinted of a serene blue.

A song began to play: Earth, Wind & Fire's "That's the Way of the World."

Hearts of fire/

Landris suddenly appeared on the right-hand side. Everyone looked his way.

creates love desire.

Landris was dressed in a white tuxedo with a full-length jacket with a center vent and no lapels, a satin stand-up collar, self-flapped pockets, seven buttons lining the front, and white double-pleated pants—an Andrew Fezza White Apollo. He and Johnnie Mae became like two powerful magnets being drawn by a mutual force toward each other.

The song continued, *Take you high and higher/to the world you belong./Hearts of fire/creates love desire./High and higher/to your place on the throne.*

They reached the center at the same time. Landris presented her with a bouquet that included her favorite, Moroccan roses. They locked into one another's gaze.

We've come together on this special day/, the song continued, *To sing our message loud and clear./Looking back, we've touched on sorrowful days./Future pass, they disappear.*

Landris pressed his lips tightly together before smiling at Johnnie Mae.

You will find/peace of mind./If you look way down,/in your heart and soul./Don't hesitate,/'cause the world seems cold.

Stay young at heart, Landris mouthed the words along with the song. They both smiled, neither seeming to desire even a glance away from the other.

'Cause you're never/never/never/never/old at heart./That's the way/of the world./Plant your flower/and you grow a pearl.

Johnnie Mae quickly wiped away a tear that threatened to fall.

Landris took her gloved hand, brought it up to his mouth, kissed it, and shook his head as he continued to grin. The song trailed off until there was only silence.

They turned to the minister; the audience took their seats. The minister began by praying.

There were no *Who gives this woman?* or other traditional things that people may have expected.

Pastor Landris recited to Johnnie Mae an excerpt from Song of Solomon, Chapter 4: " 'Behold, thou art fair, my love.' " His deep voice stopped, and he smiled and pressed his lips together at the words *my love*. " 'Behold thou art fair; thou hast doves' eyes within thy locks: thy hair is a flock of goats, that appear from mount Gilead. Thy teeth are like a flock of sheep that are even shorn, which came up from the washing; whereof every one bear twins, and none is barren among them. Thy lips are like a thread of scarlet, and thy speech is comely: thy temples are like a piece of a pomegranate within thy locks. Thy neck is like the tower of David builded for an armory, whereon there hang a thousand bucklers, all shields of mighty men. Thou art all fair, my love; there is no spot in thee.' "

Johnnie Mae smiled, then quoted from Song of Solomon, Chapter 2: " 'I am the rose of Sharon, and the lily of the valleys. As the lily among thorns, so is my love among the daughters. As the apple tree among the trees of the wood, so is my beloved among the sons. I sat down under his shadow with great delight, and his fruit was sweet to my taste. He brought me to the banqueting house . . .' " she turned and looked warmly back at the castle, " '. . . and his banner over me was love. Stay me with flagons, comfort me with apples: for I am lovesick.' "

She skipped down to verses 10–16. " 'My beloved spake, and said unto me, Rise up, my love' "—she smiled, then continued— " 'my fair one, and come away. For, lo, the winter is past, the rain is over and gone. The flowers appear on the earth; the time of the singing of birds is come, and the voice of the turtledove is heard in our land. The fig tree putteth forth her green figs, and the vines with the tender grape give me a good smell. Arise, my love, my fair one, and come away. O my dove, that art in the clefts of the rock, in the secret places of the stairs, let me see thy countenance, let me hear thy voice; for sweet is thy voice, and thy countenance is comely. Take us the foxes, the little foxes, that spoil the vines: for our vines have tender grapes.' " She accidentally smacked her lips after the word 'grapes.' " 'My beloved is mine, and I am his: he feeded among the lilies.' " She grinned, then turned back to face the minister.

The minister proceeded with the vows of commitment and love.

As they exchanged rings, Johnnie Mae spoke first as she quoted Song of Solomon 7:10, " 'I am my beloved's, and his desire is toward me.' "

Landris followed by quoting Song of Solomon 7:11–12. " 'Come, my beloved, let us go forth into the field; let us lodge in the villages. Let us get up early to the vineyards; let us see if the vine flourish, whether the tender grape appear, and the pomegranates bud forth: there will I give thee . . .' " he paused and grinned, then finished, " '. . . my loves.' "

"For as much as Johnnie Mae Gates Taylor and George Edward Landris have consented together in holy wedlock, and have witnessed the same before God and this company, pledged to each other and have declared the same by giving and receiving a ring—by the power vested in me, I pronounce that they are husband and wife in the name of God the Father, God the Son, and God the Holy Spirit. Amen."

"Amen!" the audience said with enthusiasm and in unison.

The presiding minister smiled. "I am pleased to present to you, for the first time, Mr. and Mrs. George Edward Landris." He turned to Landris. "Pastor Landris, you may kiss your brand new wife."

Landris smiled and laid a kiss on Johnnie Mae that those in attendance would be talking about for weeks to come.

As the newly married couple strolled down the center aisle together for the first time as husband and wife, their guests took the lids off the small, velvet boxes they'd been given upon entering, as they'd been instructed to do after the ceremony. A legion of soft, lovely petals of various colors and sizes ascended over and upward—crisscrossing at times before disappearing completely.

Butterflies—a symbol of transformation and resurrection. Butterflies—a divinely special blessing for a divinely special day.

CHAPTER 35

Marriage is honorable in all, and the bed undefiled.

(Hebrews 13:4)

The reception, made for a king and queen, was held in the banquet room with several beautiful, crystal chandeliers more than adequately illuminating the room. Each table was graced with a tall vase packed with single-colored roses (red, yellow, pink, and white) and candle arrangements specifically complementing that table's assigned color scheme.

The four-foot-tall wedding cake appeared to overflow with marzipan flowers down its side and onto the table like a cascading fountain running over. The groom's cake, topped with a golden crown and gold ribbons and white on the outside, which really set off the gold color, was the traditional chocolate inside.

The reception was a full-course, sit-down dinner. Hors d'oeuvres included fresh crab cakes with Cajun remoulade, smoked salmon mousse, shrimp cocktail, and cheese quesadilla with sun-dried tomatoes. They had chosen the Gatsby Style Menu, which offered stations from which the guests could choose—the salad station; the carving station with marinated flank steak or roasted turkey with cranberry compote; and the chicken station with chicken Francaise, chicken Marsala, wild rice, and mixed vegetables.

Honey and Sister, longtime friends of Johnnie Mae's, cornered her early on at the reception to share their congratulatory wishes.

"J. M., this was something! I promise you it felt like I was dreaming," Sister said.

"Well, if I'm dreaming, I sure don't want to wake up. I am so proud for you!" Honey said as she hugged Johnnie Mae just a tad too tight.

"Thank you both for coming. I'm really glad you were able to be here," Johnnie Mae said, giving them another quick hug.

"I know some people who were trying to buy their way into this wedding," Honey said. "But seriously, everything has been fantastic. There aren't words to tell people about this." Honey suddenly stretched her neck to look around Johnnie Mae. "Whoa! Who is that fine brother talking to your husband over *there?*" Honey asked.

Johnnie Mae turned around. "That's Landris' older brother. Thomas."

"Gurl, please tell me that he's not married?" Honey said, grinning.

"He's not. But he is here with someone."

"Well, if they ain't married yet, or at least engaged, then he's still available in my book!" she said. "Excuse me, I think I'm getting a little thirsty. Sister, aren't you feeling a little thirst coming on?" Honey walked toward Thomas, Pastor Landris, some other folks, and the sparkling, bubbling, overflowing beverage fountain.

Sister started laughing. "See, I told you not to invite her." She touched Johnnie Mae on the arm. "But it really was a beautiful ceremony. And I really am happy for you. I hope life gives you all of the desires of your heart."

"Well, you know that's my confession," Johnnie Mae said.

"I won't keep you from your other guests. There's a group waiting to speak to you now. I'll go over there and try to keep Honey from embarrassing us." Sister hugged Johnnie Mae again. "Be happy, okay."

Johnnie Mae nodded. Her brother Christian and his family; her sister Rachel and her five children greeted her with accolades of how wonderful everything had been. But she couldn't help but laugh at Honey. *The girl doesn't give up, that's for sure,* she thought.

* * *

A few hours later, Landris and Johnnie Mae went upstairs to the honeymoon suite he'd reserved specifically for their first night together.

"I got you a gift," Johnnie Mae said, teasing him with the box she held out.

"You got me something?"

"Yes." She was beaming. "You wouldn't let me do anything for the wedding, which, by the way, was the most beautiful and spiritual thing I've ever experienced." She placed the box gently in the palm of his hand.

He smiled, then looked her up and down as though she were wrapped with a ribbon. Opening the box, he was a little shocked by its contents: a gold Rolex™ watch with 47 round-cut diamonds encircling the outside of a hunter green, oyster perpetual face.

He put it on. "My goodness, this is striking!" He then walked over to the sofa table, retrieved a large box beautifully wrapped, and handed it to her. "And this, my love, is for you."

"Landris, you've already done too much."

He touched her lips to quiet her, and gestured for her to just open it, which she promptly did. Inside was a royal purple-with-gold, satiny-silk, floor-length robe. He took it from her hands and held it. "In the old days," he said, "when people entered into a covenant . . . you know, an agreement between two or more people . . ."

"Like a marriage?" she said, grinning while trying to contain her giddiness.

He grinned back. "Yeah, like a marriage. Well, when they entered into a covenant, they would exchange weapons to signify that all their strength, power, and war capabilities were now available to the covenant partner. Like our exchanging of the rings. Then there would be exchanging of coats or garments where the more powerful partner in the agreement . . ."

"I suppose that would be you right now?" Johnnie Mae asked still smiling as she listened to him unzip her wedding dress, then free the crystal straps from her shoulders.

He had her turn away from him as he helped her slip her arm

in one sleeve of the robe, then the other before allowing her wedding dress to fall to the floor. As he turned her back toward him, keeping his eyes on her eyes, he pulled the robe together— left, right—and tied the sash with love and care. "As I was saying . . . where the one partner would make a vow to the other, basically stating that 'all that I own, everything that belongs to me, now belongs to you.' Let's see now, we've exchanged names, whereby you have the authority to use my name as though it were me. We've shared the covenant meal showing deliverance. I suppose the only part of the covenant process that hasn't been addressed is the shedding of blood, so to speak." He looked at her.

She moved in closer to him. "Now that we're finally married, consummating this union is not only encouraged but perfectly allowed. We'll have to improvise on that shedding of blood part." She smiled mischievously. "However, there is that covenant Jesus made for us with His blood."

He nodded, went to turn on the stereo, and released a special tune into the air. His selection: "Love's Holiday," to set the tone for the beginning of their first night as one.

"You do know that I love Earth, Wind & Fire's music," Johnnie Mae said.

"Yeah. I know." He began to dance with her.

Would you mind/if I touch/if I kiss/if I held you tight in the morning light, Earth, Wind & Fire sang. *Would you mind/if I said how I felt tenderly tonight, again 'cause."*

Landris twirled her around. *I never ever felt this way in my heart before./Love has a holiday in my heart tonight.* He sang along with the song.

Would you mind/if I looked into your eyes till I'm hypnotized, Landris and Earth, Wind & Fire continued singing. He stopped and gazed deeply into Johnnie Mae's eyes as the song went on.

Would you mind/if I make love to you till I'm satisfied again 'cause . . . I never ever felt this way in my heart before./Love has a holiday in my heart tonight.

He kissed her: a long-awaited, but-now-finally-my-wife kind of kiss.

The next song, "Reasons," by Earth, Wind & Fire, began to

play, although neither one of them, at that point, was completely listening anymore.

"Marriage is such a spiritual, heavenly ordained thing," Johnnie Mae said to her husband.

"Especially," Landris whispered in her ear, "when it's with the one you truly love."

Philip Bailey hit his signature part of "Reasons." After that, "Praise Is What I Do" by Shekinah Glory Ministry came on just as Landris had programmed it to do.

Landris scooped Johnnie Mae up and into his arms, carried her into the bedroom, and *that* was all she wrote.

CHAPTER 36

Now faith is the substance of things hoped for.

(Hebrews 11:1)

Lena and Maurice were packed and ready for their trip to New York City. Maurice was scheduled to meet with the television producer at 8 o'clock, Monday night. Lena's scheduled appointment was confirmed for Tuesday morning, 7:30 A.M. on September 11.

Memory was staying at Theresa's, with Bishop Jordan and Beatrice available should Theresa need them for anything.

"Don't worry, you guys. I'm not feeling any pain," Theresa said as she hugged them while they waited inside the airport. "So go, take care of your business, and get on back. The baby and I will wait on your return before we start anything." She looked down at her stomach. "You hear that, baby?"

"And you didn't need to be doing all this walking," Lena said. "We told you it wasn't necessary for you to see us off. That's the very thing most women do when they *want* to go into labor."

"What's that—go to the airport?" Theresa teased.

"No, walk. Walking can set off labor. Sapphire, will you get her home and make her behave until we get back? I declare, I'm on pins and needles here. I don't know why I let you talk me into this ridiculous trip in the first place," Lena said.

"Maurice, take care of Mama. I think she starts babbling like this when she gets nervous." Theresa gave him a quick peck on the cheek and half-a-hug.

"Is that all a brotha gets? A peck on the cheek and a hug?" He smiled at Theresa.

Theresa looked down at her stomach. "Yeah, that's all a brotha's going to get."

A call for a flight to board came over the intercom. "Well, that's us," Maurice said, helping Lena up.

"Now, Mama, please don't go up there worrying about me. I'm feeling fine. It will probably be another two weeks before this baby decides to make its entrance."

"Well, you call us the first sign of a twinge of pain, and we'll hop on the next plane back here: finished or not," Lena said. "Maurice, you got your cell phone, right?"

Theresa hugged Maurice again and whispered in his ear, "Don't let her come back before she has seen that lawyer. This could turn out to be something really good for her."

Theresa and Sapphire watched as they disappeared into the tunnel. Not fifteen minutes later, they watched the gray and red metal bird as it took flight.

"Now," Theresa said to Sapphire. "Tell me all about the wedding."

"Are you sure you want to hear this?"

"No, I'm not sure. But I'm supposed to be past all of this. Right? And honestly, I'm curious about how things went." They walked slowly back to the parking deck.

"I will say this: That was some wedding! Simple, yet royally elegant. Real spiritual."

"So, what do you think of Thomas?" Theresa glanced at Sapphire's face just in case she was planning to conceal anything feelings-wise from her about him.

Sapphire smiled. "He seems nice enough. I get the impression he may have done something that has him in a slight bind. But he's not sharing details about it with me."

"What do you think it might be?"

"I don't know, but a few things he's said to me makes me believe it has to do with some money he might owe to Pastor

Landris. Although it sounds like he's gotten some of it straight-ened out, he's squirreling around to fix the rest." She stopped and looked at Theresa. "Are you sure you're going to make it? You're not having pains, are you?"

Theresa continued walking. "I'm good. But if you'd like to go get the car and meet me at either the baggage-claim pickup or the enplane drop-off area, I promise I won't give you any argu-ment about it."

Sapphire thought that was a good idea. Theresa waited while she got the car and picked her up outside the baggage-claim door area.

"What's up with . . . ?" Sapphire thought a second. "Is she your grandmother?"

"Memory? Yeah, she's my grandmother. But all of us just call her Memory. She's not crazy about that name. She'd prefer being called Elaine or Sugar, but that's not going to happen." Theresa reclined her seat back.

"Are you sure you're feeling okay?"

"Yeah. I'm just a bit uncomfortable."

"And your baby is due tomorrow? September eleventh?"

"Yes."

"And you were the one who insisted that both Maurice and Lena go out of town *now?*"

Theresa glanced over at Sapphire as she changed lanes to get onto the freeway ramp. "I'm not going into labor tomorrow, all right."

"What about now? This evening?"

Theresa laughed. "I'm not in labor now."

"Just checking. Because it makes no sense for me to carry you home when you're in labor, and I could just run you on by the hospital and drop you off like a piece of check-in luggage at the curb." She turned off her blinkers.

"I told you, I'm just feeling a little uncomfortable. But then, you would too if you had gained 35 pounds—"

"Thirty-five pounds!"

"Must you say it like that?"

"On another note: You left Memory at your house alone?" Sapphire asked.

"Yeah. There's not much for her to get into." Theresa thought about the necklace. It was in a safe deposit box at the bank. She had set it up in her and Lena's name. Lena still hadn't contacted the people about it. Theresa couldn't understand that either. *A million dollars and she's not even curious to see if it's the necklace they're looking for or not.*

"Earth to Theresa," Sapphire was singing.

"What?"

"You must have been really into some deep thoughts. I was asking how much longer is Memory staying?"

"Oh. She's going home the day after tomorrow. She agreed to hang around until Lena and Maurice got back. I think she's about as ready to leave as we are for her to go."

"Is she that bad?"

"Not that bad. Not lately anyway. She stopped calling us 'dearie' so much. That was grating my last nerve! And she's not as insulting as she was when she first showed up. I think going to church those few times we got her to go has made a dent in her attitude. She seemed bitter when she first arrived—unforgiving and vengeful."

"I'll tell you, if anyone has a right to be bitter, it's Lena," Sapphire said, taking the exit to Theresa's house.

Sapphire stopped in the driveway and Theresa struggled to roll out. "Maurice finally got those pictures developed we took at the gala. You want to come in and see them?"

"Sure," Sapphire said, turning off the engine and grabbing her purse as she got out.

Memory was watching TV in the den. "You're back so soon," Memory said. "They got off okay?"

"Without a hitch," Theresa said. "This is my friend Sapphire. Sapphire, this is Memory Robertson."

Sapphire extended her hand to Memory. "Pleased to make your acquaintance."

Memory shook her hand. "I see you have those things like your pastor. How on earth do you keep your hair clean?" she asked.

Sapphire smiled. "The same way you do. I wash it."

Memory took a closer look. "Do you have to tangle it back up when you finish?"

Sapphire smiled. "No. It's just like polyester: wash and wear."

"Fascinating."

Theresa handed Sapphire the pack of photos. "I'll get us something to drink."

"Have a seat. I'll get it for you," Memory said. "What would you like, Sapphire?"

"Water, please."

"Water? Well, that's a first around here."

"What? Water is not only good for you, but essential to your body and its operation both inside and out," Sapphire said.

"I never said it wasn't good for you. It's just you're the first person I've come across who, when offered a free beverage, chose something they could get easily out of the faucet for virtually nothing." Memory turned to Theresa. "Orange juice for you, missy?"

Theresa smiled and nodded. "Vitamin C for the baby and me."

"Wow, she is something," Sapphire said when Memory was out of hearing range.

"Oh, and she's being *nice* these days."

Sapphire sat down next to Theresa. "I see what you meant about her," she whispered. They giggled. Sapphire started shuffling through the different photos. "Oh, this is a good picture of Maurice." She handed Theresa the picture.

"Yeah, he's quite debonair-looking."

Memory came in and handed each her glass of beverage. "What you got?" Memory asked, peeping at a picture. Memory stopped in her tracks with alarm and tension, but, just as quickly, recouped. "That's a nice picture of you and Maurice, Theresa." Memory took it to get a better look. She smiled after staring at it for a minute and handed it back. *The necklace. Theresa is wearing the necklace: the alexandrite necklace! It is in Theresa's possession.* Memory's grin broadened. "Can I get you ladies anything else?" She looked from one to the other.

They shook their heads. "Then, I think I'll retire to my room. I need to be sure I've packed everything so I'll be ready to leave day after tomorrow."

"So, you're not staying for the baby's arrival?" Sapphire asked.

"No, babies were never my thing. Besides, it could be another two weeks before Theresa has the baby. And I need to be moving on." She smiled again. "Well, 'night you two. Or three, as the case may be."

Memory went to her room. *Theresa has the necklace. Now all I need to do is figure out how to get it back before tomorrow. Where could it be?* She grinned to herself. *Why, of course!* She made a phone call to someone in Atlanta.

"I need you to do something for me."

"What is it this time?" the man on the other end asked.

"I need a paper leaving all my worldly goods, a living will, or something like that," Memory said.

"Sugar, what exactly are you up to?" Her acquaintance called her Sugar, as he always did. "Tell me what you're trying to do here."

Memory explained what she was ultimately trying to accomplish.

"Then, why didn't you just say that? When do you need it?"

"Tonight if possible."

"Not possible."

Memory sighed. "First thing in the morning, then? I have to have it in the morning at the latest. I don't have much time."

"In the morning is possible. Do you want me to bring it over to where you're staying?"

"No." Then Memory thought a second. "On second thought, that would be perfect. Having my *lawyer* bring the papers here would be just perfect. And make it early. Say . . . sometime around 7 o'clock. And don't slip up and call me Sugar, either. It's Elaine Robertson. Ms. Robertson to you, in fact."

Memory gave him the address again in case he'd forgotten it, hung up, and hurried to pack. "Thank you, God," she said. "Things are starting to look like they're finally going my way."

CHAPTER 37

The waters wear the stones.

(Job 14:19 (a))

"Memory, someone is here to see you," Theresa yelled upstairs. She rubbed her back. It had been bothering her most of the night. "She'll be with you in a moment."

"Thank you," the middle-aged man said.

"Yes?" Memory said when she came to the door.

"I'm from Phelps and Phelps. You spoke with me the other day over the phone about some papers you needed."

"Why, yes. Come in. Come in." Memory opened the door, allowing him to walk past her. "So, are you Phelps or Phelps?"

He laughed. "I'm the junior Phelps. Christopher Phelps the second."

"Well I know you're a busy man, so I won't keep you," Memory said, standing near the now closed door.

He handed her an envelope. "I believe this is as you requested. If you'll look it over and be certain, I'll be on my way."

Memory pulled the information out of the envelope and looked over the four pages. "Perfect, Mr. Phelps. I'm not a woman of great means, but I sure appreciate you handling this for me on such short notice."

"Not a problem. Now, would you prefer to pay for that with cash or a check?"

Memory looked at him strangely. "I beg your pardon?"

"I was wondering if you wanted to settle this bill by cash or check?" He smiled.

"What? You can't bill my home address in Detroit?" she tried to say evenly through clenched teeth.

"Oh no ma'am. But we do take credit cards." He offered her an even bigger smile. "Whatever is convenient for the client."

"So, how much is my bill?"

"Fifty dollars. And rest assured, we've already applied our senior citizen rate and a special discount." He cocked his head to the side; attempting to appear sincere.

She laid the envelope on the table. "I suppose cash, then, since I don't have my checkbook in town with me." She went upstairs and scrambled up some cash.

"Now, are you positive you can't bill me? I'm leaving tomorrow, and I really hate giving away my cash so close to a trip."

"Well, now, if it's better for you, I'll be glad to take the package back to my office, and you can mail me the payment when you get home. Detroit, you say? Then I can mail this paperwork to you in Detroit afterward."

She handed him the money. "No, this is something important I need to handle while I'm in the city."

After he left, Memory turned to Theresa. "Well, I guess you've figured out I'm up to something."

"No. I just can't believe you got a lawyer to come here so early in the morning."

"He told me he would stop by and bring this on his way to work. I suppose he's an early riser." Memory picked up the envelope. "Theresa, can I talk to you for a minute? Woman to woman."

"Sure," Theresa said. "Can we do it in the kitchen, though? I'm really hungry, and I didn't sleep well at all. That's probably what's got me so cranky."

They went to the kitchen. Theresa fixed herself a piece of toast and cut up some fresh pears and peaches while Memory sat at the table and talked.

"I don't know if you realize this about me, Theresa. But I've not had an easy life. I got pregnant at fourteen. Had a child when I was fifteen years old. Ran off with my first true love at sixteen, only to have him run off on me before I turned seventeen.

My mother took my baby from me and wouldn't allow me to raise her unless I stayed under her roof. She thought I was too young to be off by myself, and she didn't think it was right for me to drag a baby around with no money and no real home to call my own."

"I can appreciate that," Theresa said as she went to take the toast out of the toaster oven.

"Oh, I understand it more now that I'm older. I never knew my biological father. Looking at my white skin and my mother who was quite dark skinned, I have been left to conclude that my father must have been white. Especially since Willie B, the man I grew up believing was my father, was as dark as my mother. She tried convincing me that there was just white in our blood, and that's why I turned out so light. I probably would have bought that story had it not been for that white lady Madear called Mrs. V, who often visited our house. I overheard her one day when she was giving Madear a fancy box with a necklace inside. She specifically told her, 'When you decide to give this to Memory, let her know it's from Grace.' Once, I thought her name might have been Grace. Later, I came to believe she might have been referring to this little town called Grace."

"Why are you telling me this?" Theresa asked as she spread peach jelly on her toast.

Memory smiled. "I'm sure you can't possibly know what it feels like to be ridiculed by the people in your community. To feel like you don't belong anywhere. But I do."

Theresa softened. *Of course I know.*

Memory looked at her face and continued. "I was too white to fit in with the blacks, and too black to fit in with the whites. I looked like a white child, but I wasn't white. And everybody made me feel like it was my fault. It was hard on me." She picked up a banana and peeled it. "I didn't always hate Madear. But that white woman knew something and somehow she wanted me to have something worth having in life. Madear took what she brought for me and kept it. I don't know why she kept it from me. But I do know what I heard. Whether it was something my real father sent me by that woman, I can't say. But I know

Madear refused to let me have it. Maybe she felt it would be a clue to my father."

"Memory, what does this have to do with me or that lawyer who was just here?"

"I don't own much in life, Theresa. But I have become quite close to you and Lena since spending time with the two of you. I don't know how long I have on this earth. But I wanted to be sure I did right by both of you. So I asked the lawyer to fix me up something whereby I could leave what I do have to you and Lena. I know Lena, though. She hasn't totally warmed up to me. She doesn't trust me, and honestly, I can't say I blame her. But I was a different person when Madear died. I was angry, hurt, and confused. That kind of combination can cause anyone to make bad decisions."

Theresa searched Memory's face. *Is she being sincere?*

Memory touched Theresa's hand and handed her the package. "As I said, I don't have much. But I want y'all to have it if something happens to me. I wanted you to know what I was doing. So the lawyer said for me to sign this, and let you or Lena sign it affirming that you understand what's going on."

"Understand what?"

"That I'm leaving my earthly belongings to Lena, and if she's unable to receive it, then to you. You can read that paper; it's not all that long. Then I'll sign it where I'm to sign it, and you can sign it saying that you understand what I'm doing."

"Why do I need to sign it?"

"You don't have to. It's just because I'm assigning things to Lena. And you know if she knew I was trying to do this, she wouldn't go along with it. You saw yourself how hard it was to get her to go to New York." Memory took out a pen, signed her name on the third page of the document. "Read over it. It's in pretty simple terms. Nothing required of you. It just means you're aware that you're the, what's it called? beneficiary? No. Executor? Yeah, the executor. All you have to do is sign the last page. That's it."

Theresa looked it over. It was pretty straightforward. "I sign the last page?"

"Yes," Memory said. "Right on that line there." She pointed to the line on page four.

"Why didn't they put the line on page three where you're signing?"

Memory looked at it again. "Looks like they reached the end of that page. I suppose they could have put it for me to sign on the last page too, but who can say why lawyers do what they do? Here, I'll also sign page four if that makes you more comfortable." She smiled and signed above where Theresa would be signing. "You don't have to sign it. If you don't care about Lena getting what's due to her, I can only say I tried."

Theresa wasn't feeling so well. She rubbed her back, took the pen, and signed her name so she could go lie down.

"Is your back bothering you?" Memory asked. She took the signed paper and hurriedly put it inside the envelope.

"A little."

"Are you having contractions, maybe?"

"Not that I'm aware of." She rubbed her stomach. "My stomach just feels like the baby is balling up in a knot periodically."

Memory came around and placed her hand on Theresa's stomach. She massaged her shoulders seconds later. "Theresa, I hate to tell you, but I think you're in labor, dearie."

Theresa had a pained look on her face. "Please don't say that." She looked at the clock on the wall. The phone rang. She jumped, then quickly answered it.

"Hey, Tee. How are you feeling?" Maurice asked.

She forced a happy face. "Oh, great! Everything's great. How about you guys?"

"We're at the World Trade Center now. Tower One. I just left Lena in the lawyer's office. I'm running a quick errand, since she'll be in there for the next hour or so. In fact, I'm walking down the stairwell to the seventy-eighth-floor elevator that will take me to the lobby even as we speak. I was just checking in on you—"

"Oh!" Theresa yelled before she realized the sound was even about to escape her mouth.

"Tee? What's wrong?"

She breathed a few times until the pain began to subside. "Oh, nothing," she said, still trying to fake a smile.

"Are you having contractions?"

"Who, me? Having contractions while you and Lena are in fabulous New York City, at the World Trade Center no less? Which tower are you in again?" she asked, trying to buy some extra time to breathe.

"Tower One. Theresa, if you're in labor, I need to know. Don't play with me, now."

Just then, her water broke. "Oh my," she said. "Maurice."

"What is it?"

"My water just broke." She looked down, then over at Memory. "I'm going to get off the phone now."

"Theresa, I'm going back to get Lena, and we're catching a plane out of here."

Theresa looked at the clock again. "Maurice, it's almost 8 o'clock. I'm not having hard contractions. It just started. Don't interrupt Mama, because if you do, you know she'll get up and leave, she doesn't care what. Another hour is not going to make much difference. Okay? Besides, there may not be a flight coming this way before the one you already have scheduled. Go, run your errand, and let Mama finish up. Then come back."

"Theresa, are you sure?"

She laughed. "Yes! Yes," she said calmer. "See, I'm feeling better already. Memory's here and my father and Beatrice are not far away. We'll be fine. You just make sure Mama doesn't freak out and that she finishes what she went up there to do. When you arrive here, you'll probably end up still having to wait. Just please, don't mess this up for Mama. It's not much longer now."

"Just don't have the baby until we get there. Okay?"

She laughed. "Okay. Right. Got it!"

"Theresa, about my marriage question—"

"Not now, Maurice." She took short, quick breaths. "Goodbye, Maurice."

"But Tee, I'm serious—"

"Good . . . bye," she said and hung up.

"Memory," Theresa said, making her way out of the kitchen. "Can you take me to the hospital?"

"Oh, I don't drive, dearie." Memory looked around. "Who do you want me to call?"

Theresa went to the telephone and dialed. "Mother, this is Theresa. Do you think you can take me to the hospital? Yes . . . Now . . . I'll see you in a few minutes . . . Thanks. Bye."

Theresa looked at Memory. "They're coming right over."

Memory let out a whistle. "Boy, that was close. Because you know I would have found a way to get you there if I had to."

"Yeah," Theresa said.

"Where's your bag?" Memory asked.

"A packed suitcase is in the closet. But I need to change these clothes."

Memory started for Theresa's bedroom closet. "You change. I'll get your bag."

When Theresa came back downstairs with her purse on her shoulders, she heard a car horn blow. "That's them." She looked and saw Memory's suitcase, too. "Are you not coming with me?"

"No, dearie. I think it's best I not be here while you're at the hospital. The last thing I need is for something to come up missing, and you suspect I had something to do with it." Memory picked up Theresa's bag and her own and set them outside while Theresa locked the door. Memory carried Theresa's bag to the car. She hugged Theresa. "I'll check on you. I'm not planning to leave the city just yet."

"Thanks, Memory."

"No, dearie. Thank *you*." Memory went back, got her suitcase, and started to walk away.

"Would you like me to drop you off somewhere?" Beatrice asked her.

"The bus stop would be nice. I need to pay a visit to the bank."

Memory got in. Beatrice dropped her off at the bus stop on the way to the hospital.

"Tell Lena I really do love her," Memory said when she hugged Theresa after she got out. "Tell her I hope she finds it in her heart someday to forgive me."

"Sure," Theresa said, confused. "When she comes home, why don't you just tell her again yourself?"

"Yeah. We'll see." Mcmory smiled and sat on the bench to wait for her ride: the ride that would hopefully carry her to what and where she'd been trying to get for years.

CHAPTER 38

Every good gift and every perfect gift is from above.

(James 1:17)

Landris and Johnnie Mae had spent two days at Oheka Castle. They were scheduled on a flight from New York City on Wednesday for their honeymoon in Bermuda. Tuesday, September 11, Landris and Johnnie Mae had plans to see more of the city.

"I have a surprise for you," Landris said.

"More? I don't know if I can stand any more."

"Yes. More. Don't block your blessings. We're having a special breakfast on top of the world."

She laughed. "What?"

"Okay, maybe not the world, but you'll be able to see most of New York City from there. I reserved a conference room just for us for breakfast at Windows on the World." He hugged his wife. "It feels so good holding you." He looked down lovingly at her.

"What feels good?" she said, teasing him by leaning a little more into his embrace.

"Holding you like this."

"Then, maybe we should stay here and continue to work on this a little more."

"Nope," he said, grabbing up her purse. "We need to visit some places while we're in the city. Let's get going. I've already paid for it, and I don't like to just waste money."

"Excuse me? Did you happen to see that wedding production you just pulled off?"

"Yes, I did. And that was not a waste of money. That was using what God has blessed me with to enjoy some of the desires of my heart. You know, we are allowed to have life and to enjoy it abundantly whether others believe we are supposed to or not."

"True. And I will be the first to admit, I have absolutely loved every minute of the desires of your heart."

"Woman, you're tempting me to lose that money over there if you don't behave." He started pulling her along. "Come on, let's get going. You also know I hate being late."

"That I do. I feel like I'm forgetting something, though. Or something is missing . . . I don't know."

"We're coming back. If you've forgotten anything, we'll get it before we check out."

They reached the World Trade Center, Tower One, at 8:00 A.M. The express elevator that would normally take them directly to the 106th floor was out of service, so they had to take the elevator to the 78th floor, then change elevators.

"Pastor Landris, Mrs. Landris," Maurice said. "What a surprise seeing you here."

"Maurice, isn't it?" Pastor Landris said, attempting to match his name with his face.

"Yes."

Pastor Landris shook his hand. "So, what are you doing so far from home?"

"Taking care of some business. And I'm also here with Theresa's mother. She had business with a lawyer in this building. I just left her, in fact."

"Well, everybody ain't able." Pastor Landris teased him.

"The lawyer actually picked up the tab for this trip. Lena's supposed to be here about another hour. I'm on my way to a shop a few blocks from here real quick. Taking care of some other business while Lena finishes up. Then it'll be back to Hotlanta."

"Sounds good. Tell Ms. Patterson I said hello. Well, we're off to a romantic breakfast for two at Windows on the World," Landris said. He pulled Johnnie Mae closer after he noticed a strange, nauseous-looking expression suddenly creep over her face.

"Oh, and congratulations," Maurice said, shaking both of their hands. "You two got married this weekend, didn't you?"

"Thank you. Yes, we did," Landris said. Johnnie Mae only nodded and smiled.

"Like you said: Everybody ain't able." Maurice laughed. "Well, I won't hold you. I want to get there and back so Lena won't have to wait any longer than necessary. It shouldn't take me more than twenty minutes. I just got off the phone with Theresa—I believe she may be in labor."

"And you guys are here?" Johnnie Mae asked.

"You know how Theresa can be. She was set on us handling this, and by George we will handle it! Baby due, coming, or not." He smiled and caught the next elevator going down.

Landris and Johnnie Mae went to the elevators. A woman named Beatriz Genoves was a greeter for Windows on the World. Since the lobby's express elevator was out of service, she was greeting patrons on the 78th floor and assisting them to the correct elevator to carry them nonstop to their Windows destination.

Landris and Johnnie Mae stepped into the elevator, not really noticing anyone other than each other. Johnnie Mae's troubled expression was now gone.

CHAPTER 39

Let us hold fast the profession of our faith without wavering.

(Hebrews 10:23)

Beatrice got Theresa to the hospital in fifteen minutes flat. She was definitely in labor. B and Sapphire found Theresa in Labor and Delivery, both friends having arrived in the parking deck at almost the same time.

"How are you feeling?" Sapphire asked.

"The pains are about fifteen minutes apart," Theresa said. She looked over at the monitor she was now attached to. "They're pretty strong when they hit. Thank goodness, they aren't lasting too long." She tightened up for about two minutes.

"Is that one?" B asked, watching the penlike needle of the monitor quickly spike upward and record a straight line on paper that trailed behind it.

Theresa nodded while holding her breath.

"Aren't you supposed to be breathing, panting even, instead of holding your breath?" Sapphire asked.

Theresa let out a long sigh of air. "Yeah. But since my labor coaches are out of town, I suppose you guys will have to remind me."

"Have you told Maurice you're in labor?" B asked.

"Yeah. In fact, I was talking to him when my water broke. He and Mama were finishing up. I figure they'll have plenty of time to get here before the baby arrives."

B turned on the TV. "What would you like to watch?"

Theresa glanced around the room. "I don't care. Put it on whatever you want."

"What time is it?" B asked Sapphire, who was the only one wearing a watch.

Sapphire glanced down at her watch.

"B, there's a big old clock on the wall," Theresa said, pointing in front of them.

"8:45 A.M.," Sapphire said with a smile.

"This is just too early in the morning for me." B curled up in the chair. "Y'all know I am not a morning person."

Two minutes later, Theresa let out a groan.

"Theresa, it's 8:47. Didn't you just have a contraction around 8:40? That's only been seven minutes. You shouldn't be having another one so soon, should you?" Sapphire asked as she searched Theresa's face.

"It wasn't a contraction," Theresa said, massaging her heart. "I just had the weirdest feeling around my heart. Like a sharp pain."

"Could you two keep it down? Some of us are trying to get a little shut-eye around here before the main event commences," B said without even looking up.

"Sapphire," Theresa said, in search of a distraction. "Finish telling me about that Honey woman who was at the wedding. The one you said was trying to talk to Thomas."

"I mean she came over there like I was invisible. I'm talking, girlfriend was bold! Thomas got away so fast; it wasn't even funny. Pastor Landris, his mother, and Deacon Thomas were laughing so hard, Deacon Thomas got choked, and he wasn't even eating."

A few minutes later B looked up at the television. She had muted it earlier so it wouldn't disturb her. "What show is that on the TV?" she asked, rudely interrupting.

"You're the one who turned it on. I thought you had it turned to one of the morning shows. Maybe it's a preview for an up-coming movie," Theresa said.

"That's one of the Twin Towers. I remember from when I visited it years ago," Sapphire said. She retrieved the remote and turned the sound up so they could hear it.

When the sound came on, they saw it was the news. A plane had flown into the World Trade Center, Tower One. The scene was being replayed over and over again.

"Oh no!" Theresa said as she sat straight up. "Turn it up some more! That's really happening, y'all! It's not a movie promo. It's real!"

B sat up and watched the screen better. "It's a plane, all right. I wonder how it managed to get so off-course like that."

"I have to call Maurice!" Theresa was reaching for the phone. "Give me the phone! I've got to call Maurice and Mama!"

"What is it? What's the matter? Is it the baby?" B asked.

"No," Theresa said as she attempted to press the right numbers. "I can't think. I can't think! What's his cell number? B, what's Maurice's cell phone number? I can't think!"

"Calm down," B said, stepping over to her. "Are you in *that* much pain?"

"B, the plane. It hit the tower!" Theresa was crying. The monitor started registering another contraction.

"Theresa, don't get yourself upset, now." Sapphire began brushing her hair back with her hand. Theresa seemed to be really losing control.

"B, please dial Maurice." Theresa pleaded.

"Oh my Lord! Another plane just hit the other tower!" Sapphire said, stopping to watch what was showing on the screen now.

"Theresa, Maurice and your mother are fine," B said calmly. "They're in New York, but I'm sure they're both just fine. They're nowhere near those buildings—"

Theresa looked at B. "Yes they are, B. Mama is meeting the lawyer in Tower One."

"What?" B said. "Well, I'm sure they were already out. Or maybe they hadn't even gotten there yet. I bet you, knowing my brother, they're at the hotel, chilling out—"

"Maurice called me early this morning. They were in the building. Mama wasn't due to be finished until around nine o'clock." Theresa began to massage her stomach. "It's . . ." Theresa pointed to the clock on the wall; it was 9:07 A.M. Theresa began to cry more even though she needed to relax for the contraction.

B called Maurice's cell phone number. Nothing. She tried again. Still nothing. She flopped down in the chair. "No." She shook her head. "Please God, please no. Please don't let them have still been there. Not my brother. Let Maurice and Lena be all right."

"B, you can't fall apart," Sapphire said. "Theresa, y'all have got to pull yourselves together now. Come on, let's pray. That's something we *can* do. Pray. Pray angels be dispatched to assist all those in those buildings. Let's touch and agree. Lord, launch a legion of angels. In Jesus name, angels go forth. Protect them. Watch over them. Keep them safe."

B pulled herself into a ball and continued crying. Theresa had tears flowing, but Sapphire kept talking to her, telling her that she had to believe, then act on that belief.

"What did Pastor Landris preach the other Sunday?" she said, reminding Theresa of the sermon. "Believing is good, but we have to act on what we believe for it to be faith."

"So, I'm supposed to act like all is well?" Theresa said, wiping tears from her eyes.

"What's your alternative right now, Theresa? You have a baby who needs you to keep it together. If you get upset, you could cause your blood pressure to rise. You do that, and you could put the baby and yourself in danger. What we need now is 9-1-1."

"Nine-one-one?" Theresa said. "You want us to call the emergency unit for help? But how can calling 9-1-1 in Atlanta help anybody in New York?"

"9-1-1." Sapphire pulled out a small Bible, flipped the pages, and turned to Psalm 91:1. She began, " 'He that dwelleth in the secret place of the Most High shall abide under the shadow of the Almighty.' " She then turned to Proverbs 9:11 and read, " 'For by me thy days shall be multiplied, and the years of thy life shall be increased.' Now, we need to thank God, because we know that 'Thanksgiving is the voice of faith.' We thank you Lord for hearing us always," Sapphire said, nodding to Theresa and B to join her.

"Thank you, Lord." Theresa wiped at her tears. "Act like the

Word of God is true," Theresa said, nodding back at Sapphire. "Act like the Word of God is true."

Beatrice walked in. "Baby? Why are you crying?" She hugged Theresa. "Your father is outside and wants to know if he can come in and see you." Theresa nodded.

Her father came in. Bearing a contraction, Theresa breathed, focusing on Beatrice, then her father, then Sapphire. B, still curled up in the chair, continued to rock.

"9-1-1: 'He that dwelleth in the secret place of the Most High shall abide under the shadow of the Almighty,' " Theresa said as she panted out short breaths. "9-1-1: 'He that dwelleth in the secret place of the Most High shall abide under the shadow of the Almighty.' 9-1-1: 'For by me thy days shall be multiplied, and the years of thy life shall be increased.' "

When Theresa's contraction passed, Beatrice asked Sapphire to step out with her.

"Do you know if Maurice and Lena were near those buildings?" Beatrice asked.

Sapphire nodded. "They were inside of Tower One, the first one that was hit."

"Has Theresa been able to speak with Maurice yet?"

"No."

"What do you think, Sapphire?" Beatrice asked.

"I think B needs to leave the room right now. She's not handling this well. And frankly, I don't think we need her in there upsetting Theresa like she's doing."

Beatrice nodded. "I agree. I'll see what I can do to get her calmed down. Maybe I'll take her to get something to eat in the cafeteria. Something."

"Mrs. Jordan, we don't need people around who aren't believing and agreeing with us. Theresa doesn't need that. I have her quoting Psalm 91:1 and Proverbs 9:11. We have to put our faith to work, because faith without works is dead. We've had too much Word at church. It's times like these when you put that Word to use. This is where the test comes, but we've already been equipped with the right answers. We're having a test right now and we have to prove it out using the correct answers."

"That's a good word, Sapphire. I'll get B. Either she'll pull it together, or she'll not be in there with Theresa. For now anyway. Sometimes when your right arm offends you, you just have to cut it off in order for the rest of the body not to be lost."

Sapphire hugged Mrs. Jordan. "I'll stay with Theresa."

"I won't be long with B. I sure don't intend to miss the birth of our first grandchild. I know B is hurting. But there is too much at stake right now. She has to be speaking right. Satan is hanging on our every word, waiting for us to talk wrong so he can use our words against us. We don't need B talking about them being lost, hurt, or dead. She needs to speak life or just shut up! And Theresa sure doesn't need to hear her negative talk."

"My sentiments exactly," Sapphire said.

CHAPTER 40

Fight the good fight of faith.

(1 Timothy 6:12)

Beatrice walked back into the room, kissed Theresa, and told her she'd be back shortly.

"Your father needs to go home for a bit. I don't want to tire him out," Beatrice said.

"I'll keep you posted to make sure you're back in time," Sapphire said.

"B?" Beatrice turned to B, who was still crying and in a human ball. Beatrice reached down and helped her to her feet. "Come on, honey. Why don't you come ride with me? We can get some breakfast if you like. We'll come back later."

B looked up at the television again. They were replaying the scenes of the plane going into the first tower, then the second. It still didn't seem real.

"Come on, B. Get your bag. We'll go to my house for a little while, then come back. Okay?"

B nodded as she stood up. "I know I don't need to be here like this. I'm not helping Theresa." She walked over and squeezed Theresa's hand. "We know they're fine. I just know they are." Theresa nodded. Then a strong contraction hit. B watched it register on the monitor. "You okay?" Theresa nodded while taking short breaths. "Take care of my little niece or nephew. Maurice is going to be so proud when he sees that little bundle."

Although the contraction eased, Theresa only nodded again, not wanting to trust her voice in case it revealed her true feelings.

Sapphire hugged B. "I'll keep you posted and let you know in enough time to be back before things get too close, if you're not back by then." Sapphire's cell phone rang.

"I don't think they allow you to have cell phones on in the hospital," B said, recalling a sign she'd read when coming in Theresa's room.

Sapphire answered it. Not many people had her cell number, and with all that was going on, she figured it was probably important. "Hello."

"Sapphire, it's me. Thomas."

"Thomas?" They'd had a nice time together at the wedding. Everybody who'd attended had left for home by Sunday night. She and Thomas had flown back together and had a good long talk on their way home, but hadn't had a chance to touch bases since. From their conversation, he understood that Sapphire was different from most of the women he had dated in his past.

"I'm sorry to bother you, but I had to talk to somebody."

"What's wrong?"

Thomas hesitated. "Maybe nothing. But I've been trying to reach George with no success. They were still in New York and scheduled to leave for Bermuda tomorrow."

"Okay," Sapphire said as she watched the others watching and listening to her while trying to pretend they weren't. She shrugged to let them know she didn't know any more than they were hearing about what was going on.

"George called me around 8:05 this morning." Thomas let out a deep sigh. "He and Johnnie Mae were on their way to this special breakfast he had arranged at Windows on the World. That's located at the very top of Tower One of the World Trade Center."

"And you haven't heard from him since he called you?"

"I've tried calling his cell number but it keeps saying 'the subscriber is unavailable.' I called to his room at Oheka Castle and a recording says all circuits are busy. This isn't looking too good."

"Thomas, don't panic. You're going to have to speak the Word of God now. You can't be speaking wrong. Not at this point. This is too important for you to give place to any wrong thoughts. All is well, okay. Just pray that angels encamp around about them. Believe all is well, then act like what you believe is true."

"That's what George preached the other Sunday. It's something, huh? How he would preach a message that today seems so relevant. Almost like he knew—"

"Thomas, listen to me. Put a watch over your words. Okay? Don't say anything contrary to what you truly desire. Do you understand me? Speak only your desire."

"Yeah, I hear you."

"It's important that you do more than just hear me, Thomas. I'm sure wherever they are, they're praying, believing, and saying what God says: 'A thousand may fall at my side and ten thousand at my right hand, but it shall not come nigh thee.' That's what we have to do: agree with the Word of God. This is where the wind meets the wings. You can hear the Word all day long, but what ends up coming out of your heart? 'Out of the heart, the mouth speaketh.' " Sapphire looked at Theresa first, then B.

They both smiled and nodded. "Listen, Thomas. I've got to go. I don't think we're supposed to have cell phones on in the hospital. I'll give you the phone number here in my friend's room." She looked on the telephone beside Theresa's bed and gave him the number. "If you hear anything, call me. If I don't answer, call the hospital to see if Theresa Jordan has been moved to another room with a different phone number. I plan to be here awhile. You know what? Just leave a message on my home answering machine. I'll check it periodically. That will probably be the best way."

"Thanks, Sapphire."

"Thomas, get a scripture to stand on. Check Psalm 91, the whole chapter in fact."

He laughed. "Between you and George, I don't know if I stand a chance of slipping back to my old self. By now, I would have fallen apart. You know, I prayed many years ago for God to save my sister. She was to speak at a church. Talking about Jesus. The 'Christians' there literally drove her out of the church. 'They weren't allowing no 12-year-old and female at that, to *preach* to them about Jesus.' She ran out. Crying. Upset. A speeding car that lost control and ended up in the church's parking lot struck her. When she died from that, these same folks said, 'That was God's justice, and what happened was God's way of setting things straight.' Now, it's like it's happening all over again."

"That's why it's important you only speak what you truly desire to come to pass. Thomas, you have to fight the good fight of faith. Not the bad fight where you lose, or get beat up, or beat down. But the good fight. The fight of faith where you win!"

Sapphire hung up. All eyes were now focused on her, eager for all the details.

"It seems Pastor Landris and Johnnie Mae were in Tower One around the time the plane hit. They were at a restaurant called Windows on the World. Pastor Landris phoned Thomas when they were on their way up. Now Thomas can't get in touch with him."

"Lord!" Beatrice said. "The devil might be busy, but my God is busier! Angels, we loose you right now in the name of Jesus. Go!"

Sapphire looked at Theresa with a reassuring smile. "It's already all right." She gently brushed down her friend's hair again with her hand. "It's all right. Right now."

CHAPTER 41

But speaking the truth in love.

(Ephesians 4:15)

Mrs. Gates and Princess Rose had flown back on the same flight as Marie, Donald, and all of their children. Mrs. Gates had gotten upset when Marie insisted that Princess Rose should stay with her until Johnnie Mae came back from her honeymoon.

"You don't think I'm capable of taking care of my own grandchild?" Mrs. Gates had said when they were riding from the airport.

"Mama, that's not what I'm implying at all."

"Well, did Johnnie Mae tell you not to trust me with her child?"

Marie sighed. "Mama, Johnnie Mae hasn't said anything to me about this. She's concerned about you just like the rest of us. But I thought you just might be tired from the trip. I called myself giving you a break. That's all. I didn't know you'd get upset."

"Well, I'm perfectly capable of taking care of a child! I raised every one of y'all and some of your children if you really want to go there."

"Mama, please. Let's *not* go there. I'm tired. I don't want to fight you," Marie said.

"Then it's settled. Princess Rose goes to my house with me."

"Mama—"

"Unless Johnnie Mae specifically told you not to let me keep her, I see no reason for her not to stay with me as she's always done."

Marie looked at Princess Rose, whose head was going back and forth between the two of them as though she were watching a rally in a tennis match.

"Fine, Mama. Princess Rose can go home with you. Are you satisfied?"

"Yea!" Princess Rose clapped and cheered.

Marie looked at Princess Rose and at her mother, then laughed. She shook her head. "Only, if you need someone to go to the store or something, let me know." She smiled. "Okay?"

"Fair enough. If that will make you feel better."

So Princess Rose was at her grandmother's house when the planes hit in New York. The last thing Mrs. Gates was worried about was Johnnie Mae's being in danger. She had no idea Johnnie Mae and Landris had gone to Windows on the World for breakfast that morning. She knew they were leaving for their honeymoon on Wednesday.

Mrs. Gates would later replay in her mind that early morning phone call she'd received from Johnnie Mae on Tuesday, September 11.

"Mama, how are you and Princess Rose?" Johnnie Mae had said.

"I'm fine. She's fine. Still sleeping. I suppose all the excitement these past few days plum tuckered her out. But it's early yet." Mrs. Gates looked at the clock. "In fact, what are you doing up calling so early? I'd think you'd be sleeping in late yourself."

"Landris planned us a special breakfast on top of the world, but I'll tell you about it. Besides, it's later here; we're an hour ahead of you. Mama, I need to ask a favor of you."

Mrs. Gates looked at the receiver. "Is everything all right? You sound a little funny. Rushed."

"Everything's fine, Mama. I just need to ask you to do something really important for me. I don't have a lot of time, okay? But I really need this."

"Sure," Mrs. Gates said, hearing the urgency in her voice. "Tell me what you need."

* * *

Memory's friend, Christopher Harris, came and picked her up from the bus stop just as they had planned the night before.

"Well, did you get it?" he asked.

"Yes, I got it. And what do you mean charging me $50, 'Christopher Phelps the second, of Phelps and Phelps'?" Memory looked at the paper with Theresa's signature, pulled out a key, looked at it, and smiled.

"I wanted to make it look authentic. What lawyer do you know who will do work and not look to be paid immediately, if not before?"

"Yeah, but you could have said you'd bill me," Memory said, putting the paper carefully back inside the envelope. "That would have been just as convincing."

Christopher Harris looked at Memory and laughed. "Honestly, you don't look like someone I would trust to bill and get paid my money. Besides, it worked, didn't it?"

"Yeah. Now give me back my money." She held out her hand.

"Nope. I've earned that $50. And you never pay me like you say you're going to."

"Keep it then. I'll take it from your cut. So, what do we do next?" Memory asked.

"We go to my place. I add a few choice sentences to that paper your dear, trusting granddaughter signed. You go to her bank. The way you snooped through things without them suspecting anything, finding out Theresa had just acquired a safe deposit box and getting the key to it, was something, Sugar. You'll give the note I'm doctoring up to the person at the bank who authorizes access to the safe deposit boxes and show them you have the key. I hope you can be convincing enough to finish what you came here in the first place to do . . . before you started getting all sentimental with your family, that is. Then we vanish without a trace before anyone even discovers the necklace is missing."

Memory stared out of the window. This *had* been her idea to begin with. She was close to getting back what was rightfully hers. But she couldn't help thinking about the bonding time she had shared with Lena and Theresa—her real family. The way they had treated her, even though they had every right to turn her away. Lena was out of town now, counting on her to take care of the child she had almost given her body to be burned for. Theresa was about to bring Memory's first great-grandchild into the world: a little girl. Memory knew it was a girl. *How did I get so caught up?* she thought. *God, help me.*

"What are you thinking about over there, Sugar?" Christopher asked as he drove down the street.

She looked at him and smiled. "Oh, nothing in particular."

"Well, in just a little while, you can daydream all you want. You'll have enough money to do whatever your heart desires. And everything will be right with the world."

"Yeah," she said. "Everything will be right with the world."

CHAPTER 42

For ever, O Lord, thy word is settled in heaven.

(Psalm 119:89)

"Well, you know the Lord gives and the Lord hath taken away," a man with a balding spot in the top of his head idly said as he stood in the vestibule of the church.

"That's not true," a young woman said in reply to his statement.

He looked her up and down. "What's not true?"

She looked at him. "It's not true that the Lord gives and the Lord takes away."

"The Bible says so."

She walked over to him. "It is true this statement is recorded in the Bible. It is true that Job said it. It's true that Job believed it when he said it. But it's *not* a true statement regarding God."

"Oh yeah?"

"What did Pastor Landris teach us on that?" she said, searching for a sign he had been present for this particular message.

"You mean that God is the giver and Satan is the taker? That Jesus came that we might have life, and not just life, but life more abundantly. That if we believe God gives, then turns around and takes it back, we can't rest in the assurance of God. We can't fend off the attacks of the devil if we believe something is coming from God that's not." The man enjoyed a moment of pride in the ease of his recollection before continuing: "That

Satan comes but for to steal, kill, and destroy. That if we want to know whether something is from God or from Satan, we need to check the fruit of what is to be produced by it."

The woman smiled, pleased that she wouldn't have to explain all of this to him. "Job didn't know what was going on behind the scenes when he said what he said. He thought what was happening to him was God's doing. So he resigned himself to it, when in fact, it was Satan who came to God desiring to put all of this on Job."

"And Job didn't realize that although God had a hedge around him, when he spoke out of his mouth his fears, Satan's army was listening, looking for something to report back to use against him," the man said, still reeling off words originally spoken by Pastor Landris. "Job didn't realize that his speaking the wrong things gave Satan a toehold into his life. A place for Satan to be able to come in and out at will."

"Job revealed a lot to us when he said, 'And the thing I feared the most has come upon me.' Yes," the woman said, "death and life are in the power of the tongue. Job didn't know that his speaking words contrary to what God's Word says allowed Satan access to mess in his life. It wasn't God trying to test Job, it was Satan who was allowed—because of Job's words of authority being used in the wrong way—a small enough crack to get in the door."

The man smiled and nodded. "Thank you, sister. You are right. Thank you for reminding me of this. It's so easy to stray if you're not mindful."

She smiled and nodded back. Then her smile quickly faded. "I still can't believe what folks are saying. I can't believe Pastor Landris is really gone. It's just not fair."

He shook his head. "I know. I can't believe it either. But I'm pretty sure it's true: Pastor Landris is no longer with us."

"The true mark of a good teacher, though, is that when he's not there with you in the storm or the rough spots, you were taught enough of the Word to bring you through."

"And Pastor Landris definitely taught us the Word of God. He also educated all of us that when others are teaching, we should judge what they say to ensure that it lines up with God's Word and God's nature."

"I suppose I'd better get inside," the woman said. "I don't want to be late. I hear Minister Huntley has been appointed the interim pastor. I'll see what he has to say."

"You think he'll be the one to end up replacing Pastor Landris permanently?" the man whispered.

"Who knows? I know there are several on the board who have been pushing for him to be pastor since even before Pastor Landris came. I don't expect anything less than an all-out campaign now to make him the official pastor of Wings of Grace Faith Ministry Church." The woman shook her head. "I'm still a member for now, so I plan to give him or whomever is named the pastor a fair opportunity."

The man shook his head. "It's just not going to seem the same without Pastor Landris, here though. That man truly had a heart for God."

"Oh yeah?" someone said, walking up behind the man and woman as they talked. "And just look where it got him."

The man and woman turned around to see who had so rudely barged in on their conversation.

"What an awful thing to say," the young woman said to an older woman.

"Awful maybe," the older woman said with a smile, "but true. I figure, he just got what he had coming to him. Reaping some of what he'd sown maybe? He wasn't perfect, you know. Too bad for him." She pushed past the two of them and strolled cheerfully inside.

CHAPTER 43

If two of you shall agree on earth.

(Matthew 18:19)

Since Theresa would not be released from the hospital until after Saturday, she wouldn't be able to attend the funeral. Life and death: like a door that one enters and one exits through, her baby had entered the door: a little girl; and another dear one had exited.

Theresa couldn't believe her eyes when they placed that small bundle, her newborn, in the crook of her arm. This tiny being, who didn't have a clue what was going on in the world on this day, didn't have a care in the world. This baby she had carried inside of her and felt as she kicked, got hiccups, and elbowed her was now gazing at the world for the first time from the outside.

"Hi, little one," Theresa said as she played with her fingers. She didn't count them as she'd heard many people say they had. This perfect little being, who had already made a change in her life, was causing her to better understand how her own mother had felt about her. And she knew from the first moment she held her that she would go through the fire herself for this one's sake if she ever had to.

"There are things we have to take care of, but you'll have plenty of time to spend with her later," the attending pediatric nurse said as she gently took the baby from her.

Theresa had run into complications during delivery: her

blood pressure had escalated too high. Stress, everybody figured: the stress within and the stress occurring without. She'd had a C-section, the very thing she hadn't wanted—not because she had a problem with them cutting her, but because Lena and Maurice hadn't arrived yet. She and the baby were trying to hold on until they came. And they were coming. She just knew they were. It didn't matter that she'd seen the towers collapse with her own eyes . . . they'd replayed that footage over and over and over again. Sapphire eventually turned the television off, telling Theresa she didn't need to keep watching it. "You have to protect your eye gates," she'd said. But Theresa's brain was finding it difficult to process it as something that had really happened. That's why she watched it when they replayed it. She kept looking for the nightmare to change—as if she would wake up, then fall back to sleep and change the dream to go the way she'd like it to. That's what she was expecting: this nightmare's ending to change.

Yes, she knew Maurice and her mother had been there. That Maurice had called from inside the building. She saw all the lives affected. But Sapphire told her she didn't need to have these images in her mind. So Sapphire turned off the TV and, true to form, pulled out a book by Charles Capps, *The Tongue, A Creative Force*. And Sapphire read confession after confession to Theresa— over and over and over again, until her voice began to give out. But like a warrior, she kept on; and Theresa's spirit appreciated hearing those anointed, power-filled words. It calmed her. The nurse reported Theresa's blood pressure had dropped, but the doctor had already scheduled the C-section.

So, Maurice and Lena weren't there for the birth of the baby. But Theresa's father, Beatrice, B, and Sapphire were all on hand, standing in the gap. Hours passed, leaving Theresa to constantly check the time.

"Have you heard from them yet?" Theresa asked after the baby was born and she was out of recovery.

"Not yet. But we will," Sapphire kept saying.

B eventually lost it completely. "I've got to get home," she said. "I can't take this sitting around waiting like this anymore." So she left.

Exhausted from the day, Beatrice and Bishop left shortly after B. Sapphire stayed.

"Sapphire, why don't you go on home?" Theresa said. "You've been here all day. I'm fine. Really I am."

Sapphire smiled, rubbed her friend's head, and sat in the chair next to her. "I don't have anywhere else I have to be except here. I'm staying, not because I don't believe you'll be fine. But because I'm your friend and I choose to stay."

Theresa smiled, then tears began rolling down her face.

"What's wrong?" Sapphire said as she leaned in closer.

"Nothing. I just don't understand. Why does God allow things like this to happen to good people? believers? His people, even?"

"Some say God allows what *we* allow. That it rains on the just and the unjust."

"But it's not fair that bad things happen to innocent people. Children are starving in places while we have food stockpiled and going to waste. And then stuff like this?"

"Theresa, now you know that God is not the god of this world. God is God, but Adam essentially handed it over to Satan, and now Satan is the god of this world."

"But we have power and authority, don't we?"

"Yes. Having it is not enough. We must exercise our authority. We have to do something. It's our job to love and to do for one another. God has already done His part. We have to do our part. Do *our* part." She squeezed Theresa's hand. "And our part, right now, is to take care of each other, to say what God says over our circumstances and situations, and to do what we can to show God's love to others. That's what we *can* do."

"Have you talked with Thomas any more?"

Sapphire nodded. "He hasn't heard from Pastor Landris still, and he's having a hard time with it. He had a sister that died when he was young. He told me how much he had prayed and believed for her to live back then just as he is doing now. He admitted his bargain with God: that if God would save his sister, he'd serve him for the rest of his life." Sapphire handed Theresa the water she was trying to get. "She died, and Thomas lost his confidence in God. He figured either God didn't hear him or

God didn't care. Either way, what was the difference? Now he's again praying and believing."

"Does he understand better now?"

"He understands that God does hear and He does care. I explained that there are some things we just don't know or understand. But God is still God. And when we are in the family of God, in the end, we win no matter what Satan does or tries to do or make us believe. Even when we make the transition from these earthly vessels to our heavenly home, 'to be absent from the body is to be present with the Lord.' So we still win. I think Thomas has it now, confessing his desires and not speaking the problem. If people could only see how there are times we tie God's hands when God wants to do something or to work on our behalf. But we're so busy saying the wrong things. God will only honor His Word and not just any old thing we're saying or praying that doesn't line up with it."

"I believe all is well," Theresa said, smiling and putting her words to work.

"And I agree with you, my sister."

Theresa rested for a few hours. Her phone rang, startling her, minutes after 8 P.M.

"Is there a Theresa Jordan there and able to come to the phone?" the voice on the other end said when Sapphire sleepily answered it. "There's been an accident."

CHAPTER 44

Seeing then that we have a great high priest, that is passed into the heavens, Jesus.

(Hebrews 4:14)

So, the door of transition to the other side of life had opened and received one who was dear to many hearts.

"What happened?" Theresa asked, then began to cry. Sapphire stood and looked on.

Theresa started crying harder. Sapphire fought the urge to take the phone out of Theresa's hand, even though Theresa's eyes seemed to be pleading for her to do so. Theresa laid the receiver on the bed and cried more. Sapphire picked up the phone to see if anyone was still on the other end. Only a dial tone remained.

"Theresa," Sapphire said softly, hanging up the phone and taking her friend's hand. "What did they say?"

"An accident. A lady ran through the light. She hit Beatrice and my father's car." Theresa took a deep breath and continued. "They were on their way home. Apparently a woman was talking on her cell phone. She wasn't paying attention. The light was red, and she ran it going top speed. Beatrice and my father were coming through the intersection at the time. She was going too fast to stop, and she hit them. Hard."

"So, what hospital are they in?" Sapphire asked.

"Hospital?" she said in a daze. "Beatrice is dead."

Sapphire sank into the seat. "What?"

"Beatrice is dead!" Theresa completely broke down. "Dead, Sapphire. Dead . . ."

Sapphire began to cry as well. "And your father?"

"He was in the emergency room. But the woman who just called said he's fine."

Sapphire took out her book with confessions and began to read them aloud.

"Sapphire, please. I don't want to hear them now. Beatrice is dead. Maurice and Mama were in the World Trade Center and nobody has heard from them yet. I don't feel like hearing words of confession right now. Okay?"

Sapphire kept reading. Louder. Like whoever she wanted to hear her was hard of hearing.

"Did you hear me? This is not what I need right now!" Theresa looked at Sapphire, who had stopped reading to stare back at her.

Sapphire hugged Theresa. "Theresa, I love you. I truly do. But this is *exactly* what you need. It's what we both need right now. We can't allow Satan to win! We can't let him steal our joy. We can't let him steal our faith. We cannot allow him to win! Do you hear that, Satan?! You're already defeated! Defeated! You're under our feet!"

Theresa cried harder and nodded. "You're right. We can't let him win! We can't!"

Sapphire laughed and went back to reading, loudly, the Word of God confessions.

The next morning, Theresa felt a kiss on her forehead. She opened her eyes.

"Morning, baby."

Theresa blinked, believing she was merely dreaming. "Is it really you?"

Lena nodded. "Yes, it's really me."

Sapphire woke up. "Miss Lena?"

"Good morning, Sapphire."

"Maurice?" Theresa said, sitting straight up now. "Where's Maurice?"

Lena frowned. "That's a bit tough to have to answer right now."

"Tough?" Theresa said.

"Yeah. You see he wanted to go by and see *his* baby first, while I wanted to come up and see *mine*." She smiled.

"He's with the baby?"

"Yes. And I'm planning to go see her, but I had to come see you first."

"Mama, we were praying and confessing, but we didn't hear anything—"

Lena squeezed her hand. "I know. We felt the prayers. Believe me, we felt them."

"So, what happened?"

"It's a long story. I'll tell you about it later. Okay?"

There was a knock on the door. Maurice stuck his head in. "Is it okay if I come in?"

Theresa held open her arms as he made his way to her. "Maurice. Oh, Maurice." She began to cry. "I was so worried. The baby was coming. We tried to hold on . . ."

"I just saw her. She is so beautiful."

"Mama, I'll have the nurse bring her in here so you won't have to go find her."

Lena nodded.

"How are you feeling?" Maurice asked Theresa.

"I feel fine. The baby's wonderful. I tried to reach you, but—"

Sapphire stood up. "Look. I'm going to go and give you guys some time alone."

"Sapphire, you don't have to leave on our account," Lena said.

"Oh, I've been here since yesterday morning. I need to go home and get cleaned up. I don't want the baby thinking Auntie Sapphire stinks." Sapphire kissed Theresa's head again. "I'll be back later today. I'll let one of the nurses know you want the baby on my way out." She smiled. "Are you going to be all right?" Theresa nodded. Sapphire left.

"When did you get here?" Theresa asked, looking from Lena back to Maurice.

"Just got in. In fact, we came straight here when we reached the city."

"Reached the city?"

"Yeah. We couldn't get a flight out of New York. All the planes were grounded, and we barely were able to find a rental car available. I drove almost nonstop." Maurice kept caressing Theresa's hand.

"I know he's tired," Lena said. "But he insisted this be the first place we come. So here we are."

"Then, you haven't spoken with Daddy?"

"No. But I'm sure he's beside himself about this baby," Lena said as she stood up.

"Mama. It's Beatrice." Theresa's countenance changed.

"What's wrong with Beatrice?"

"She was in a car accident yesterday. Mama, Beatrice is dead." Theresa started to cry again.

Lena held her. "Oh, baby," Lena said softly. "Oh, my precious baby."

"Daddy was in the car, too, but he's okay. They kept him in the hospital overnight for observations. I wanted to go see him to make sure he's all right. But I can't. And my blood pressure's back up."

"I'll go," Maurice said. "Theresa, just don't get yourself worked up about it."

"Could you go now? I mean, after they bring in the baby."

The nurse came in with the baby, rolling her in a see-through, portable bed. "Ms. Jordan, here's your sweet little one. Just call when you're ready for us to come take her back to the nursery."

Lena quickly washed her hands and picked up the baby. "Look a' here," she said with a coo in her voice. "Isn't she beautiful? So, what did you name her?"

"Mauricia Grace Jordan."

"Oh, that's pretty," Lena said, looking down at the baby.

"Mauricia after her father," Theresa said. "And Grace, to acknowledge God's unmerited favor."

Lena and Maurice stayed another thirty minutes.

"Well, Tee, we're going now. I'll go check on your father before I go home, get myself cleaned up, catch a few winks possibly, and Lena and I will be back as soon as we can."

"Maurice," Lena said, touching his forearm to stop him from leaving. "Wasn't there something you wanted to do when we got here?"

Maurice looked at Lena, the baby, then Theresa. "Maybe later," he said as he managed a half-smile. "Maybe later."

CHAPTER 45

Preach the word; be instant in season, out of season.

(II Timothy 4:2)

The elders and board of directors were all assembled in the conference room at Wings of Grace Faith Ministry Church. With three sides made of glass, allowing the sun to shine in, it projected the type of atmosphere Pastor Landris had strived to create: "An airy presence, so as not to make others feel the world possessed the power to hem you in."

"We can only offer the position on an interim basis," Elder Fuller had said on that Saturday following September 11. "You do understand that, Minister Huntley?"

"Oh, no problem. Whatever I can do to help. You all must know that I'm willing to do whatever I can for God's work." Minister Huntley had a solemn, yet sincere look on his face. "If you don't mind my asking, though, how long do you believe the interim position will last before you actually look to permanently fill it?"

Elder Fuller looked around the room. Several members of the board had not arrived yet, and truthfully, they shouldn't be discussing so much business without them. But he couldn't see the harm in telling Minister Huntley at least what he believed would be taking place over the next few months.

"Well, Minister Huntley. We want to fill the position as

quickly as possible. A church this size shouldn't be without a permanent leader. People need stability."

"I agree. And as I have said, I'm willing to do whatever I can to move this church forward. Pastor Landris certainly infused this place with his vision. I know there is still much left to be done, and I believe my having been a faithful follower under his tutelage made a positive impact on me being able to step promptly into his shoes."

"Nobody can fill Pastor Landris' shoes," Deacon Thomas said as he came in.

Minister Huntley smiled. "Of course. I didn't mean any disrespect to Pastor Landris or what he has accomplished. I was only pointing out my faithfulness to this church and to the vision. Granted, Pastor Landris and I are quite different in many ways."

"I know that's right," Mother King said as she hobbled in. "Sorry I'm late. I had to take care of some business before coming here. I'm figuring we'll be here awhile, and I don't want to feel rushed."

"It's quite all right. You're actually ten minutes early. And there are a few more members due to arrive," Deacon Perkins said, swiveling short turns in his chair.

"That's one thing about Pastor Landris. He despised slothfulness. Thought it was a disrespect in the process of time," Deacon Woods said in a reflective tone. "That's one of the things I admired most about him. Eleven o'clock service began at eleven o'clock. Not eleven-oh-one. It didn't matter if he was the only one here to start, we began on time."

Mother King started laughing. "Yeah, I remember the first time he did that. You talking 'bout some mad folks up in here." She threw her head back and sighed.

Deacon Woods joined in the laughter. "Do any of you remember Sister Ida Jean?"

"Ida Jean Pickett?" Mother King said. She sucked her teeth.

"Yes, Lord. That woman almost blessed Pastor Landris out when she arrived at church at her usual 11:15 A.M. time and found she had missed the prayer and praise time of the service." Deacon Woods began imitating Ida Jean Pickett: " 'What do you mean, Reverend, by starting church when the majority of the members haven't yet arrived?' Man, she was fired up, and I don't mean the-Holy-Ghost fired up either."

"That woman!" Mother King said. "When Pastor Landris told her to sit down while services were still going on and he'd address it after church, she really clowned. 'I ain't sitting down nothing! I missed praising my Jesus! You owe us an explanation now.' "

"Well, me personally, I don't see the harm in starting a little late if you have a need to," Minister Huntley said. "Things do come up beyond folks' control. I'm sure God cares more about us praising Him than the fact that we started on time."

Deacon Thomas cut his eyes at him. "See. Now that's where you're wrong. It shows a lack of respect when we are slothful. Besides, people need to be able to count on your word. If you say eleven o'clock service begins at eleven o'clock, then it should begin at eleven."

"Minister Huntley," Mother King said, straightening up her wig. "The problem is when people come at the time you say a thing starts, and it doesn't. You disrespect those who had the integrity to come, as everybody should have. If you're continuously late, then people learn they can't count on what you say. They form a habit of coming late to catch you when you do start, and you end up starting late because you're waiting on them to come. It becomes a cycle. So, you see, it comes down to respect and keeping one's word. I hope your intentions aren't to carry us back to that catch-22." One eyebrow rose, as though that were a question to be answered.

Minister Huntley smiled. "Oh, no ma'am. As I stated earlier, I just want to be a blessing to this church. A servant. Of course, I have my own style of doing things. But I know my place around here. Pastor Landris indeed was truly a visionary—"

"What do you mean *was*?" a familiar voice boomed from the back of the room.

Everybody turned and looked toward the door. "Pastor Landris!" Elder Fuller said. "Good to see you, sir." He looked around and noticed that two people still hadn't arrived. "We'll be starting the meeting in about five minutes."

Pastor Landris walked in and took a seat. "It appears you guys have already gotten started, from the sound of things." He smiled. "Don't let me interrupt. Now, what were you saying about 'Pastor Landris was'?" Pastor Landris faced Minister Huntley. When Minister Huntley looked away, he searched other faces around the room. Not many would return his look.

"Pastor Landris, we'd like to give the others time to get here, since this is an emergency scheduled meeting."

Pastor Landris touched his moustache. "I assume so, since I'm supposed to be out of town honeymooning right now. And were it not for the events of 9-11, I'd still be gone."

The other members arrived. Pastor Landris sat back in his chair and waited.

"Pastor Landris," Elder Fuller began, "we all want you to know what a blessing you have been to us individually and corporately. You have taken us both spiritually and physically as a church farther than we ever dreamed possible. As you know, there were only a handful of us when you came on board as pastor. Under your leadership, we have seen growth that has literally exploded, with people flocking here from near and far."

"That's very true," Deacon Woods said.

"So, why are we having this meeting?" Pastor Landris said as he began to study the faces of Elder Fuller, Mother King, Deacon Perkins, Deacon Woods, Deacon Thomas . . . He stopped at Deacon Thomas when he noticed the pained look on his face.

"Pastor Landris," Elder Fuller said, "it's with regret that we find we must ask you to step down as the pastor of Wings of Grace Faith Ministry Church. Effective immediately."

"Step down?" Pastor Landris said, exhibiting his surprise.

Elder Fuller nodded. "Yes."

"You're firing me?"

"Well, let's just say we feel you're not the right person for this position any longer."

Pastor Landris leaned forward. "Go on. I'm listening."

"Well, Pastor," Elder Fuller said, as he stood straighter. "We voiced our feelings about your choice of Minister Fulton filling in for you while you were to be away."

"You mean your not approving of my decision to allow a

woman preacher to be in charge?" Pastor Landris sat back in the
chair and began to play with his fountain pen.

"Look, Pastor," Deacon Woods said. "You have all these radical ideas about church and serving God. You believe in healing.
You got our womenfolk believing they're equal to us as opposed
to being servants the way God intended them to be."

Mother King sat up and began to wiggle her chair and cause it
to squeak. It was obvious she was fighting to keep from saying
anything. Her moving didn't go unnoticed.

"Not everyone agrees," Deacon Woods said, eyeing Mother
King. "But the majority of us feel like you're too radical, and the
majority rules. We need a pastor who'll stay in line with our doctrine and the traditions that have been in place since this church
began."

"So, you're saying you don't believe God really wants us
well?" Pastor Landris said.

"No, not every saint. I say we all got to die from something,"
Deacon Perkins said.

Pastor Landris shook his head and laughed, although nothing
was funny. "So, when the Bible says, 'By his stripes, ye were
healed,' God didn't mean for *us* to be healed?"

"Now see, I'm not saying that. I'm just saying maybe sometimes God does, and maybe sometimes God doesn't," Deacon
Perkins said, looking for someone to help.

"So, then, you're saying, it's a game of chance? Roll the dice?
Maybe God will, maybe God won't. Let's take a chance and see?
Is that what you're saying?"

"And your telling folks that God wants us to have," Deacon
Woods said. "Well, my Bible tells me, 'Only the poor in spirit
shall see God.' 'It's easier for a camel to go through the eye of a
needle than for a rich man to get into heaven.' Jesus was poor, so
we should follow His example and be poor. At least that's what
some of us here believe."

Pastor Landris laughed out loud. "As it is written, 'I have
come that you might have life and life more abundantly.' 'Beloved,
I wish above all things thou mayest prosper and be in health.' So,
Jesus was poor, huh? Okay. Then how many poor people do you

know who have treasurers following them? Yeah, you know Judas? The one who betrayed Jesus? The one who carried the bag? The *money*bag? Jesus said in Matthew 26:11: 'For ye have the poor always with you; but me ye have not always.' Doesn't sound like Jesus thought of himself as the poor. So, my wrong looks to be that I dared preach the Bible?"

"A woman preacher in charge was the last straw, Pastor," Elder Fuller said. "We asked you, and you paid us no mind. That was the bottom line. Minister Fulton is an anointed teacher. Powerful. She has blessed both the men and the women of this church."

"The Bible study she teaches on Tuesday on our authority in Jesus," Deacon Perkins said, "has been awesome, and to be perfectly honest, has virtually changed my life."

"We just don't agree with you allowing her in the pulpit," Deacon Pritchard pointed out. "I know what you say, but God created man first, then woman. That proves women shouldn't be over men. They have their place." A few heads nodded in agreement.

"God created animals before He created man," Pastor Landris said. "So, I suppose the point you're making is that the first created, rules?" He shook his head. "My, Lord."

"See. Now that right there is why we're here talking about this, Pastor Landris," Elder Fuller said. "All we're asking that you do is adhere to what we believe to be right."

"That's all? Just adhere to what you believe is right? Disregard what God might be saying to me?" Pastor Landris stood up. "Well, since it seems you all have already made a decision based on whether or not I agree to 'adhere,' it has been a pleasure to have been the pastor here, serving God, and serving this congregation."

"Pastor Landris, this is ridiculous! All you have to do is agree to abide by a few simple rules," Elder Fuller said. "How difficult can that be? Then we can drop this whole matter. We don't want to lose you. Minister Huntley agreed to step in only because you don't seem to want to follow a few simple requests by the majority of this board. Well, Minister Huntley has expressed his willingness to abide by and to work with us."

Pastor Landris looked at Minister Huntley, who turned away. "Yeah," Pastor Landris said. "Yeah, simple requests." He walked away from the conference table.

Minister Huntley looked up at Pastor Landris. "This is not your church, Pastor Landris. You don't own it, and you should respect the leadership's wishes here."

Pastor Landris looked back at Minister Huntley. "I never said it was my church. In fact, the last I heard, Jesus said, 'Upon this rock I will build *my* church.' I was under the impression it was God's church, and that I was only the shepherd. A steward." He walked over to Minister Huntley and touched his shoulders. "I pray it turns out to be all you believe it to be." He smiled, then graciously shook each member's hand on his way out. Mother King and Deacon Thomas, two of the five minority votes that let him know they hadn't voted against him, hugged him tightly and didn't seem to want to ever let go.

"Well, that's that," Deacon Woods whispered to Minister Huntley when they were away from the others. "Congratulations on becoming the interim pastor. If things go as planned, you'll be the pastor of this church before the year is out good."

Minster Huntley smiled and patted Deacon Woods on the back.

Pastor Landris went straight home. Johnnie Mae greeted him at the door.

"Well? What was the emergency meeting all about? That's if you can tell me."

"They're officially letting me go as pastor."

"You're kidding?" She hugged him. "But how can they?"

"The majority decided they preferred staying with the way they've always done things. They say I'm not the right person to lead them to the 'Promised Land,' " Landris said with a laugh. "Can't leave their traditions. You know, you can take the people out of Egypt, but you can't take Egypt out of some of the people."

"Thomas called," Johnnie Mae said as they walked to the kitchen.

"Did he say what he wanted?"

She shook her head.

"Just what I need," Landris said. "Something else."

"Well, he did make good your money to pay your taxes. Maybe

something good is happening with the rest of your money. He said it was important that he talk with you as soon as possible."

Landris kissed her. "Let's forget all this. Now about our honeymoon . . ." He grinned.

"Landris, a place does not a honeymoon make. We'll go. Later. When things settle down." Johnnie Mae thought back to September 11, when so much had transpired. "But by the grace of God, we might not even be here now," she said. *But by . . . the grace of God.*

CHAPTER 46

And they overcame him by the blood of the Lamb.

(Revelations 12:11 (a))

On the morning of September 11, Johnnie Mae and Landris had been on their way to the 106th floor of the World Trade Center when they saw Theresa Jordan's friend, Maurice Greene. He mentioned he was in New York with Theresa's mother, Lena.

"Tell Ms. Patterson I said hello," Landris said to Maurice before they left.

It was hearing the name, Patterson, that triggered a thought in Johnnie Mae's head.

"Landris! We've got to go back to our suite at Oheka Castle," Johnnie Mae said.

"What?" The numbers of the floors ticked off as they ascended.

She looked at him. "I know you've planned this wonderful breakfast for us. I know you hate to waste money. What if we just get them to put it in a carryout or something and take it back to our suite?"

"Johnnie Mae, why would we want to do that?"

"Lena's last name is Patterson. I know it's a long shot, but I need to check on the possibility that Lena might be related to Sarah's old friend I've been searching for."

"Sarah? The woman at the nursing home?"

"Yes, the woman at the home I told you about. The one who believes her family is trying to keep her hidden away. She had a friend named Mamie Patterson. According to Pearl in Asheville, a woman named Mamie had a child and, if what Pearl says is true, Mamie may have ended up with Sarah's little girl. I need to check on something, then call my mother." Johnnie Mae was talking a mile a minute. The elevator stopped. They were at Windows on the World. Johnnie Mae hushed and glanced around. It was beautiful just from where they were standing at the moment.

"Johnnie Mae, I'm not going to let you ruin our breakfast. We are going to eat a nice, romantic meal. Then, if you like, you can call your mother or do whatever it is you're feeling compelled to do."

When they reached their conference room, Johnnie Mae couldn't believe how wonderful everything had been set up for them. She felt bad having almost ruined what Landris apparently had spent a lot of time and effort arranging for the two of them.

Landris excused himself, leaving her quiet minutes to take in the breathtaking view.

"Johnnie Mae," Landris said, standing and holding a wicker basket. "Let's go."

"What?"

He held the basket up again. "We're going back to Oheka Castle."

"Oh, Landris. I didn't mean to ruin this. We can stay. I love it here. I really do."

He smiled. "Listen, all I want is to spend time with you. We'll take this back to our room, but only if you promise to finish whatever it is you're trying to do in one hour's time. One. After that, no more work. No more thinking. No more wheels turning inside that head of yours. You will focus on me while I focus on you. Tomorrow, we'll leave for Bermuda. I would just like for you to hurry up and get this out of your system. All right?"

She smiled as they walked back to the elevator. "All right. And I promise, I'll wrap this up in one hour. No, less than one hour!" She hugged him. "Then I'll be all yours, Mr. Landris."

"All right. I'm not playing now," Landris said, staring her down. "One hour."

They were out of the building, unknowingly, fifteen minutes before the crash of the first plane. It was only after they were back in their suite at Oheka Castle that they learned just how close the two of them had come to the devastation of that day.

Johnnie Mae called her mother as soon as she got inside the living room. Knowing she had only an hour, she was in a hurry to finish. Just like she'd promised.

"Mama, I need to ask you to do me a favor."

"Is everything all right?" Mrs. Gates said. "You sound a little funny. Rushed."

"Everything's fine, Mama. I just need to ask you to do something really important for me. I don't have a lot of time, okay? But I really need this."

"Sure. Tell me what you need."

"I need you to get in contact with Sarah Fleming. She was that woman at the home we visited. The last one. You remember?"

"You mean Ms. Azile's little friend?"

"Yes, Ms. Azile's friend. Tell Sarah I'm not positive, but I may have a lead on her daughter," Johnnie Mae said.

"You want me to tell her that?" Mrs. Gates asked. "But what if you're wrong?"

Johnnie Mae thought about it a second. *What if I am wrong?* "You're right, Mama. Tell her I may have a lead on her old friend Mamie. I need to be sure she'll be there when I get home. I don't have a lot of time to work on this. We'll be leaving tomorrow morning for our honeymoon. But when I get back, I'm going to check out a few things. Mama, this is important. Tell Sarah if she feels like she's in danger of her family moving her where I can't find her, she'll have to find some way to get in contact with me and let me know where she is. Mama, it's vital she understands that if I find her family then lose her . . ."

"I'll tell her, Johnnie Mae. Please don't worry about this. You just got married. Look. This will keep until you get back. Spend some time with your new husband. You know how you can be about things. A man can only be so patient for so long."

Johnnie Mae laughed. "I thought you were supposed to be having memory lapses?"

"My mind works fine when it chooses to. Now you have a good time with that husband of yours. Don't worry about me or Princess Rose or even Sarah . . . what's her name? Fleming. Yeah, Sarah Fleming, for that matter."

"Okay, Mama. Just be sure to tell Sarah. Thanks for everything. Really."

"Sure," Mrs. Gates said.

It was only after Johnnie Mae hung up with her mother that Landris told her about the planes hitting the Twin Towers.

"Lena and Maurice? Do you think they made it out?"

"I pray they did. The news showed some people getting out. I don't know where they were at the time. We just have to pray that they're safe."

It wasn't long before both towers collapsed to the ground. Landris and Johnnie Mae postponed their honeymoon. It took them two days to get out of New York. When they got home late Thursday night, there was a message for Landris on his answering machine. The church leaders wanted to set up a meeting with him as soon as possible. And Thomas, who had agreed to housesit while Landris was gone, was AWOL.

Landris also learned upon his return that, contrary to what he had scheduled, Minister Fulton had not preached on Sunday, but instead it had been Minister Huntley. When he called Minister Fulton, she told him she didn't know what was going on—that a few on the board of directors had called her in and informed her that there had been a change in plans. That was all she knew. Then Landris was hit with the news of Beatrice Jordan's untimely death. The funeral was scheduled for that Saturday morning. Landris was told Theresa Jordan delivered her baby, but because of high-blood-pressure complications, she was still in the hospital. The doctors advised against her even trying to attend Beatrice's funeral, citing a number of medical reasons.

Landris called Elder Fuller to find out what was going on with Minister Fulton and the meeting he wanted to schedule.

"Pastor, it's just best if we meet with you as soon as possible.

Whenever it's convenient, the sooner the better. You know how rumors can grow legs and mouths and start running and talking all over the place. There are some things we need to discuss before anything gets out there or back to you, wrong."

"Then can you at least tell me what it is pertaining to?"

"The direction of Wings of Grace Faith Ministry Church," he said. "And that's all I'm at liberty to say at this time."

So Landris agreed to a four o'clock, Saturday afternoon meeting: "the sooner the better."

It was there he had been informed; he was no longer the pastor of the congregation he had worked so hard to help grow both physically and spiritually.

Everything coming down in one instant: just like that.

CHAPTER 47

But where sin abounded, grace did much more abound.

(Romans 5:20)

"Theresa, where did Memory go?" Lena asked. "Did she say?" She had avoided the subject after hearing about Beatrice. Three days had passed since the funeral on Saturday. Theresa was finally home adjusting to caring for a newborn baby.

"I don't know," Theresa said, realizing Memory's disappearance hadn't crossed her thoughts. "She left the day I went to the hospital; I haven't heard from her since."

"Memory didn't go to the hospital with you at all?"

"No. Some lawyer stopped by to bring her some legal papers she'd requested, early that morning. When I went into labor, Daddy and Beatrice—" She stopped, thought about Beatrice, looked up at the ceiling, and began to gently, but mindlessly rock the baby.

"Legal papers? What kind of legal papers?" Lena had to keep Theresa's mind focused on the discussion at hand. *Something's not right.*

"She was saying something about wanting to leave you her things in case anything happened to her. She believed you probably wouldn't accept them, so she wanted me to sign it as a witness to it, or be like the executor of her will. Something like that."

"The necklace!" Lena looked at Theresa. "Did she find out you have the necklace?"

"No. She tried talking about it, but I never let on that I knew what she was talking about. There's no way she could know I have it. It's been in the safe deposit box since after we received that reward information." Theresa suddenly got quiet. "The pictures."

"What pictures?"

"The ones Maurice took at that gala we attended." She covered her mouth with her hand. "There was a picture of me wearing the necklace."

"Did Memory happen to see it? Think, Theresa."

Theresa fell back against the stacked pillows and began to rub her head. "Oh, Mama. She saw it. That's why she was in such a hurry to get out of here. She saw the pictures when I was showing them to Sapphire. The day we took you and Maurice to the airport. I didn't think anything about it because I was only showing them to Sapphire. I forgot I'd even worn it. The necklace never crossed my mind. Memory walked in, glanced at a few photos, then quickly excused herself to go pack. She saw it. She must have." Theresa shook her head. "I can't believe this! Then, while I was in the hospital . . ."

"That quote-unquote legal paper, Theresa? Did you sign it?"

"I signed a page that was blank about halfway down." Theresa sighed. "She set me up, didn't she? I don't believe my own grandmother . . . and she set me up!"

Lena patted Theresa's hand. "Don't beat yourself up about it. You're not the first."

"Mama, go to the bank and see if it's still there. I need to know. I can't believe I let her do that to me." Theresa stared into space as Lena left and came back with her purse.

"Theresa, you can't blame yourself," Lena said. "That's just how Memory operates."

"Mama, I've not asked you yet, but that lawyer in New York, did you get a chance to find out what he wanted before everything happened?"

Lena nodded. She patted Theresa's hand again. "We'll talk later. There's been too much going on these past weeks. It's just something else to think about, so let's not, right now." Lena stood up. "I'm going to run to the bank so I can check for myself. You know what's funny is: I'll still need to find Memory, whether she's taken that necklace or not."

"Whatever is going on, it must be pretty big."

"It is. And I'm not sure whether it will have a happy ending or not. But I don't want you worried or thinking about anything except little Grace there."

"Why do you call her Grace instead of Mauricia?"

"Ah!" she said waving her hand. "You know how old people are. Grace is easier to handle than . . . Mau . . . ree . . ."

"Mau-ree-see-a," Theresa said. "Like Maurice with an 'e' and an 'ah' at the end."

"You young folks tickle me making up names people can hardly spell or pronounce."

"Mama, you never did tell me how you and Maurice got out of the World Trade Center that day. Can we talk about that?" Theresa knew she was stalling. She didn't want to know for sure what she believed Memory had most likely done. Not yet anyway.

"Long story short. You could say an angel prevented us from being there longer than we were. Maurice had gone to get something for you, but then you went into labor with little Grace. He ended up coming back to let me know. You know I had already made my feelings very clear about the baby. The lawyer had planned to take me to another floor to retrieve something from a vault when he was interrupted to take an important call. After Maurice came and told me you were in labor, I told that lawyer I was out of there. He got off that phone in a hurry and rushed me to the other floor. Maurice came, since I told that lawyer I wouldn't be wasting any more time than I had to. Turns out little Grace there saved not only Maurice and me due to her impending arrival, but also the lawyer. You see, the floor we went to ended up being that plane's initial impact. Had I not been in such a hurry to leave, we would have been in there at precisely the time that plane hit."

"Mama, you don't know how glad I am that the two of you are all right."

Lena smiled. "Theresa, do you love Maurice?"

Theresa smiled. "Yes. I do."

"Then, let him know. Okay?"

Theresa nodded.

"It's important to let people know how you feel about them. Learn to live a life with no regrets. Don't regret not having thanked a person. Having forgiven someone. Or let a person know how much they mean, not meant, mean to you. Never find yourself saying what you wished you had said or done. Say it. Do it. Live a life with no regrets. Take Maurice, for example: What if he hadn't made it back here?"

Theresa instantly became reflective. "If Maurice had died, I would have regretted him not knowing how much I really do love and appreciate him."

"Then, tell him now. While and when you can, as often as you can."

"Mama, do you know something I don't?" Theresa watched Lena put her purse on her shoulder and walk toward the door.

"I always know something that you don't," she said, laughing. "I'll be back."

"You're going to the bank? Right now?" Theresa asked.

"I'm walking to catch the bus that will take me to the bank."

"You don't have to do that. Walk, that is. I'll call someone to come take you." She picked up the telephone.

The doorbell rang. "I'll get it, then I'm gone," Lena said, winking at Theresa.

"Good morning, Richard," Lena said to Bishop Jordan at the door. "How are you?"

"Making it," he said. "And where are you off to so bright and early?"

"The bank."

"So, you're finally driving?"

"Oh no. Catching the bus."

"That's quite a walk to the bus stop," Richard said. "I'd be happy to drop you off there personally. Just let me holler at my baby and grandbaby real quick."

"That's okay. I'll walk. You can just go on up. She's in her room."

"I don't mind carrying you to the bus stop, Lena. Really I don't. I'd even be happy to take you to the bank. I don't do a whole lot of driving still, but I can hold my own."

"Yes, you have recovered from that stroke extraordinarily well."

"I still get tired from time to time. But I think it may be more old age than anything." He chuckled.

"Tell me about it. You're preaching to the choir now, Richard." She smiled. "Well, I'll be back shortly. Do you need anything while I'm at the bank?"

"I'm not going to even go there, Lena girl. You know I could do that old corny joke about bringing me back a few twenties, fifties, and hundreds. But I'm not going there."

"Thank goodness!" Lena laughed.

"Daddy!" Theresa yelled. "Is that you?"

"Yes, baby girl. It's me." He yelled back.

"Daddy, will you take Mama to the bank?" Theresa asked.

Lena shook her head vigorously and opened the door. "Go on up. Hurry! Run!" she said, laughing as she hurried and closed the door behind her.

"Daddy! Did you hear me?"

"I heard you, baby girl. But it's too late. Lena has . . . already left the building."

CHAPTER 48

There remained therefore a rest to the people of God.

(Hebrews 4:9)

Johnnie Mae had been doing searches on the Internet and various other places. She wanted to be sure her working theory wasn't too far out there. Patterson wasn't a common name like Smith or Jones, but it wasn't rare by any means either.

She'd gone to Birmingham and gotten Princess Rose. Her mother had come back to her house in Coffee, Alabama, to help out. Johnnie Mae had already moved many of her things to Landris' house in Georgia, but she had a lot more packing to do. Her decision to keep her house in Alabama was only until she knew for sure what she wanted to do. She had considered getting her mother to stay there with her brother Donald—just thinking of different ways they could keep an eye on Mrs. Gates without her feeling she had to go to a home. Donald didn't care to stay with his mother at hers, his, or Johnnie Mae's house.

"Too much of a stereotype attachment, Johnnie Mae," he had said. "Do you have any idea how women feel about scrubs these days? They are brutal if they find out you live with your mama. They don't care if you make it sound honorable. You live with mama."

"So you care more about what people think than our mother?" Johnnie Mae said. "Do you not realize she's trying to put herself into a nursing home? A *nursing* home."

"It's not a nursing home, Johnnie Mae. She's just downsizing her living space and expenses. What's wrong with that? Mama knows what she's doing." He sighed. "Why aren't you after Marie, Rachel, or Christian about her living or visiting with one of them? They all have children at home. It would probably help them out just her being there."

"Don't you think I've tried? Everybody says they're too busy to look after her. Like they would really have to take care of her. She's the one who usually does the taking care of. I guess I'll try harder to talk her into coming to live with me in Georgia."

"Johnnie Mae, now, you know how we all feel about that. None of us wants Mama to leave the state. We'd like to be able to see her when we get ready. Personally, I don't want to drive to Georgia to visit her when she could stay around here and be close by."

"Oh, so you don't want to put yourself out, huh?" Johnnie Mae said. "Nobody wants to be put out to take care of her should she need it, but you want her conveniently close by *should* you decide you want to stop by or need her?"

"See, now, there you go. Always creating some hullabaloo, Miss Drama Mama!"

Johnnie Mae invited her mother over to her house as she attempted once more to convince her of the benefits of moving to Georgia with them.

"Princess Rose needs somebody to look after her, Mama. You'd be doing me a tremendous favor if you moved to Georgia and stayed with Landris and me," Johnnie Mae said as she typed on the computer. "I really do need you. At least for a little while."

"And what does Pastor Landris have to say about all of this?" She stood over Johnnie Mae watching various screens pop up on the computer monitor when Johnnie Mae pressed a key or clicked the mouse.

"He would love for you to come live with us."

"Yeah. Right. The man just got married, when he takes you on top of the world, what are you doing? You're trying to figure out how to get back to your room so you can check your notes and call me to find some woman you hardly know, who may or may not still be there, and she wasn't. Then you come home without going on a honeymoon at all—"

"We had a honeymoon while we were in New York. That does count."

"Like I said, you didn't go to Bermuda on your honeymoon as planned, and now you're here in Alabama instead of in Georgia with him, trying to find out what again?"

"Trying to find out if Lena Patterson might be any kin to Mamie Patterson."

"Yeah, right. And if you know this Lena Patterson woman, why don't you just pick up the phone, call, and ask her so you can be done with it?"

"I've tried that, Mama. Look. Lena lived in North Carolina, but it was Winston-Salem, not Asheville. That's where Sarah said she was from: Asheville. Landris was trying to get Theresa Jordan's phone number, but she moved recently and her number is not listed. He was going to get it from the church, but then he was asked down as pastor."

"Lord, I still can't believe they let that man go. After all he's done for that church and the community, and what do they do? Turn him out like a reversible leisure suit."

Johnnie Mae looked at her mother and laughed. "Reversible leisure suit, Mama?"

"Yeah . . . well, you get my picture."

"Landris called Bishop Jordan, since he still had his phone number, to see if he could get Theresa's number from him. When Landris learned that his wife Beatrice had died, we didn't want to worry him about it, so we just left my number for him to pass on to Theresa."

"So, you're here on this here World Wide Web, as you call it, searching for what?"

"Anything on Mamie Patterson. And, so far, I've come up with zilch."

"Since Sarah Fleming was gone by the time I got there, I don't know why you're bothering about this. Even if you find her family, you don't have a clue where she is."

"This is so complicated." Johnnie Mae stopped tapping keys

and laid her head lightly on her desk near her keyboard. "Maybe you're right. Maybe I should forget this whole thing."

"Well, I gave Ms. Azile your phone number like you told me." Johnnie Mae looked up at her mother.

"I told her if she finds out where Sarah Fleming is or hears from her, to give you a call. Maybe something will turn up soon."

"Mama, let's try one more thing. Let's go see Ms. Azile one more time. Maybe she'll remember something or can tell me something that will help me locate Sarah. Anything at this point would be helpful. Because I'm not getting anywhere this way."

CHAPTER 49

The kingdom of heaven suffereth violence.

(Matthew 11:12 (a))

Lena got to the bank and showed her ID and key to get into the safe deposit box.

"Empty," she said, staring at the bottom of the box.

She went to the person in charge. "Excuse me, could I look at your records to see who was the last person to access our safe deposit box?"

Lena was shown the sign-off card. "Elaine Robertson," Lena said, pointing to the signature. "How could you possibly allow someone to go into this box if their name was not listed to have access to it?"

The woman looked at the name, then pulled some other record. She smiled. "Ma'am, it seems Theresa Jordan gave Ms. Robertson written permission to access this box."

"But how is that possible? Elaine Robertson had no legal right to access this box."

The woman showed her a paper that in effect allowed Elaine Robertson onetime access to the box: 'I am presently having a baby. Since I and my mother Lena Patterson are the only two people listed and my mother is out of town on an emergency, I need for my grandmother, Elaine Robertson, to have onetime access to retrieve something of grave importance on my behalf out of the safe deposit box number listed below.' Ms. Patterson, as you can see, the signature for Theresa Jordan on record matches the one here. There was no reason for us to doubt this. Ms. Jordan has been a faithful patron for years. We were well aware she was pregnant, so there was no cause to suspect anything."

Lena sighed.

"Is there a problem to be reported? Was Elaine Robertson not her grandmother as she claimed? She seemed sweet and sincere enough. She provided me an ID and a key."

"She is Theresa's grandmother. Technically. I won't comment on how sincere she is." Lena stood to leave.

"Ms. Patterson. If you like, we can report this to the authorities. Although it is hard to prove what was inside the box, at least it can be reported as stolen."

Lena shook her head. "I'll let you know later. First I need to go home and talk with my daughter. We'll get back with you should we desire to press this any further."

The woman smiled. "I do apologize. But as I stated, there was nothing wrong in what we did here."

"Except if the person's name was not on the form or added by the principal holding person, you shouldn't have allowed anyone access to it. This isn't even notarized."

The woman stopped smiling. "Except what she brought was, in fact, as though Theresa Jordan had come in and added her to the form herself. In my opinion."

Lena got a copy of the "authorization letter" and went home. Theresa was already feeling bad thinking she had allowed Memory to possibly get one up on her. *How am I going to tell Theresa that Memory indeed took the necklace from the safe deposit box?*

But Lena had other things to deal with. She had in her possession information that Memory had no idea existed and a locked box, given to her from the person who had been responsible for Lena being in New York in the first place. She needed to locate Memory; there was something else Memory had no knowledge of. Something important. Something the lawyer had shared with Lena.

"Mamie Patterson was not Memory's biological mother," Mr. Hatcher had said.

CHAPTER 50

And the violent take it by force.

(Matthew 11:12 (b))

Thomas called George.

"Good news, bro," Thomas said.

"Man, where are you? I got home and you were gone."

"I told you I'd be out of there by the time you got back from your honeymoon. When you called me to let me know you were all right and that you'd be home, I didn't want to be hanging around. You're newly wedded. Who wants somebody hanging around while they're trying to get to know each other better?"

"Yeah, but Thomas, this situation was different. And besides, we're trying to get Johnnie Mae's mother to come live with us. Johnnie Mae is in Alabama at this moment, trying to persuade her. You know there's plenty of room here," George said.

"Unless you live in a mansion with separate everything where a person could go in and out for days and never pass another soul, it's just not cool. Not for me, anyway." He inhaled a heavy dose of air. "Listen. I have some good news. Seems like a few of those rollover, reward-type investments I ventured on—"

"With my money and without my permission." George added, lest he forgets.

"Yeah, yeah. I think I've gotten that message loud and clear. Anyway, I'm here with Sammie and there are a few things beginning to happen on this side. I don't want to discuss it prematurely, but one seems to be a done deal. Just waiting on the paperwork. When this one comes through, you'll find yourself owner of a pretty cool business." He paused to give George an opportunity to comment. When George didn't, he continued. "The other thing that seems to have panned out is a certain necklace that has finally surfaced."

"A necklace? Okay, so you're telling me all the money I had is still locked up? With the exception of the money you put into those few T-bills and CDs that fortunately amounted to enough to pay my tax bill due with just a little bit left over—which I should also point out has generated more income, with taxes now due on that portion."

"Yeah, I know. You have to pay taxes on the additional money that grew on what you paid your taxes with. Personally, I'm just glad the government is not looking for *me* at this point. I know you—you love me, but with you, right is right. You would have handed me over to the authorities if that portion of the money hadn't turned up when it did."

"Okay, so we agree that you're a crook; we're just haggling over how much of a crook you are?" George said, laughing.

"Man, quit speaking those negative words over my life."

"Oh, you're right. I apologize. You are a man of integrity," George affirmed, smiling.

"I'm a new creature in Christ. Old things have passed away," Thomas said, his thoughts quickly flashing to Sapphire.

"I see Miss Sapphire has made quite an impression on you."

Thomas smiled. "How did you know I was thinking about her?"

"I didn't. Sapphire is a good woman. I've seen so much growth in her in just the past year alone. She's hungry for the Word. Sitting at my feet whenever I teach, and under Minister Fulton's feet every chance she gets."

"Minister Fulton? She's the woman preacher? Yeah, I sat in on one of her lesson sessions. Her teaching is 'off tha hook!' as the young folks say. I've learned a lot from her myself. I can begin to imagine who I could become in the Lord if I hung around you folks at Wings of Grace Faith Ministry Church for any length of time."

George had yet to tell Thomas about his being asked to step down as the pastor.

"Back to that necklace," George said, steering Thomas back to his original thought track.

"Yeah, the necklace. Sammie said they got a call from one of the reward packets his people sent out months ago. Apparently, someone is claiming to have possession of it. The reward offered was a million dollars. But the people who want it are offering two million. That's a million dollars profit, minus Sammie's ten percent fee, of course."

"What kind of a necklace could be worth two million dollars?"

"One with some history and a little mystery. An alexandrite. Rare. Valuable. Hard to find. Missing for decades. Sammie says these people are desperate for its return. He thinks we might be able to up the price to include his fee. That would be one million profit—two million coming your way." Thomas waited. "So, why aren't you excited?"

"Let's see: I believe that was six million and some change recovered that went to pay taxes, penalty fees, with two hundred thousand to me. And if this pans out, that would be another two million. We're up to a whole eight million dollars and some change now. I'm only at a loss of what . . . twenty million dollars? You're right. So, why *am* I not more excited?"

"Now, don't forget about that other thing that seems headed toward a done deal."

"Yeah. We're waiting on paperwork on a business I might possibly be owning."

"But it's valued at around ten million dollars. Whether you realize it or not, owning a business will provide you with some much needed tax breaks," Thomas said with pride.

"Right," George said with a touch of skepticism. "Let's see: I'll be up to eighteen million dollars and some change with that. Oh, that's *if* this comes through."

"Come on, George. Give me a break. I *am* trying. And there are some other things Sammie and I are checking into that might bring even more of your cash back. I have my faith out there on this. I'm believing, have confessed it, prayed the petition prayer—"

"Petition prayer? How do you know about petition prayer?"

"Sapphire and Minister Fulton. Petition prayer is asking God once, in the name of Jesus, your desire. After that, you don't ask again because if you do that shows you didn't believe you received the first time. So now I just say, 'I believe I have received.' And I thank God that it is already done."

"Already done." George smiled. "Our God is a right-now God. Not a past-tense God, except when we ask and it's done. Not a future-tense God who *will* do it later."

"But a present-tense God. An 'I am' God. An 'I supply' God," Thomas said, smiling. "It feels great walking by faith and not by sight."

"Amen."

"So, George, please don't put me down. I have my faith on all that the devil stole from you being restored to you one hundredfold. I believe that, and that's what I'm thanking God for every chance I get. God is faithful. The taxes have been paid. You had money for your tithes and for that elaborate wedding. And since God is a God of abundance, I believe you're about to step into a whole 'nother realm. I believe God has something bigger for your life than even you planned."

George thought about what his brother was saying. "Are you giving me a Word of Knowledge here?"

"Word of Knowledge?"

"Yeah. That means to tell me what is to come."

"If that's what a Word of Knowledge is, then I suppose I am."

George smiled. God was confirming a Word He had already placed in George's spirit. "Then I receive it, my brother," George said. "And I agree."

"As soon as I wrap up things here, I'll be catching a bus headed your way. I know the church was glad to have you back early. I know I've certainly missed your teaching, and I haven't been under you for nearly as long as many of the others have."

George became quiet.

"George, are you still there?" Thomas asked.

"Yeah, I'm here. Thomas, I've been asked to step down as the pastor."

"What? Man, stop joking around. Step down? Dismissing you? Man, please!"

"I'm not joking."

Thomas abruptly stopped laughing. "What happened? I don't understand. All I've heard since I've been there are wonderful things about you. Old and young alike think you're something special: 'A true gift from God. An anointed teacher, preacher, and pastor.' "

"Well, a few of the elders and the board of directors—let's say the majority of them—think otherwise. They don't feel I'm adhering to rules, doctrines, and traditions set forth by men who have predestined them to be so."

"So, you're gone? You're no longer the pastor there? Just like that?"

"Just like that. One elder called the other day to say they wanted to give me an appreciation. Seems there's a groundswell of support beginning, now that the word about me not being there is spreading. If I know some of the people, they are going to have a lot of displeased members. A lot of them were really getting what I was teaching. It was changing their lives. Making a difference in their quality of life. I'm sure the leadership won't tell the church the real reason I'm not going to be there: that they didn't care for the direction in which I was taking the church.

"Growing the membership was fine. Building a bigger facility was grand. Establishing the hearts, minds, and spirits of men and women in the Word of God was a noble undertaking. 'Just don't teach and preach the parts we don't believe in.' " George mocked the sentiments he felt were really being expressed. "Excuse me. 'We believe it, but we don't believe it applies to us Christians. We believe in healing, but not for everybody. We believe in women working in church, just keep them in their places. We believe in equality, as long as it's not applied equally across the board.' Let me stop," George said.

"Conforming instead of transforming the mind?" Thomas asked.

"Precisely."

"Well, I've got work to do. George, you know I love you, right?"

"Yeah."

"And you know I never meant to do anything against you? With the money and all? I just thought it was a good get-rich thing that could work and profit both of us in the end."

"God is a God of progression. First the seed, then the blade, then the ear, and then the full corn in the ear," George said. "Miracles are good, but we weren't made to live off miracles. God will—notice I didn't say can, but will—God will take you from glory to glory if you'll do what you're required to do and trust in Him to do His part. Really trust Him."

"Amen," Thomas said. "Now that was a Word!"

CHAPTER 51

And let the peace of God rule in your hearts.

(Colossians 3:15)

Theresa listened as her father talked about how he was doing since Beatrice's death. His mind was still sharp. And if you hadn't known it, you wouldn't have guessed he'd even had a stroke, with the exception of a slight dragging in his left leg when he walked.

Her thoughts were in and out: inside with him and outside with her mother, who had gone to the bank two hours ago and hadn't returned yet. *What did she find when she reached the safe deposit box?* Theresa wondered. *Could Memory, our own flesh and blood, really do something like that to us after we opened our home and our hearts to her? Surely not. Please God—let Mama come back with a good report. Please . . .*

"I got a call from George," Bishop Jordan was saying when she tuned back in to his words. "His wife wanted to know if she could have your phone number or if you would call her. Johnnie Mae's her name. She said it was important; not life threatening, though. I have her phone number here if you want it." Bishop Jordan held out a slip of paper with two phone numbers he had written down.

Theresa took it and looked. *A Georgia and an Alabama area code*, she thought. *Dual homes.* She snickered slightly.

"You okay?" Bishop Jordan asked as he leaned closer.

"Yeah. I just wish Beatrice was still alive."

"I know. It feels like I'm forgetting something or someone everywhere I go and in everything I do. It's like you lose a part of yourself. I have to catch myself from asking her where something is." He smiled. "When I got ready to come here, I started to call for her to come on so we could get going. She always drove wherever we went, so it feels funny sitting on that side of the car. I miss looking to my left and seeing her sitting there wiggling to adjust herself better in the seat. She hated to wear a seat belt; thought it was too constraining. But she wore it, just kept tugging at it to loosen it from time to time."

Theresa took her father's hand. "I miss her like that too, Daddy. And she was so looking forward to this baby."

"I'm just glad Beatrice got to see and hold her. Our little Grace," he said.

Lena came in the door and yelled. "Yoo-hoo! Where is everybody?"

"Upstairs in my room still," Theresa yelled back.

Lena came up with a broad smile on her face. Theresa searched to see what she had found. Lena turned away and looked at Bishop.

"So, Richard, what do you think about that there grandbaby of ours?" Lena's voice was full of cheer. Theresa let out a sigh of relief.

"I think God is good. She is a beautiful little thing and a good baby. She reminds me of you, Theresa, when you were a baby. Doesn't she, Lena?"

"Yeah. And it doesn't seem so long ago either," Lena said.

Bishop Jordan stayed a while longer. They laughed and played with the baby, mostly holding her, feeding her, and biting at her toes. After Bishop left, Theresa stared at Lena.

"What?" Lena said, feeling eyes that seemed to be bearing down to the core of her soul.

"What did you find at the bank?"

"Nothing," Lena said.

"Nothing as in nothing? Nothing as in something? Or something as in nothing?"

"Stop the merry-go-round," Lena said, laughing. "You're making me dizzy!"

"Just tell me, Mama."

Lena sighed. "The necklace is gone."

Theresa began to rub her head and shake it. "I can't believe it. How could Memory do it? How could I be so stupid? You warned me. It was that paper I signed, wasn't it?"

"That was part of it. They only let her in the safe deposit box because, legally, it seemed she had something from you stating it was okay."

"But nothing was on that page when I signed it." Theresa got up and picked up the phone. "I'm calling them. I want to swear out a warrant for her arrest. Mama, I know she's your mother, but I don't care. What she did was broke the law. You can't forge a document, then steal people's belongings. You just can't!"

Lena took the phone out of her hand. "Theresa, let's talk."

"No, Mama! You're not going to talk me out of this. You're just too nice a person. You let people run all over you. It's not right! God doesn't require you to allow people to make you a doormat just because you're a Christian. She broke the law, and she needs to pay! That's it. There's nothing you can say to me that will make me see this differently."

"Theresa, you can't steal what technically belongs to you," Lena said.

Theresa stopped and looked at her. "What? But Big Mama gave it to you. You said so yourself."

"That necklace . . ." Lena began, then stopped. "My trip to New York . . ."

"Yeah?" Theresa was mentally attempting to pull the words out of Lena faster.

"The necklace, Theresa, technically does belong to Memory." Lena patted the bed beside her. "Come. Sit. Now is a good time to tell you what I found out in New York."

CHAPTER 52

But the wisdom that is from above is first pure, then peaceable, gentle, and easy.

(James 3:17)

Johnnie Mae and her mother went to visit Ms. Azile.

"Hey, sugar. Where have you been?" Ms. Azile asked as soon as she saw Mrs. Gates. "I thought you were planning to move in here soon."

"I'm still considering my options," Mrs. Gates said.

"And I'm still trying to convince her to come to Georgia and live with me," Johnnie Mae said.

"Georgia? Well, that ain't too far. And it's good when family wants you. Lord knows I ain't got nobody to take me away. Wish I did—like my friend Sarah Fleming. She wasn't here long before her nephews and a niece came to take her home."

Johnnie Mae looked at her mother, who nodded for her to go on and ask her. "Ms. Azile . . . about Sarah. You say her family came and got her?"

"Two nephews and a niece. Not the warm and friendly type, neither. In fact, they had a time convincing Sarah they were kin to her. I sat right there watching while they were talking. I overhead most of what was going on," Ms. Azile said, whispering the last part. "I didn't like the way they came in here like they owned the place. Not while Ms. Azile is around, no siree. So I just hung around enough to hear what was going on without them knowing it. 'Cause if they hadn't been on the up-and-up, there would have been a few bodies to be picked up around this place when I got finished. You don't hurt my friends."

Johnnie Mae smiled. "Ms. Azile, can you tell me what you overheard? Not everything, just anything that might help me to find Sarah. I really need to talk to her. It's extremely important. It's something she asked me to do for her."

Ms. Azile looked up at the ceiling. Sorting through words, searching for just the ones that might help Mrs. Gates's daughter: the daughter who loved her enough to want to carry her to Georgia with her even though she was newly married, with a new husband.

"Let me see now. They told her that her mother had passed. Then there was something about a will. And that she had to come with them. They were trying to act like they really cared about her, but even I could tell that was only an act. From what I was able to put together, from what they said and the things they didn't say—"

"Didn't say?" Mrs. Gates said, looking suspiciously from Ms. Azile to Johnnie Mae.

"What people don't say sometimes can be just as important as what they do say," Ms. Azile said, nodding and smiling. "Y'all better hear what Ms. Azile is saying."

"So, what do you think was going on?" Johnnie Mae asked.

"I think they were in a bind legally. Apparently, their part of the inheritance was tangled up in Sarah's part. They needed her back in . . . Asheville, North Carolina."

"Are you sure they said Asheville?" Johnnie Mae asked.

"Yeah, because Sarah talked about that place all the time. About that castle that was there. She said we'd go if she ever got a chance to get back home. That she'd come back and bring me for a visit if it were ever possible. But I figured she was talking. Dreaming like the rest of us. Thinking family will come back for you. So I was surprised when them three showed up and were going on and on about taking her home to Asheville."

"Ms. Azile, did Sarah seem to you like she really wanted to go with them?"

"After they talked to her awhile, she seemed like it was okay with her. I think she would have done anything just to go home one more time. I don't think she believes she has long on this side of the calendar."

"Ms. Azile. One more thing: Do you have any idea what their names were? Any of them? A last name would be great. But anything to help me figure out who she might be with right now would be so much appreciated."

Ms. Azile looked at Johnnie Mae. "You're sure she'd want this?"

Johnnie Mae smiled. "Ms. Azile, I give you my word. This would be a prayer answered for her. I assure you that much. She asked me to help her, and I said I would. Now I need you to help me keep my word to her."

Mrs. Gates nodded when Ms. Azile looked at her for additional approval.

"Powell," Ms. Azile said. "When the guy came to the desk to ask for the director, he said his name was Montgomery Powell the second."

Johnnie Mae hugged Ms. Azile and got up to leave.

"Oh, baby," Ms. Azile said. "One more thing I think might be important. They kept asking her about Alexandrite. I don't know if that's a person or what. But the young woman with them, they called her Maggie, she kept asking Sarah about the whereabouts of Alexandrite. And one of the nephews practically grilled her about a wings of grace."

"And what did Sarah say?" Johnnie Mae asked.

"Sarah kept saying as far as she knew, the wings of grace had to be somewhere safe. She whispered, it looked like to me, 'Wings of grace is safe now.' Then she smiled."

Johnnie Mae and Mrs. Gates thanked Ms. Azile as they left.

CHAPTER 53

Let us therefore come boldly unto the throne of grace.

(Hebrews 4:16)

"Mama, I have to go to Asheville. I shouldn't be there but a day or two. But I have got to try and locate Sarah or something that makes sense in all this," Johnnie Mae said.

"Wings of grace," Mrs. Gates kept saying over and over again. "Why does that seem to mean something to me?"

"I don't know, Mama. Did Sarah say something when you and she talked?"

"Wings of grace. Wings of grace." Mrs. Gates looked outside the kitchen bay window. "Wings. Wings." She began to sing, " 'Some glad morning when this life is . . .' " She stopped and looked at Johnnie Mae, who, at that point, had a worried look on her face. "Johnnie Mae, the box!" Mrs. Gates said.

"The box?"

"Yes, the gold-and-wooden box Sarah told you to keep. Remember? She told you to keep it safe for her. She didn't want it with her because she was afraid her family might—"

"Come take her away and get the box!" Johnnie Mae started smiling and ran upstairs as quickly as she could to her bedroom closet. She returned to the kitchen just as fast.

"Wings," she said, holding the box out for her mother to see. "Wings!"

"Wings," her mother said, smiling back and touching the

beautiful, detailed wings etched on the wooden part of the top of the box. "The key?" Mrs. Gates said. She was getting excited and kept touching the keyhole. "Don't you have the key?"

Johnnie Mae beamed as she presented the key. They went to the kitchen counter. Johnnie Mae placed the box on top of it and inserted and turned the key. It opened with a click.

She pulled the lid up. Mother and daughter exchanged grins.

Inside the lid of the box, carved in a brush-script font, was the word 'Grace.' Johnnie Mae pulled things out of the box. There were all types of jewelry: rings, earrings, and necklaces. There were coins inside, including an old 1913 nickel with a Liberty Head. And two thick legal documents neatly folded into thirds.

"Mama, I've got to go to Asheville. I really have to now. I've got to find Sarah."

"Do you trust me to keep Princess Rose, or would you prefer I let Marie baby-sit the both of us?" Mrs. Gates half-teased.

"Just be careful, Mama. If you feel disoriented, stay home. Call someone to come over until it passes."

"Well, I'm going home. I don't care to rattle around in this big house by myself. Take me home and you can be as long as you want in Asheville." She stopped a second. "But aren't you still supposed to be a newlywed? What about your poor husband?"

Johnnie Mae smiled. "I was just thinking that Asheville would be a real romantic place for Landris and me to visit as a couple. A newly married couple at that."

She called Landris and told him what was going on. When she mentioned the word "alexandrite," he interrupted her. "Alexandrite?" he asked.

"Yes."

"That's an expensive stone—rare, in fact. Valuable, if you can find it. Thomas was telling me something about that very stone just recently."

"Landris, you don't mind if we go to Asheville, do you? I was thinking we could get a room at the Biltmore Inn. Get a little honeymooning in while I see if I can locate some folks named Powell, and ultimately find Sarah."

"Did you ever hear from Theresa?" Landris asked.

"No. I don't know if her father had a chance to give her my message, or if she just doesn't care to talk to me."

"So you're not any closer to seeing if Lena may have some association with this Sarah person than you were before? First cousins once removed . . . twice removed . . ."

"I don't have a clue. It was a long shot, but it might have helped me figure some of this out."

"Okay. Well, I'm not too busy these days, since I'm not the pastor of a church anymore. I'm free to travel with you. I'll drive us up there," Landris said.

"Good. Mama is going to keep Princess Rose."

"You feel okay about that?"

"Landris, she hasn't had an episode in awhile. The doctor has her on a high dosage of vitamin C and vitamin E. They're still running tests to see what might be going on with her, but she's been fine. They're going to Mama's house, and I feel sure she won't take any unnecessary risks with Princess Rose around."

"As long as you're sure."

"We're not going to be gone that long. Besides, we would have been away longer than this had we gone on our honeymoon to Bermuda as planned."

"Then, I'll be ready to leave when you get here."

CHAPTER 54

For by grace are ye saved through faith.

(Ephesians 2:8)

Landris took Johnnie Mae to visit Bishop Jordan before they embarked on the road to Asheville. Landris had wanted to see how Bishop was doing since his wife's death, and to let him know that if he needed anything, he was there for him.

"I heard about what happened with the church," Bishop Jordan said. "Seems like they stirred up something over there they didn't fully anticipate in getting rid of you."

"Well, it's not in my hands anymore," Landris said.

"So, what do you think you'll do now? I'm sure you're getting offers to pastor other churches," Bishop Jordan said.

"I've gotten some inquiries. In fact, several people have approached me about forming my own church. For now, I'm just seeking God's direction. Being still, praying, and listening to what God has to say to me."

"That's good. Talking to the Lord is good," Bishop Jordan said.

"Not just talking, Bishop Jordan. Prayer is not always about us telling God; it's making way for a two-way conversation. It's listening to what God has to tell us, instead of us all the time 'telling Him all about our troubles.' As if He doesn't already know. If we'd pray, then listen to what God has to say, we'd learn a lot more, that's for sure."

"You know what they say: You don't learn by talking, you learn by listening," Bishop Jordan said.

"True," Landris said.

"So, Mrs. Landris, how's married life treating you?"

"Great, so far. There's been a lot going on lately," Johnnie Mae said. It was funny being called Mrs. Landris. Not too many people had called her anything other than Johnnie Mae since she'd said "I do."

"I heard about what happened in New York. It's been some trying times. And now there's that anthrax scare making the rounds," Bishop Jordan said as he shook his head.

"Bishop Jordan," Landris leaned forward in his chair. "Johnnie Mae really needs to get in contact with Lena. Is there any way you can possibly assist us in this?"

Bishop Jordan looked at Johnnie Mae. "I got your message, young lady, and just the other day gave Theresa your phone numbers. I guess she hasn't had a chance to contact you yet?"

"No, but I realize a lot has been going on with everybody. I just have something important I need to ask Lena. It wouldn't take but a few minutes. I don't want to appear insensitive to what's going on in people's lives, but if I *could* wait to ask, I would."

"It's all right. Tell you what: why don't I run you over to see Lena?" Bishop Jordan said. "Right now, if you have time."

"We wouldn't want to intrude," Johnnie Mae said.

"I'll call and see if it's all right. I'm sure Lena won't mind." Bishop Jordan made the call. Landris drove, as Bishop Jordan directed him. They arrived at Theresa's house about thirty minutes later.

Lena was waiting with a hug, some fresh coffee, and plenty of sweet rolls. They exchanged greetings and sat down in the den.

"This is a lovely home," Johnnie Mae said. "It has a warm feel to it."

Lena smiled. "I'll pass that along to Theresa. She's worked so hard getting things in place." There was an awkward silence. "Johnnie Mae," Lena said. "What is it you need to know? Richard tells me you have something important you need to ask."

Johnnie Mae smiled, readjusted her body on the sofa, and cleared her throat. "Lena, I met this woman a few months back. She's about eighty-six years old and originally from Asheville, North Carolina. I won't bore you with all the details, but there was a name that came up in our discussion: Patterson. I recalled you were from North Carolina. I'm curious whether you might be familiar or some kin to this particular Patterson."

"Okay," Lena said, watching Johnnie Mae with intensity. "What's the name?"

"Mamie Patterson. Have you heard of her before?"

Lena's heart beat faster; her breath became too quick and left her coughing for air.

Johnnie Mae rushed over to help her. "You okay? Do you need anything? Water? Air? Is it your heart?"

By that time, Bishop Jordan had made his way to the kitchen to get a glass of water and was on his way back. He handed Lena the glass of cool liquid.

"I'm okay," Lena kept saying. "I'm fine." She sipped the water. "I'm okay now."

"I didn't mean to upset you," Johnnie Mae said.

Lena looked at Johnnie Mae. "Mamie Patterson was my grandmother. I called her Big Mama. She was the one who raised me."

"Is she still living?"

Lena shook her head. "She died when I was sixteen."

Johnnie Mae let out a sigh. "Lena, I don't know quite how to tell you this. But I think I may have met your grandmother."

"You mean Mamie?" Bishop Jordan said. "That's impossible. I went to her funeral."

Lena shook her head. "Richard, she's talking about my biological grandmother."

"Biological?" Richard said. "I don't understand. What are y'all talking about?"

"Mamie was not Mama's real grandmother, Daddy," Theresa said as she walked into the room carrying her baby in her arm.

"What in the devil are you people talking about?" Bishop Jordan said.

Theresa sat down. "Good morning, Johnnie Mae. Pastor Landris. Daddy."

"Good morning," they all said in unison.

Lena stood up. "Mamie was not my biological grandmother. I went to New York about a month ago," she said, mainly to Johnnie Mae. "A woman had me named in her will with explicit instructions on how things should be carried out. She didn't want me learning about it in a letter, so she made a video for me. And one for my mother."

"Your mother?" Johnnie Mae said. "Do you know where your mother is?"

"My mother was here about a month ago, although that was purely a coincidence. Actually, she came searching for something she believed was taken from her years ago."

"You?" Johnnie Mae asked Lena.

Lena laughed. "No, she didn't come for me. It was a necklace, if you care to know. An alexandrite necklace, to be exact."

"Alexandrite?" Landris said. "You have an alexandrite? An alexandrite necklace?"

"Had," Theresa said. "The operative word is *had*. Lena gave it to me last year. We received a package a few months back about a million-dollar reward for a necklace—"

"Oh . . . my . . . Lord," Landris said, covering his face with both his hands.

"I know. A million dollars will make a lot of people call on the Lord," Lena said.

"No, you don't understand." Landris looked at Johnnie Mae realizing he might have some vital information on this matter. "My brother called me just the other day about a necklace. An alexandrite. He's working with someone I guess who fronts reward money, sort of like a bounty, in the recovery of valuable items. Someone contacted them claiming to have an alexandrite necklace. They received a million-dollar reward for it."

"You . . . are . . . kidding me," Theresa said, actually laughing at the irony of it all.

"But back to Mamie not being your grandmother," Bishop Jordan said. " 'Cause you people got my head spinning like a spinning top right now."

"Okay, here's what I know," Lena said, deciding to lay the information she had on the table. "Grace Fleming had a daughter named Sarah. Grace's husband had two sons from a previous marriage. Sarah fell in love with a black man named Ransom Perdue, got pregnant, somehow he was tricked, sent away, and never heard from ever again. Sarah had the baby. Her half-brothers connived against her, mainly to keep her from her inheritance. Sarah's father was in bad health, and the sons figured out he didn't have long to live. When Sarah's baby was born, she was told her baby died. Then her father died shortly after that. Sarah had such a strong personality, her half-brothers plotted to have her sent away. They claimed she'd had a mental breakdown. That alone reduced any credibility she might muster in getting anyone to take her claims of foul play seriously. Grace controlled some things after the death of her husband—none to the delight of her stepsons, of course. The only thing was: Grace didn't know where Sarah was, because the sons controlled all of that, and they refused to let her know. That was their way of keeping her in line. Or so they thought."

"Sarah," Johnnie Mae chimed in, "naturally believed she had been abandoned by everyone, including her mother. Whenever she tried telling anyone the truth, she was quickly medicated or put in isolation. Then she'd be transferred to a new facility."

"Her mother eventually hired a private investigator to find her daughter," Lena said. "But every time she got close, Sarah would be moved and the search had to begin again."

"But Sarah had a box hidden with a woman named Pearl Black in Asheville, North Carolina," Johnnie Mae said, picking up the story she was familiar with. "Sarah kept the key while Pearl held on to the box. Pearl was the midwife when Sarah delivered her baby: a girl. Told her baby was stillborn, Sarah had some idea but no real proof that her baby didn't die. She never knew what really happened or that her baby had been just down the hall, four doors away from her, being cared for by her dearest friend in the world."

"Mamie," Lena said, "who not only raised my mother, a child that wasn't hers, but me, my mother's child. Mamie stopped working at the house after her 'twins' were born. Everybody figured Grace had fired her, since it was no secret they couldn't stand each other. It turned out to be a perfect cover," Lena said.

"Grace had intended to make everything right, but the stepsons had other plans. If they had known Sarah's baby hadn't died per that brother Heath's instruction, they might have found a way to make it so later. Heath was just that evil."

"So, Grace saved the baby?" Landris asked.

"Yes, it was Grace. She was the one who came up with the plan of passing Sarah's baby off as Mamie's: 'Twins, born hours apart.'" Lena shook her head. "Grace gave a special-made box with wings on the outside of it to Mamie. Inside was a rare alexandrite necklace. She had given an identical special-made box to Sarah earlier, on her eighteenth birthday. Inside were the ring, bracelet, and earrings that matched the necklace, along with some other valuables and important documents."

"Among other things," Johnnie Mae said, fully aware of the contents inside of the gold-and-wooden box.

Lena looked at her. "How would you know that? Did Sarah tell you? But she couldn't have, according to Grace. Grace said Sarah wasn't to open it until her thirtieth birthday. It was a tradition. But nobody could find the box after Sarah was sent away. Grace believed it had been stolen by one of the brothers. Or maybe Sarah had somehow gotten rid of it, although she couldn't see that as a possibility."

"She didn't get rid of it," Johnnie Mae said. "She gave it to Pearl for safekeeping. Sarah didn't trust anybody in that house. She believed Pearl really cared about her. So she gave the box to her to keep safe until she found a way to leave. She knew there was some jewelry inside of it. She even suspected portions of the legendary Alexandrite Collection might be inside. But she never opened it. And she never knew what happened with her friend Mamie: why Mamie stopped working there; why she never came back to even visit her; how someone could love you and not come console you when you've lost a baby that they knew you desperately wanted. Sarah didn't understand why Mamie had deserted her when she needed her most. The two had been closer than blood sisters."

"Mamie sent word she had something important to tell Sarah," Lena said. "She had sent a message by a cook who was to give the note to Pearl to give to Sarah when she was due to perform her checkup. Grace figured Mamie might try and back out of their pact. She had told Mamie not to let anyone know the truth about Sarah's baby. No one. Not until it was safe to do so. In fact, she had gone to see Mamie the very day Mamie was about to tell her husband, Willie B, the truth. Willie B didn't have a clue what was going on, but he knew one of the twins was just much too light. He had accused Mamie of being unfaithful to him, and with all people, Mr. Victor Fleming, senior, the husband of the wife who showed up just when Mamie was about to confess the truth about Memory."

"Mamie eventually did tell Willie B the truth: that Memory was Sarah's baby. But it was long after Sarah was gone." Lena drank some of her water. "One thing was sure: Grace didn't let that baby lack for anything. She insisted on paying Mamie still, since Mamie was technically taking care of Memory full-time. Grace didn't care for the name Mamie had given the baby: Memory Elaine."

"Why?" Landris said. "Although I'll admit Memory is an unusual name."

"It wasn't the name Memory she took issue with. It was Elaine," Lena said. "Elaine is also Sarah's middle name. People with secrets have a tendency to be nervous. Grace was afraid one of her stepsons would figure out the truth, harm that child, or worse: kidnap her and have her sent away just like they'd done to Sarah. Grace loved Memory and would have done anything for her. Feeling, essentially, she'd failed her own child."

"You almost need a score card to keep up," Bishop Jordan said, scratching his head.

"When I went to New York, the lawyer gave me a videotape Grace had made. She filled two journals, explaining as much as she possibly could. Grace also left one more box with wings on it. I'm supposed to find Memory, if possible, and open it with her."

"So, there were three wings of grace boxes?" Landris asked.

"Yes. Mamie had one with the alexandrite necklace inside it that Grace had given her for Memory," Lena said. "For years, she brought things for Memory—her inheritance. Just in case her stepsons won in the end, Grace wanted to ensure Sarah's seed would receive that to which they were entitled. Grace left us her last and final box, etched with her signature crest of strength, yet elegance—*Wings of Grace*."

"So that's why you feel the necklace I had belonged to Memory?" Theresa said.

"Originally, it did. Big Mama gave me the necklace," Lena said, "because Grace had made it clear it was our family's entitlement. Memory was still making irresponsible decisions. She was hanging out with the wrong crowd. Big Mama never intended to take Memory's inheritance from her, but she knew Memory would sell anything worth money the first chance she got. Big Mama said Memory broke into her house a few times, trying to steal something to sell. I'd wager she was after that necklace. That's why it wasn't in the box. Memory or whoever took the box thought valuables were inside. But Big Mama had emptied it of anything of value, fully expecting Memory might try that very thing."

"Man," Bishop Jordan said. "What a story! You know, this would make a good book." He looked at Johnnie Mae. "You should think about turning this into a novel."

"The reason Big Mama gave the necklace to me was because she believed I had a right to our inheritance," Lena said. She didn't think it was fair that Memory might take it and essentially throw it away. Grace never objected to it being passed down. In fact, she encouraged that. She gave it to Memory, intending for Memory to pass it on to me someday, and then I would pass it on to my offspring. Which, in truth, I did do."

"And now Memory has taken it back," Theresa said. "And that's mostly my fault."

"Theresa, it's not your fault. Memory came with one purpose, and she fulfilled it."

"So, where is Memory now?" Johnnie Mae asked Lena.

"I haven't a clue," Lena said.

"Do you know where Sarah is?" Lena asked Johnnie Mae.

Johnnie Mae laughed. "Funny, huh? We finally figure this out, and the key players are missing in action. I don't know where Sarah is. Last I saw of her, she was in Alabama."

"Then, let's start looking for her there," Lena said.

"Her family came and took her away about six weeks ago. I believe she's in Asheville, North Carolina now," Johnnie Mae said. "Actually, Landris and I are on our way up there today. I just wanted to try one more time to see if the name Mamie Patterson had any meaning to you," Johnnie Mae said, looking directly at Lena.

Bishop Jordan relaxed his body. "Well, it indeed looks like you hit pay dirt," he said.

Johnnie Mae looked over at Landris, who nodded as though he were reading her mind. "Listen, if you'd like to go with us to Asheville," she said to Lena and the others, "we have room."

Landris smiled. "Yeah, I'm driving, so it won't be a problem."

Theresa laughed. "You have room for all of us?"

"Yes," Landris said. "I'm taking the Denali. It'll comfortably seat six."

Lena looked at Theresa.

"Of course, I'm going!" Theresa said to Lena. "I feel fine. Me and the baby are up to riding."

Lena nodded and smiled. "We're going. Give us time to throw a few things in a bag . . ." She looked at Bishop. "Say, Richard? You want to ride to Asheville with us?"

A smile crept over his face. "Me? Why I wouldn't miss this for the world," he said.

"We'll come back later this afternoon and pick you up around two o'clock?" Landris said, checking each face to see if that was enough time for them to be ready.

"Two o'clock sounds good," Lena said with excitement. *Memory, where are you?*

CHAPTER 55

Looking unto Jesus the author and finisher of our faith.

(Hebrews 12:2)

The shiny Denali, black with tan leather interior, rolled into Asheville on that first Monday in October, which just happened to also be October first: clearly a day of firsts, especially if Johnnie Mae and Lena were to have their way.

Everybody got settled into his or her hotel room. An electric charge was in the air, although a lot of it had to do with the staff at Biltmore Castle gearing up for the Christmas crowd who would soon flock there for their fill of holiday spectaculars.

Johnnie Mae had been here before. She knew the first order of business, and probably the most profitable with the least resistance, would be a visit to Pearl's house. Not wanting to just show up unannounced, she called. No one answered.

Johnnie Mae decided to swing by Pearl's house anyway. Lena and Theresa piled into the Denali to keep her company, since it was already dark out.

As Lena walked up the porch stairs, she asked, "Who did you say lives here again?"

"Pearl Black. The midwife." Johnnie Mae knocked. Nothing. She knocked harder and longer when she didn't hear any movement inside the house. Still nothing.

"Try again," Lena said when no one came after the second

time Johnnie Mae knocked. "She's got to be pretty old. How old did you say she was?"

"Ninety-eight to be exact. But she has a great-granddaughter who lives here with her." Johnnie Mae knocked on the wooden door hard once again.

They waited. Still no one answered. Johnnie Mae became a little concerned.

Early the next morning, Johnnie Mae tried calling, hoping to catch Pearl's great-granddaughter, Angel, before she left for work.

"Hello," a voice said, obviously in too big a hurry to be bothered.

"Hi, is Angel in, please?" Johnnie Mae said.

"Speaking."

"Angel, I'm not sure if you remember me, but my name is Johnnie Mae Taylor." She glanced just in time to catch Landris' frown after she said her name. "I met you a few months ago. I'm the one with the key to that box your great-grandmother had."

"Of course I remember you!" Angel said. "It's not every day someone famous stops by and gets Great-granny all excited."

Johnnie Mae smiled. "Listen, I'm here in town for a couple of days with some acquaintances of mine. I'd really like to stop by and chat with Pearl. I promise not to hold her long. It probably won't be for more than an hour."

"Oh, I'm sorry, Ms. Taylor. Great-granny died," Angel said.

"She what?"

"Yes, she died a few weeks after you left, in fact. It was as though she really had been waiting on someone to come reclaim that box so she could feel free to go on home and be with the Lord."

"I'm sorry to hear that, Angel."

"Oh, don't be sorry. Great-granny lived a full life. She reached the minimum seventy years God promised us in the Bible, and then some. We celebrate daily the time God gave us with her, and keep living the life we know we ought and were taught."

"Well, Pearl was a remarkable woman," Johnnie Mae said. "Truly remarkable."

"Yes, ma'am. And she thought the world of you, Ms. Taylor. In fact, she left something here for you. I was planning to send it to you. Then I got an offer for a job in Birmingham, Alabama, and figured I could just contact you when I got there and bring it to you myself. But since you're in town," Angel said, "I can give it to you here."

"Would it be possible for me and two friends to come by sometime today?"

"Well, I have to go to work, but I can get with you this afternoon when I get off. In fact, I could just come by your hotel."

"I don't want to put you out."

"It won't put me out. I manage a radio station. This is my last week at work. I had planned to come to Biltmore before I left anyway. You're at Biltmore Inn, aren't you?"

"Yes."

"Good. Give me your room and phone number, and I'll call you when I'm on my way."

"Are you sure?"

"Oh, perfectly sure. Ms. Taylor, is there something pressing you needed to know before I get off the phone? I'm sensing there's something you want to ask?"

Johnnie Mae smiled. "Well, I was curious. Have you ever heard of Montgomery Powell the second or Victor Fleming the third?"

"The Powells and Flemings? Yeah, who doesn't know them around these parts? Their family's mega-rich and mega-powerful."

"Angel, it would really help if you could tell me how to get in touch with them."

"I can do you one better. Why don't I take you to meet Montgomery personally?"

"That would be great. But could you do me one small favor?"

"What?"

"Don't let Montgomery know my name. I'm not sure if somehow he might be expecting me, and he might possibly not let me in the door," Johnnie Mae said.

"This wouldn't have anything to do with that elderly woman they brought back with them, would it?"

"They brought back an elderly woman?"

"Yeah. Word on the street is she's a little cuckoo. Slightly touched in the head."

Johnnie Mae placed her hand over her heart to muffle its loud beating. "Angel, would you happen to know her name by any chance?"

"Nope. I hear they kind of keep her in a room. Apparently, she doesn't care to have visitors. She's eccentric. They say she's had mental problems. They don't expect her to live much longer. The family wanted her to be able to spend her last days in the home she grew up in," Angel said. "Listen, I have to get out of here. I'll call you this afternoon."

When Johnnie Mae got off the phone, she clapped her hands. "Praise Him!"

Landris walked up to her. "So when are you planning to start using your new last name, Mrs. Landris?" he said with a smile.

"Landris, some people only know me as Taylor. It's just hard having to explain things at certain times. Angel met me when I was still Johnnie Mae Taylor and—"

"Hey. Slow down. I was only asking a simple, innocent question."

"I'll start, okay. But Landris, I suppose now is just as good a time as any to say this. I'll probably still use Johnnie Mae Taylor on my books. It's established, you know."

He nodded, but his smile slightly faded. "Whatever you think is best," he said. "Just as long as *you* know: You're Mrs. Johnnie Mae Landris as far as I'm concerned."

CHAPTER 56

Let the Lord be magnified, which hath pleasure in the prosperity of his servant.

(Psalm 35:27 (b))

Landris' cell phone rang.

"Hey, where are you?" Thomas asked.

"I'm in North Carolina."

"What are you doing there?"

"Checking up on something with my wife." He smiled, liking the sound of that.

"Well, listen: I've got some good news and some great news. Which would you rather hear first?" Thomas waited.

"Man, quit playing. If they're both good, it doesn't matter."

"Okay, the good news is: one of the reward bounties came through."

Landris gasped. "The alexandrite? The one those people were willing to pay—"

"Two million dollars, my brother! Sammie and his people got the necklace, made sure it was the genuine thing—and it was. The people got their million-dollar reward. Sammie said they acted like they made those type of transactions every day. Then the other buyers were contacted, transaction completed, and you are now a cool two million dollars richer than you were only an hour ago."

"Thomas, do you know where we can find her?"

"Her who?"

"The woman who had the necklace. The alexandrite necklace. I need to find her—"

Thomas got quiet. "I don't know anything about a woman having that necklace." Thomas paused. "George, don't tell me you're wanting to do the right thing and give her or whomever the whole two million dollars. Come on now, this is business . . . a legit transaction. Somebody had the necklace. We put up one million, we sold it for two."

"Thomas, I'm not trying to ruin the deal. Somebody turned in the necklace. They were paid their money as promised. Everybody's happy. I just need to find that person."

"Everybody's happy, including the ones who just paid to get that necklace in their possession. Sammie said they were so glad to get it that they gladly paid the extra he charged. So you're getting the entire two million, my little brother."

"Thomas, I need to find the woman who turned in the necklace. I'm not looking to cause problems for anyone. Will you see if you can get a number, a mailing address—"

"They don't keep that sort of information on file," Thomas assured him. "Apparently, that's why they have such a high recovery rate. People appreciate the anonymity of doing business this way. It keeps everybody out of trouble. 'You got it. We want it. Let's deal. No questions asked.' After that: untraceable cash and transaction complete. Delete. Nothing to trace back to anyone ever. And why do you think it was a woman?"

"Will you at least see what you can find out? For me? Look, I'll even throw in a bonus if you can help me find the person who turned in the alexandrite necklace."

"A bonus? What's that? Ten percent of what you're already paying me for all my troubles? Let's see now, ten percent of zero is . . ."

"Thomas, I'm serious. Just see what you can do. Please. This is really important."

"So, do you want to hear the *great* news or not?" Thomas asked.

"Go ahead."

"That other deal I told you might be coming through? Well

the ink is drying as I'm flying. When you get home, I'll bring the paperwork over for you to look at and sign."

George laughed. "Sounds great, Thomas. I'm going into a business I didn't initiate, you can't tell me exactly what it entails, and I'm supposed to be excited about it?"

"Yes! Have a little faith, will you? I know I messed up big-time before. But I believe you're going to agree with me on this one. I don't want to tell you about it and prejudice you against it before you've even had time to really look at it and give it a chance."

"And if I don't like it?"

"Then, you don't sign."

"And my money that apparently has already been committed without my prior consent?"

"You'd get some of it back, but you know there is that good faith clause, so of course they keep a good chunk."

"But at least I'd get something back. Right, Thomas? And something is better than nothing? Right, Thomas?"

"Only *you* can find a way to make great news sound bad. I'm going to get off the phone now and work on some more things. When will you be home? I want to time my visit so I can get in and get out without you newlyweds ever realizing I interrupted."

"Probably tomorrow or the day after."

George got off the phone. He found Johnnie Mae staring out of the window at the beautiful, majestic blue mountains.

"It's wonderful up here, isn't it?" Johnnie Mae said. "Beautiful. Breathtaking."

"Indeed. And the mountains aren't bad either." He had his eyes fixed totally on her.

She looked at him and playfully slapped his hand. "You are bad."

"So, what's on your mind?" He cradled and rocked her softly inside his arms.

"I'm supposed to be getting together with Angel this afternoon. She knows this man named Montgomery Powell the second and hopefully can get me inside his home to see him. But after I get in there, I haven't a clue what to do next."

"What do you mean?"

"I believe Sarah might be in there. How do I get them to let me talk to her if she is?"

"Johnnie Mae, God has brought you this far. Just trust Him to help you once you get inside." Landris squeezed her tighter. "Thomas just called me on my cell phone."

"What's he talking about now?"

"He wanted to let me know I am practically the owner of some business that he can't even tell me what it's about. He's bringing the paperwork to look over when we get back." Landris held Johnnie Mae a little tighter. "Thomas also told me someone claimed a reward on an alexandrite necklace. It had to have been Lena's mother. I just know it. I asked him to see if he could locate the person who claimed the reward, but he says they don't keep that kind of information on record. Something about a 'no questions asked' clause. So, I don't have much faith in anything coming of it. But it won't hurt to try."

"At least you're making an effort. Right now I'm just praying I can get to Sarah and let her know we've found at least some of her family. She deserves that. Sarah's been through so much, it's only fair that she experience some good from all of her struggles and efforts."

"I believe she will," Landris said. "I'm putting my faith out there that she will."

CHAPTER 57

And the prayer of faith
shall save the sick.

(James 5:15)

Angel came to Biltmore Inn as promised. She insisted on driving, so Johnnie Mae rode in her two-seater sports car. They arrived at the mansion twenty-five minutes later.

"This is it," Angel said. "I told Montgomery I was bringing someone from out of town with me. He wasn't thrilled until I told him you were slightly famous and promised we wouldn't stay long. That's another reason why it was best that only you came."

"Thanks."

"No problem. I just hope this works out for everybody concerned."

Angel rang the doorbell. They were escorted inside. Montgomery Powell II, a suave, middle-aged patrician, was a gracious host. Awed by the fact that Johnnie Mae was an author, he felt that if he impressed her enough, she might take an interest in writing his life story. He showed her various rooms and explained the historical value contained in and surrounding each of them.

Johnnie Mae brought up little facts she knew about their family history. It was he who was now impressed.

"I see you've been checking up on us, Mrs. Landris," Montgomery said.

"I just did some research on the area for a possible novel." She smiled, since it wasn't a lie: Sarah had told her that if this didn't pan out, she could use the information in a novel. Johnnie Mae pulled out her junior-sized, leather holder with the yellow legal pad and made a big to-do about looking over her notes. "Your grandfather, Victor Fleming senior, from all accounts, was a pretty shrewd and industrious businessman, I see."

Montgomery smiled. "Yes, my father often told us of our heritage. We indeed have much to be proud of."

"Indeed." Johnnie Mae smiled again.

"Excuse me, but my memory is not what it used to be. What did you say your last name was again? I know Angela said you were an author. I was curious whether I've read anything you may have written?" He scratched one of his thick, wild, scraggly eyebrows.

"My name is Johnnie Mae Landris. But I write under the name Johnnie Mae Taylor."

He appeared to be flipping through a mental Rolodex, then smiled. Apparently, she wasn't famous enough to register admiration or concern.

"Well, my family and the blacks around here have always gotten along splendidly. But, listen, Mrs. Landris—"

"Oh please, call me Johnnie Mae." She smiled pleasantly, then cocked her head to the side.

"Johnnie Mae, listen. I really have some matters I need to attend to. So, I hope you don't think me rude—"

"Sarah Fleming," Johnnie Mae said in a firm, matter-of-fact tone of voice.

He looked at her with piercing eyes before they softened a bit. "What about her?"

"I was looking for her and was wondering what, if any, light you might be able to shed on her current whereabouts?"

"Why would you be looking for her? It's common knowledge she was committed over sixty years ago. Our family has always been dutiful to take care of her. When she got better, my father and uncle ensured that she stayed in the finest facilities in the South."

"Would you happen to know where she is at this moment?" Johnnie Mae watched him as he began to physically squirm.

"Look, Mrs. Taylor or Mrs. Landris or whatever name you choose to go by: My great-aunt is of no concern of yours. We as a family don't really care to discuss her, as she is a very sensitive issue for us. But then, every family has one—certainly, no big deal to someone like you, since I'm sure you can relate."

"I only asked where I might be able to find her. Surely you've nothing to hide?"

"I just don't want you upsetting our dear great-aunt. If you must know, she is deathly ill. We don't expect her to be with us much longer. We brought her home, and I refuse to subject her to being hounded by some money-hungry writer who would blatantly disregard the welfare of a dying old woman just to sell a few books!" He started toward the door and opened it. "It's been a pleasure, but at the moment, I have matters to attend."

Johnnie Mae looked over at Angel as they reached the door.

Johnnie Mae turned around. "Mr. Powell. Let me let you in on a little secret," she said softly. "I've spoken with Sarah quite extensively already. I know a lot more than I'm sure you'd care for me to know. Sarah was doing fine the last time I saw her. Here's the deal: If you don't produce her to me by tomorrow morning, I will use all the influence I can muster to bring attention to this situation. And Mr. Powell, trust me, the information I have accumulated so far would not cast a pretty picture on you or your loving, caring family." She stepped out of the doorway. "In fact, should Sarah meet death before I see her, you may well find yourself answering to suspicions of foul play."

He laughed. "You do have some kind of an imagination, I'll give you that much. I suppose that's why you're a . . . novelist."

She glared at him, then wrote down her hotel room and phone number on her business card. "Here's my card. I desire to speak to Sarah. You have until the morning. After that, I don't think you're going to care too much for the results this *novelist*," she mimicked his tone of voice, "*not* seeing her will produce."

He forced a smile as he deftly snatched her card. "I will check with my great-aunt to see if she cares to speak with you. If she is able, I'll have her call you and let you know her desires herself. Then I would ask that you not ingratiate yourself into our lives ever again. Is that understood?" He presented her with another one of his smirks.

"Tell her: Alexandrite and wings of Grace." Johnnie Mae then turned to walk away.

"Just a moment," he said as his grin fell to the ground and he grabbed her by the arm. She looked down at his hand. He just as quickly let go. "What do you know about that?"

"Enough. I know enough. And trust me, I have all the proof necessary to blow you and your family clean out of the water if I am forced to. Is *that* understood?"

"Aunt Sarah," he mumbled under his breath. "But how? How did you do it?"

Johnnie Mae smiled. "She's not crazy. She never was. She's not sick either, unless you and your family have done something to her since bringing her here. I pray, for your sake, you haven't, because, Mr. Powell, when something is important to me, I don't play, and I don't quit. You have until morning. After that, you'd better pray to your god to help you. Because me and my God will be doing everything in our power to help Sarah. Right is right. I don't know if you know that. Sarah has been on the wrong side of justice and fairness for far too long. The scales have now tipped. So, don't fool yourself. Oh," she said with a smile. "If you think this is an idle threat by some passive *Black* woman, with a capital 'B,' don't make one more mistake and misread this one."

Johnnie Mae and Angel walked away and got in the car. Angel hastily drove away.

CHAPTER 58

For the word of God is quick and powerful, and sharper than any two-edged sword.

(Hebrews 4:12)

"Are you out of your mind?" Angel said as they rode back to the hotel. "Do you not realize you're in the South? And you were threatening a white man? In his house? And not just any white man, but one who has the power and probably the people on his payroll who could still possibly make you disappear?"

Johnnie Mae looked at her with an assured calmness and smiled. "He's not going to do anything. He doesn't know what all I really have. Right now, he's scrambling trying to figure out what his next move should be. I just pray, for Sarah's sake, I'm not too late already."

"But aren't you afraid?" Angel said as she looked from the highway to Johnnie Mae and back again.

"Afraid? No."

"Why not?" She laughed nervously.

Johnnie Mae touched her arm softly to help her compose herself. "Because 'God has not given me a spirit of fear, but of power and love and a sound mind.'"

"Bible verses? You go to a man of power, threaten him, accuse him of practically kidnapping his own great-aunt with the possible intent to kill her, and you quote a scripture as to the basis for why you're not shaking like I am right now?"

Johnnie Mae smiled. "Either I believe it or I don't. There's no straddling the fence. Either I believe the battle is not mine but the Lord's, or I believe it's mine. If it's mine, it might be mine alone to fight. If it's His, He'll send legions of angels—" Johnnie Mae looked at Angel and smiled even more. "Like you, Angel. He put you in my path. If it hadn't been for Pearl and you, I don't know what would have happened. Sarah's counting on me now. She's been praying to God for years, believing sometimes that He wasn't hearing her. But she never gave up. Many of us would have a long time ago, but she didn't. God works through people, and sometimes it takes us a little longer to say 'yes.' Sometimes we hear God tell us to do something, but we tell Him 'no.' God uses people, but He doesn't force us. So when we say no, He then has to speak to another's heart."

"Is that why sometimes it seems to take forever for a prayer to be answered?"

"Yes. Then there are times when we pray and God has dispatched an angel to handle it. But we stop God and the angels from working on our behalf because we give up or quit too soon or begin to speak words God can't give His support to. Do you recall in Daniel 10 when Daniel prayed and it seemed like God wasn't answering his prayer?"

"Daniel 10?"

"Yes. You see, an angel had been dispatched. And the angel was coming for Daniel's *words* . . . what Daniel had said. But the prince of Persia was trying to keep the angel from reaching Daniel. Many times it's the enemy who is trying to stop things. It's not God's doing at all. But as long as Daniel didn't speak anything contrary—"

"You mean like when we say, 'Maybe God didn't want me to have it' or 'Maybe God said no,' when in fact God didn't say no at all? Or when we start speaking negative confessions?"

"Exactly. Our words cause things to happen in the spirit world. When we don't see anything happening, we have to be careful that we don't start talking wrong. The wrong words can stop what the right words put into play," Johnnie Mae said. "That angel told Daniel he had been fighting twenty-one days trying to get to him. Then the archangel Michael showed up to help, and that angel was able to reach Daniel. Just imagine what a different outcome would have transpired had Daniel started saying negative things. That angel would no longer have had any authority to come to Daniel."

"So, you're saying the reason you can be so bold is because you believe God is on your side?" Angel asked.

"I'm saying, 'They that be with us are more than they that be with them.' And I believe that. But I have to believe it enough to act on it. Because that's what faith is: 'Acting on what you believe.' "

Johnnie Mae and Angel arrived at the hotel.

"You want to come in?" Johnnie Mae asked.

"Sure." Angel parked the car. "So, what are you going to tell the rest of them when you go inside?"

"The truth. This may or may not work. We could be in for a real fight. But the battle is not ours—"

"It's the Lord's!" Angel said with a shout of triumph.

When they went inside, Landris led them all in a word of prayer. They prayed the prayer of agreement, then touched in agreement on their desired outcome.

"Lord, tell old Pharaoh to let your people go," Landris said. "In Jesus' name, amen."

"Amen," they said together.

"Now, let's thank God that's it's already done," Landris said. "Let's give voice to our faith."

CHAPTER 59

But he giveth more grace.

(James 4:6)

It was 11:58 A.M., and Johnnie Mae hadn't heard from Montgomery Powell II.

"I suppose he called your bluff," Bishop Jordan said as they loaded their belongings into the Denali to head back to Atlanta.

Johnnie Mae smiled. "It wasn't a bluff. I fully intend to pursue this when I get home."

"And I'll use whatever resources I have at my disposal to help," Landris said.

Lena looked discouraged. "I can't believe we were so close," she said.

Theresa hugged her. "Don't give up. Hold fast and keep confessing your desire."

Lena smiled. "I'm not giving up."

As they rode down the freeway, Johnnie Mae turned to Landris. "Get off at the next exit," she said.

Landris looked at her and back to the road. "Why? Did we forget something?"

"I have to try one more time. I just have to."

"We're going to the Powells' house?" Landris said, turning on his blinkers to move over the two lanes necessary for him to be able to exit.

"Yes."

"What if they call the police?" Landris said.

"Then, that might be a mistake on their part. But I feel in my spirit we should go."

They found the house without any problems. Lena and Theresa sat quietly, the baby asleep in her car seat, and Bishop Jordan leaned forward to get a better look outside.

"This is it," Johnnie Mae said.

Theresa's feet were the first to touch the cobblestoned drive-way. "Wow," she said, looking around leaving Lena to take the baby out of the car seat for her.

They all went to the door. Johnnie Mae rang the doorbell. A middle-aged woman around Lena's age appeared.

"Can I help you?" She stopped and looked at Lena, whose face was turned so that only the side that had not been scarred was visible. The woman stepped back for a moment, not believing how much Lena resembled her oldest sister.

"We're looking for Sarah Fleming," Johnnie Mae said.

"She's eat—" The woman had been staring so hard at Lena she'd almost slipped up. "Who's asking?"

Johnnie Mae was about to say something when Lena stepped forward. "Her granddaughter," Lena said, her scar now completely visible to the woman.

The woman stepped back again, although Lena wasn't sure if it was from seeing her entire face now or the impact of the words she had just spoken.

"Her granddaughter?" The woman laughed. "That's impossible. She couldn't possibly have a granddaughter. She never had children. So, who are you? Really?"

"My name is Lena Patterson. My mother's name is Memory Patterson."

"See, my great-aunt never married. She has forever been a Fleming. And there were never any Pattersons in our family tree. But even more to the point: You're black."

"Young lady, I've been through a lot in my life. We've come to find Sarah Fleming, my grandmother, and we're not about to let you or anyone else stop us."

"You're after the inheritance, aren't you?" the woman accused them. "That's it. You must have heard how everything our family owns has ended up in Sarah's name. I don't know how you found out. So you're here trying to scam your way into her fortune. How much are you after? I want you to know, we'll not allow you to take our great-aunt through some mess over money. She's been through a lot herself. And you should be ashamed of yourself coming to take advantage of a defenseless old woman!"

"Where's Montgomery Powell the second?" Theresa demanded, saying his name bitterly.

"He went into town to take care of some business. He should be back shortly. And I can assure you, he's not going to take kindly to you when he hears about this."

Johnnie Mae took a small step forward. "You seem to be a pretty decent person. Maybe you really don't know what's been going on. Would you just let Sarah know that Johnnie Mae Taylor is out here to see her? Tell her, and you'll see she'll say it's okay. Sarah asked me to help her. Please, just tell her I'm here."

The woman looked at them standing at the door. "How do I know I can trust you? How do I know you're not up to something? trying to con your way into our home?"

Johnnie Mae looked in her purse, pulled out a gold snuffbox with a drawing of the Russian emperor Alexander I and empress Elizabeth on it, and handed it to her. It had a double-headed eagle holding two glory wreathes over the couple's heads, and inscriptions in Russian whose meanings Johnnie Mae didn't have a clue of.

The woman read aloud the inscriptions on the left shield and on the empress's side of the box: " 'Peace in Europe Year 1814.' " She read the other side: " 'Your fortitude saved Europe.' " She then read the inscription on the right shield. " 'Your victories brought peace.' " She looked at Johnnie Mae. "Where did you get this? We have another one identical to this one put away. I had heard we once owned two of them, but no one has been able to locate the other one in the past several decades."

Johnnie Mae promptly produced an earring and demonstrated its color change from sunlight to indoor light. "An alexandrite," the woman said. "But where did you get it?"

"It belongs to Sarah. All of these belong to Sarah," Johnnie

Mae said. "Now please, let her know that Johnnie Mae Taylor is here asking for her. And would you hurry."

The woman looked at the snuffbox and the earring again, then nodded as she handed them carefully back to Johnnie Mae. "I'll be right back," she said as she closed the door, leaving them outside to wait.

"What now?" Lena asked as she turned and surveyed the immaculate grounds.

"We'll just have to see what happens next."

A car drove up. Montgomery jumped out before it could even be parked. "What are you doing here? I will have you arrested if you don't leave my premises immediately!"

"Hey, calm down," Landris said, stepping up to cut him off before he got too close to the others.

"And who are you?" Montgomery fumed, looking Landris up and down.

"I'm George Landris, Johnnie Mae's husband. And frankly, I don't care for the way you happen to be yelling at her at this moment."

"Then, I would suggest y'all leave."

"We're not leaving, Mr. Powell, until we see Sarah," Johnnie Mae stated.

"Yes, you *are* leaving! I spoke with Sarah yesterday—after you left. She said she's never heard of you. She has no idea how you know what you do. So, you can't possibly have anything to hold over me or my family's head, or to use against us in any way."

"Is that what she told you?" Johnnie Mae said.

"It's exactly what she told me!"

"Do you think maybe she was afraid to tell you the truth? Thinking maybe you'll send her away again like you and your family have been doing for decades?" Johnnie Mae said as she stared at him. "Why don't you ask her when she feels safe? Ask her while witnesses are around. Let's go in and speak to her together."

"You mean you and your gang here?" He laughed. "Fat chance. This one here," he pointed at Landris, "looks like he was just released from prison and is already strung out on drugs with that ungodly looking hair of his. This is America; get yourself a hair-cut!" He turned back to Johnnie Mae. "Well, I'll have you know I've taken out a protection order to keep you away from Sarah and my premises. But in the spirit of my Christian upbringing, I'm giving *you people* two minutes to get loaded up and off my property." He looked at his watch and patted his foot to a sound-less beat.

The woman inside the house returned and opened the door.

"Elizabeth, call the police!" Montgomery barked out the words. "Ask specifically for Gerald, if he's there. Tell them we have tres-passing thugs on our property, and we'd like a squad car here im-mediately to remove them!"

Elizabeth stood there. She didn't budge.

"Did you hear me?" Montgomery demanded.

Elizabeth looked from Montgomery to Lena to Johnnie Mae. Then she opened the door wider and nodded for them to come inside.

"Elizabeth, what are you doing?" he yelled. "Are you re-tarded? I just told you to call the police!"

Sarah suddenly appeared at the door, and the blood practically drained from Montgomery's face. "Aunt Sarah, now what are you doing up? You go on back upstairs, Aunt Sarah. These peo-ple here mean us no good." He started toward the door en-trance.

"Don't you take another step toward me," Sarah said. "Or I'll have *you* arrested!"

"Aunt Sarah, what are you talking about?" Montgomery laughed as he continued toward the door.

"I mean it," Sarah said. "I'll have the authorities here so quick it will make your head spin."

Montgomery laughed again as he came closer. "And who's going to believe you, old woman? A little old woman that every-body knows is a little touched from days of old. What are you going to tell anybody, Aunt Sarah? Who has believed you in all these years? I watched my daddy and his brother have you shuf-fled from one place to the other. Who saved you then? And your mother, Grace, she was about as loony as you. She actually be-lieved she was a match for Daddy and Uncle Victor. Then me.

And now look: You have a bunch of . . ." he said the 'n' word, then spat on the ground. "This here circus of folks ain't gonna help you none! Look at them. They're *black*, Aunt Sarah! What can a bunch of blacks do to help you? Huh? What?"

"Sarah," Johnnie Mae said as she approached her. "I found them." She was beaming.

"Found what?" Montgomery sputtered.

"You found them?" Sarah asked as her face began to soften.

"Yeah. And I came back to tell you, but you were gone." Johnnie Mae grinned as she gave Sarah a quick hug. "Sarah, I'd like for you to meet Lena Patterson."

"Lena?" Sarah said as Lena moved toward her open arms.

"Elizabeth, I'm not going to tell you again. Call the police. Now!" Montgomery commanded.

Lena hugged Sarah back. "I'm your granddaughter," Lena said as they embraced.

"My granddaughter? I have a granddaughter?" Sarah hugged Lena even tighter as she looked over at Johnnie Mae for an answer and tenderly touched Lena's face.

Johnnie Mae nodded. "Lena is your daughter's child. This is Theresa Jordan, your great-granddaughter; and Mauricia Grace, your great-great-granddaughter."

Bishop Jordan and Landris stayed out of the way. Sarah stood back, looked, then hugged them before starting the cycle all over again. "My family? Oh God. My family! God has answered my prayers with a triple portion."

"Family?" Montgomery seemed astounded. "But how can that be? You never had children. The only child you had died at birth. My father told me so! He told me what he'd done—"

Sarah looked to Johnnie Mae. Johnnie Mae began to explain. "Memory—that's your daughter's name—is alive. And *she* had a daughter named Lena." She pointed to Lena.

"But that can't be! *This is lunacy!*" Montgomery headed for the house. "I'll call the police myself! I'll not let you thieving, scheming people come out here and try to take all that my family has worked so hard to build. And you!" He stopped at Johnnie Mae and drew back his hand. "I'll see you in—"

"Man, have you lost your mind!?" Landris said with eyes blazing as he grabbed Montgomery's wrist just as his hand was about to come down on Johnnie Mae. "I am a preacher. Please don't make me have to ask God's forgiveness for something you're tempting me to have to do to you. Because if you raise your hand to any of these women here, and *especially* my wife *ever* again, I'm afraid I just might have to lay my religion down for just about two minutes." Landris stared him down, then he let his wrist go.

After the police arrived, they quickly learned that Sarah actually held the legal right to the house, whereas Montgomery did not. The police escorted Montgomery, not without protest, off the property as per Sarah's expressed wishes. Sarah then invited everyone to come inside.

"Memory. Where is my daughter?" Sarah asked after they had settled in.

Lena looked at Sarah. "We don't know. She was in Atlanta about a month ago, then she left. We haven't heard from her since. I'm sorry; I know how disappointing this must be for you after so many years and now being so close."

They sat in the parlor. "My family," Sarah said pensively. "I'm seeing y'all with my own eyes, and I still can't believe it's real. And look at that baby. May I hold her?" Sarah held out her arms to receive Grace from Theresa. "What time is it?" Sarah asked as she smiled at Grace.

Theresa looked at her watch. "It just turned two o'clock," she said.

Sarah smiled, nodded, and rocked the baby as she sang a song she hadn't sung in over 67 years. She stopped in midstream and asked, "What time is it now?"

Theresa looked down at her watch again, not understanding why Sarah was so obsessed with the time. "It's now 2:03," Theresa said.

When Sarah finished the song, she smiled at the baby, who had fallen fast asleep, looked up at the others, and said, "What time is it now?"

"2:07," Theresa said, not wanting to sound too annoyed.

"Why do you keep wanting to know the time?" Lena asked, fully understanding how age can affect thoughts.

Sarah smiled. "I was thinking about time. How we fret about it or regret time we think we've lost or that's been stolen from us. But sitting here with my family right now, I realize no matter what time the clock says, it's always now. All we ever in reality have to live or experience life in is now. We can't go back and change or redeem the past. We can't live in the future. All we ever have is now. And now I have all of you here. I thank God for what I do have, and I'm not going to worry about what I don't have."

Sarah then turned to Johnnie Mae. "Thank you so much. I was afraid you would leave and decide it was too hard to continue trying. I prayed this morning that you would come: just take a chance and come by. When Montgomery came to me last night asking about you, I couldn't let him know anything. If he had even suspected something, he would have had me out of here before I could have blinked my eyes twice." She nodded. "I prayed God would send you today. And He did. And now look." She laughed.

"Auntie Sarah," Elizabeth said. "I am sorry. I had no idea. I really didn't know."

Sarah touched the baby's cheek gently with her finger. "Now you know. And I can spend time with my family." She looked at Lena, then Theresa. "How long can you stay?"

Lena looked at Johnnie Mae, then Theresa as though one of them had her answer.

"Mama, why don't you stay a day or two, and me and Daddy can ride back today? Then Maurice and I will drive up in a few days to visit and bring you home."

"Are you sure?" Lena asked. "I promised I'd help you with the baby."

"And you have. We're fine." She looked over at Grace resting in Sarah's arms. "Grace and I will be just fine."

"Mother's name was Grace," Sarah said. "Did you know that when you named her?"

"No, not when I named her." Theresa stood up and looked toward the door. "What about your nephew? What if he comes back and makes trouble like he said he would?"

Elizabeth answered. "Montgomery knows the jig is up and his time has run out," she said. "They won't be doing any more of their dirty work. I've already called one of the top lawyers in the state for Auntie Sarah. And, wouldn't you know: he happened to have grown up with her? They were once childhood friends. He's already working on getting things straight."

"I'll call when I get home to let you know when we'll be back up," Theresa said.

Lena grabbed Theresa's hand and pulled her away from the others. They stood near the curving, iron stairway out of earshot. "Theresa, Maurice is a good man. Now, I can't tell you what to do. But if he *should* ask, do me a favor—follow your heart."

"Ask? Ask what?" Theresa said.

"He bought you a ring while we were in New York and had planned to officially ask you to marry him when he returned. But after all that happened, he decided he didn't want you agreeing to marry him out of pity or wrong emotions."

"Pity? Wrong emotions?"

"Yes. You keep turning him down. He's trying to live for the Lord now. He wants to do things right. I'm not telling you to say yes if it's not in your heart. But if your heart says yes, don't play games with him. That's all I'm saying. Okay?"

Theresa smiled and hugged Lena. "No matter what time the clock says, it's always now. I hear you, Mama. *Now*, if Daddy should ask you to marry him, follow *your* heart."

"What?" Lena pulled back from Theresa and her silliness.

"Daddy. He's thinking about asking you to marry him. I probably shouldn't be telling you this, but I suppose *now* we're even." She laughed.

"Where did you get such a ridiculous notion?" Lena said, one hand on her hip.

"I suggested Daddy come live with me because I didn't want him living alone," Theresa began. "He then informed me that he had plans for his life. He doesn't think it looks right to ask a woman he loves to marry him, then they move in with his daughter. I don't know. I suppose it's a man thing. He said he doesn't want to appear like a 'scrub.' " She laughed again. "Anyway, he says he's perfectly capable of taking care of himself. So he's definitely not looking for a nursemaid."

"Well, I should hope not," Lena said, blushing.

Theresa smiled. "So, *should* Daddy ask you to marry him—listen to your heart. No games, okay? Because no matter what time it happens to be, it is and will always be *now*."

"See, now you know you're wrong. Taking what I said and using it against me."

Theresa hugged Lena tightly. "Whatever it takes and by whatever means necessary."

They rejoined the group already in the midst of saying their goodbyes.

"Thank you, Johnnie Mae. I know God sent you into my life," Sarah said. "I almost missed God by not talking to you. Things might be different now if I had done it sooner."

"I'm just glad everything worked out. Sarah, I have your box, the one with the wings of Grace, in the SUV. Would you like it back now?"

Sarah shook her head. "Just hold it. Wings of Grace. My box. Memory's father made those boxes for Mother: three of them. She got the idea for her box to have wings actually from the Book of Ruth, second chapter, verses 10 and 12: 'Then she fell on her face, and bowed herself to the ground and said unto him, Why have I found *grace* in thine eyes, that thou shouldest take knowledge of me, seeing I am a stranger.' " Sarah stopped and took Johnnie Mae's hand. "That verse pretty much sums up just how I felt that day when you said you would help me. Then the twelfth verse says: 'The Lord recompense thy work, and a full reward be given thee of the Lord God of Israel, under whose *wings* thou art come to trust.' And that is my prayer for you: that the Lord *recompense* your work, and a *full* reward be given to you," Sarah said with falling tears.

CHAPTER 60

The righteous shall inherit the land.

(Psalm 37:29)

Landris and Johnnie Mae took Theresa and Grace home first, then Bishop Jordan. He had a mischievous grin on his face.

"God is good, ain't he, Pastor?" Bishop Jordan said as Landris walked with him to his door. "What Satan often means for bad, God will turn it into good. We just have to trust God to be God."

"Okay, Bishop Jordan. Where are you headed with this?" Landris said.

"Oh, you mean, let's stop beating this batter with a spoon and bake the cake already? Nothing, son. I just wanted to remind you that prayer is a two-way street. We can tell God what He already knows, or we can listen to what He knows that He wants to tell us."

Landris smiled. "You know God has been really speaking to my heart, don't you?"

"Well, I certainly hope so. I also hope you don't let the devil knock you down for the full ten count. You can't always see your entire journey at one time, but if you can just see far enough in front of you to get to the next place, then the next, I hear you can make a whole trip that way." He winked.

When Landris and Johnnie Mae got back to the house, she called to check on her mother.

"How are they?" Landris asked when he saw Johnnie Mae's troubled look afterward.

She twisted her mouth a little. "*They're fine*," she said, mocking the way they had sung it to her, as though "We're fine!" were a new hit song.

"Johnnie Mae. Let's go get your mother," Landris said, holding her in his arms.

"Landris, I've tried. She doesn't want to move here. And my other siblings are giving me so much grief about me even pushing the issue. Mama really wants to live in her own home in Alabama. And all I want is for her to be safe and happy."

"Johnnie Mae. Let's . . . go . . . get . . . your mother," he said again.

"Didn't you hear me?"

"I heard you. Now you hear me. Let's sell this house and move, me and you, to Birmingham to live." He smiled.

"I don't understand. I thought you were seriously considering starting a church here. You have a ready-made congregation. Not that I'm wishing anything bad for the church that kicked you out because you had the nerve to literally take God at His Word."

"Now you're sounding a little bit bitter, sweetheart. You need to work on that."

She nodded. "You're right. But there are people right now just waiting on the word from you, and you could be back as pastor of a church before next week is here good."

He hugged her around the waist. "A wise man once told me, 'There are times we don't always see our entire journey at one time, but if we can just see far enough in front of us to get to the next place and then the next, we can make a whole trip that way.' In my prayer time with God, He's been leading me, by faith, to go in a different direction."

"To Birmingham, Alabama?"

"I'm not sure, but I believe so. What do you say?"

"I say, as Ruth said to Naomi: 'Entreat me not to leave thee, or to return from following after thee: for whither thou goest, I will go; and where thou lodgest, I will lodge: thy people shall be my people, and thy God my God.'"

"Johnnie Mae, do you have any idea how much I love you?"

"I'm beginning to get some idea," she said, laughing while he bombarded her with pellets of kisses. The doorbell chimed.

"Hold my place," Landris said as he went to see who was interrupting his playtime.

"George, my brother!" Thomas gave George an envelope and strolled in. "This is on the wire transfer for the $3 million: 2 from the necklace and another million Sammie finally got from one other transaction." He showed George a stack of paper. "Now you can be the proud owner of a radio station in Birmingham, Alabama—FM, R & B. Keep in mind that after you sign this, it will officially be yours to *change* as you please."

"Nice, but I don't recall saying anything about wanting to own a radio station."

"Okay, so you're not as excited as I thought you would be. But you don't have to know much about running the station. They just hired a woman who really knows the business of managing radio. She starts in two weeks, and I hear she's a real angel."

"Is that right?" George said. "A real angel, huh?"

"Seriously. She's a real angel. Her name is Angela Gabriel, but she goes by Angel."

"Angel Gabriel. I met an Angel Gabriel recently. I wonder if she's the same one?"

'*I met an Angel Gabriel recently.*' *Now he's trying to be funny.* Thomas smiled, but George only stared at him. "Okay. So here's what I think. You are always looking for ways to contribute to building up the kingdom. If you own an FM station in the South, why not do something radical and change it from say . . . an R & B station to a 24/7, all-day/all-night, contemporary gospel station?"

"Thomas, listen, I appreciate you. But—" He stopped, then started laughing. "Okay, God, I hear you. I hear you now . . . loud and clear! I . . . hear . . . you!"

"I'm talking gospel on FM," Thomas said. "Reaching thousands of people, clear, day and night. Blessing people with alternative music they can drive to work and home to."

George laughed harder, which had Thomas totally confused.

"What?" Thomas finally said. "What is so funny?"

"Thomas," George said between laughs. "That's a great idea. And they've already hired someone, Angel Gabriel, who can pull this off with a spirit of excellence?"

"Yes. They say she's excellent. Highly recommended. She'll be starting in two weeks. So you're saying that you're beginning to like this idea?" Thomas said.

"Yes. In fact, I love it! It's like a Word from God. What an awesome way to put money to use! And it's in, of all places, Birmingham, Alabama!"

"Okay, so what am I missing here?" Thomas's eyes physically roved as they searched George's face. "George? I've finally pushed you over the edge, haven't I? Ah, George . . . man."

"Thomas, I'd like to offer you a job." His laughs transformed into short chuckles.

"Me?"

"Yeah, you. But you'll have to move to Alabama. I'm thinking about making you general manager of operations at this radio station. But no more impulsive decisions."

George looked stunned. "Yeah. I've always been interested in radio. And I suppose you will be needing someone there to watch things while you're here."

"No," George said, slapping his brother on the back. "I'll be in Birmingham, too."

"You? But how? Why? What are you planning to do in Birmingham, Alabama?"

"That's where God seems to be pointing me. I believe it's called a Holy Ghost setup. That's when you have a plan and God has a plan, but God's plan is grander. And to be honest, Thomas, I can't wait to see what God has planned for me in my next chapter."

CHAPTER 61

And have tasted the good word
of God.

(Hebrews 6:5)

Lena and Sarah sat down at the dinner table that evening. "Sarah," Lena said.

"Would you mind calling me Grandmother?" Sarah asked. "I know it might feel funny having just met me and all. And if you'd rather not—"

"No. Grandmother is fine." Lena smiled. "Grandmother." *It does sound funny*, she thought. "Were you serious about the things you said to Montgomery earlier today?"

Sarah looked up. "You mean when I suggested he be careful about who he insults based on color?"

"Yeah."

"Serious enough to cause him worry, if that's what it took."

"So, is it true? the paper you held up when his lawyer and the sheriff were here? Does it really prove what you were insinuating as being possibly true?"

Sarah reflected on her showdown with Montgomery—specifically, the period that led up to her causing Montgomery's smug expression to literally fall to the ground.

*   *   *

"I'd be careful about slinging those words around if I were you," Sarah said after Montgomery proudly rolled off a few racial slurs toward no one particular person.

"I just call 'em like I see 'em," Montgomery said with a look of pure disgust.

Sarah took out a folded paper and held it up. "Then, what would you have to say if I told you that this paper will prove you're not as white as you think you really are?"

"*What*?" Montgomery cocked his head incredulously, turning now to square off against Sarah.

"What if I were to tell you that you're not white? that your grandfather was the son of a black person? that he passed for white and no one ever suspected differently? that here inside this paper is proof positive?"

Montgomery focused in on the folded paper Sarah held. "You're as crazy as they claimed you were." He snickered. "There's no way we came from slaves. I'm white. Pure white! Look at you! *You're* white! Look at Elizabeth! And the rest of our family. White!"

Sarah smiled. "And your point is?"

"There's no way—" He began to stumble backward as he attempted to run away from words that contained, at that moment, an alternate possibility of his life.

"Oh," Sarah said. "Did you know that before black folks were slaves, some were kings and queens? The architects of advanced civilizations? So much history that's not taught. Brilliant people. A richness." Sarah smiled and turned to the sheriff. "Sheriff, did you know Egypt is actually in Africa? that diamonds come from Africa? I don't understand how people keep losing sight of the facts." She looked at them staring at her.

"Oh well," she said, placing the paper back in her shift pocket. "Leon? Is that your name? Do whatever is needed to keep Montgomery and his crew from ever stepping foot back on *my* property without *my* permission again," she said to Montgomery's lawyer.

"You can't do this!" Montgomery said. "You crazy old bat! I'll see you in court!"

"Oh, I can't?" Sarah said. "Well, I do declare. I believe I just did." She turned to the others as the sheriff and his lawyer escorted Montgomery off to the side to explain to him exactly what had transpired, and what it meant as far as he was concerned. "Would y'all care to come inside for something refreshing? I'm sure y'all are famished," she said.

Sarah smiled and nodded at Lena as her thoughts returned to the present. She took out the paper. "So you want to know if what I said to Montgomery about our ancestors not being full-bloodied white is true?"

"Yes," Lena said.

"Does it really make a difference? I mean really? In the scheme of things?"

Lena thought for a second. "When I look at you, I see a white woman."

"And if it turns out I have 'black' blood, would anything change about who I am?"

"In truth, it would."

"Why?"

Lena thought again. "I don't know. It's like the way society is. I can sit here and look at you and think you're white. See that you look white. But if you were to say that you have even a trace of black in you, the world would immediately classify you differently."

Sarah laughed. "That's so funny . . . so utterly, utterly funny. Many believe the Bible is the Word of God. That it is the truth. Genesis says God created Adam and Eve. Not a black Adam and Eve and a white Adam and Eve. Just Adam and Eve." She placed the paper near her heart. "Sounds like to me if that's true, all of us—black, white, yellow, and red—originated from the same two people. Yet, we still see each other as separate, failing to see how much we're really all related." She handed the paper to Lena. "If it's important for you to know, read it, and see." Sarah touched Lena's shoulder, then left.

Lena looked at it for several minutes. She went into the kitchen, turned on the stove, lit the paper from the burner, then watched the fire devour it in the sink. She smiled and walked away without having read what truth it might have conveyed. *Answer it truthfully. Why does it matter?*

WINGS OF GRACE

VANESSA DAVIS GRIGGS

ABOUT THIS GUIDE

The questions and discussion topics that follow are intended to
enhance your group's reading of WINGS OF GRACE by
Vanessa Davis Griggs. We hope the novel provided an
enjoyable read for all your members.

1. In the *Prologue*, Mamie ponders whether she should answer Willie B's question or whether she should answer the question he should have asked. What question should Willie B have asked?

2. How did certain events shape and/or affect Sarah Fleming's life?

3. What were your feelings about Memory showing up at Theresa's home?

4. The necklace played a significant role throughout the story. Discuss the necklace. Do you believe Memory was entitled to it? Was there a better way for Memory to have handled the situation surrounding the return of the necklace to her?

5. George Landris' brother, Thomas, managed George's stock portfolio for him. Do you fault George for the position he found himself in regarding the money from the sale of the stock and his situation with the IRS? Why or why not?

6. How should have George responded, being a minister and a Christian, in regard to his brother having taken his money?

7. When the governing board of the church requested that Pastor Landris get someone else other than Minister Fulton (a woman preacher) to be in charge during his absence, should Pastor Landris have complied? Why or why not?

8. Prior to reading this, what beliefs did you have about women preachers? Women being submissive to men? After reading this book and hearing Pastor Landris, are your views the same?

9. When Memory told Theresa, as Theresa was leaving for the hospital, to tell Lena that she really loved her and that she hoped to be forgiven, do you believe she meant it?

10. Do you think Memory had any regrets about deceiving her family having gotten to know them as she had?

11. Should Lena have allowed Theresa to report Memory for forging the document that ultimately allowed her illegal access to the safe deposit box? Did Theresa bear some of the burden for signing that paper?

12. Talk about Johnnie Mae meeting Pearl Black, the various things she learned about Sarah's past, and the locked box.

13. Discuss Pastor Landris and Johnnie Mae Taylor's wedding. What symbolisms did you see in the wedding having Johnnie Mae and Landris come together from the side and meet each other halfway? Their vows? Their honeymoon night?

14. Discuss the happenings of September 11 regarding the following characters: Johnnie Mae and Landris; Lena and Maurice; Theresa, Sapphire, Thomas, B, and Beatrice.

15. As in real life, there were several losses in the story. Discuss your feelings regarding the loss of (1) Pastor Landris as pastor, (2) Pearl Black, (3) Beatrice, and (4) Memory leaving without having learned the truth about who she really was.

16. Was Pastor Landris wrong to have grabbed Montgomery's arm as he was about to strike Johnnie Mae? Why or why not?

17. Do you feel it's too soon after the death of his wife for Bishop Jordan to be thinking about marrying Lena? Why or why not?

18. Sarah gave Lena the paper that would answer whether there really was black blood in her family tree. How do you feel about Lena burning it without looking at it? Does it really make a difference? Expound.